will you won't you want me?

ALSO BY NORA ZELEVANSKY

semi-charmed life

NORA ZELEVANSKY

will you won't you want me?

 ST. MARTIN'S GRIFFIN ▲ NEW YORK

WILL YOU WON'T YOU WANT ME? Copyright © 2016 by Nora Zelevansky. All rights
reserved. Printed in the United States of America. For information, address St.
Martin's Press, 175 Fifth Avenue, New York, N.Y. 10010.

www.stmartins.com

Designed by Anna Gorovoy

Library of Congress Cataloging-in-Publication Data

Names: Zelevansky, Nora, author.
Title: Will you won't you want me? / Nora Zelevansky.
Description: First edition. | New York : St. Martin's Griffin, 2016.
Identifiers: LCCN 2015045664 | ISBN 9781250001276 (softcover) |
    ISBN 9781466850187 (ebook)
Subjects: LCSH: Single women—Fiction. | Life change events—Fiction. |
    Self-realization in women—Fiction. | BISAC: FICTION / Romance /
    Contemporary. | FICTION / Humorous.
Classification: LCC PS3626.E3564 W55 2016 | DDC 813/ .6—dc23
LC record available at http://lccn.loc.gov/2015045664

Our books may be purchased in bulk for promotional, educational, or business
use. Please contact your local bookseller or the Macmillan Corporate and Premium
Sales Department at 1-800-221-7945, extension 5442, or by e-mail at MacmillanSpecial
Markets@macmillan.com.

First Edition: April 2016

10   9   8   7   6   5   4   3   2   1

for andrew. who turns my tears to laughter, even on sunday nights

will you won't you
want me?

Flip
By Marjorie Plum, age 10

One morning, a girl awoke and discovered that she was two-dimensional. She was an illustration in a book.

She couldn't budge from her page, suspended in motion, stepping off a sloped curb. She was ink sinking into tree pulp, bound by the glue and string of a longer tale.

It wasn't until someone opened the book and saw her that she realized her own potential. There were versions of her on every page, waiting to move. She was part of a flip book that told her story.

Sometimes, when somebody flipped through the pages too quickly, her particular image was skipped and yet the story was still told. Other times, the reader's thumb rested at the corner and, for a moment, her image became the only one.

Every day she waited to hear that sound: _flip, flip, flip_. It meant she was coming alive.

Then, one day, she heard _flump_ instead.

The book had fallen into a bathtub filled with soapy water and the wet pages stuck together. The pictures blurred, but instead of disappearing, she became whole.

THE END

1

Marjorie Plum was the most popular girl in school, but it had been a decade since anyone cared.

Untangling earbuds, she rushed down the sidewalk past duos in bowler hats. Her heeled clogs trampled fallen cherry blossoms, surprised in trails midexodus to the gutter.

She did not notice a yellow cab squealing to a halt when she jaywalked or the driver shouting, *"Tu madre es una puta fea!"* She did not sense, as she hustled past an occupied stoop, the tension between a round-faced girl, who had professed romantic love, and her crush, who had in turn pronounced himself gay—*confused* at least.

Just hours before, the writer Nora Ephron had died of cancer. Somewhere along the campaign trail, the presumptive Republican presidential candidate, Governor Mitt Romney, and his advisers were brainstorming ways to avoid releasing tax returns. In Syria, Arab Spring had spiraled into civil war. England was enjoying Elizabeth II's Diamond Jubilee but also a meteoric rise in cases of gonorrhea.

Across the Manhattan Bridge in Brooklyn, a young girl struggled with her creative-writing assignment over a dish of carrots and hummus at the kitchen table. In palm tree–lined Los Angeles, a misanthropic film buff packed for his flight back east.

Like every other, this day was at once important and insignificant in the scheme of things. Unaware of what was to come, Marjorie would likely have rated it forgettable.

Had she bothered to note the date, though, she might have realized that this warm June evening in 2012—when the first tendrils of summer heat snuck behind the bunched knees of pants, prompting the overdressed to adjust, readjust, and adjust again—was ten years to the day when her tenure as Queen Bee had ended at high school graduation.

Just eighteen years old then, while exiting the auditorium onto the sidewalk after the ceremony, Marjorie had mocked her maroon graduation cap and gown with a "too cool" performative snort. Afterward, she watched kvelling parents—clutching red rose and baby's breath bouquets—shoot warning looks at younger offspring, who whined in hungry anticipation of special occasion brunches. Her chemistry teacher, Mr. Bender, checked his watch. Underclassmen, noting Marjorie's arrival outside, gossiped and giggled more loudly, building the nerve to approach with yearbooks like autograph collectors.

And, suddenly, loss wheezed at the edge of Marjorie's consciousness, something more than precollege jitters. Eyes welling, she paused to memorize the scene like a character turning off the proverbial lights on the finale of a stale sitcom.

That day, she *knew* life was about to change—for the worse.

Marjorie ("Madge" to friends) had mastered those teen years, traumatic for a disproportionate many. She loved the drama, the constant shuffling of romantic couples, firsts from cigarette smoking to second base. She felt no kinship with popular kids of teen movies who pumped pompoms and bullied future tech CEOs. Still, at high school's end, she could sense her impending devolution into "Faded Prom Queen" (though she had skipped the taffeta-inspired event and headed straight to the after-party).

As her parents presented her with an engraved Tiffany necklace in congratulations at her own eggs Benedict brunch, she had promised herself she would not white knuckle that metaphorical tiara. But the descent into unimportance proved brutal nonetheless.

Now, at twenty-eight years old, as she ducked through reclaimed church doors into the new Lower East Side gastropub, DIRT, it occurred to her that suburban housewives did not have the monopoly on quiet desperation. Once, a night out had left her smelling of astringent liquor and Big Red gum, buzzing with nicotine and reverberating bass. She and cherry-lipped friends breezed past gargantuan bouncers who reeked of Cool Water cologne; they mooched off strange men's VIP bottle service vodka, sat atop banquettes instead of *in* them, and smoked cigarettes under gaudy Gothic chandeliers, emerging purple and filthy into pale early mornings, carrying a destabilized vibration like a badge. These days, life was *civilized* and deadly predictable thanks to early nights, the disappearance of attached female friends, and $17 mixology cocktails with mint foam from rooftop herb gardens. DIRT—a high-ceilinged Manhattan rebuttal to Brooklyn's farm-to-table nooks—was no exception, with its predictable knotted mahogany bar, white subway tiles, 1950s signage and chalkboard menu.

Marjorie nudged her way toward a lone empty barstool: "Excuse me, excuse me . . ." and then *"Excuse* me." She eyed the crowd: Vera was late. Odd. The bartender was busy rustling his handlebar mustache in hipster mating ritual at a blonde in a vintage baby doll dress.

The girl pouted. "I went to U. Penn. That's Ivy League!"

"Barely. That's barely Ivy League." He winked.

His inattention notwithstanding, Marjorie drew glances. The stray cherry blossom hitching a ride on her caboose was in part to blame. But she was also striking, tall and lean in her scoop-necked T-shirt, high-waisted miniskirt, and well-loved ankle boots, a favorite unostentatious but It bag slung across her chest. Her long auburn hair was swept into a sloppy topknot above high cheekbones, small pink lips, pale, sporadically freckled skin, and wide hazel eyes—accentuated with black liquid liner. Her resting expression could be mistaken for a frown, but the slightest smile revealed a rotated right-hand lateral incisor that upgraded her from pretty or cute to interesting, even beautiful. A small scar under her left eye was the result of three stitches after smashing headfirst into glass doors at her grandmother's Palm Beach condo at the advanced age of fifteen (advanced for that sort of accident, at least).

Among those to clock Marjorie was a foppish man of roughly her age, leaning against the wall as if in his own living room. He paused midsentence, losing interest in the brunette before him. Then, adopting an expression of purpose, he straightened his skinny tie, retousled his perfectly mussed dirty blonde hair and excused himself, sidling up next to Marjorie—a free seat always appears for men of this kind— and performing a nonchalant, "You alone?"

Answering was the path of least resistance. "Aren't we all?"

"So deep." The corner of his mouth curled upward with pleasure at his own gall. She refused to return his smile, no matter how adorable he fancied himself. Which was very adorable indeed. "Well? No need to be rude," he pressed.

Marjorie turned to face him. "*I'm* not rude. You're rude."

"Listen, *Madgesty,* it's customary to say hello when you see some-one you once French-kissed on Spider-Man sheets. Why the cold shoulder?"

It had been ages since Marjorie had last seen MacDonald O'Shea— named like a law firm by moneyed parents who had seen him mostly as a business venture—and longer since anyone had invoked her high school nickname.

The truth was she *had* seen and studiously ignored him when she walked in—along with two polished wooden booths of guys she'd both tailed and avoided during her teenage years, many of whom now stuffed wedding rings on meaty fingers and baseball caps on balding heads. She had felt too at sea, too atomically unstable, to engage them.

She gestured toward the button-nosed young woman he'd aban-doned, who pretended not to stare after him. "You looked busy."

"Never too busy for the one who got away."

"One of ten to fifteen who *ran* away, actually."

"See? Rude. Correct, but rude. Anyway, what's a guy gotta do to get a hello already?"

Marjorie had to smile; Mac never changed. She leaned in to plant a peck on his straight-razor-shaven cheek, and, before she realized, he whipped around and kissed her square on the mouth. Electricity shot through Marjorie's body; she chided herself, recoiling. To relish his at-tention was amateurish. Her resolve against his sleaze—unappealing

on paper but nonetheless powerful—was a point of pride. "You're impossible."

"Most women say *irresistible*. But then you've always been strange."

She groaned.

"Aw, sweetie. Bad day?"

"Nothing a lobotomy wouldn't cure. Or copious alcohol."

"One strong drink coming up."

"Make it two, if you succeed. And good luck getting the bartender's
attention."

"Watch me." She watched as he backed toward the end of the bar
and, within moments, was distracted by a wannabe model in batik
harem pants.

Mac's confidence was not due to classic good looks. Of medium
height, he maintained a narrow build with rigor. His face was intelli-
gent, not handsome, thanks to a protruding chin and a too-fair complexion. But his birthright—a cocktail of charisma, entitlement,
insatiable need, and absent ethics—made him a social giant. His chosen objects—men, women, children, even dogs—were made to feel
like members of an elite club, out of which everyone else had the misfortune of being cast. Once they got a taste of his flirtation, they *needed*
Mac's Technicolor personality to subsume them, to fill the gaps where
boredom and insecurity lay, to make them feel significant. And when
he lost interest—and he *always* did—he left them feeling hollowed out,
like they'd failed. Any Psych 101 novice could see that he craved approval after years of chasing his chilly family's affection, which—in his
darkest but clearest moments—he knew was only rumored to exist,
like some emotional Bigfoot. But that fact did not dilute his power.

Feeling suddenly vulnerable, Marjorie plucked a red plastic stirrer
from the bartender's stash and bit down on it.

Where is Vera?

She swiveled on her stool in search of her friend, making inadvertent eye contact with an old acquaintance, John, who sat thirty feet
away clutching a sweating beer stein. The last time she'd seen him,
she'd probably been wearing a crystal beaded choker and dancing to

SexyBack—it had been that long. She forced a smile; he nodded in return.

Oh, thank God.

Through the throngs of tattooed sleeves, she caught a glimpse of a French-inspired J. Crew striped top, a favorite of her roommate's. By design, Vera's crisp uniform and sharp black bob disguised her roots—more burnt toast than croissant—thanks to a quirky ex-hippie single mother.

Vera arrived beside Marjorie at the same time as a bearded young man in an ironic New Kids on the Block T-shirt. He gazed at her in silent plea. He'd been waiting for an empty stool; his new oxfords were rubbing his toes raw. Vera gave him the once-over, decided she could take him, and sat. He limped away, defeated.

She performed an exaggerated double take at the table of former high school guys. "What's with the aging extras from *Boyz in the Hood*? I'm like choking on a mushroom cloud of Drakkar Noir. Isn't theirs more of a cheesy Meatpacking scene?"

"I didn't realize they'd be here."

Approaching with drinks in hand, Mac caught sight of Vera from behind, shot Marjorie an annoyed look, and feigned a gag. Then he plastered a grin on his face and cleared his throat. "They're here because I'm an investor."

Vera's snarl morphed into a smile, as she turned to face Mac. "Sorry. I didn't realize . . ."

"Wait, you *own* this place?" Marjorie shook her head. "Cheater! I thought you were procuring cocktails based on your charm!"

"And I thought you were drinking alone." He clenched his teeth. "But here's Vera. Surprise, surprise."

Vera had always been a hard-trying beta to Marjorie's breezy alpha. Those roles had developed organically when, as eight-year-olds, they started a secret Care Bear Club. Marjorie was named President and Vera VP.

At the time, Marjorie's mother, Barbara Plum, had felt concerned about the children playing nicely and asked, "Why do you need *titles* in a club with only two members?"

A young Marjorie had shrugged. "So we know who's boss."

Her mother loved that story.

Mac was unimpressed with Vera from the beginning. When he started at their middle school, he ignored the Care Bear VP because of her "ferretlike" pointy chin, hooked nose, and wide-set eyes. (Marjorie defended to no avail the way a smile broke through her best friend's features like unexpected sunshine on an overcast day.) Vera claimed to hate Mac back, yet in his presence she transformed into someone too ready to laugh and agree. Nothing depressed Mac more than an easy mark.

These days, Vera had no reason to kowtow. Unconstrained by the golden handcuffs of early social success, she had spread her wings and evolved into a thriving "finance person." Marjorie had no clue what that meant except that Vera was shackled to both her work-sanctioned BlackBerry and personal iPhone and expensed pricey dinners.

Mac leaned against the bar. "So, Vee. Long time no see. How's old Grinch doing?"

"Grinch passed away. Like seven years ago." Vera smiled, flattered at his memory.

"Sad story. He was a good dog."

Marjorie rolled her eyes. Mac made a point of learning a single fact about every acquaintance to bring up later in a performance of intimacy. He often asked after Marjorie's great-aunt Gladys with whom he claimed to have "hit it off" at a Plum family New Year's Day party years before. No one hit it off with Gladys. She had a foul attitude and five o'clock shadow.

He might have met Vera's mangy mutt *once* in total during a short-lived tryst. After junior year in college, Vera returned from a semester abroad in Barcelona with stories of a hot Spanish carpenter named Juan Carlos. Mac felt the man was garnering too much praise, his name too cliché to let stand. So, despite being Vera's lifelong detractor, he showered her with attention, then, sans a challenge, dropped her.

"Congratulations, BTW," Vera simpered.

"On?"

"This place."

"Just the money guy." Mac shrugged.

"But you have amazing instincts. I mean, has anything you backed been *un*successful?"

Marjorie snorted. "I'm pretty sure the sashimi 'burlesque' club wasn't a big moneymaker. Or that floating restaurant in Gowanus? With the sulfur smell? Or—"

"I think we get it," Mac snapped.

Marjorie picked up her drink, served in a mason jar with a sprig of rosemary, took a sip, and flinched. "Ugh, Mac. You got me some sweet girly drink! Don't you know me at all?"

Mac sighed. "That's *mine*. It's a Hamptons Julep from the mixology menu. I got *you* a vodka soda." He gestured toward a stemless glass of clear carbonated liquid, an acid green lime slice perched on the rim.

"Oh, I see." She plucked the stirrer from her mouth and pointed it at him. "I didn't realize you'd pledged Delta Gamma. Where's this year's spring formal, you slut?"

Mac glared at her. "It's not a girly drink. You're evil. I'm going back where I'm appreciated."

"No, no, no! I was joking!" Marjorie called after him, laughing. En route back to the brunette, who waited chest foremost, Mac peered over his shoulder and shook his head at the rare failed exchange.

"What's with you?" asked Vera. "Not that I mind seeing O'Shea tormented, but . . ."

"Sorry. Bad day at the office."

Vera assumed an expression of practiced patience, readying for her friend's *Ground Hog's Day* laments. In her mind, Marjorie chose prolonged misery over action, much like Vera's own long-suffering divorcée mother, to whom she had offered hours of unheeded advice. Now she grunted, "What happened *today*?"

"Ugh. It's bad. We're handling PR for the launch of this new liquor company, Snow Lite. Flavored vodka that promotes weight loss."

"Right. 'Cause that makes sense."

"It's not only fraudulent, it's also disgusting. Anyway, I forwarded an e-mail about the newest infusion flavors to our intern, Herb: *banana, peanut butter, pork belly*. I was continuing a joke from earlier about how the press release should promote bulimia as the diet plan, since the smell makes you want to barf . . ."

"Funny." Vera did not smile.

"I could have sworn . . . but whatever . . . I guess I clicked Reply. The e-mail went to Snow's CEO. Turns out, he wasn't amused."

"Oh, God." Vera covered her face with her hands. "Did Brianne throw a mug at you again?"

Marjorie shook her head. "She's off coffee at the moment."

The notorious Brianne Bacht-Chit had encountered Marjorie in the early aughts at the opening of one of many white-on-white-wallpapered restaurants with mismatched "Mad Hatter" chairs and industrial sconces. Figuring that the adorable, even recognizable, twenty-something might lend *joie* to her firm, Brianne offered Marjorie a part-time "consulting" job, then began resenting and punishing her for the same reasons she was hired. Brianne was a little abusive and then a lot, and finally, for twisted reasons neither could fathom, she hired Marjorie full-time.

Marjorie sighed. "Instead, she got creepy quiet, then said, 'When I met you, you seemed like *someone*. I was wrong. Consider yourself on probation. You're welcome.' Wow. I was able to repeat that verbatim. Is that a marketable skill?"

"Madge. For the eight hundredth time: You need to quit. You're self-sabotaging."

"Too bad about that pesky rent."

"You'll find the money somewhere."

"Easy for you to say."

Vera's mouth dropped open. "What's *that* supposed to mean? I work my *ass* off for what I have." Her face contorted and her voice rose, as her rage escalated. "You sit around feeling sorry for yourself, making careless mistakes. No one hired me because I was cute at a cocktail party. If they had, I guarantee I wouldn't have squandered the opportunity. If you're unhappy, make changes! Or stop talking about it!"

Marjorie swore she felt plates shifting below her feet then, as if the world was turning upside down and she was powerless to stop it. It was a day for pots boiling over, for straws breaking camels' backs. Amoebic spots squirmed before her eyes; she didn't dare glance at the table of high school boys. "Whoa, Vee. I meant it was easy for you because you're so together. I envy that in you."

Vera opened her mouth, then closed it again, twice, then sighed. "I actually have something to share too."

Marjorie took a long sip of her drink. "Sounds promising."

Out of pity or perhaps because he now realized he was dealing with an owner's friend, the bartender appeared and gestured toward Marjorie's empty tumbler. She smiled despite herself, as an alcohol-induced lightness rose in her head, a welcome dulling of edges. She nodded.

"It's good news, actually," Vera was saying. "This isn't quite how I planned to tell you, but . . . Brian and I are moving in together!"

Marjorie struggled to reconcile the pendulum swing from anger to enthusiasm—a bit bipolar. "That's great, Vee. I'm so happy for you guys."

"Good. Because there's more."

Where is that drink?

"We found an apartment."

"Already? Wow. So quick!"

"Well, not *that* quick."

They were silent for a beat. "I . . . How quick, Vera?"

Vera mumbled something incomprehensible into her bony hand.

"What was that?"

"We've been looking for like two months, okay?! I didn't tell you 'cause I wasn't sure how you'd react. You're not the biggest fan of change."

"So, you're moving out." Marjorie glanced down at her palm, where she'd crumpled her napkin into a stress ball. "When?"

Vera avoided her gaze. "This weekend."

"*This* weekend?" Marjorie choked. "Vera, it's Thursday! Rent is due next week! What am I supposed to do about the other half?"

Vera glared. "This isn't about *you*! For *once*!"

"Giving me notice would have been just normal, common courtesy!"

"Well, things haven't been *normal* between us for a while." Vera stood and grabbed her tote; her blunt bob maintaining military formation. "Look, I can't do this right now. I've gotta go. Just keep the apartment or something."

"You know I can't afford it alone!"

"Find a new roommate."

"Where?"

"Online."

"Have you not heard of the Craigslist Killer?"

Vera's lips wobbled guiltily before forming a resolute line. "I knew you'd try to make me feel bad about this. You can't stand that I found someone before you did."

Marjorie shook her head. "This isn't a Lifetime original movie, Tori Spelling. I think our twenty-year friendship deserves a slightly more nuanced interpretation."

"Whatever. Brian said you'd act this way."

Brian. Motherfucking short, squat Brian with ruddy cheeks that suggested cheeriness but were more likely the result of respiratory distress from too many pizza burgers. Self-serving, rude, blowhard Brian with his long hair that he fancied "hip," his requisite black Audi, boilerplate East Hampton house (not big enough to be "impressive" but within the boundaries of "the right hood").

He was the first male to show consistent interest in Vera, who was too smart not to know that she was settling. So Marjorie had struggled to hide her disgust, enduring hours of drivel about the cost of Brian's boxy suits and Yankees season tickets (he didn't even follow baseball!). Though she considered him Satan's spawn, he actually grew up in Cherry Hill, New Jersey (not hell per se), the unremarkable child of a housewife and a discount furniture manufacturer who sat *on the bench* of his school's mediocre football team, winning him enough status to feel entitled but also cheated. Perpetual frat boy Brian, who invaded Marjorie's personal space one drunken night in their apartment's narrow kitchen after Vera passed out and tried to stick his fat white-spotted tongue down her throat, promising—between saliva strands—that it would be "their secret." Brian, whom Marjorie had rebuffed with too much obvious revulsion.

"Vera. Be reasonable," Marjorie coaxed. "You're leaving me homeless with only a few days' notice."

"It's pathetic to live with a roommate at twenty-eight years old anyway. I'm saving you from yourself."

In that moment, Marjorie saw Vera's rodent resemblance, after all. "Seriously?"

"Things can't always go your way, *Madgesty*." At that, Vera stormed out, leaving Marjorie alone in DIRT. (The irony of the name could not be ignored.)

The bartender arrived with Marjorie's drink, waving her debit card back into her wallet, as Mac sat down beside her. The guy in the oxfords missed his chance at a stool again.

"You okay?"

Marjorie shrugged. The day was both important and unimportant. She was both fine and unfine. With her balled-up napkin, she stanched a tear before it realized its potential, then raised her glass. She and Mac both swigged.

And, as the world teetered imperceptibly on its axis, the blossom attached to Marjorie's bottom fluttered to the floor.

2

Marjorie's popularity came in middle school like an early birthday present—not totally unexpected but a treat nonetheless.

One afternoon in seventh grade, she arrived late to an assembly led by a self-defense expert named Terry in high-water sweatpants and a

T-shirt that read SAFETY FIRST; DANGER WORST. She was accompanied by a life-size dummy named Carl. (Some recent muggings were being blamed on kids from a nearby juvenile hall, though the perpetrators were actually a bad seed foursome from the school's own sophomore class—a truth that had yet to trickle down to the teachers' lounge.)

The metal door sighed as Marjorie entered the gym-cum-auditorium; several students turned to look. The history teacher, Ms. Carroll, approached. "It is unacceptable to hold us up like this." Marjorie's friends—clutching each other like life preservers—waved her over with gummy-bracelet-encircled wrists. As she tiptoed past, seas of fifth through eighth graders parted with reverence. Boys roughhoused; girls peered down at once favorite shoes in doubt. Even Terry stopped to watch Marjorie take a seat.

"Okay, kids," said Terry, "let's get started. Are you ready to FIGHT BACK? TO STOP BEING VICTIMS? Let me hear you!"

"Yeeeaah . . ." came a halfhearted collective reply. An eighth-grade class clown yelped a delayed, "YEAH!" and then cracked up.

That's when Marjorie realized: they had waited for her. Even the teachers had stalled, feeling unconsciously that the group was incomplete.

Sensing eyes on her back, Marjorie turned. Mac sat behind her, grinning. He was new at school but had already secured his role as critic and jester, adored and feared.

"All hail Her *Madgesty*," he mocked, with a bent head and a flourish. The girls around him—there were always girls around him—giggled.

"Shut up," Marjorie whispered. "Shut up, shut up."

"That's totally your new name," Vera said, "*Madgesty*." Mac eyed her with boredom, then winked at Marjorie.

Marjorie claimed to hate the name, yet she answered to it. Just like that, reality plummeted down the chasm between the truth and what one tells oneself, never to be seen again.

In fact, she became reliant on, paralyzed by, and wholly defined by the unearned adoration, got drunk on its ease, feared its disappearance, and protected its power, erecting a wall of reserve that separated her from those who could safely behave like humans (going to the bathroom, getting pimples, tripping down stairs).

She snorted now—a lone unsquelched nerdy habit—as Mac delivered his story's punch line from his barstool, "And it *was* blue gym socks. I swear!"

"No, it wasn't! It couldn't have been."

"Well, it was."

"But how did you know?"

"I didn't. Wild guess. But I won the bet; he had to give me his *own* copy of his Rookie card."

"Mac, I don't even believhue you."

"Was that even English? You're slurring, you lush."

The bar's clientele had morphed. The kitchen was closed, baby carrots, new potatoes, and broccolini stalks tucked safely away in Tupperware cribs for the night. The happy hour crowd had left to catch *Girls,* the end of the Yankees game and, in more evolved cases (or so they felt), *The Colbert Report.* Mac's "boys"—even the one mysteriously nicknamed "Plug"—had gone home to their pregnant wives and plump girlfriends. Now younger drinkers with wallet chains debated the merits of emocore bands.

Marjorie sighed and looked at Mac, who repeated "socks!" and started her snorting again. She was on probation at work, soon to be homeless, and losing her best friend to a late Elvis doppelgänger. The laughter was a relief.

"You're a dork." He shook his head. "Why don't people realize that? But seriously, do you believe me? The story?"

"Of course not!"

"Why?"

"Because I know you and you're a liar!"

Mac's mouth dropped open in mock—perhaps tinged with real—hurt. "No way. You're coming with me." He grabbed Marjorie's arm, pulling her up off her stool.

"Where are we going?" Struggling to keep her balance, she snagged her bag, then followed him toward the back. "Oh, lovely! A scenic tour of the janitorial closet!"

Near the fire exit, he opened a pockmarked door, ushering her inside what was clearly the manager's back office. A card table was topped with a landline and piles of papers, someone's organized chaos; the wall above was pinned with interior design inspirations and a schedule. At center slumped a ripped fat black leather couch. Mac shut the door, muffling the festive sounds, and began searching a file cabinet drawer for the card he'd supposedly won off a chagrined Mets pitcher.

Marjorie leaned against the wall for support. Standing had demonstrated the depth of her drunkenness. "Did you find this furniture on a street corner? You're charging twenty dollars a drink. You could at least spring for IKEA in here."

"Said the girl who's been freeloading all night." He touched his hand to something sticky and grimaced. "Ugh. These guys are filthy. I'm gonna have to talk to them."

Marjorie eyed Mac, who was crouched over, wearing a look of determination. He had always hated a mess. As a teenager, when she first glimpsed his pressed jeans draped over hangers like slacks, she assumed that his live-in housekeeper was to thank. But over time, she noticed that he pulled high-tops from his closet and straightened his pens on the table at school with precision. Now, his narrow button-down was pulled taut in just the right places—no doubt custom. Marjorie realized he was dressed up, even for him.

"What's with the tie?"

"Huh?"

"Why so snazzy?"

He didn't look up. "Meeting."

"With whom, may I ask?"

"No, you may not."

"Must have been someone important to merit Brioni. Now I'm curious. Hot date with a tranny? Corporate espionage ring?" She raised an eyebrow. "Court date?"

He shot to standing. "Jesus, Madge. Just leave it alone!"

Marjorie started to apologize, for what she wasn't sure; her head swam too delightfully to figure it out. Mac sighed. "Stop, stop. Forget it. I might as well tell you . . . it's Natalie."

"Oh. Mac, you don't have to—"

"No, it's fine. I shouldn't have snapped." He tugged at his earlobe, a longtime nervous tick. "She got arrested last week, for possession. Again."

Mac's older sister Natalie had struggled with drug dependence since her late teens. Stints at myriad domestic country club rehab centers and two in Switzerland plus a short-lived Outward Bound program in Utah had not helped. (She'd spent her two-day solo mission picking psychedelic mushrooms from cow fields.)

"Today was her court date. Had to appear as the saintly brother. Good guess, by the way. But for future reference, I'm not much into transvestites."

"I'm really sorry, Mac. You didn't have to tell me."

"It's fine. Let's face it: I always wind up confessing to you. You have that effect on me. It's probably those big doe eyes." They locked stares for a strange, tense second. "Or that big rack."

Marjorie snickered, despite herself. Mac turned back to the cabinet as if to resume an unfinished conversation. "Okay, I'm gonna find this. And prove that I'm not a liar!"

"Not a liar about *this*."

"Right! About this." Mac sorted methodically, placing each scrap in a designated pile.

For reasons she was not ready to confront, Marjorie was reminded of her one lapse in judgment with him. She was fifteen years old and at the height of her reign. In New York City, social circles spread beyond private and public school classrooms to neighborhoods. When she and her friends were not at clubs full of peers, they hung on Riverside Drive with older hip-hop- and grunge-obsessed boys, many of whom were washed-up quarterback equivalents who had rebuffed college in favor of pot and video games.

At school, she was crushing on an eleventh grader named Bryce, a soccer player but also a smoker—so not without edge. Marjorie did not fall easily. Her infatuations lasted only until her affection was returned with clumsiness or if the object wore lame sneakers. However unconsciously, she could not afford to show weakness for fear of falling from her pedestal. Flaws, even by association, were unacceptable.

Her inner circle was chilling by the park after school one day. One by one, they slipped off to orthodontist appointments and dreaded tutoring sessions at algebra-textbook-littered tables. Eventually, only she and Mac remained. He offered to walk her home, an old-fashioned suburban cliché rooted in the city by honking cabs and homeless people pushing supermarket carts. The concrete sidewalk—spotted with ancient bubble gum wads turned black—sparkled; weeds reached defiantly up through cracks toward the late-afternoon sun. The October weather was unseasonably warm. They walked along Riverside Drive, mindless of wind off the Hudson.

A million miles away, in Nigeria, a pipeline exploded, killing over 1,000 people. Across the country, in Silicon Valley, offices were being set up for a little start-up company called Google. In exactly two years and 330 days, the world would change forever when hijacked planes hit the World Trade Center, rocking the city to its core, traumatizing the United States' roughly 285 million inhabitants in one instant and rendering it forever impossible to meet a relative at an airport gate. But here, at this moment, in this preserved neighborhood in New York City, the kids were all right.

Mac had just finished an impression of their English teacher, Mr. Eisenstein, oinking about *Animal Farm*. He stole a glance at Marjorie, then, with forced breeziness, asked, "So, you like that new kid?"

"What new kid?"

"You know, that soccer douche bag. Brass. Or whatever."

"His name isn't Brass. It's *Bryce*. And you play soccer!"

"Whatever. You know who I mean."

Marjorie was well aware. They trudged in silence for a beat, hearts pounding, threatening to betray their adolescent performances of normal.

"So, do you like him or not?"

"Who?"

"Seriously? I'll take that as a *yes*."

Young Marjorie stopped and turned to face young Mac, forcing her thumb deep beneath the scratchy nylon strap of her messenger bag. "Don't take that as a yes. It's not a *yes*."

Mac rolled his eyes. Even the dimmest observer could see what was brewing between Bryce and Marjorie: him pulling on her short plaid skirt and calling her "Britney Spears" when they passed in the hall; Marjorie feigning disgust and shoving him lightly back. (The singer's first single ". . . Baby One More Time" had just hit the airwaves, and her accompanying Catholic schoolgirl video was all over MTV. The world was at once revolted and enamored.)

"I heard he got a girl pregnant at his old school."

Bryce had not gotten anyone pregnant. Bryce had not yet had sex. Either way, his reputation might only have benefited from that rumor.

"Mac, that's ridiculous, even from you."

"Just admit that you like him. It's obvious that you do!"

"I don't. Don't. Don't. Don't."

"You're the worst liar."

"Just don't tell anyone!" she blurted out. It was a mistake born of panic. She'd confirmed Mac's suspicions. He would be on the phone spreading the dirt before that night's episode of *Dawson's Creek* began. She waited for his joyous exclamation of "I knew it!" Nothing came. They had stopped next to an old stone fountain on Riverside Drive and 76th Street, so much a part of her everyday landscape that she barely knew it existed.

"Why do you care anyway?"

"I *don't* care." It sure looked like he did. He tugged at his earlobe like he was signaling to some half-blind pitcher.

"Then why are you asking?"

"I heard he likes Sarah Kaplan anyway."

"Please. Everyone knows Sarah Kaplan is hooking up with Eric Martinez."

He stared at her hard, sighed, and then looked up at the blue sky and across the street at a bicyclist pedaling hard toward his next Chinese food delivery.

"Fine! I like you. Okay? I do. And that Bryce guy is a loser."

Marjorie was shocked. She had written Mac off long before and assumed that he'd done the same with her.

"Oh."

His opponent knocked off balance, Mac grew suddenly confident. "I think you would like me too if you gave the idea a chance. We'd be unstoppable."

"It's not a competition."

"Sure it's not." He rolled his eyes. "Here's the deal: I'm going to kiss you now. And you're not going to say anything afterward, until you give this some thought. But you have to give me this chance. It's only fair."

No one had ever told Mac O'Shea that *life* wasn't fair.

Marjorie had set her sights on Bryce, and Mac was hardly boyfriend material. But she found herself wanting to say *yes* on a gut level she'd not experienced with boys before but would later with *men*. She felt an uneasy flutter reverberating through her, a warmth, a pull.

"I'm not sure about this," she admitted.

"Why?"

"I think you might be . . ."

"What?"

"A bad idea."

Mac laughed. "That's for sure." And before she could gather her wits, he'd stepped so close that she got distracted by the light tips of his dark eyelashes. "So, can I kiss you?"

She nodded a quick assent, though her brain screamed *no*. He leaned in, his lips finding hers, at first a bit awkwardly, as she panicked. But then the kiss intensified and she was surprised by her shudders as his hands found her waist. And when he let go, because it was he who ended it, she wasn't sure how she felt. Embarrassed, sure. Dizzy, yes. Like maybe she wanted him to do it again?

Before she could do anything, he tipped an invisible hat in her direction, grinned, and stalked away in the direction of home.

That night, Marjorie couldn't focus on the latest episode of *Felicity*, ate only half a steamed artichoke (her favorite), and couldn't comprehend her Algebra 2 homework, even after consulting notes. She wasted an hour doodling squiggles in lively conversation with geometric boxes. The next morning, she spotted both Mac and Bryce in the locker area, caught first one guy's eye, then the other's, and ran.

By seventh period, she was queasy and still unsure but was finding it difficult not to think about that after-school kiss, when Vera reported the first rumors: "I'm telling you this because I would want to know." Despite her complicit audience, she couldn't disguise her gossipy glee. "Mac is telling everyone that you made out with him yesterday. He says you practically *raped* him into kissing you, and he isn't even into you."

Knowing what she did about Mac, Marjorie shouldn't have been surprised that he had fabricated a half lie that would both humiliate her and sabotage any relationship with Bryce, or that he never approached to apologize or acknowledge her silent treatment when she ignored him for the next *three weeks* before slipping back into their former—if not as close—acquaintance. Nor should she have been alarmed when he befriended Bryce as his closest pal, even into adulthood, and adopted for him the nickname "Brass." Still, she'd felt hurt and confused.

In the end, she'd dated Bryce anyway for the next two years, until she started twelfth grade and he left for Tufts. Then they played and inevitably lost the long-distance game.

Between Marjorie and Mac there had been just one more incident, an innocent dare during a party game with friends in his childhood bedroom—that kiss on the Spider-Man sheets.

Now Mac closed the file cabinet and arched his back to stretch a crick. "Guess I'm gonna have to live with you thinking I'm a liar. The card is MIA."

"I would have thought you were a liar either way, if it's any consolation."

"You know? It is."

He walked in a slow, wide circle around the disproportionate couch and leaned against the wall beside her. "So, what now, Her Drunkenness? Wanna rejoin the hordes for another drink?"

"I dunno."

"What don't you know?"

"About another drink."

"Got somewhere to be?" He turned toward her, his head cocked sideways. The unanswered question hovered in the air between them.

"I just think it's probably a bad idea."

He smiled. "Oh, yeah? I remember you once thought I was a bad idea."

"I still do."

This time, he didn't ask. Mac kissed Marjorie hard, pressed her expertly against the wall. He tasted, she thought with amusement, of that Hamptons Julep. For a moment, he broke away and peered into her face, as if confirming her existence, probably memorizing her expression to better tease her later. And Marjorie thought then that life is inevitable. That this had been fated since she first walked into the dumb gastropub earlier that evening. She and Mac were arrested peas in a pod. She had one last thought of fleeing to her bedroom, next door to Vera and Brian. Nothing had ever sounded so lonely.

Mac ran his palms down the sides of her hips, then thighs, and she trembled a little at the strangeness of it all. Then, a bit tentatively for him, he slid his hand up under her skirt and between her legs. He traced his name against the lace of her neon yellow Hanky Panky underwear, and then she was toast.

3

Even as a preteen, Marjorie had never been a fan of sleepovers.

First, a cry fest was inevitable. After activities like watermelon Bonne Bell Lip Smacker application and Slam Book making (which involved girls anonymously scribbling each other's flaws on pink stationery with bubble hearts above the *i*'s), some underdog would feel "left out" having had her nose called "big" (knowing *full well* who wrote that!). An argument would ensue; girls took sides. Enter angry parent at 3:00 A.M. with electrified hair and robe knotted off-center, issuing a stern warning about how it's "bedtime!" and the kids better "be quiet!" That reprimand would rebond the group. Only then would the girls—tucked inside worn Strawberry Shortcake sleeping bags—drift off into sound REM cycles, a couple even having remembered to wear their retainers.

Most of all, Marjorie hated waking up surrounded by someone else's stuff, eating strange pancake breakfasts governed by that household's rules, waiting for her parents to appear and chaperone her home. It was a feeling that persisted even as she grew up.

The next morning was no exception: She collapsed onto the cold tile floor of Mac's bathroom, having sprinted from his bed, her clothing in hand. Anything to avoid confronting him naked in daylight. She'd already entrusted him with way more than was wise. In a surge of adolescent paranoia, she imagined him at DIRT, talking trash to those boys about what she'd said and done the night before. *Shit. Shit. Shit.*

The throbbing bass in her head was accompanied by a falsetto of C-sharp sinus pains and a tenor of nausea. Not long ago, she would have erased the drunken night with a large Diet Coke, BLT, and steak fries. But grease was no longer a miracle cure. She would pay in exhaustion and mild blues for the entire day, at least.

That's when she remembered it *wasn't* Saturday.

"Fuck!" Marjorie smacked a hand over her mouth. She cracked the door and peeked out.

Mac was still sprawled on his stomach, cheek pressed into a cock-eyed pillow, lips parted. She could see the rise and fall of his back, bare but for a trio of healing mosquito bites. A tangled sheet covered any risqué bits, thankfully; they hadn't closed the shades when they stumbled in, giddy and half stripped of clothes. She fought down images from the night before: clawing kisses on the pavement outside DIRT and in the taxi as they sped up 10th Avenue. For now, her memory was mercifully fractured into blurry shards.

He had kicked the cream-colored comforter off the king-size platform bed so that it lay in a heap on the otherwise immaculate bamboo floor. Summer had just arrived, but, ever meticulous, he had already switched to his lightweight duvet.

This room—like the rest of Mac's too-slick loft—had an unused, boutique hotel quality, with more empty square footage than any city dweller might rightfully expect. A bearskin rug at the foot of the bed was one kitschy nod among "tasteful" interior-designer-approved pieces. Above modernist leather library chairs, white built-in shelves held first-edition Hemingway tomes and coffee table books from *Annie Leibovitz at Work* to a *Beastie Boys Anthology,* stacked both horizontally and vertically by color (as was the current trend). Marjorie doubted that Mac had read any besides the *Sports Illustrated Swimsuit Portfolio* and a hardcover volume of *Batman* comics.

Marjorie shut the door softly and set to work fastening her bra. Her shoulder felt stiff; she hated to think why. If only she had gone to yoga instead of meeting Vera. She stood and grabbed her skirt, shimmying it up to her waist, and slipped on her shirt, then realized with disgust that her underwear was missing.

What stared back from the Art Deco mirror was not pretty: Her eye makeup had bled into raccoon circles; a near dreadlock had formed at the back of her head from pillow friction. She sighed and opened the medicine cabinet, revealing a stash of packaged guest toothbrushes; she opted not to dwell on why they existed. The rest of Mac's face products were as high-end as her own but scented like Gillette deodorant, branded with names like "Black Ice" and packaged in silver and blue to signify to male consumers that no raw masculinity was lost by instituting a skincare regimen.

Cold water on her face was a revelation. Once finished with her ablutions, she tucked any evidence into the bottom of the garbage pail, eschewed peeing for fear of a loud flush, and sat on the closed toilet seat to pull on her socks and boots.

Perhaps she would survive, after all. She pulled her phone from inside her tote; it was dead.

Marjorie slipped out the bathroom door and spotted her underwear tucked beneath Mac's left thigh, standing out against the white sheets like a cheerful announcement of her bad choices. *Fuck.* They were unextractable without waking him. She sorted through her bag, for once thankful that she toted around everything she owned, and pulled out an old cotton "period" pair of extras—not cute. She crept close to the clock on Mac's bedside table: 12:23 P.M.

"Late" didn't express it.

Fuck.

Seized with panic, Marjorie tripped to the doorway while pulling on her spare underwear, catching a boot in one leg hole. Falling toward the floor like a felled tree, she caught herself on the doorframe, untangled her foot, yanked the stubborn garment up, and started out. Behind her, an insufficiently groggy voice said, "Later, Madgesty."

She turned to see Mac smirking back at her, bed head rendering him no less self-satisfied.

Fantastic. He could now cap off his madcap Madge story with a description of her tripping over grandma panties.

With as much dignity as she could muster, Marjorie retorted, "Later." At least it felt like a retort. And she marched—once out of sight, *scurried*—from his apartment into the freight elevator and onto the street.

At least the humiliation is over, Marjorie thought, as she hurried east, her skirt tucked into her faded underwear.

4

It was a glorious blue-skied, sunny June day, against which Marjorie stood in stark contrast.

It is an unwritten rule that the more disgusting one feels, and even perhaps looks, the more fat, pockmarked men on the streets of New York City whistle and shout lewd remarks. Maybe this is the universe's way of making up for a bad night with recognition of resilient beauty. Or perhaps these men find a pretty woman, disheveled and vulnerable, suddenly more in their league. In Marjorie's case, her exposed butt may have been to blame.

Either way, Miss Plum jogged the first blocks of her walk of shame to work amid mostly good-natured jeers and invitations, appraisals of her "jugs," and relentless reminders to "Smile!" (As if any woman wants to be instructed to grin when the morning merits nothing of the sort.) Then, as there was no simple subway route from the far West Side to Midtown, she flagged down a cab.

The driver, Adolfo Moris Díaz, was born in Astoria, Queens, to a Dominican family and named for nineteenth-century Spanish poet Gustavo Adolfo Bécquer, not the murderous founder of Nazism. Still, he went by "Mo." As in "Mo Money, Mo Problems" his fellow drivers at the taxi dispatch liked to joke. And Mo *was* hard luck, often catching fares to remote areas of Staten Island and Long Island City, where there was little to no chance of picking up a return fare. And, of course, there was the poor luck of being named Adolf in a city full of Jews.

Mo was in a particularly bad mood today, having been kept awake all night by his newborn son (safely named Joe), then starting his shift at 4:00 A.M. First thing at dispatch, mind clouded by exhaustion, he'd tripped over an orange safety cone and spilled coffee down his slacks, inspiring taunts from fellow cabbies about having pissed his pants. He'd also stained his lucky Jorge Posada Yankees jersey, a prized possession since the catcher (whom Mo considered similarly underappreciated) retired.

Marjorie slid onto his scarred leather backseat, thinking it cold through her nonexistent skirt. She prayed that she wouldn't throw up. If Mo had known the extent of her queasiness, he would have prayed too.

"Thank goodness you stopped!" She glanced at his license. "Today . . . Adolfo, you saved a woman's life."

Normally, Mo might have managed a smile, but he was in no mood to placate some spoiled slut who wreaked of booze. And he didn't appreciate the use of his full first name. He opted for stony silence.

"Okaaay, I'm going to 11 West 42nd Street."

"Eleven?"

"Yes, 11. 11, 11."

"Wait, what? 111111?"

"No. Sorry. Just ignore that last bit."

"So, just 1111?"

"No. Just 11."

"Lady, *where you going?*"

"Sorry. Just 11 West 42nd Street between Fifth and Sixth Avenues . . . and make it snappy! That was a joke. That last part. Not the address."

Mo pulled violently from the curb as Marjorie gazed out the window, racking her brain for an excuse for showing up to the office at one o'clock in the afternoon in yesterday's clothing: an emergency doctor's appointment? A plumbing problem so dire that she'd had to plug the toilet with her foot and couldn't get to a phone?

On the upside, work could hardly get worse. Long before, Brianne had begun saddling her protégé with demeaning tasks: coffee fetching, copy making, collating, and lunch ordering—even once, during the annual boozy Christmas party, "bathroom upkeep." Occasionally, Brianne rolled Marjorie out in a short dress to work the door at boutique openings or swag-filled parties, where she would shout about some invented mistake (*The VIP list is in the wrong font, you idiot!*) before an audience of waiting guests.

At first, Marjorie had been seduced by Brianne's horsy smile and hard sell, by an infamous tyrant's deference, and by money because, unlike many of her peers, she didn't come from a lot. But she couldn't say why she continued to take the abuse. The truth, tucked between deep layers of gray matter, was that—after her post-high-school plummet from grace—she felt like too much of a failure.

Marjorie was more defeated each day, less capable of picking her purse up off the concrete floor of their lofted office and marching out the door. And, in self-fulfilling prophecy, she grew worse at her job: She jammed the copy machine, stapled paper stacks on the wrong corners, delivered them upside down on Brianne's desk, and awaited her next reaming.

When Mo finally pulled up to her office building, Marjorie sank lower into the taxi's palm, awash in both relief and despair. The driver felt the former: the way she stuck her head out the window was a classic hangover move. And this girl looked like a puker.

She excavated the insides of her bag, digging past empty packs of mint chocolate chip Extra Sugarfree Gum and wadded-up receipts, before uncovering her wallet. The bills inside were covered in sticky leaked lip gloss. She handed them to a thoroughly disgusted Mo, who looked to his taped-up photo of Shakira for support.

In the lobby, Bill, the building's long-enduring daytime security guard, looked meaningfully up at the antique wall clock, then winked a little sadly at Marjorie.

"I know," she murmured. "I know, I know."

"Miss Plum! Miss—" She disappeared into a waiting elevator car before he could clue her in to her exposed bottom.

Marjorie shot upward, her stomach left floors behind. Fellow passengers carried salads with dressing on the side from the downstairs commissary; the naked lettuce depressed her. They studiously ignored each other, arranging themselves at an optimal distance.

What felt like an eternity later, the doors opened with a *bing!* and she disembarked into the reception area at Bacht-Chit PR (that was "Bat-Shit" to those who knew Brianne). From behind an enormous spaceship of a desk, adorned with a single cruel orchid, Tina the receptionist looked Marjorie up and down, taking in the day-old, rumpled attire. "Oh, no." Her pudgy cheeks sank inward. "Madge! What happened?" she stage-whispered, gesturing her friend closer.

From one of the waiting area's white Eames chairs, a man—in the same Brioni tie as Mac's, his hair side parted and slicked back like Rhett Butler—followed Tina's gaze. He crinkled his nose in offense and returned to his *New York Magazine*.

Marjorie grimaced. "Is it bad?"

"Is it *bad*?" Tina repeated. "No, woman, it's apocalyptic! I was hoping you'd been delayed for a *real* reason: maybe a sprained leg or a tiny car accident." She emphasized the smallness of the hypothetical crash, holding the purple, bedazzled synthetic nails of her thumb and index fingers an inch apart. "Didn't you get my calls?"

Marjorie lifted her useless phone. "It's dead."

"Well, girl. So are you." Tina gestured toward the inner offices. "Might as well have at it. She's not getting any less mad. Crazy bitch."

Normally, Tina disdained harsh language, not for fear of Brianne's disapproval (the woman couldn't survive without her) but to practice the good manners she preached to her two daughters. Today's exception did not escape Marjorie's notice and, instead of bolstering her, it made her more nervous: The situation must be nuclear. She took a step toward Brianne's office.

"Wait!" Tina yelped. "Your skirt is tucked into your drawers."

Marjorie closed her eyes, decided not to review the number of people who had peeped her underwear that morning, and untucked herself.

She marched like a condemned criminal toward Brianne's door and knocked. Herb, the intern with whom she'd joked about Snow Lite the day before, whisked it open from inside. Sunlight reflected off his greasy forehead. (Brianne had taken to calling him "Slick" behind his back, a nod to his oily skin.) Marjorie was relieved to see a friendly, albeit unattractive, face. But when she tried to make eye contact, he averted his gaze. She was too toxic to acknowledge.

The lady herself sat behind an enormous desk, head bowed over a magazine spread. A selection of beauty product samples with floral packaging were clustered in front of her beside a transparent canteen of ominous green liquid. Apparently, Brianne was on another juice cleanse; her mood would be exponentially foul from food deprivation.

Some happy client had sent a "good luck" bamboo plant, plucked from a Canal Street stall—a perfect gift for Brianne, who considered herself "spiritual" because, once in a blue moon, she paused mid-venom spew to do Downward-Facing Dog. An unused yoga mat dotted with peace signs leaned below a closed window; the air reeked of sage.

Brianne wore the usual *meaningful* jewelry: an eighteen-karat-gold breast cancer ribbon, Peace dog tags, a diamond hamsa prayer bracelet hung with charms of the Chinese character for truth and the astrological symbol for Taurus: a bull. And yet the concept of karma conveniently escaping her grasp. As was the fashion, to manifest success, she believed she need only proclaim her desires out loud.

Not long before, Brianne had attended a group meditation led by Amma, "the Hugging Saint." (Gwyneth Paltrow was supposedly a fan.) Receiving the first genuine embrace after years of air kisses, she pronounced herself a devotee, espousing wisdom but never bothering to attend another gathering. On her desk's corner was a framed quotation attributed to the guru: "Bliss is not to be found outside of us; it exists within us."

Bliss was nowhere in sight.

The door banged shut. Marjorie glanced back: Herb appeared to be blocking her exit, the world's puniest bodyguard.

"Look who decided to grace us with her presence, Heeeerb."

"Marjorie finally showed—"

Brianne shot him a menacing look: This was her show. He pressed his lips shut. She pulled off her reading glasses, smudged with bronzer. Supposedly into "natural beauty," she fried herself at tanning salons, then spackled her hide with crusty foundation. The aesthetic was left over from a mournful adolescence spent wandering Akron's Summit Mall, staring longingly after popular girls with high bangs on movie dates with boys named Chip.

In fact, the PR bigwig tortured Marjorie as proxy for her Ohio high school's prom queen, Krista Midvale. Brianne had been an obese teenager. She had not been tormented, but she still resented the kids who thrived as she sat at home on her couch, watching reruns of *Remington Steele*. At graduation, she swore success-based revenge. Unfortunately, Krista aspired only to have a loyal husband, two or three nice kids, and a part-time real estate career—all of which she had quickly achieved. At the one reunion Brianne dared attend, clutching an Hermès bag as a shield, Krista flashed the former fat girl (whom she barely recognized) a pageant smile, wishing her all the best. *Bitch*.

"Brianne, I'm so sorry I'm late," began Marjorie. "I was out last night at Mac O'Shea's new place, DIRT. I thought maybe he'd let us throw some events there . . ."

Brianne shook her head sharply. "Nope."

"So, there was this plumbing issue and . . ."

Brianne wasn't listening. She clicked an icon on her computer, and the printer sputtered to life, sucking a virgin sheet of paper into its jaws.

"Um." Marjorie said. "Um. Um."

Brianne signaled to Herb, who scurried to extract the page. She took it from him, then held it out to Marjorie, before dropping it "accidentally" to the floor.

"*Oops, oops, oops,*" Brianne cackled.

Full of self-loathing, Marjorie bent down, picked up the document, and skimmed it. As she read, horror set in.

"It's all set to send out as a mass e-mail," said Brianne. "But the printed letterhead added something special for the presentation to *you*."

The letter read:

Dear Colleagues,

It is with great regret that I am writing to inform you of a rift within our Bacht-Chit Public Relations & Events family.

Many of you have had occasion to work over the last seven years with an employee of mine named Marjorie Plum. I'm afraid there is no positive way to express this:

Effective June 14, I was forced to terminate Ms. Plum's employment, as a result of unsettling and erratic behavior, the exact nature of which I am not at liberty to divulge. Suffice it to say that our support and thoughts go out to her family during this trying time, and to Marjorie, as she seeks the lifetime of treatment she clearly requires.

I want to take this opportunity to apologize for any unseemly or unprofessional interactions you may have had with Ms. Plum. I took her under my wing originally as a special mentee and felt it was important to give her several chances to right herself before closing our doors to her. I suppose I may have shown poor judgment in that empathic act.

Most important, should Ms. Plum try to contact you, for your own good, I strongly urge you to ignore her calls and e-mails. Do not engage or reply. She is unpredictable, and I would never want to feel responsible for any negative or even dangerous occurrences.

If you have any questions, please don't hesitate to be in touch.

Yours in Peace, Love & Harmony,

Brianne
Brianne Bacht-Chit, Founder & CEO

"I particularly like the part about your family," said the demon behind the desk. "Good touch, if I do say so."

Marjorie was stunned. "I don't understand."

"Then you're even dumber than you look."

"Why would you do this?"

"Well, you're fired, if that isn't obvious." Brianne smoothed her overprocessed mop. "I could have let security escort you out; the prospect is amusing. But I can't risk you badmouthing me. Unfathomably, people seem to *like* you. It's probably a pity thing . . . Where was I?"

"She's fired!" yelped Herb.

"Right. You're a waste of oxygen, Madge. You may now leave. And if you say one nasty thing about me, I'll send this out."

Panic and rage coursed through Marjorie. "You can't do this."

"Actually, I can. You gave me 'cause' yesterday. BTW, kudos for taking absurdly long bathroom trips, so that Herb could hop on your computer and resend that e-mail to Snow Lite's CEO from your account. What do you *do* in there?"

Marjorie *knew* she hadn't e-mailed the client. But her gut instincts had been undermined long before.

Her face pulsed with adrenalin and shock. "You're questioning my sanity? You're the one who's lost your mind! You can't just make things up. It's called 'libel.'"

"I'm not so worried about that." Brianne cracked her neck, side to side. "You're a shoddy employee. Now you've shown up in yesterday's dreary clothes, hours late, reeking of alcohol, so it's plausible that you have a drinking problem—only a hop, skip, and a jump to a psychotic break." She grabbed her green juice, captured its straw in her mouth, and sucked, eyes smiling above the dredge. The liquid had tinged her tongue black.

Brianne nodded to Herb, who crossed the room and reopened the door.

"Leave, please. Thanks." She returned to her magazine.

Fury rose in Marjorie's chest. "Drink up, Brianne. You'll still look like a giant rotting pumpkin. I hope you choke to death on your LOVE pendant." She turned and stalked out of the room.

"Did everyone hear that? Herb, please take note. The crazy girl *threatened* me." Brianne shouted, "Madge, darling! Just FYI. This is me hitting Send."

Marjorie didn't stop at her desk. She walked back down the hallway, past a wide-eyed Tina at reception, down the elevator, past security and out onto the street, then she threw up in a garbage can atop three empty Starbucks cups. Only then did she realize that her skirt was still caught in her underwear.

5

An hour and two minutes later, more by instinct than design, Marjorie found herself riding the elevator up to her parents' apartment, thanking the doorman gods that she didn't recognize the guy on duty. He had put aside the *New York Post* sports section and greeted her with formality.

Her parents had bought their place decades before, when middle-class families could afford Manhattan living. Longtime members of the building's staff were like distant uncles, offering wisdom and kindness as Marjorie grew up—helping her stash uncool wool hats pre- and postschool and warning her when yellow "alert" forms arrived from school reporting her misconduct.

The day she got accepted to NYU, her father had shared the good news with their favorite doorman, Tommy, who dubbed her "Smarty Pants Plum." She couldn't have faced him today. The smell of the lobby alone—a familiar combination of Mr. Clean, honeysuckle, and Hungarian food—threatened to undo her.

At the front door, Marjorie pulled out her keys and let herself in. No one was home. Her parents wouldn't be surprised to see her anyway; they all had plans for dinner together that evening. She was exhausted, having walked from Midtown, the subway tunnels seeming too close to the depths of despair.

She pulled an extra phone charger from a junk drawer in the pantry, then walked down the hall to her childhood bedroom and plugged it in. She stood at center, taking in her surroundings. A million years had passed since she painted one wall red and thumbtacked up pictures of Jared Leto in *My So-Called Life* and Scott Speedman in *Felicity*. Where was she when everyone else was getting a life?

Marjorie crossed to a gray speckled bookshelf, filled with children's staples like *Encyclopedia Brown* and Judy Blume's *Forever,* classics like *Pride and Prejudice* and *Little Women,* comics from *Archie* to *The Adventures of Tintin.* The shelf's disorganized twin bookended the bed. On the bottom was a defunct record player, and records from Marjorie's early childhood—not cool enough to be dubbed "vinyl" by baseball-capped DJs—leaned against the side: *Free to Be . . . You and Me, Really Rosie,* Hans Christian Andersen.

Behind that teetered a tower of small rectangular books. Marjorie felt a pang. When she was seven years old, her father bought her a black-and-white flip book of Charlie Chaplin duck-walking down the street, nearly beheaded by a passing lady in an enormous feathered hat. Despite the simple story, Marjorie had been taken by the still images launched into motion. She started collecting flip books, even making her own. She pulled out an original now: a roughly drawn flower growing from a seed. *Flip. Flip. Flip.*

Random objects and loose papers cluttered the shelf above. (No one ever accused Marjorie Plum of neatness.) Lime green brocade peaked out. Curious, Marjorie plucked the item from beneath the layers and turned it over in her hands: *That's right!* She and her fourth-grade classmates had written their own books. For the cover, she had chosen a material fit for a nineteenth-century English manor's drapery. "Oh, my God," she said, laughing.

Suddenly, she felt like she'd fallen through a wormhole. She could distinctly recall crafting some story about a girl stuck inside a flip book (what else?). She'd left indelible teeth marks in many a pencil while her mother suggested big words like "imperceptible" and then instructed her to "look them up." Now she thumbed to the book's back, finding an About the Author written in her then unpolished hand (clearly ignoring any editorial guidance from the teacher, since the story itself was without mistakes) beside a Polaroid of her ten-year-old self in a flowered sundress and clunky New Balance sneakers.

Marjorie Plum is a riter and artist. She will one day live in a big blue glass house, where she will rite storys for movies and books. She will have two cats named Bimpy and Bop, and a million freinds will visit to do art projects together. She will be very happy. She will never eat cooked carrots, EVER.

Marjorie could hardly bear the innocence.

Next, she excavated a blue leather coin-collecting kit with slots for pennies, their open mouths waiting to be fed. Mac, she thought, would relish this proof of her inner geek. *Mac, Mac, Mac.* Had he cornered the market on contentment? Was that the secret: spending nights tanked, mornings alone drinking high-end espresso, your only guiding principles anonymous sex and a good personal trainer?

Marjorie's phone finally sprang to life, a flurry of *bings, bongs,* and *whooshes.* Picking it up, she scrolled through: mostly texts from Tina, before and after the insanity.

Massaging her aching head, Marjorie pulled her hair out of its bobby pins. Amid the nausea and upset, she realized with alarm that on some twisted level she'd been disappointed that the messages were not from Mac. She allowed herself for the first time that day (and she hoped the last time *ever*) to think about the night before: how they'd laughed after Vera left, how he'd looked at her after that first kiss, how they'd lain drifting off to sleep, pillow to pillow, his hand warm and comforting on her lower back. What felt right under the cover of night now seemed so misguided.

She shook her head clear and looked around. She had been a child with interests beyond her own complexion and next vodka tonic. Where had she gone *wrong*? (One might point to a certain day in June 2002, when—in a silly maroon cap and gown—she accepted her diploma but never actually left the auditorium.)

As if in response to her question, a photograph fluttered from the messy bookshelf onto the floor: A sixteen-year-old Marjorie sat on a neighborhood stoop with Vera and their other friend Pickles, swigging from a forty-ounce bottle of Olde English malt liquor. Pickles blew smoke rings, in challenge, at the camera. Marjorie's crimson-smeared lips pushed against the bottle's mouth. She looked like a child playing dress-up, cheeks full, eyebrows unplucked, free.

Marjorie had distance from most of her teenage memories, which dropped away with her baby fat and abandon. But, for an instant, she was inside the picture, feeling the rough concrete under her thighs, smelling chocolate croissants baking at Zabar's, nearby. And it was too painful. She dropped the photo, walked to the bed, and lay down on her side, exhausted. Tucking her legs up toward her belly, she pressed her hands together at her cheek, as if in prayer.

6

Marjorie awoke, disoriented and creased, to the smell of garlic sautéing in olive oil.

Her outlook after a rare midday nap—when she rose to find the sun slipping away—was bleak, even on a good day. Now, as reality set in, she was miserable. What was she going to tell her parents? Should she wait until the end of dinner? Until second glasses of wine? *Shit*. She should have come armed with unemployment statistics and complaints about "big business!" (That was a thing, right?) Was it too late to occupy Wall Street? She never did like camping.

She walked to the bathroom and looked at her disheveled self in the mirror. The Tiffany necklace she'd worn since high school graduation had left a red indentation on her chest—a scarlet heart. She borrowed white jeans and a slouchy French blue button-down from her mother's closet, showered, dressed, then crept out into the living room. The Plums were nowhere in sight. The family feline, Mina the Cat—a Siamese with grace but not poise—leapt off an antique chair. She rubbed her spindly body against Marjorie's legs and let out a gravely grunt, more smoker's cough than mew.

"Hi, Goof!" Marjorie scooped up the runt, who began grooming her human pal with her sandpaper tongue. "Okay, okay, okay. Thank you, but that's enough." The cat settled against Marjorie's chest, a purring, kneading fur ball.

Taking a deep breath, Marjorie crossed the spacious living room into the open exposed-brick kitchen: sweet potatoes baked in the oven, a roast chicken cooled in its juices atop the stove, a pot of artichokes steamed.

"Mom?"

"Marjorie?" The voice originated from a small adjoining office, once the maid's quarters, typical in a classic eight New York apartment. "Is that you, sweetie?"

"Well, I certainly hope so. Otherwise someone's broken into your house and is kidnapping your cat."

Mina the Cat, unconcerned, snuggled in closer.

"Coming, coming! Are the sweet potatoes ready?"

"How would a person know that exactly? You know I burn water."

Barbara Plum appeared from around the corner, looking surprised—as she frequently did—by the delight she felt at seeing her daughter. Marjorie had not been a "miracle baby" per se, but she was a last-minute decision and the couple's only child. Barbara had never liked babies and thought she wouldn't want one, but, as she was fond of quipping, her biological clock simply ran slow.

For dinner's sake, she opened the oven with a checkered mitt before greeting her daughter. "They'd be brown and crispy, almost caramelized." She had changed from workday clothes into a black T-shirt, yoga pants, and shearling-lined L.L. Bean slippers. Her gray-streaked, chin-length hair, once auburn like Marjorie's, was tucked behind her ears. "Everyone burns everything until they learn to cook. You have to be bad to get good."

Just another reason to feel inept, thought Marjorie. Her mother had gone to Fairway Market, bought food, and prepared a no doubt amazing meal—no big deal. Where had Marjorie been at that time? Pulling on underwear in Mac's doorway? Getting fired?

She stroked Mina the Cat in silence, as her mother lifted the artichoke pot's lid, pulled off a leaf, and handed it over. Marjorie tasted it and nodded.

Turning off the burner, Barbara faced her in proper greeting, brushing her fingers through her daughter's hair. "You look pale. Are you feeling okay?"

"Um," began Marjorie, suddenly undone by her mother's touch. "Um, um, um."

Barbara's forehead crinkled in concern, and it occurred to Marjorie that she might have caused the three jagged lines traveling faintly across her mother's otherwise youthful face. "What's wrong, sweetie? Did something happen?"

Through crossed blue eyes, Mina the Cat stared her in the face too.

"I'm okay—" Marjorie's voice faltered. "I just didn't have . . . a very good day." A single tear rolled down her cheek, trailing off into the dry creek bed of her jaw. She wiped it away. What a disappointment she must be. "It's nothing."

As if sensing a coming storm, the cat leapt off of Marjorie and scampered to the safety of the living room.

"It doesn't look like nothing."

"I'm fine." Marjorie exhaled, a vibrato wheeze. "Only, I think I can't breathe."

Barbara put an arm around her daughter's shoulders and led her to the couch. "It's okay," she said. "*Are* you okay?"

That's when Marjorie's father arrived. And, from the look on his face, he wished he'd waited a couple minutes. Chipper Plum disliked confrontation; he contributed opinions—gruffly—only on politics and TV. Years before, he'd perfected the art of zoning out when tension arose between his two favorite women, answering *"What?"* with genuine confusion when asked to take sides. Now, with his long limbs and pale skin, he stood by, evoking a birch tree. But there was no hope of escaping undetected. Instead, he adjusted his round wire-rimmed glasses and ambled to Marjorie's unoccupied side. "What happened?"

Marjorie took another shaky, accordion breath. She needed to offer an explanation, lest her parents imagine something catastrophic. Anything but the truth would do. "It's the Middle East," she tried, covering her eyes with her palm, "It's just so messed up over there."

"Over where exactly?" asked her father doubtfully.

"You know. There! Syria, Egypt, Morocco . . . whatever."

The Plums exchanged a look.

"If it's any consolation, sweetie, Morocco is in an unrelated part of Africa," said her mother. "They really did a horrible job of teaching geography at that school of yours."

"Well, it's everything. I mean, what's wrong with this world? Did you know that they might cancel *Parenthood*? Sometimes I just want to give up."

"You're having suicidal thoughts because of a TV show?" said Barbara.

"It's not like it's *Cheers*," said Chipper seriously, whose deep love of television history made the complaint more plausible.

"Oh, forget it," Marjorie wheezed. "I can't even lie effectively! I got fired. That's why I'm upset . . . fired, fired, *fired*."

"Okay, sweetie. Stay calm." Barbara pulled a travel-size Kleenex pouch from her purse and offered a tissue.

"Mom. I'm not crying! I'm hyperventilating!"

"Right. Remember what I learned at that seminar about anchoring yourself in the present when you feel anxiety? Look around the room and identify what's physically here to stop the emotional spiral."

"Mom!"

"Just try it!"

As a life coach, Barbara Plum stayed abreast of current self-improvement trends. (She did not, however, adopt New Age fashion or beauty principles—never a tribal pattern or patchouli-scent did infiltrate.) Long before, she had audited a Mindful Meditation class, which framed her approach not only to unhinged clients but also to her daughter, who had begun having panic attacks thanks to Brianne's flagellation. Marjorie resisted these strategies, mostly because her mother suggested them.

"C'mon. We'll do it together. There is the oak farm table with a splintered slat protruding from one leg. There's the black leather Austrian Thonet chair with scratches from Mina's nails down one side, and the Kilim Persian rug with . . . Oh Christ, did the cat throw up over there?" She turned to face her husband. "Chipper, our living room is a mess! We need to get *everything* fixed!"

Marjorie sighed. "I think we've strayed off topic."

Chipper scratched his head. An anxiety attack wasn't terrible—not by comparison to a fight. Still, raw emotion was not his forte, having grown up in Darien, Connecticut, where people had the courtesy to use restraint. Residents wore Docksider boat shoes, blue button-downs, and pleated khakis, and had the inbred good sense not to sob or shout in public, except on rare occasions when they mixed white wine spritzers with the wrong prescription pills.

Chipper's family was unique in that they weren't Episcopalian or even Protestant. His people were *Mayflower* Jews with nicknames like Fifi and Mims, who decorated a suspiciously large and cone-shaped pine "Hanukkah bush" in blue and white lights every holiday season. Rumor had it that Plum had been changed from Plumberg by Chipper's great-grandfather *"Just call me Mike!"* Moishe, though the family retold a vague story (accompanied by dismissive hand gestures) about immigration through Ellis Island. "How fortunate," one dense neighbor commented to Chipper's mother, Judy, "that your name was changed for the better and not worse! Where did your family emigrate from? Dublin? I much prefer Plum to O'Plummer!"

Having overheard this exchange at ten years old and having a general, albeit unclear, idea that dishonesty was at play, Chipper henceforth referred to his mother as "Mrs. O'Plummer," which drove her nuts. (She may not have wanted to advertise her Judaism, but that didn't mean she wanted to be Irish!) And, as an adult, he felt a connection—not the irritation of a phantom limb—when he glimpsed his missing foreskin, solidarity instead of self-loathing in the face of anti-Semitism, pride not envy when he read the works of great Jewish scholars and intellectuals like Hannah Arendt and Martin Buber, literary figures like Saul Bellow and Philip Roth. He worshipped Sandy Koufax, lusted after Lauren Bacall and, later, modeled his humor after Lenny Bruce. He *felt* Jewish.

In his teens, he joined the 1960s revolution and became his version of a hippie (all politics; no suede fringe), though he grew his straight blondish hair—which seemed to confirm his family's passing lie—out to his shoulders. It was not until the late 1970s, when he was twenty-nine years old and still eschewing bell-bottoms, that he met Mrs. O'Plummer's worst nightmare: his Brooklyn College teaching assistant, Barbara Davida Schwartz (Marjorie's mother). He fell in love and, within weeks, was learning hands-on about his own heritage from her deeply Jewish family: "Try the gefilte fish! It's a vehicle for horseradish!"

Ultimately, Chipper and Barbara took their religion lightly, hitting synagogue only on high holidays (*"L'Shana Tova!"*), and stocking the fridge with sour dill pickles. Marjorie was bat mitzvahed (more gifts of sterling silver Tiffany jewelry). And her Grandma Plum did attend, though she declined to don a doily on her graying head during the service.

Chipper rebelled in another way too: Instead of studying law like his older brothers, he became an academic, a media studies professor. His infatuation with radio, film, TV, and other "vast wastelands" had been fostered every time his parents felt lazy and plopped him in front of the boob tube as a child. "Lucille Ball was my babysitter," Chipper was fond of saying, though he mostly watched precursors to modern reality shows, like *Queen for a Day,* on which women spun sob stories in exchange for sympathy and *fabulous!* prizes.

Chipper had shed any residual affection for the golf shirts and bow ties of his youth. But his aversion to emotion remained. And so now he fought the urge to flee.

Barbara shot him a stern, knowing look. He returned it with a growl, but they both knew she was right. And Chipper always did the right thing.

Marjorie had calmed down enough to tell the (edited) story.

"What a nightmare," sighed Barbara afterward.

"How can that horrible woman do such a thing?" cried Chip.

Ultimately, they decided, over drumsticks and artichokes, that a change was for the best. At least Marjorie believed that until her mother agreed.

"It's a terrible industry anyway."

"Mom. Brianne is horrible, but let's not damn them all."

"You should have quit ages ago. I mean, *ages.*"

"Maybe I am better off," said Marjorie, "but I don't have a job or money or any idea what to do next. I can't work in PR, and that's all the experience I have!"

"Fake it 'til you make it, Bozo," suggested her father. Suddenly, the term of endearment felt downright insulting. "Do whatever's necessary. Take a cue from *Tootsie!*"

"Dress up like a man?"

Born into extreme privilege and having always known his path,

Chipper had never worked a nine-to-five office job in pursuit of a dream. He gave terrible career advice.

Barbara sighed. "We're talking about a *real* career instead of bar-hopping for a living."

"Hold on. You encouraged me to take this job!"

"You were nineteen."

"This is insane revisionist history! You were over the moon. It was like your ship had come in—and docked at the top of the social stratum."

"We're not talking about my ship. We're talking about your dinghy."

"Suddenly there's a difference?"

Marjorie had accepted Brianne's job offer and remained for many reasons, but her mother's elated whoop at the news of her rising status had contributed.

"We thought you'd have moved on by now."

"Fine." Marjorie was revolted by her own petulance. "But what am I going *to do*?"

This question was a misstep. After all, people paid Barbara Plum to answer it.

"I'll get a piece of paper. We'll make a list!"

"Barb," Chipper pleaded. But the train had left the station. She was already at the counter, sifting through an old cookie tin for a working pen. He turned to Marjorie for reason: "This seems like a poor idea."

She shrugged. "Maybe I need to do this."

Giving up, Chipper grabbed the *New York Times* for protection and leafed to the op-ed page, where there would likely be less dissent. Barbara sat back down, her chair screeching against the tile floor in warning.

"Let's begin with a list of obstacles. Then we can address next steps, one by one, so as not to overwhelm."

"Well, let's see . . ." considered Marjorie, sprinkling her sweet potatoes with coarse salt.

Barbara caught her daughter's hand midshake. "Enough."

"Really, Mom? Right now, you want to lecture me on sodium intake?"

"If you want to be bloated on top of everything else, go ahead."

Both women rolled their eyes.

Consumed by appearances, Barbara was more like Chipper's own mother than he allowed himself to suspect. She came from a working-class Queens family, whom she loved and respected, but she wanted more. She had fallen for Chipper based on animal magnetism and shared sense of humor, but had also likely been attracted to his obvious smarts (glasses!), upward mobility, and those same WASPy looks his mother fostered.

There had been another man before Chipper: a carpenter, who dreamed of owning a peach orchard upstate. Barbara fantasized with him about the pies she would bake, the fires he would build. But she knew she could never be satisfied with that life.

With Chipper, Barbara built the future she'd imagined and gave birth to a beautiful daughter, whom she couldn't help reminding to stay as perfect as she'd come out—to capitalize on those looks, brains, and private school connections, to remember lipstick, stand up straight, get back on top!

Still, once in a while, when Barbara bit into a ripe peach, she felt a pang for the path not taken, though she did not remember why. One could live only one life and hers would be with the well-bred professor, who could never pass up an episode of *M*A*S*H*.

"The first problem is that I have no money," said Marjorie.

"Okay, got it. *No money.*" Barbara scribbled on the yellow notebook paper in cursive.

"And nowhere to live."

"Nowhere to live."

Marjorie looked hopefully at Barbara; Barbara looked back blankly.

"What else?"

"Mom."

"Yes?"

"I have nowhere to live."

"I know." Barbara scanned the list, checking her work. "I got that one."

Marjorie steeled herself. "I may need to move back in with you guys, just while I save some money."

Barbara set down the pen and folded her hands in front of her in a "professional" way that drove Marjorie insane. "That may be a problem."

"A problem? Why?"

"Because we're renovating your bedroom."

"Into what? A gym?"

"No. Into another bedroom. For guests, who aren't sixteen."

"You're converting my bedroom into a *bedroom*?"

"That's right."

"When were you planning on telling me that?"

"Tonight."

"So the artichokes, my favorite, were to butter me up?"

"No. I don't need to butter you up. This is *my* house."

Mina the Cat sauntered into the room, caught a whiff of the tension, and raced away, ducking under the radiator. Chipper pulled the newspaper closer to his face.

"You know, Mom, you don't need to make me feel *more* alienated."

"I wouldn't dream of it."

"When is this starting?"

"Wednesday."

"Wednesday?"

"Yes. And I realize this might not be convenient, but I need you to go through your stuff and decide what you want."

Marjorie turned to father and instead found herself face-to-face with an article about drops in coffee prices in relation to Colombia's economy.

"Dad?" Chipper did not respond. "Dad!"

"Yes?"

"Did you know about this?"

"Of course, he knows about it! It's his home," said Barbara. "And you haven't stayed over in six months. Were we supposed to dedicate your room as a shrine?"

Marjorie covered her face with her hands. "Okay, okay, okay. What am I going to do?"

Barbara looked surprised. "Well, honey, that's why we're making a list!"

"Mother! I don't need a list! I need a job, never mind an actual *career,* but those issues seem less pressing, since I have nowhere to *live!*"

"Well, that's sensible."

"I can't tell if you're being sarcastic."

"No. That *is* sensible. And I have an idea."

Barbara disappeared into her office and returned with her iPhone in hand. She copied a number on a fresh sheet of paper and handed it to her daughter.

"What's this? The number for the nearest mental hospital?"

"Very funny. It's my friend Patricia Reynolds's info. You remember her from the symposium at Bard."

Marjorie racked her brain. "Wait. The drum circle woman? With the hemp recipe book?"

"She's very nice."

"Mom!"

"Well, she is. Anyway, Patricia just sent out a message saying that her youngest, Fred, is looking for a roommate."

"A mass e-mail? That sounds desperate."

Barbara's look said, *Takes one to know one.*

"Have you met this kid?"

"No."

Marjorie examined the paper, as if it might offer a glimpse of her future. "Mom. This number has a 347 area code."

"Yes."

"That's *Brooklyn.*"

"I believe that's true."

"Mom! Please, stop playing dumb. You're the one who says we 'don't do' Brooklyn."

"I didn't say that."

"Actually, you did," Chipper said. The coast seemed clearer now, and he did love ribbing his wife.

"Well, fine. That's right. *We* don't do Brooklyn." Barbara paused. "But now *you* do."

Barbara and Chipper grinned at each other across the table.

"That's funny?" said Marjorie. "Why is that funny?"

Chipper snorted—Marjorie had inherited that habit from him—sending both elder Plums into hysterics.

"You guys are insane!"

They just laughed harder. Eventually, Marjorie joined in. It was either that or cry.

7

Marjorie left her parents' house with the best of intentions.

On the train, as a one-man band played "Empire State of Mind" on his accordion and kazoo, she typed another list on her phone:

TO DO
- Get job.
- Save money.
- Consider deep-seated psychological issues behind sleeping with M.
- Figure out what to do with life.
- Learn to tolerate Brian, so oldest friendship isn't over.
- ~~Never drink again.~~
- Don't drink for a week.
- Buy face wash. You're almost out. (Not life-changing, but acne isn't going to HELP your future.)

The passengers opposite nodded off or read books from *The Hunger Games* to *Fifty Shades of Grey* (safely hidden inside e-readers); they skimmed bibles—New Testament, Old Testament, Koran, Weight Watchers points booklets.

Marjorie liked to invent backstories for these strangers: Someone somewhere yearned to kiss the sixteen-year-old girl in the brown suede moccasins with dangling tassels. Someone had surely had his heart broken by the young man with hair gelled into a static tsunami. Someone remembered a youthful crush on the elderly Asian woman, stoic beside a rolling cart filled with plastic bags of unusual vegetables.

She caught Marjorie's eye, frowned, and spit a wad of phlegm on the subway car's floor.

Once downtown, Marjorie walked east on Houston's broken sidewalk, emboldened by a possible solution. She bypassed NoLIta and walked toward the Lower East Side. The one-time Jewish ghetto had been childhood home to Marjorie's grandfather Jacob; there, he had attended the city's oldest synagogue, bought lox and pickled herring at the still thriving Russ & Daughters. Now the neighborhood was packed with hipster boutiques and restaurants with forty-five-minute waiting lists, and, of course, bars like DIRT.

Marjorie stood outside, suddenly doubting the wisdom of her idea. She wound her hair into a twist and then let it fall. She turned to leave. But just then, up walked John. Their shared nod from the night before was the most interaction they'd had in eight years; now they'd be forced to make small talk.

"What's up, Madge?" He shot her a lazy smile. These days he was a gentle giant at six five and round. He bent way down and pecked Marjorie's cheek. "How you been?"

"Fine." She bit her lip. "I got fired today." What possessed her to share?

"Oh, man. Sucks. Been there. Bunch o' assholes. Or, I don't know, but I'm sure."

"Thanks, John. That's sweet."

"Surprised that happened, though. Always seemed like things came easy to you."

"Oh. Did it?" Shame so innate that Marjorie barely knew it existed bubbled up and threatened to spill. "I guess not anymore."

"Ah, well. Bet you could use a drink. Where you coming from?"

"Dinner with my mom and dad." Why did that feel embarrassing too—like she was thirteen years old and needed to pretend she didn't *have* parents?

"I always liked your ma."

"You did? That's nice."

"Yeah. Nice rack too."

Marjorie's mouth dropped open in disgust. But, as John pulled open the door, she had no choice but to walk through.

She paused on the threshold. Everything felt like a bad omen: askew piles of napkins bearing the gastropub's logo—a vintage-style hoe; men with fresh pints entranced by flat screens, the word "fussili" misspelled among the chalkboard specials.

The same mustached bartender looked up at her, then glanced nervously over to where Mac was standing with the brunette—a poor man's Jessica Alba—from the evening before. *Of course.* Marjorie forced a breezy smile.

Actually, she was enraged. He couldn't have waited twenty-four hours before whoring himself out again? Mac and John exchanged pounds in greeting. He turned at John's gesture and—spotting her—waved without qualification, and approached. He looked uncharacteristically sloppy: shirt buttoned wrong, cuff stained.

"What's up, Madgesty?"

"Nothing, Mac. Cute girl you got there." She couldn't resist a comment.

He glanced back at Alba 2.0. "She's no you." He grinned. "Speaking of which: you back for more?"

"Did you really just say that?"

"You better believfe it."

"You're wasted."

"Not too washted . . . to, you know, perform."

"I'm gonna go." Marjorie turned to leave.

"No, stay, stay. I'm just fucking around! Have a sense of humor already. What's up?"

Marjorie took a deep breath. She had nothing left to lose. "I was wondering if Tom Selleck needs a barkeep."

"'Scuse?"

"The bartender with the mustache. I need work, quickly. I got . . . I had to leave my job today."

"What do you do again?"

"Mac, seriously? We've thrown three different opening parties for your restaurants."

"Right. I see what you're saying." He sank into the closest booth.

"What am I saying?"

"That you need a job, so . . . okay."

"Really? It's that easy?"

"Sure."

"Oh, my God, Mac." Marjorie exhaled. She could keep her Manhattan apartment! She'd find a roommate online, murderers be damned. She resolved to buy an extra coconut water at the corner bodega to demonstrate her commitment to the neighborhood. "This means so much."

"Don't mention it. I'm shhure you'll find numer-, numer-, ugh, fuck it, *many* ways to thank me."

Marjorie froze. "Wait. What?"

"Looking forward to being your boss. You know what I mean."

"In a horrible turn of events, I think I do know *exactly* what you mean."

He winked—like he had an affliction—then leaned across the table to where she stood and slipped a finger through one of her belt loops. "Why don't you come to the back room and sign your paperwork."

Marjorie stepped back, yanking his hand from her jeans. "Wow. What a disappointment. Even for *you*." She started toward the door.

"This is not a good way to start a working relationship!" Mac called after her. He tugged at his ear, smirked, then braced himself, as he fumbled to standing.

Glancing back at him, it occurred to Marjorie that getting back on her own feet would prove more difficult than she'd imagined too.

8

At 11:30 P.M., Marjorie fit her key in the bottom lock at her apartment, 2B. The number had prompted many a nervous (and immediately regretful) date to quote Shakespeare. She nudged the door open with her hip.

The lights were out in the living room. The air smelled of extinguished fig candle, a neighbor's yellow rice and red beans, and something familiar that defied description: *home*. Marjorie let go a sigh, equal parts relief and despair.

She had always imagined moving back to the Upper West Side after college, but the area had transformed from J. D. Salinger leftist to "might as well be Westchester" suburban, overrun with yoga-clad bankers' wives. In looking, she discovered that there wasn't another neighborhood with so many wide avenues, parks, beautiful prewar buildings, and tree-lined streets, bookended by half-century-old businesses from shoemakers to florists.

But NoLIta—nicknamed for its proximity to NoHo and Little Italy, a pipsqueak of a neighborhood itself—offered compensation in the form of the occasional tree boxed in by wire fencing but also sweet independent boutiques and cafés, all windows, Deco details, and understated signage.

The two-bedroom apartment with tinged plaster walls and parquet floors seemed like a gift from God but was actually inherited from a midlevel executive at Vera's firm, who had amassed enough cash for less square footage in a new high-rise off the West Side Highway with amenities that tend to go unused, like an indoor pool and a lobby lounge.

Now Marjorie threw her purse on the couch and tiptoed to the kitchen to wash subway grime from her hands, noticing, with fresh misery, ownership stickers on most of the furniture that bore the initials "V.G." for Vera Granger. *For the movers.*

Marjorie had never made enough money for big-ticket home items and piddled away any small surpluses on taxis and takeout. But Vera, with her subscriptions to *Lonny, Dwell,* and *Domino,* had insisted on upgrading from dorm-appropriate, afghan-covered couches, and living like the adults they were becoming.

Marjorie scanned the room: *Good-bye heather Room & Board couch, "LOVE" poster, and white shag rug that Vera somehow kept clean. Good-bye gold-stitched Moroccan poof.*

Did nothing belong to her? From a shelf across the room, a stuffed Uglydoll toy mocked Marjorie with its adorable fangs. "What are *you* looking at?"

The only items of hers were on that same shelf: a delicate glass bird with which she'd fallen in love at a design store on Wooster, a postcard of a painting of an evil little girl by Japanese artist Nara, and a rhinestone starfish from a jewelry designer friend. A bottle of expensive champagne lay in Vera's wine rack, a "cheer up" gift from an exboyfriend, one of the many times she chickened out about quitting her job. In a grunge-era distressed Anthropologie frame was a photograph of Marjorie and Vera from elementary school. Her head was tipped onto her best friend's shoulder. Both girls grinned, dwarfed by their oversized teeth and backpacks. *Little girls.* Something broke apart inside Marjorie just then.

She and Vera had fought before. A friendship doesn't span two decades without misunderstandings and growing pains. But this time felt different. Was Marjorie jealous that Vera had found someone? Maybe. Did she feel abandoned and alone? Perhaps. Did she believe that Brian was a steaming pile of crap, an option worse than settling? YES.

In her bedroom, Marjorie tossed her clothes on the desk chair and changed into an old tank and Pepto-Bismol-colored sweatpants, give-away swag. She plopped down on her bed, steeled herself, and then did the only thing left to do: She texted Patricia's drum circle spawn about the Brooklyn apartment. Living with a random guy in an outer borough was better than being homeless.

She opened her laptop, searched "Williamsburg," then stared at the Google map that emerged of meaningless street names and grids.

9

By design, Marjorie slipped out before her roommate emerged in the morning. In fact, Vera arrived in the living room moments later, sniffing like a bloodhound at the scent of still wafting Issey Miyake perfume.

Shortly thereafter, Marjorie panted up the train station stairs at the corner of President and Smith Streets. She wondered at the idiocy of calling a subway stop "Carroll" that doesn't stop exactly on that corner and promptly judged Brooklyn for it.

Her inherited snobbery toward the outer boroughs was particu-larly absurd considering her mother's Astoria upbringing. Marjorie had spent many blissful days at her grandparents' loudly furnished, plastic-covered, brick row house in Queens before she turned twelve and they moved to West Palm Beach, Florida—the place, her grand-father had quipped, "where people go to die." That had unfortunately been the case.

Only months before, Marjorie had ventured across the bridge (al-though which bridge she could not say) with Pickles—who, pregnant at the time, craved deep-fried food but would sooner subject her unborn child to anthrax than processed treats—to Williamsburg's gourmet vegan donut shop, Dun-Well. (Being first to visit a new Brooklyn culinary destination was social currency for Pickles, who would return to her Upper East Side mommy group with boxes of "healthy" artisanal peach chamomile and green tea donuts.) Young hipsters had roamed past in outfits that had lapped ironic and become earnest again: neon ankle socks, suspenders, retro lanyard bracelets obscuring inner wrist tattoos, even top hats.

Marjorie figured she could handle Williamsburg. But Fred's address seemed to be in a totally different and unknown neighborhood: Carroll Gardens.

So far, admittedly, even the subway platform was comparatively nice. Beneath requisite filth, white tiles shined. Exiting passengers looked like-minded and roughly her age, with earbuds firmly planted in their ears and their noses in paperbacks. Main drag, Smith Street, was dotted with independent storefronts; President grew more idyllic as she walked, following her iPhone's directions.

By the time Marjorie reached Fred's building, a quaint gray-blue row house with a bright red door and maple tree out front, she'd started to wonder if she'd been transported: Was this Portland, Oregon? Madison, Wisconsin? Why was it all so . . . pretty?

She was studying the buzzer, trying to recall Fred's last name, when a stout older woman in a track suit, with hair dyed so black it was blue, barreled out the door, wielding her Louis Vuitton knockoff purse like a weapon.

"Who you lookin' fawr?" It wasn't so much a question as an accusation. Marjorie was still in New York, after all.

"Fred!" the Manhattanite squeaked.

"Figures. Top of the stayas." She held the door open. Marjorie slid inside, as the woman disappeared down the street, a charging bull.

The building was simple but well maintained. Climbing to the second-floor landing, Marjorie wondered if taking the stairs daily might tone her butt (a silver lining!). There was no obvious doorbell; she knocked.

"One second, one second!" shouted a muffled voice from inside.

Marjorie heard a bang, a curse, then heavy footsteps. The door swung open to reveal . . . no one. She shifted her gaze downward and laid her eyes on a tiny waif of a girl with a pixie cut, wearing what looked like a vintage evening gown and motorcycle boots.

"Hi," said Marjorie, wondering if she had the wrong apartment. "I'm looking for Fred?"

"You found me!"

"You're Fred?"

"In the flesh!" The girl fluttered like a moth. "Fred. Short for Fredericka, which is a mouthful, so no one calls me that. Did you think I was a boy? Are you disappointed? It's misleading."

Not waiting for an answer, Fred ushered Marjorie down a hallway, yanking the door closed behind them. "It doesn't shut unless you slam it. Rule numero uno de la casa: Slam the door! It makes Roberta mad, but that's just an added bonus!"

"Roberta?"

"The woman who lives downstairs. Dark hair, nasty snarl, yea big." Fred drew her arms up into a large circle. The gesture felt descriptive rather than mean-spirited, as if it never occurred to Fred that calling someone "fat" would be offensive.

"I think I met her outside."

"Probably. She's no problem. All bark, no bite. She brings me homemade Italian cookies twice a week. The ones with the pine nuts, you know? I haven't had the heart to tell her I'm allergic to almonds, and they're just thick with marzipan. It kills her that I'm small. She thinks I don't eat!"

Fred did look a bit like a child playing dress-up. Marjorie felt obliged to respond, though she had nothing to add, "I like cookies." She sounded like an idiot. Fred didn't seem to notice.

"Come in, come in. Welcome to 'the Hellhole.' No, just kidding, but I haven't had the chance to clean in anticipation of your arrival. Sorry!"

Fred led Marjorie into a large, open living room and kitchen. Along its seams, original crown moldings bore Art Deco flourishes. Sunlight streamed in from the backyard and fell across polished wood herringbone floors. Apart from some woven tapestries, dream catchers, and pagan good luck amulets hanging about, this apartment was more lovely than any in which Marjorie had lived as an adult. She and Vera had sacrificed niceties—charm, character, space—to live among the beautiful people.

"This is it! Where the magic happens. What do you think?"

"It's really pretty." Marjorie knew she sounded stiff. She sometimes felt offbeat compared to her old friends, but next to this frenetic bohemian, she was plywood.

Fred smiled. "Thank you. Or, I should say, my aunt Maggie thanks you. Mags bought this place back in the day, and it turned out to be a good investment. She got transferred to Pittsburgh, and now, here I am! It was paid off years ago, so the rent is mostly a formality, to pay for upkeep. Feel free to look around! By the way, I really admire your hair." She ruffled her own. "I keep mine short because I can't figure out how to *do* it, you know?"

"Thanks. It's not much work, once you get the hang of it." Marjorie crossed to the kitchen window, careful not to knock over the two guitars—an old, loved acoustic and a pink electric—leaning against the sill. The backyard was abundant with hydrangea, honeysuckle, vegetables, herbs, and what looked like blueberry bushes.

"Roberta is the original farm-to-table chef. It's her garden."

Marjorie had to admit, it was beautiful. That was something, at least. "Oh, by the way, how much is the rent? I realize I never asked."

"It would be six hundred a month."

Marjorie spun around to face Fred. "Seriously?"

"Yeah. It's only fourteen hundred a month total, and you'll pay less because your room is smaller."

"But . . . I hope you don't mind me asking, but if it's so cheap, why do you even want a roommate?"

Fred laughed loudly, like a pirate. "Good question. I'm trying to make a real go of my music career, so I want to be responsible for as little financially as possible. Very rock n' roll, right?"

That explained the esoteric 1970s posters of Joni Mitchell and Harriet King. Marjorie suddenly felt depressed. Would she be obligated to attend sad coffeehouse shows, where her singer/songwriter room-mate would sing in falsetto clichés about some greasy-haired, patchy-goateed guy who dumped her?

Maybe her poker face needed work because Fred said, "We have a practice space. Don't worry, I don't 'jam' with the band here." The air quotes suggested a sense of irony, despite the surrounding evidence of goddess worship.

"Oh, I wasn't worried," lied Marjorie. "So, what's your . . . day job?"

"You name it!" Fred leaned against the kitchen island. "I'm a part-time receptionist at Cornerstone Healing down the street—it's an acupuncture and herbal medicine clinic. I help my brother out at his film company sometimes. And I—OMG. OMG. OMG!" Fred shot up and began pacing like a mental patient in solitary.

This is it, thought Marjorie. *This is when I find out that she's not just "quirky." Thanks, Mom.* "Are you okay?"

"I have practice in twenty minutes!"

"Oh, well, go ahead. I can run upstairs, see the room and I'm good to—"

"No, you don't understand. I double-booked. My other job is as a tutor, and I have my first session with this girl in Park Slope today! Also at ten thirty."

"Shit. Can you cancel either?"

"No, we have to learn a new song for a gig this week." Fred sank onto the tattered couch and closed her eyes, groaning, "Why am I like this?"

It was funny to be around someone who seemed even less together than Marjorie. "Is there anything I can do?"

"Really?" Fred sat up. "Thank you!" She leapt off the couch, grabbed her acoustic guitar and woven backpack, and sprinted for the door.

"Wait! Where are you going?"

"I owe you big time! I'll text you the address."

"Address? For what?"

"For the tutoring session. They pay in cash, so if they let you stay once you tell them you're not me or part of the program, you'll make money at least. Make sure you tell them that this time slot won't work for me going forward, so they can request a replacement."

"Wait, Fred, seriously?"

"Please! I can't tell you how much I'd appreciate it."

"What about the apartment?"

"You can move in whenever. Just call me and we'll work out the details. My ma says you're kinda broke, so I can help you move with my band's van." She paused. "Oh, I mean, assuming you *want* to move in."

Marjorie hadn't even seen the room, but what choice did she have? "I'm in. In, in, in."

"Great, great, great!" Fred bounded back over to Marjorie, crammed a set of keys into her hand, and surprised her with a hearty hug. "This is going to be amazing!"

"But Fred! I don't even know how to get to Park Slope."

"Follow the quinoa crumbs!" Fred slammed the door behind her.

Marjorie stood shocked for a moment, then trotted up the steps to see the extra room. Judging by the absence of Fred's clothing heaps, hers would be the one at the end of the corridor. It was small but clean, and had a window overlooking the garden. Marjorie felt mildly relieved. It would do just fine.

She walked back down the stairs, grabbed her own bag, and headed out to cover this strange girl's tutoring session.

Maybe this would work out after all? Marjorie had her doubts.

10

A text from Fred—a mess of undecipherable typos and fragments—listed where and whom to meet but ignored the purpose of the tutoring session, which was likely to go poorly regardless since Marjorie couldn't stand kids.

Precious shops lined 5th Avenue; up side streets sat idyllic brown-

stones, inside of which Marjorie assumed residents were home brewing beer and pickling vegetables for wild composting sessions.

As instructed, she waited outside a vegetarian café. Gatherers,
watching thirty-something women push enormous strollers past,
trailed by pasty men with offspring strapped to their fronts like
kangaroo pouches. Telltale dead eyes—puffy with sleep deprivation—
confirmed that the babies had finally won.

Their uniform attire suggested limited primping time: Women
marched in Crocs (a feat never before realized) toward yoga classes
to fight emergent hips. Men wore "Brooklyn" T-shirts, alerting themselves to their current location.

On the corner, a woman huddled over her screaming infant in his
stroller, repeating, "C'mon, Davis, C'mon, Davis!" as if he might listen to reason. Engrossed, Marjorie did not notice an eleven-year-old
girl and her mother sitting inside by Gatherers' window, staking out
the entrance, until the elder—a stocky woman with a chest like a shelf
in her sports bra—walked outside and tapped Marjorie on the shoulder. "Excuse me! Are you the tutor?"

It would occur to Marjorie later that the mother, Harriet, never
asked her name, a surprising oversight by someone so protective of
her only daughter. For now, Marjorie sized the woman up, as she began rattling off instructions. Harriet was an older parent—early fif-
ties. Wiry gray hair bordered her makeup-free face in haphazard
squiggles.

"Let me introduce you," she was saying, "so you can get started
and I can get to my chiropractor appointment. We live around the
corner, so Belinda can walk back alone. Just please remind her to look
both ways before crossing the street!"

Marjorie shook hands with Belinda, hovering tableside. The
girl's long dark hair was pulled back in a flowered headband, and
her big green eyes peered suspiciously from behind tortoiseshell
glasses. She wore a nonsensical T-shirt that read HAPPY DANCE! above
a smattering of rainbows and stars and bootleg jeans, baggy on her
prepubescent chicken legs. Her sneakers looked far too big for her

frame, belying—like a puppy's enormous paws—a taller adulthood than her mother enjoyed.

". . . So that's the gist," Harriet finished. Marjorie hadn't been listening. Maybe this was why most of her friend's tutors growing up had proved inept?

"Okay. You guys have fun!" Harriet smiled and frowned, smiled and frowned.

"Well, I don't know about fun," joked Marjorie. Harriet squinted at her. Apparently this was a humor-free zone. "Because, we're doing homework." Nothing. "Which isn't—you know what? Have a great chiropractor appointment. I've got it from here."

Harriet nodded curtly. "Oh! One last thing." She dug inside her canvas Whole Foods tote, pulled out some folded sheets of paper, and stuffed them into Marjorie's hand. "You have my number in case of emergency, right, Belinda?"

"Yes, Mom." These were the first words from the girl's lips. Harriet didn't leave a lot of dead air.

"Don't forget to look both ways on your way home!"

"Mom!" Belinda flushed, out of either embarrassment or frustration. "I don't even have to *cross* a street."

"Well, be careful anyway!" With that, Harriet left, peeking back through the window only twice for consolation.

Marjorie felt relieved, until she sat down and realized she was stuck with this child for the next . . . wait, how long was this? And what the hell were they supposed to do? If it was math, they were both in trouble.

"Hi," she tried.

"Hello." Belinda stared her down.

"So . . ."

The kid rolled her eyes. "So, what?"

"So, is she always like that?"

"Who? Mom H.?"

"Mom H.?"

"Yeah. That's what I call her."

"That's weird. Why?"

"Belinda has two mommies."

Marjorie studied the girl for a beat. "Are you being funny or are you . . . special?"

"Did you really just ask me that?"

"So you don't normally talk about yourself in the third person?"

"Do *you*?"

What was with the attitude? Marjorie watched Belinda toy with the ripped corner of a paperback copy of *Go Ask Alice*, the diary of a teenage drug addict. It seemed advanced for an eleven-year-old.

"Are you reading that for school?"

"No. For life."

"Okay, then." Out of ideas, Marjorie unfolded the papers from Harriet and found a typed list, long enough to overwhelm Santa Claus:

ALLERGIES

Tomatoes: Tongue swelling, rash, upset stomach, sneezing.

Bee Stings: Swelling, itching, anaphylactic shock.

Peanuts (Nuts in General): Tongue swelling, anaphylactic shock. (CALL 911!)

Soy: Upset stomach, bloating, flatulence.

Gluten: Upset stomach, bloating, flatulence, diarrhea.

Dairy: Upset stomach, bloating, flatulence, diarrhea, vomiting.

Nitrates: Migraine headaches, searing pain at the jawline, stomach pain.

Cats/Dogs: Sneezing, congestion, swelling of the tongue and throat.

Nightshades: Abdominal pain, asthmatic episodes, congestion.

Chocolate: Hyperactivity, abdominal cramping, rash, vomiting.

Berries: Rash, itching, swollen throat, asthmatic response.

That was page one.

Alarmed, Marjorie looked up at Belinda, who sat with her arms crossed, unconcerned.

"You have *all* of these allergies? Shouldn't you be living in a bubble or something?"

"No. I'm not allergic to anything. Except spicy food makes my head itch."

"Wait. Then why do you have this?"

"It's a list of *possible* allergies. My mom says they can develop overnight."

"For real?"

"For real."

"Wow. Belinda, your mother is a little nuts."

To Marjorie's relief, Belinda giggled. "She's totally crazy." For a moment, the girl dropped her cool façade, as she couldn't help adding: "Have you heard of helicopter parents? This is their landing pad. You think my mom's bad? One girl in my class isn't allowed on playdates because she once scraped her knee during one. Three *years* ago."

"That's just distressing." Marjorie refolded the list. "Let's put this aside for now. I'm hungry. You?"

"Kind of, yeah." Belinda began rummaging through her purple canvas backpack, then placed a minicontainer of Sabra hummus and a bag of carrots in front of her.

"That's what the kids are eating these days?" Marjorie eyed the snack.

"That's what my mother gave me."

"You know it's weird to eat your own food in a restaurant, right?"

"I'm a child. I do what I'm told."

"Okay. Well, I'm going to have iced tea and one of those massive cookies on the counter. You're sure you don't want that instead?"

Belinda examined her hummus, weighing whether to remain aloof or go for the sweets. She confessed, "I'm not allowed to have iced tea because of caffeine—Mom H. says it stunts your growth—and no sweets before dinner. Or processed sugar ever."

"I appreciate your candor. Let's just make it a treat for today. We're living on the edge!"

"What about stunting my growth?"

"Your mother is under five feet. What does she know?" Marjorie stood to place their order at the counter. "Chocolate chip or peanut butter?"

"Can I have the one with the M&Ms?" Belinda asked shyly.

A college kid in a patterned bandana took their order. When Marjorie returned, Belinda's reserve was back in place.

"So, what do people call you?"

"Belinda, remember?" She shot Marjorie an impatient look.

"No nickname? Belle? Lindy?"

"My mother doesn't believe in them."

"Seriously? No one ever shortens your name?"

"Some boys at school call me 'Blender,' as in 'face caught in a,' but I don't think they mean it as a compliment." They sat in silence for a beat. "Aren't you going to tell me that boys only say that because they like me?"

"No. Do you want boys to like you?"

"I guess so."

"Then lose the headband. It's cute, but it screams little girl. Girl, girl, girl."

"Really?" Belinda's hand flew up to her head.

"Get out a pen and paper," said Marjorie, suddenly inspired. It was too late to save herself, but maybe she could help Belinda. "I'm going to give you your first assignment."

The girl pulled out a spiral notebook, covered with doodles of stars, and opened it to a fresh page. "Ready."

"Go to your school library and take out a book called *He's Just Not That Into You*. Only read half. It's repetitive."

"And that's going to help me?"

"One day."

"It's fiction?"

"No. It's more like . . . a reference book."

Belinda scribbled down the instructions.

"Also, download a Liz Phair—that's with a 'ph'—song called

'Girls' Room.' Listen to the lyrics. Everyone has to cope with girls named Tiffany someday . . . or, for your generation, Madison maybe. Now, wanna tell me what we're supposed to be working on?"

"You don't know?" Belinda narrowed her eyes. "So, technically, I could lie? And avoid working on the thing I hate most in the world?"

"You could, but something tells me you won't."

The Kid shrugged. "I can't do it, so we might as well give up now."

"What are we giving up on?"

"Creative writing." *Thank God.* It had been Marjorie's best subject. Maybe she *could* help this kid. "We had this assignment at the end of last year to write a short story based on themes from books we'd read like *The Catcher in the Rye, Frankenstein,* and *To Kill a Mockingbird,* you know? About growing up and transforming and stuff."

"And?"

"And I couldn't do it." Belinda seemed to deflate, a popped balloon.

"Why? You seem like a smart kid."

"It's the glasses. They make me look smarter than I am."

Marjorie snorted. "I think it may be more than the glasses."

"You want the truth?" Belinda stared hard at the table. "I have no imagination."

"What? That's crazy!"

"No one believes me, but it's true! One girl in my class, Estella, wrote a story about baby dragons. This boy Waldo wrote about zombies. But I literally couldn't make anything up."

"And your teacher wasn't sympathetic?"

"No. So now I have to write the story over the summer . . ." Panic filled Belinda's eyes. "Otherwise, they'll hold me back a grade."

"They're not going to hold you back."

"They said they might!"

"You're way too advanced. But we do need to get you writing. Here's what I think—"

The barista arrived with their cookies and iced teas. "Marjorie?"

Marjorie nodded, as the waitress set the snacks down.

Belinda frowned. "I thought your name was Fredericka?"

Only then did Marjorie realize that—in the chaos of meeting Harriet—she had neglected to explain the switch and Fred's future scheduling conflict. "Oh, no. Fred was supposed to be your tutor, but she couldn't come. So I did. Marjorie. Madge, actually."

"Can I call you that?" Belinda bit into a cookie the size of her head, leaving a trail of chocolate on her upper lip.

"You can."

"Cool. I don't know anyone with that name."

"It's after *Marjorie Morningstar,* my mother's favorite book. Your name is unusual too."

"I was named after Belinda Carlisle, the singer. She's Mom H.'s favorite."

Neither girl knew the full backstories that had compelled their respective mothers to choose their names: Barbara Plum (née Schwartz) had fallen in love with Herman Wouk's novel because she aspired to the main character's life—a Jewish girl, far away from Queens on the sophisticated Upper West Side, experiencing adolescent adventures instead of helping out at the family's dry cleaning store.

Meanwhile, Harriet had grown up with a passive mother and an emotionally abusive father. Only when periodically whisked to her grandmother's house as a teenager was she permitted to close herself off in a room and blast music, to let noise overwhelm thought. Granny Gloria had taken a surprising liking to the Belinda Carlisle songs, so Harriet played them often to please her. And, when Granny died, Harriet made sure to play "Heaven Is a Place on Earth" at the funeral. Thus, her daughter became Belinda, and no nickname would suffice.

Marjorie took a long sip of iced tea. "You know, I could have told you my name was Fred and that would have been fiction."

"Um, no. That's a lie."

"Same thing."

"I'm pretty sure you're not supposed to teach me to lie."

"How much time do we have?" Marjorie glanced at her cell phone:

4:45. The kid was a decent distraction, but she needed to coordinate her move. Her stomach flipped just thinking about it.

"We have five minutes left."

"Okay. I'm going to ask you some questions about yourself and you answer. Ready? Do you have brothers and sisters?"

"No."

"Do you wish you did?"

"Sometimes."

"What would they be like?"

"Actually, I have half siblings somewhere because my sperm donor was also used by other women besides my moms. But they don't want me to meet them . . . yet."

What a strange new world. "See? There's a lot of interesting things about you. Go home and make a list of five experiences you've had. They don't have to be major. We'll find the basis for your story in no time."

Belinda looked doubtful, as she licked the last cookie crumbs from her palms. "Isn't that cheating?"

"Absolutely not. Write what you know. Ready to go?" Marjorie handed Belinda half of her own cookie, wrapped in a napkin. "Why don't you have the rest?"

"Really? Thanks!" Belinda stuffed the treat into her backpack for later, then handed an envelope to Marjorie. "My mom said to give you this."

"More allergies?"

"I think it's money."

Marjorie was grateful for the cash.

Outside, it was early evening, but still bright and warm.

"So, I'll see you next week?" said Belinda.

"Oh." Marjorie absorbed Belinda's hopeful expression, felt the heat of the envelope in her hand. "I'll be here!" she said before she could think better of it.

"Bye, Madge!" chirped Belinda, as she disappeared around the corner.

"Look both ways before you don't cross the street!" Marjorie called back.

When Belinda got home, she opened her spiral notebook and reviewed her to-do list:

Belinda's Tutoring Assignments

1. Lose the headband. Figure out how to do hair like Madge's.
2. Convince Mom H. to stop giving people that dumb allergy list.
3. Download Liz Phair "Girls' Room" song.
4. Write list of 5 things that have happened to me.
5. Borrow "He's Just Not That Into You" from the library.
6. Get a nickname.

Bolstered, she decided to try, one last time, to write her own short story:

Belinda's Attempt #6,002

~~Once upon a time, there was a girl boy dog cat~~
Once upon a time

~~Long ago…in hell…In a land far~~
~~In Park Slope, Brooklyn~~
BLEH!

Once upon a time, a girl had no imagination. She never went anywhere or became anyone. She got kicked out of school before she was 12 and spent eternity in a pink headband, begging people to stop calling her "Blender."

THE END

11

Leaving Belinda, Marjorie realized that she was not in the midst of an anxiety attack about her future. That seemed like a feat.

True, she was moving to a galaxy far, far away (from anyone she knew, anyway) to live with an alien hippie and had just impersonated a tutor, offering advice despite being *bad at life*. She would have to rely on her half of the returned security deposit from her old place to pay rent. *Pathetic.* Plus, she would probably never see her favorite pair of neon yellow underwear again.

But it was a glorious day in Brooklyn, a community that suddenly seemed not unlike *Sesame Street*. Folks—like so many Big Birds— chatted about whatever (*sleep training, victory garden composting, due dates, renovation plans*), blocking the sidewalk with giant strollers and laundry carts. Manhattan's postwork crowd began to drizzle from the subway, plodding cheerfully toward couches, takeout, and Netflix.

Marjorie was distracted by all this, which was probably why her brain registered alarm long before she consciously understood what lay ahead. By then, it was too late: On the corner of Dean Street, a residential stretch straddling gritty and sweet, three men clustered in conversation. She made eye contact with the slim dirty blond among them. And all smugness vanished on both sides as recognition set in.

Mac rearranged his shocked expression into a grin as he broke off conversation. The other men—one in jeans, work boots, and a worn T-shirt, and the other, the diametric opposite, in a suit and tie— followed his gaze.

Marjorie had no choice but to stop. She adjusted the tote on her shoulder, praying that her dark circles from exhaustion were less visible in direct sunlight.

"Madgesty. Fancy meeting you here."

"And here I thought you didn't dare set foot in the outer boroughs, thought I was safe!" She crinkled her nose adorably.

Mac looked sheepish. "Yeah, well, duty calls. This is Hank and Keith." He gestured toward his companions. "We just met with the Barclays Center people about having a DIRT annex there, down the line." (The brand-new stadium had caused uproar, as locals feared it might disturb the peace—scalpers loitering in corners and such. The developers had yet to deliver the neighborhood improvements they promised in exchange for permission to build. Protesters stood behind a barrier outside, wielding signs and shouting at workmen, who weren't in a position to change anything.)

Marjorie shook hands with Mac's friends, assuring them with her brightest smile that it was a pleasure to meet them, while planning her escape.

"So." Mac rocked back on his heels. "What are *you* doing here? I didn't think you hung out in Brooklyn either."

"Well, there's an Everest-high mountain of things you don't know about me, so . . ." She forced an even wider smile.

Mac lowered his voice, leaned in. "Are you mad at me, Madgesty?"

"Why would I be mad at you, Mac?"

She was struggling to be civil. He represented everything wrong in her world.

"Weird that you ran into each other, since you both never come here," inserted Hank, the casual of the two and DIRT's executive chef.

Actually, Mac and Marjorie—like two electrons magnetically drawn together—had a long history of accidental meetings: in the Miami airport, a Chicago hotel, an outdoor café in St. Thomas, the painkiller aisle at a Duane Reade pharmacy uptown, long after they'd both moved south. "We always run into each other," said Mac. "It's fate, right, Madgesty?"

"I think the kids call it *stalking*." She winked.

"Not when it's an accident."

"That's what all the stalkers say."

The men laughed. Mac did not. There was an awkward silence.

"What's wrong, O'Shea?" asked Marjorie. "Cat got your tongue? And by that I mean, 'Some stripper named Kat give you oral herpes?'"

"I like her. She's funny," said Hank. Keith nodded, enjoying the show.

"Well, I better be going. Going, going, going."

Mac, off his game, seemed desperate to stall and right the exchange. "Oh. Um. Where are you—I mean . . . sorry. Are you headed back to the city?"

"I'm getting the train at Atlantic. Why? Are you guys heading that way too?"

"No. We're going to that new Pork Slope BBQ place."

"Oh. Did you just want to tell me that or—?"

The guys laughed again. And Mac was suddenly reminded of an instance in fourth grade, when the housekeeper was off and his mother sent him to school with a paper bag lunch of Carr's crackers and Camembert cheese. Kids teased him about the smell for weeks.

"Anyway. Okay, bye," said Marjorie. "Nice meeting you!"

Mac bent to kiss her cheek, but she stepped away, stranding him midpeck. Performing her best Miss America wave, she headed toward the subway, cursing their synchronicity. She hoped her anger hadn't been too obvious; she didn't want to be the "crazy pissed chick" they discussed when she left.

As it happened, she *was* the object of speculation once out of earshot.

"Should we go?" Mac sighed, struggling to shake off the chance meeting.

"Um. Who the hell was that?" asked Hank.

"Nobody. Let's go."

"Dude. I'm not moving 'til you tell me what's up."

"Just some girl I went to high school with. She's—nobody."

"She's hot," said Keith, Mac's financial adviser and resident dickwad. He stuck a finger in his collar for effect . . . and ventilation. It was a warm day.

"You like her?" pressed Hank.

"Is this seventh grade? Do I *like* her? Do I want to play Seven Minutes in Heaven with her?"

"I do." Keith grunted.

Hank studied Mac's face. "So you aren't into her?"

Mac shrugged. "We used to hook up sometimes." It was a minor exaggeration, really.

"Then give me her number," oozed Keith. "I'm a sucker for a fire crotch."

"She's not really a full-on redhead."

"Whatever. Don't matter if the carpet matches the drapes."

Ignoring Keith, per usual, Hank shook his head. "I never thought I'd see the day. You're actually into her, which is a first. And, I don't know what you did, but she's pissed. You better find a way to fix that or you'll regret it."

Hank spoke from experience: His wife, Clara, was once a casual fling, whom he messed with between other conquests. It wasn't until she cut him off to date an architect (and Bradley Cooper doppelgänger) that he realized he'd let someone amazing slip away. He groveled for seven months before winning her back. They were married within that year and were now rarely apart despite his late hours. It was always him with the baby strapped to his chest, her making self-effacing jokes about her cooking, them hanging in a beer garden with friends.

"It's fine. *I'm* fine," said Mac. He was far from it, at once embarrassed and tortured by the memory of her lips, parted in question, and her glare, in vivid opposition to the encouragement she'd whispered against his ear just nights before.

"You stuttered, man. The guy who can talk to anyone just fucking stuttered."

Keith finally lost patience. "Enough with the girl talk. My balls are sweating. I want an overpriced IPA from some shitty second-rate city like Portland. Now. Let's go."

And with that, a conversation that might have lasted hours among three emotionally evolved women ended as the (mostly stunted) men moved on.

12

On the walk from the train to her apartment, Marjorie's phone signaled a text from Vera with a furious *bong!*

> U need to have apt cleaned. Keep my
> half of deposit. Will more than cover cost.
> Assume u r moving. I let Victor know. He
> says leave keys inside apt when u leave
> Weds. I leave tomorrow.

Marjorie would have loved to tell Vera to shove her half of the security deposit, but pride was above her pay grade. She had thirty-six hours to pack before slumlord-in-training, Victor, started charging some inflated day rate.

In the building's dingy basement that smelled of dead *something,* she miraculously remembered the storage unit's padlock code. Vera's belongings were gone. Inside sat only a broken skateboard—a gift from one ex-boyfriend, broken by another during a failed ollie—and some empty cardboard boxes Vera had called her a "hoarder" for keeping.

Once upstairs, Marjorie surveyed her bedroom and considered climbing into the closet to hide forever. Then she dove in.

The time limit meant no nostalgic pit stops along memory lane: no rereading yearbook entries (*"Have a good summer, beatch!"*) or staring at photographs of herself with rounder cheeks and self-cut bangs. No scanning passages from favorite books by Jane Austen, Joan Didion, and J. D. Salinger. No time to read the apology letter from the boyfriend who broke her skateboard.

Marjorie did linger on one twenty-first-birthday card: Vera and Pickles had thrown her a surprise dinner at a friend's West Village bistro. The note—scrawled in Pickles's left-handed chicken scratch on letterpress stationery—read:

Our Dearest Morningstar! (Get it? You will when you see the present! And then you won't even care because it's so awesome—ha!)

We love you, baby. Trio for life! Happy birthday and a million more—at which we'll STILL be toasting with you at 2B (or not 2B!).

Love you 4-eva and eva! xoxoxoxoxo S & P

The gift had been gold stud earrings in the shape of stars, specked with tiny diamond chips. Marjorie loved them so much that when she wore them, she obsessively pressed her earlobes to make sure they hadn't fallen out.

Suddenly, she felt so alone that she couldn't breathe. She leaned back against the side of her bed and, desperate, tried her mother's tactic: *There's my desk, there are my books, there, beyond that door, Vera is finishing packing.*

Marjorie grabbed her purse and fumbled for her phone, dialing.

"Hello?" The voice was less harried than expected.

"Pickles? It's Madge."

"Madge! It's positively heaven to hear your voice."

Pickles Marie Schulman, whose real name was Priscilla, had a flair for the dramatic and a vernacular more suited to a 1920s screen siren than a contemporary New York City housewife.

"I'm surprised I caught you."

"Me too, sweetie. Me too. Surprised to function most days with these rug rats harassing me! But you called at precisely the right time: Riley just went down after her afternoon feed. Just need to note which boob she nursed on in this app, then I'm yours. How the hell do iPads work, anyway? Which boob, which boob," she sang. "I'm like a cow, sweetie. A total *cow*!" She let loose her shrill laugh, rumored to have shattered crystal at Bill Clinton's second inaugural ball. "He can inaugurate me anytime," a young Pickles had sassed at the time, having no real idea what she meant.

The Schulman family—bolstered by generations of Schulman Farms packaged deli meat money—had been longtime Democratic delegates, although Barack Obama had caused internal struggle for the older generation. Claiming not to be racist and actually *tolerating* a young black man as president of the United States turned out to be different beasts. But then Pickles's older brother came out of the closet and, with gay marriage in the balance, the family had no choice but to succumb. Plus, Pickles's Grandma Rue had to admit that "the homosexuals" did throw the most well-orchestrated weddings. The family got over the hump. In fact, Pickles's mother, Binky, was—at this very moment—choosing between peonies and roses for a fundraiser supporting the incumbent POTUS.

Binky's involvement was in part at Barbara Plum's suggestion long before. At the height of Clinton's economic boom, hordes of wealthy women—including Mrs. Schulman—descended on the Plums' apartment every Tuesday morning at 10:00 for Fairway muffins and direction toward enrichment with solutions ranging from new hobbies (political activism!) to divorce. The girls had first met as preteens at one of these "boring" life-coaching seminars, when Pickles's mother forced her to tag along while she was on spring break from school. They became fast friends, sharing a love for cropped tops, caprese salads, The Notorious B.I.G., Smashing Pumpkins, the movie *Clueless,* and "Serial Killer Week" on Discovery Channel.

"One second, hold on, almost there, okay! Go!" Pickles rambled. "I've turned the blasted thing off and am ready to convene. How are you? Did I ask how you are?"

Marjorie had to smile. Pickles's enthusiasm was contagious, even if it meant she sometimes forgot to listen. Her closest friends knew that on the flip side there could be low lows, punctuated by hopeless sobbing. But mostly she was the picture of joie de vivre.

"I'm fine. You?"

"Divine, honey. You know how I do. Only you don't sound *fine* at all. You sound down in the depths. Am I right? Are you Dumpster diving? Do tell. Let Mama fix it."

"I'm not sure where to start."

"At the beginning. Where else?"

"Okay. You know Mac?"

"I haven't lately been lobotomized, despite what pregnancy brain might suggest, so *yes*."

Of course she knew Mac. When Pickles got caught with pot and unceremoniously kicked out of her Upper East Side girls' academy, she was accepted at Marjorie's high school. (The new Schulman Athletic Center was erected the following year.)

"What's up, sweetums? I'm not gonna lie. Mentioning Mac is ominous from the get."

Better to rip off the Band-Aid. "I slept with him."

Silence.

"It wasn't like me."

"I was going to say. Historically, you leave the poor decision making to me."

"I'm going through a tricky time; try not to judge."

"Not me, sweet pea. We're all just trying to get by. A little worrisome, though. You know I love to live vicariously through your single lady antics, but . . ."

For years, Marjorie had played rapt spectator to wild child Pickles. She wasn't beautiful (though she never knew it) but projected effortless sex appeal, a by-product of minor damage. Below sly almond eyes and an otherwise nude face, her wide lips were always brightly painted. And thanks to her flat belly and heart-shaped "French" butt, she looked as hot in a fitted T-shirt and low-slung bell-bottoms—skin peeking out between the two—as most do in black microminis.

Pickles made bad choices, falling into (and out of) love too easily. She dragged on cigarettes like lifelines, tossed back whiskey without wincing. She developed obsessions—often inspired by new boyfriends—like opera or video art or helping starving children from Haiti to Detroit. Then, as the shimmer faded and reality set in, she would decide that her causes didn't need help as much as she did and she'd swoop Marjorie away to a Schulman compound in Sun Valley,

Idaho, Tuscany, or St. Barts. Boundless resources had not helped tame her.

But almost six years prior now, Pickles had made another, less expected plunge: She got married, youth be damned. She'd made a shockingly strong choice. Her husband, Steve—an MBA, absorbed quickly into the family business—was sweet, smart, stoic, and took pleasure in Pickles's flights of fancy. Soon after came children.

The kids changed Pickles. One minute she was treating some boy toy to Vegas lap dances and the next she was taking bourgeois pole-dancing classes with her "mommy group." Marjorie was glad that Pickles ditched her old ways, having feared that her old friend might panic and flee when confronted with the sometimes ugly realities of marriage and motherhood. It was just hard to picture her covered in spit-up—that didn't originate with some wasted drummer.

Ultimately, Pickles dove into child-rearing full throttle too, which proved obnoxious. For the first time, she had followed through with something, and that made her miraculous—worthy of applause. During the first pregnancy, Marjorie shared her friend's excitement, shopping months early for impractical baby clothes from J Brand jeans to Steven Alan dresses. But the obsession proved exponential. Before the baby's birth, Pickles had already spurned anything that wasn't bamboo, organic cotton, hemp, or deemed otherwise acceptable by holier-than-thou mommy blogs. If possible, she would have constructed her whole world from kale.

And it only fed the beast when—out of politeness—an acquaintance called pregnant Pickles "glowing," referenced "the miracle of life," or acted as if her health was of national importance. Both Vera and Marjorie began dreading Pickles's phone calls, during which she bragged about how easily she got pregnant (*"The first time we tried, sweetums!"*), as if the act had required skill instead of biological luck.

Leading up to labor, she'd preached about natural birth (*"Who needs medication? I've done enough drugs!"*), quoting her doula and midwives (yes, plural). When push *literally* came to shove, though, and the baby refused to budge after five hours and enough Pitocin to induce a small elephant, she settled for a C-section. And for that too she was self-congratulatory: *"I'm so relieved: Everything is still intact down there!"*

Her son Jasper's actual arrival did nothing to quell the beast, though perhaps the self-adulation had quieted down some since the more recent birth of Riley. By then, she had lectured so much about fair trade sweet potatoes that even her mother, Binky, had to roll her eyes—no easy feat with all that Botox. And Marjorie had started reaching out less and less. This call was a wary crossing of a burning bridge.

"The Mac thing is a hot mess, but it's actually the least of my problems. Are you ready for this? Vera is moving in with *Brian*." Marjorie awaited commiseration. None came.

"Right, right."

"You knew?"

"I did."

"For how long?"

"Gosh, I'm not sure. Maybe she told me six weeks ago at brunch? This lovely raw food spot near me. The best flaxseed—"

"You had brunch? Without me?"

"It's not unheard of to convene without one of the trio, love. You and Vera have been living together for years without me." Pickles hesitated. "She specifically wanted to see me alone."

Alarms blared in Marjorie's head. Phone cradled between her shoulder and chin, she crossed to her desk and began shoving stacks of unread books into a box. "So what did she say about me?" she asked with forced calm.

A palpable pause. "About you?"

"Pickles, I'm not dumb. She obviously wanted to vent."

"She mentioned being worried about you, that's true. But mostly she wanted to talk about what was happening in her life . . . without having to feel bad."

"Wait, what does that mean?"

Pickles sighed. How had she happened into this mine field? One day, these girls would have babies and realize how way too exhausted she was for this.

"She feels—mind you, I'm not saying this is *true*—that you aren't happy for her successes. That you're still struggling with not being high school 'Madgesty' anymore, wondering why you can't have your heart's desire without effort. That you're drowning and pulling her down with you to the bottom."

"The *bottom*?" Marjorie choked.

"*Bottom,* so to speak."

"This is all because I don't have a boyfriend. Being single at our age is like her worst fear. I'm a cautionary tale to her."

"Now, Madge. No one said that.'"

"No one said that *out loud*."

"We just feel that, with your lack of direction, you're a bit . . . *immature*."

"Oh, now it's *we*? Why? Because I haven't settled for a Brian? Because I don't have kids?"

"Yes."

"Yes?!"

"You're a bit developmentally arrested."

"Is that like being mildly retarded?"

Pickles lowered her voice to a whisper: "'Retarded' is really not the accepted word these days."

"What else did you diagnose me with?"

"Nothing. We finished our kombucha mimosas and left. I took Jasper to samba class and—"

"Jasper takes samba?"

"He's very graceful."

"He's three."

"Look, sweets. I didn't mean to upset you. You can always talk to me."

Marjorie took a shuddered breath and collapsed into the ergonomic desk chair her father had insisted on her having; it served mostly as purgatory for dirty clothing. "Sure."

"So when is Vera moving out?"

"Tomorrow. But she didn't tell me until yesterday, which is crazy because—"

The baby started crying in the background. Marjorie could practically see her friend fading away like Michael J. Fox in that *Back to the Future* Polaroid, a movie she, Vera, and Pickles had first watched together in eighth grade.

In the face of futility, Marjorie continued, "I wasn't given any notice."

"Uh-huh," said Pickles absently.

"And, here's the thing, Pick. At work yesterday, I was—"

"I'm so sorry, love. Got to run. Riley is wailing, and if she wakes Jasper that will be the end of me, ruin tomorrow for him and the nanny. But it's been so fantastic to hear your voice; I adore you. Let's talk next week! Love to your parents!"

The line cut off with a crisp click.

". . . Fired," finished Marjorie into the deafening silence.

13

Marjorie slept as late as possible, then awoke to the sounds of packing blankets unfurling, furniture banging, and cardboard boxes being heaved into the arms of what she assumed were two burly men in lifting harnesses—"Luther and Curt of Platinum Movers," she heard them announce.

She hid in her bedroom for the rest of the morning, while Vera and Brian navigated their move. She was *developmentally arrested*. They could hardly expect more.

An hour in, Vera—the self-proclaimed model of poise and evolution—shrilled that her iPad had been stolen. (Curt had actually placed it on a window ledge out of harm's way.) Marjorie shook her head in disgust and decided to drown out the existential (and actual) noise with the final two episodes of *Downton Abbey,* Season 2.

Hours, gowns, and constitutionals later, Mary and Matthew had reached a more than satisfactory resolution despite war, mayhem, and class distinctions. Clearly, Marjorie had been born in the wrong century. She untangled her cross-legged limbs, stood and, hesitantly, turned down the TV's volume.

No sound. No Curt. No Luther. No binging of the service elevator. She cracked the door and peeked out into the living room. No one.

Maybe she should have wished her longtime best friend a disingenuous "Good luck!" But making peace would mean sharing recent setbacks with Vera, and by default Brian and whomever he told. *No way.*

She crept out, the floorboards creaking with each socked step, and slid to the front door, Tom-Cruise-in-*Risky-Business*-style. Through the peephole, the hallway looked warped as if through a kaleidoscope. There was no sign of life: no dollies, no red tape spools with serrated edges, no empty Gatorade bottles.

Marjorie exhaled and faced the empty living room; only a flea market side table and cheap IKEA halogen lamp remained. Like undesirables at a school dance, dust balls mingled at the edges with leftover surge protectors: cream and beige. A diorama of Marjorie's objects sat in one corner: the framed photo, the starfish, a broken conch shell (was that hers?), the champagne. Marjorie considered chugging it, but her recent hangover still lingered, too close.

That was when she heard a noise from the kitchen. Was that the ice maker? *Tell me that was the ice maker.*

Before she could flee, Brian—disgusting as always in his grubby Syracuse University sweatshirt—nearly plowed her down, a water glass in hand. She jumped out of the way, suddenly aware that she was braless in a sheer tank.

"Oh. You're here." He wiped his mouth with the back of his hand, then dried it on his Tony Soprano track pants.

"I just woke up," Marjorie lied, feigning a yawn. "I thought you guys had left."

"We're about to. Vera's waiting downstairs." Brian grinned, squishing his layers of neck fat together like piled jellyfish. "We figured you didn't come home last night."

She didn't like that he was smiling. "Of course I came home. Where else would I be?"

"I don't know or care, but Vera worries. I figured you were with O'Shea, but I guess he spanked some other chick at the Babe Cave this time."

Marjorie froze. "Excuse me?"

"Heard you guys mixed it up something ugly night before last at DIRT."

"Who told you that?"

"So it's true?"

"It's none of your fucking business. *Who told you that?*"

"Lighten up, Ice Queen. That's what you get for whoring. Guess I was a year too early that New Year's Eve. You were still uppity. Bet you'd feel lucky to have me now."

It took every ounce of Marjorie's will not to grab the halogen lamp and beat Brian senseless with it. " 'Lucky' isn't the word that comes to mind. Anyway, don't believe everything you hear. Like I'd go home with Mac." She snorted.

"Like you would. Like you *did*. Would have thought even you knew better."

Marjorie's laugh bordered on maniacal. "Seriously, Brian, as a last favor, now that we're getting out of each other's hair for good, tell me who told you that."

He shrugged. "I never minded you that much. You just need to learn to be more laid-back . . . like me. Say it and I'll tell you."

"Say what?"

"That you'll try to be more like me."

"Are you serious?" She bit the inside of her cheek to keep from screaming.

"As a heart attack."

She sighed. What pride did she have left? "Fine: I want to be more like you."

"You'll try . . ."

"I'll try."

"Great." He stepped toward the front door.

"Wait! Who told you that rumor about me and Mac?"

"No one."

"What?"

"Someone told Vera. No clue who. But hey! Have a nice fucking life, *Madgesty*."

Marjorie snapped. She stormed toward him, got in his face and shouted: "GET THE FUCK OUT OF MY HOUSE!" He froze, stunned, as she ripped the water glass from his hand. "This is my glass, you fat piece of shit. I just pray that one day Vera wises up and leaves you to die alone."

"I'm not the one who's alone, baby," Brian snarled, as he slipped out the door. "Enjoy whoring!" The tumbler hit the wall and shattered, missing him by inches.

Now *this* was rock bottom.

14

Fred made good on her promise and showed up at Marjorie's on moving day with her fellow band members: The bassist, Brandon, and drummer, Andy, wore matching slouchy shoulders, early Bieber hair, and chain belts. One of them had a tattoo of *Dennis the Menace* on his forearm, but which was anyone's guess. The saxophonist, Elmo, was the oldest at twenty-two, and wore a patchy beard to prove it. He played leader, admonishing the others for carrying the mattress incorrectly and not bending their knees when picking up heavy boxes. (As an out-of-work musician, he'd worked plenty of manual labor gigs.)

Marjorie had requisite pizza on hand and thanked the guys every thirty seconds until Elmo asked her to stop. "It's no problem. Fred told us you're broke. Been there."

Injured pride aside, Marjorie was grateful—even after one box broke open, revealing a collection of old Taylor Swift CDs, and the guys ribbed her.

After Brian left, she had stood, staring at the glass shards, and weighed her options. She could plot ways to murder and humiliate Vera's boyfriend (perhaps not in that order) or she could get on with her life. A third option was to die of embarrassment now that the Mac indiscretion was public knowledge. That was still pending.

The band's van was as rusted and windowless as Marjorie had expected, needing only a mattress and portable lava lamp to complete the 1970s "love shack" picture. Unspeakable fluids surely lurked below the paint-stained tarp on its floor. Some company's former logo was poorly painted over on the exterior.

Marjorie loitered beside Fred on the sidewalk, watching the boys load up the last of her stuff.

"How did that tutoring thing go, by the way?" asked the pixie. "Thank you so much! You saved me!"

"Oh, it was no problem."

"Were they mad? That I screwed up and can't do that time slot, I mean?"

"No, not at all," evaded Marjorie. "They found a solution."

"Okay, cool. Cause I actually have too many tutees right now as it is."

Changing the subject, Marjorie said, "So, are you gonna paint the name of your band on the side of the van?"

"Oh, we have. Many, *many* times. But we keep changing it. We've pledged to stop until we keep a name for at least three months."

"What are you called now?"

"The House Hunters."

"You play house music?"

The pixie's mouth dropped open. "Shit!" She flopped down onto the curb, nearly squashing a European couple's off-the-leash pug. "Ugh! Guys! We have to switch the name again! Damn. *House.*" Behind wraparound sunglasses, the dog's owners rolled their eyes. *Stupid Americans.*

Fred wore another eclectic outfit: Her black tank top was tucked into an ankle-length lace skirt with a wide leather belt and sandals so basic that Jesus might have rocked them. A red-and-black scarf encircling her neck evoked *Carmen.*

Marjorie smiled. Maybe she was sleep deprived, but this quirky girl was growing on her. She sat beside Fred. "What else has the band been called?"

"Oh, a bazillion things: the Red Plastic Cups, Filthy River, Filthier River, Filthiest River, *The* Filthiest River, the Movers, the Shakers, Pippi West End—"

"'Pippi West End?'"

"It's my stripper name: you know, the name of your first pet plus the street you were born on."

"You named your band after—?" Marjorie snorted, then burst into laughter. "I'm sorry. I'm slaphappy. I haven't slept. It's not you . . . ha!"

Fred began to giggle too. "Ha! How high must these guys have been to say yes?" The girls dissolved into hysterics and soon had tears streaming down their faces.

The boys stood by the van, hands on their hips. "If anyone cares, we're done," said Elmo.

"Women," grunted Andy. Or maybe Brandon.

"Sorry!" Marjorie stood, wiping renegade mascara from below her eyes. "I know you said to stop saying it, but thank you, thank you, thank you!"

Elmo blushed, then ducked into the driver's seat; his cohorts slid in on the passenger side. "Meet you there." Pulling away, he waved without looking back.

"There goes your chariot," said Marjorie to Fred. "You want to head back to Brooklyn on the train with me? I just need to grab my bag and leave the keys."

The apartment was now truly empty; even the white cable cord dangling from the wall had lost its sense of purpose. She set her keys on the kitchen counter.

"This must be weird for you," said Fred.

Marjorie pulled her hair back, let it drop; she took a steadying breath. "It—just happened really quickly."

"One day your life is one thing—"

"And the next you're living with Pippi West End."

Marjorie closed the door forever on apartment 2B.

15

The text barrage from Mac began later that day:

> Madgesty. It's your friendly neighborhood hedonist.

> Weird to see you in Bklyn on Mon. Good weird.

> You seemed mad.

> Do I get a chance to explain?

Marjorie deleted each message without replying.

They kept coming.

Over July 4th, she could practically smell the cocoa butter, grilled corn, and singed firecrackers that permeated the air at the Schulmans' Montauk house. She, Vera, and Pickles had celebrated there annually since they were kids. She tried not to feel hurt when no invitation arrived, but the fireworks display on the East River viewed from Fred's tar roof seemed like a sad replacement. That's when those Taylor Swift CDs came in handy.

Mac's texts—surely sent from the Hamptons too—did not help. As Marjorie unpacked, she endured *bing!* after *bing!* until the noise polluted her sleep, conjuring anxiety dreams about timed pop quizzes for which she was unprepared.

Finally, she turned off her ringer and missed several calls from her mother, who became hysterical. (Though Barbara Plum had advocated moving to Brooklyn, she hadn't visited the borough in twenty years. Despite countless *New York Times* articles to the contrary, she envisioned a neighborhood akin to Rikers Island prison.) Once she reached Marjorie, she demanded the ringer stay on.

So the texts continued:

> C'mon. Does 15 years mean nothing to u?

> Tina Fey or Amy Poehler? Quick. Choose.

> U know u love me. Deep down underneath all that anger.

> Don't u want your yellow panties back at least?

> I said *panties.* Aren't u gonna tell me that's creepy?

> Did you fall down a manhole? That happens sometimes.

> U know it was fate that we ran into each other in Bklyn, right?

I have syphilis.

Fine, I don't have syphilis. But when
someone says that, u really should call. It's
your health.

I'm being pathetic for u. Have u ever known
me to act this way?

Is this getting old yet? Just fucking text me
back.

By Friday afternoon, Marjorie was considering throwing her phone
out the window.

Fred was all for it. She knocked on Marjorie's door, ostensibly
to offer a Dr. Brown's Cel-Ray soda, even though she knew nobody
drank that besides her and some geriatric men in Boca Raton. She
was clearly starting to worry: Who was this stalker driving her new
friend bonkers? Marjorie offered a skeletal explanation about longtime friendship, a trust-fund-fueled sense of entitlement, the bad idea,
her—abridged to sound less pathetic—request for a job.

Later, she was admiring her newly set-up room (faded sheets,
well-loved books, a life reassembled, the pretense of being herself
again), when another text arrived:

Sitting in DIRT'S back office, thinking of u.

It was one too many. Marjorie grabbed her phone and typed
furiously:

Unsubscribe.

You're alive!

UNSUBSCRIBE.

You can't unsubscribe. This isn't SPAM.

Seems like junk to me.

Madgesty, c'mon.

UNSUBSCRIBE.

Madge. That isn't going to make me stop.

This is NOT some grand gesture, Mac. it's
an invasion of my fucking privacy. I said
stop it! RESPECT that!

There was a long pause. On one end of the conversation, a young man sat at the dining table he never used (not in DIRT's office at all), crouched like *The Thinker* and pulling fretfully at his ear. On the other, a young woman, still in her pajamas and nighttime nerd glasses, held her breath and wondered if she'd gone too far. Or just far enough.

Mac sighed. He couldn't see a way to win this one:

Fine.

And it was over. Marjorie felt relieved, but empty too like a sticky-fingered kid at a birthday party, watching the last balloon float up and away. She was officially untethered. She climbed into the bed—a Design Within Reach hand-me-down from her parents—and closed her eyes.

Moments later, sensing a presence, she opened one eye and found Fred peering in from the doorway: "Oh, good. You're up!"

"Fred?"

"Yes?"

"Why are you watching me sleep?"

"I have a special power that makes people do things when I stare."

"No, you don't."

"Are you or are you not awake because I wanted you to be?" The pixie bounded in and crossed to the window, overlooking Roberta's garden patch. "Looks like more tomatoes are coming in. Yum."

"Roberta shares them?"

"Nope."

"So, what? You steal her tomatoes?"

"Who are you? The produce police? It's our thing: I steal the tomatoes, she accuses me, I act indignant, she shakes her fist and threatens to set up cameras. It's our shtick!" Fred shimmied, as if jazz hands were another facet of their cabaret show.

Marjorie shook her head. "You're crazy."

"Lucky for you, I take my antipsychotics—sporadically."

Fred perched at the end of Marjorie's bed, her feet dangling a foot above the floor.

"Speaking of which, I couldn't help but notice the text-free silence."

"There will be no more texts." Marjorie laid a palm across her forehead.

"You don't seem happy about that."

Staving off tears, Marjorie inhaled a rattled breath. "I'm fine. It's just PMS."

A veteran gym class dodger, Fred knew a "women's issues" lie when she heard one. "That's it! I've made a decision!"

"About your band name?"

"You mean the Laundry Baskets?"

"*The Laundry Baskets*?"

"Forget that. No, about tonight. We're having a party."

Marjorie groaned and fell back against the headboard. "Fred, no. I mean, you should totally have a party. But count me out. I'm so tired and disgusting. I'm getting a pimple on my chin, and I'm small talk deficient. What would I tell people?"

"You're not disgusting! At least you won't be once you shower.

Seriously. You should bathe. I can't let you spend another night listening to Jackson Browne. While I approve of your choice of depressing music, the wallowing has to end. Anyway, my friends are all 'between jobs.'"

"Yeah, but I don't have some artistic passion either."

"Let's make one up—like you're really into clowning."

"Oh, my God." Marjorie buried her face in a weathered throw pillow.

"C'mon! I want to celebrate you moving in!"

Marjorie was touched. "That's so sweet of you, but please," she pleaded, "I don't feel celebratable."

"Fine. It'll be a laid-back get-together. We won't celebrate you or anything else. We'll watch C-SPAN and get bummed; we'll watch Fox News and get *really* bummed."

Marjorie mustered a weak smile. "Fine. What can I do to help?"

"Nothing. Elmo and I already stocked the van at some budget store in Chinatown. I hope you like lychee gummy candies and dried squid snacks!" Fred had never planned to take no for an answer. "Now go *shower*—notice the emphasis on that! Not to sound like your mom, or *my* mom, but you should go outside. Court Street is super-duper cute. Get a special trinket for your room to symbolize your fresh start! And, if it makes you feel better, get me some biscotti too. Just kidding. Sort of."

"A trinket requires money."

"Get something small!" Fred jumped up and skipped toward the door, then spun around to face Marjorie. "BTW, have you ever heard of 'Saturn return'?"

"Is that the next *Star Wars* movie?"

"See, every twenty-nine point five years, Saturn comes back around to where it was when you were born."

"Like the planet?"

"Yeah. It's an astrological phenomenon that spurs a wake-up call in your late twenties and early thirties: Time to grow up and become someone new. Time to change, like it or not."

Marjorie gave Fred an incredulous look. "So Saturn is causing my emotional collapse?"

"Rudolph Steiner also posited that every seven years, we change monumentally. And a lot of experts agree with that too."

"Experts?"

"Whatever. It's easy to be a cynic! All I'm saying is, whatever you believe, this is not an easy time. The more you fight the change, the larger it looms. Also you need to shower. It's time."

"You mentioned that. Thanks, Fred. You're the best. I don't deserve you."

"Few do. At least there's a light at the end of the tunnel: past its "best by" date Tsingtao to drink tonight! Okay. I'm off to practice with the Crystal Doorknobs." She disappeared, then popped her head back into view, waiting for a reaction.

Marjorie crinkled her nose.

"Ugh. Back to the drawing board. Okay! Fred out!"

She exited stage right, humming Jackson Browne's "Late for the Sky." Marjorie thought the Wacky Sprites was a more fitting name for the band.

But she took her roommate's suggestion. She showered and went wandering. Carroll Gardens turned out to be an Italian neighborhood: outside businesses with names like Sal's, Caputo's, and Monteleone's, older gentlemen in wife-beater tank tops relaxed in folding chairs. Between those old standards were newer, buzzed-about restaurants: Frankies 457, Prime Meats, Buttermilk Channel.

She kept walking, through boutiquey Cobble Hill, grungy Downtown Brooklyn, and quaint Brooklyn Heights. It felt good to be in motion. On the way back, seduced by wafting lavender and eucalyptus, she stopped into a beauty product store called Shen in search of her trinket. From a display of LAFCO candles with fragrances named for spaces (Living Room, Boudoir, Sun Room, Office, Patio) she chose one called Greenhouse (Guest Room sounded apt but depressing, and her nook did overlook a garden). She bought Fred biscotti from a hundred-year-old bakery down the street too.

Back at the house, the pixie stood out front, holding a tomato behind her back and acting indignant before a shouting Roberta. To her surprise, Marjorie felt the muscles around her mouth tug upward into a smile.

16

For Marjorie, the party did not start well.

When she arrived downstairs, the festivities were in full swing: The living room was infested with scruffy-bearded guys with varying beer bellies. Girls of all shapes—pear, apple, lollipop, straw—in ill-fitting vintage dresses and high-waisted shorts looked rockabilly or hippie, depending on their makeup application. Someone somewhere was playing a kazoo.

Fred—sporting a Cleopatra-style velvet headdress that jingled when she walked—was already drunk. She spotted Marjorie and shrieked, "Here she is! Everyone, this is the one and only, fabulous Marjorie Plum!"

So much for remaining inconspicuous. Some revelers glanced over with disinterest, others nodded hello and returned to their conversations. One seemingly out-of-place guest—more J. Crew male model than indie rocker with parted blond hair above a pastel button-down—clapped like a seal.

Fred stumbled up and clutched her roommate's arm.

"Who's that?" Marjorie whispered, nodding toward the country club transplant.

"Oh. That's just James. He's my ex-boyfriend. *Hi, James!*"

James waved but remained standing in the corner.

Marjorie raised an eyebrow. "Okay. We'll talk about *that* later."

"Yes! Later! Because now you need alcohol and to meet my brother!"

"Oh, is there alcohol left? I thought maybe you drank it all."

Fred ushered Marjorie to the liquor station—too bad LAFCO didn't have a scent for that. The kitchen counter was spotted with droplets of cranberry cocktail, lime juice, and Coke. Bags of ice sulked in the sink. Fred grabbed a red plastic cup. "Pick your poison."

"If I'm going to catch up with you, maybe a shot."

Marjorie could sense her anxiety humming beneath the surface. Maybe alcohol would help.

"Shots! Perfect!"

Fred poured vodka for ten into each cup. She passed one to Marjorie, raised her own, and toasted: "To Saturn returning, then getting the hell out!"

"To Saturn! Your home planet." Marjorie pounded the astringent liquor, ignoring the sharp burning in her chest. As she gasped, Fred gave her a funny look. "That was supposed to be several shots in one. We were going to toast again and again." She hadn't made a dent in hers. "Oh well! Come meet the bro."

Two less bohemian-looking men stood talking, maybe arguing, by the fridge.

"*This* is Michael," said Fred.

The shorter one—who evoked a teddy bear—flashed a disarming grin not unlike his sister's and gave Marjorie's hand a hearty shake. "The famous Marjorie Plum! So nice to finally meet you. I must say, you look surprisingly normal for a friend of Fred's."

"Nice to meet you too. And thanks, I think."

"And this," said Fred, "is Gus." She gestured toward the taller, tanner, dark-haired man in a thin gray T-shirt, cargo shorts, and flip-flops. "Don't let his crotchetiness fool you. Gus is the best."

"At what, nobody knows." He didn't extend his hand.

"So how did you come to live here again?" asked Michael. "My sister says you're not a musician."

Nearby, some guy began strumming Van Morrison's "Brown Eyed Girl" on his acoustic guitar and singing along, *soulfully*.

"Oh, Christ. *That* guy," said Gus.

"You know him?" asked Fred.

"I've known hundreds of him," he grunted. "I'm going outside for incense-free air. What's next? 'The Joker'? Why haven't music tastes changed since I was in college? Aren't kids supposed to have Bieber fever or something?"

Gus pushed through the crowd and disappeared.

"Don't mind him," said Michael. "He's not the most tolerant gentleman. Hating everything and everyone is part of his charm."

Marjorie raised an eyebrow. "That's one word for it."

"So, you were about to tell me how you landed at Casa de la Hermana Loca."

By now, Fred had strayed and was engaged in a meaningful debate about guitar picks with a drummer, who couldn't have cared less but thought she was cute. Marjorie could feel panic rising, despite Michael's good intentions. She debated claiming to be "between jobs" or calling herself an "entrepreneur." She couldn't bring herself to be honest.

"Are you okay?" Michael asked. "You're a little pale."

"You know, I didn't really eat today. Maybe the vodka was ill-advised."

"Ah, the danger of living with my sister, who subsists mostly on fairy dust. I think there are brownies over there, near the squid thingies." He pointed to the far end of the counter, where a silver tin did in fact contain baked goods, cut into rough sections with a butter knife.

"I should probably go grab one." She added, "Be right back!" They both knew she would not return. Not even the most sincere revelers follow through on that promise, such is the sad and lovely impermanence of parties.

Michael moved on quickly. A round girl with jet-colored hair and nails ran up and embraced him; he seemed to know her well enough to overlook her bleeding mermaid neck tattoo.

Meanwhile, mostly for show, Marjorie took a couple brownies in a napkin and sat at the bottom of the stairs, taking deep breaths. The alcohol—normally calming—was turning on her. Her pounding

heart drew her attention to the myriad valves and arteries that labored
to pump blood through her body. The more she tried to ignore it, the
more the system in her chest seemed doomed to fail, and the more
sure she became that she was about to become a cautionary tale—the
twenty-eight-year-old girl who collapsed at a Brooklyn house party.
The cause would be that she was a loser, the way people die from broken hearts. At her memorial service, the rabbi would proclaim, "Marjorie didn't accomplish much in life, but she had some nice pairs of
boots from sample sales. Ameeeeen! *L'Shana Tova.*"

Maybe food would help. She stuffed the brownie into her mouth;
they stuck in her throat. But she didn't trust herself to fill a cup with
water at the sink and return to her seat without incident.

Two girls in matching Daisy Duke jean shorts and stacked rings
leaned against the stairwell's railing, oblivious of Marjorie's state.

"Most millennials are so entitled," said the taller one. "Like, sure
my parents pay my rent, but I also have to *work*."

"You have an unpaid internship, one morning a week."

Marjorie wheezed, catching the duo's attention. They exchanged
a look: *Let's go find some gluten-free beer.*

Other snippets of conversation floated around her like smoke.

Brooklyn is so not the new Manhattan. Manhattan is the old Brooklyn.

Don't start a blog. Words are so over.

*The husband is hot, but it's like he has no genitals at all—smooth like a Ken
doll. She gives him permission to pee.*

The beating of Marjorie's heart intensified. Perhaps sugar and
chocolate, high in caffeine, were not the best cures. Was this the pre-
cursor to an epileptic seizure or, worse, an aneurysm? Who would
help her if she collapsed? Not Guitar Boy, whose sensitivity was for
show. Maybe one of the girls smoking a joint by the sticker-covered
fiddle case, if they could muster the energy.

A joint! Marjorie suddenly realized: *They were pot brownies.* True
panic set in. She had to get outside! She stumbled toward the front
door, capsizing some disembodied plastic cups, then burst onto the
landing, as a group of female revelers arrived. One—nerd glasses,

Sleater-Kinney tank, sensible face—caught her before she tripped
down the stairs.

"Easy there, girl. Gotta take the steps slowly in heels."

Marjorie managed a nod before rushing downstairs and busting
out into the night. She leaned against the building's façade and gulped
fresh air like she'd escaped drowning.

Only after a full minute did she notice Michael's friend sitting on
the concrete steps, peering up at her in amusement.

"You okay there?" he asked.

"I've been better."

"What's up?"

"I feel dizzy."

A look of concern replaced his smirk. There was authority in his
voice: "Sit down."

She did as instructed, taking a wobbly seat beside him.

"That better?"

"A little maybe. It's stuffy in there."

"Do you need to put your head between your legs?"

"I don't know. Are you a doctor?"

"No. But people do that."

Marjorie nodded. "You know, that guitar guy did play 'The Joker'
after you left."

"I don't doubt it."

She took a deep breath. "I don't know what's wrong with me."

"Maybe it has something to do with the trough of vodka you
pounded."

"You saw that?"

"I was almost impressed."

"Really? And Michael said you're not nice . . ."

"Oh, did he?" Gus smiled.

"He said, 'My friend Russ is not the most tolerant gentleman.'"

"I don't think he said that."

"He did!" she said indignantly.

"I doubt it, since my name is *Gus*."

"Same difference." They were silent for a moment. Maybe she was drunker than she thought. "You want to know the real problem, Russ?"

"Russ might. I'm Gus."

"It's twofold."

"Is it now?" Gus grinned. The girl was at least entertaining and, for a drunken mess, okay to look at. "It's been awhile since I heard something twofold."

"First, I'm a train wreck. I have no job, no prospects, no money. My parents are turning my bedroom into a bedroom."

"That doesn't even make sense."

"I know! That's why I didn't want Fred to celebrate me with this party!"

"Hard to stop Hurricane Fred once she has an idea."

"You've known her long?"

He nodded. "Michael and I are best friends from college."

"That's nice. I remember when I had friends."

"Well, that's just pathetic. Okay, so what's two?"

"Right! Twofold!" She lowered her voice to a whisper: "I ate *two* brownies. And now I'm freaking out."

Gus looked up to the heavens, as there was no one else with whom to mock her. "You're freaking out about eating brownies?"

"Yes!" she said, as if it was the most natural thing in the world.

"Marjorie. That's your name, right? Marjorie?"

"Yes."

"Do you have an eating disorder?"

"What? What are you—oh! No. The brownies are *magic*. They're, you know, *pot brownies*," she whispered. "And now I'm all paranoid."

"They're not pot brownies."

"Yes. They are."

"The nice Italian woman downstairs made them."

"Roberta?"

"Yes, Roberta. Those brownies are drug-free, clean and sober. No rehab for them. You, on the other hand . . ."

Marjorie exhaled softly. "Oh, thank the Lord. But then why am I freaking out?"

Gus sighed. "Well, I don't know you, but considering that you don't look like a friend of Fred's because there's no spike through your tongue, I'm going to guess that you're out of your element."

"That's true! I am!"

"And proximity to all that natural deodorant in there probably didn't help."

"That *was* a lot of peace and love and unplugged music in there."

"Those people are working really hard to seem laid-back." He pointed his thumb back toward the apartment, as if hitching a ride to somewhere less Kumbaya. "Maybe the universe had to compensate by giving you angst."

Marjorie had spent her life pretending to be unflappable, especially with men. But something about this guy's frankness was pushing her toward cracking, her soft-boiled sanity leaking out like so much yolk.

"It's a good point, but that's not it. The thing is, Russ, I peaked."

"You peeked at what?"

"No! I peaked. Like hit the high note. Made my best move. It's downhill for me. I'm worse than those washed-up football players in movies with the potbellies and the bald spots—Hey, why are those guys always bald? Do you think football causes baldness? They do want to instate those helmet rules."

"I don't think that's about hair loss."

Marjorie considered that, then dismissed it. "Anyway, I'm worse than them because I didn't even have a BIG game to relive or glory days. What did I do, Russ? Smoked cigarettes by the park! Skipped lines at clubs!"

"Gus."

"What?"

"Never mind."

"Did you play football, Russ?"

"Basketball."

"Yeah. You're tall. Has anyone ever told you that?"

"It's been mentioned once or twice."

She narrowed her eyes, as if seeing him for the first time. "Are you from the Midwest? People are tall there."

"I'm from Philly."

"So sort of."

He groaned. "I feel like maybe I'm going to regret asking this, but what happened? You seem, current state aside, like a relatively normal person."

"Don't I?" she asked. *"Don't I?"*

"Are you talking to me or—?"

"You're looking at a washed-up prom queen, metaphorically, I mean. I might as well be living in an old trailer, wearing a housedress. I didn't get knocked up in a '57 Chevy, but it's like that! And I've gone nowhere since then."

"Since not getting pregnant?"

"I don't know how to do anything. I can't even cook. I made quinoa once and didn't know you had to rinse it first. My roommate got like *really* sick. And the sad thing is, I don't even *like* quinoa!"

"That *is* sad."

"I am profoundly disappointing because, ironically, I never set any goals. Having more than forty-three dollars in my bank account would have been a good one. But I couldn't make one of Oprah's Dream Boards or complete one of my mother's life-coaching exercises if I tried. Not like Vera, who plans everything."

"Of course. Vera. Who is that again?"

"I assumed it would all come naturally because I was so *good* at high school, socially, I mean. I just didn't expect to be sitting here now, Russ. No offense; you seem nice enough."

"My name is Gus. Not Russ. And, for what it's worth, I think skipping the Dream Board sounds like a primo idea."

"Maybe. But now I'm in godforsaken Brooklyn, which is oddly nice, *too nice,* spilling my guts to a stranger, divorced from my past and, weirdest of all, I don't want that back either. Not even Pickles, you know?"

"I like pickles. But okay."

"They're like family to me, but we're in different places. I'm not even mad about it." Marjorie threw her hands in the air, a human goalpost. "Isn't that funny?"

"That's hard to say, since I have no idea who the hell you're talking about."

Marjorie soldiered on. "Of course, I definitely don't want my job with Brianne back."

"Of course not."

"Why would anyone want Brianne *back*?" she laughed.

"Who indeed? Good old Brianna."

"Oh, nothing good about her."

"Right. I meant, bad old Brianna."

"But I don't know what the next thing is, even though Fred says it's all about Saturn."

"Ah, Saturn. That sounds sensible."

"I just want to feel good again." Marjorie dropped her head into her hands, an epic headache building. Her breath shook like rustling leaves forecasting a coming storm. Then, suddenly, she began to cry for the first time since her downward spiral began. She shook with quiet sobs and Gus's heart broke a little for her. Tentatively, he placed a palm on her back.

"Okay," he said softly. "It's okay."

"I'm sorry," she sniffled. "This is the one thing I'm supposed to be good at. I'm social! People have called me 'charming.'"

"If it's any consolation, they may have been lying."

Marjorie laughed, the heaves subsiding, though her head remained buried. "And now I ruined your evening!"

"I'm not even sure I was having an *evening*."

She turned to face him, her eyes puffy and watery, the tip of her nose pink, which only made her prettier. Her cheek was squished against the shelf of her knees like a child. "Are you sure?"

"Marjorie, there are three twenty-two-year-old guys in there play-ing ukuleles. Let me assure you, that isn't my idea of a good time."

She giggled, despite herself, then sat up, sniffled, and wiped her face with her hands. A bit of eyeliner had been transferred to her lower lid; the imperfection of it underlined her vulnerability. "I must look like a mess."

"You look fine. Good, even. I'm thinking you've never looked bad. Let's be honest."

Suddenly, they both became aware of his hand on her lower back. He snatched it away like he'd been shocked. "Do you need a tissue? I'm sure there's one inside. Might be made of hemp, but that's the risk you take."

"I have this." She dug into her dress pocket and pulled out a crumpled white paper napkin. "From the brownies." Her breath still caught in small jolts. She dabbed at her face.

"If you want my opinion . . . which you shouldn't because you don't even know me: You're just feeling insecure. But you seem smart . . . ish and you're cute. I'm assuming you're usually more stable."

She half nodded, half shrugged.

"Here's the thing: At some point, we all go through this—growing pains are a rite of passage." Marjorie was trying to listen, but she was distracted by the appealing way his brow furrowed as he talked. He leaned in, as if sharing a secret. His green eyes, tilted ever so slightly down at the corners, suggested a puppy dog sweetness in opposition to his angled features. "This is what it feels like to be in transition. It's horrible, but it's en route to something better—unless you fuck it up."

"Hey!" Marjorie swiped at him, feeling more upbeat. He ducked away.

"I'm sure that's what Fred was talking about with her Saturn mumbo jumbo. Ridiculous as that crap is, it's true that change is hard—but also necessary if you don't want to have *peaked*. So you hit what you thought was the summit and now you've rolled back down. Next time you climb up—not to overuse the metaphor—you'll reach different . . . whatever they're called, *lookouts*. Maybe there isn't even a top. Maybe there are just these beautiful pit stops or ugly thorn bushes and rattlesnakes to get past in the road."

"This mountain is in the desert."

"So it is. Point is, what you're experiencing is a version of freedom. You can be whoever you want. This time around, you're not a kid. You get to make real choices."

"I can be whoever I want, do whatever I want."

"Within reason. Based on the way you took those stairs, I wouldn't pursue tightrope walking."

"At least not in these shoes."

Glancing toward Marjorie's feet, Gus couldn't help but notice her legs. He leaned back, resting his elbows on the step above. The streetlight's rays played on the plains of his face. He was good-looking, Marjorie thought, if you liked that kind of . . . really hot guy. Why had it taken her so long to notice? Well, that ship had sailed. She'd practically blown her nose on his shirt.

"How come you're so wise?" she asked.

"Because I'm old."

"I'm calling your bluff. Not that old."

"Old enough to be your . . . nothing. I'm thirty-two. But it doesn't take a sage to see that you're going to be fine."

Marjorie and Gus smiled at each other, frozen in a moment entirely theirs, when the banjos stopped strumming, the beer foam stopped fizzing, and the laughter—if there was any in this earnest crowd—subsided. For an instant. Everything was still.

They were captured in a spotlight, as a car maneuvered its way into a parking spot in front of them. The vehicle rumbled forward and back, then the engine died. A lean young man climbed out, then looked up, scanning the buildings. Finally, his eyes rested on the duo, sitting companionably together.

And it occurred to Marjorie that, to a stranger, she and Russ might appear to know each other, though they had just met. Musing about that, she missed the look of surprise on the driver's face, as he strode toward them.

"Hi, Madge."

She stared up at him, her mouth hanging open, then turned to Gus. "Is he really here, or am I hallucinating from the brownies?"

"For the love of God, the brownies were normal. Do you generally have a psychedelic reaction to chocolate?"

"Allergies can appear overnight."

"Well, I'm pretty sure he's real."

"I see." Marjorie turned to Mac and demanded, "Then why are you here?"

"I happened to be in the area for dinner. I didn't realize you were living here."

"Seriously? That's the best you've got?"

"We always run into to each other in weird places. Is this that surprising?"

Marjorie stared at Mac, unmoved. He pretended to examine his shoes, weighing his options. "Fine. I didn't realize you'd live on this remote a street. I thought an 'accidental' run-in would be more feasible."

"I told you to leave me alone."

"I know. But I thought if you could see me, then you'd know I'm being sincere." Mac glanced from her face to Gus's, sizing up his perceived competition. "Who's your friend?"

Marjorie looked at Gus, embarrassed. "Sorry, sorry, sorry. This is Russ. Russ, this is Mac."

Mac's handshake was a tad aggressive, but Gus decided to let the little guy flex his muscles. It's what Russ would do. Russ was such a good guy. Still, he couldn't help murmuring to Marjorie, "I thought you didn't have any friends."

Marjorie pursed her lips. "I don't."

"Madge. Just let me talk to you for one minute. I came all the way out here."

"Fine." She crossed her arms. "Talk."

Mac glanced at Gus and shifted on his feet. "Alone?"

"Oh, don't mind me," said Gus, standing up. "You guys clearly have some catching up to do, and I have a sudden yearning for bad acoustic

James Taylor covers." He winked at Marjorie, a little sad to leave her in the company of a douche bag with a silver Aston Martin, and turned to go inside.

Marjorie waved at him, then stood herself. Less wobbly now, she turned to Mac. "I'll hear you out on the way to a bodega. I need some pretzels to soak up the alcohol."

Mac shrugged. Worked for him. A drunk Marjorie was a more pliable, forgiving one. They started down the street. The air smelled sweet, like honeysuckle, but also carried the stench of rotting garbage—eau de summer in New York City. They turned right on Court Street toward the BQE's rumbling overpass.

"How did you get my address?"

"I called your mom."

"Seriously?"

"I thought you might be staying with your parents. She seemed happy that someone was visiting you."

Mac thrust his hands in his pockets, fighting the impulse to reach out and touch Marjorie. Why did she have this hold on him?

"Okay, so talk. Why are you here?"

He sighed. "Because I didn't throw up."

"Excuse me?"

"After we slept together, I didn't throw up."

"Well, gee, Mac. If that's not a compliment, I don't know what is!"

"That came out wrong, but in order to explain, I have to reveal something really personal. I need to know you'll keep it secret."

"I don't know, Mac. I'm thinking of having T-shirts made: I SLEPT WITH MARJORIE PLUM AND DIDN'T PUKE!"

"Madgesty. C'mon. Can I trust you?"

"You're asking *me* that? You have the biggest mouth in North America. You told Vera about what happened between us!"

"No! I told John. He's the only one, I swear. If he told anyone, I'm sorry."

"Just don't ask me to keep a secret, okay?"

"Fine. Point taken. Here goes." He took a deep breath, fixing his gaze on the sidewalk in front of them. "About eight months ago, I developed a problem."

"Okay . . ."

"I slept with this cocktail waitress from that midtown club I invested in. Or maybe she was from the Bowery one . . . ?"

"Mac, you've got to be kidding me."

"Sorry. Anyway, I had sex with her, and right afterward, I got nauseous and threw up."

"Maybe you had a bug." Marjorie shrugged. "It happens to us mere mortals."

"That's what I figured. Until it happened again the next week."

"Same girl?"

"No, different girl. Right afterward, like clockwork, I barfed. Then the next week, it happened again, twice, with two other girls."

"Now *I* want to barf."

"At that point, I was just bringing girls home to see if I could break the pattern. But I couldn't. Finally, I stopped trying, except maybe once a month."

"That must have taken restraint."

"You're kidding, but it did. I was freaked-out. It was like my dick was broken or something."

"Maybe you have an STD." Marjorie made a mental note to call her gynecologist and schedule a full workup.

"No. I went to a shrink, I tried hypnotherapy, medication, everything. Nothing worked. Until you."

"Until me."

"We had sex and I felt fine. We did it again an hour later, and I felt fine again. I went to sleep, woke up. We did it again. I still hadn't puked."

"Wow. It's like a real-life fairy tale: 'The Magic Vagina.'"

"At first, I was psyched. My dick–brain connection was fixed! But then I started to wonder what it meant: Why didn't you make me hurl? I panicked. I went to DIRT and got wasted—that's when you stopped by. And that's why I didn't call."

"Please. Give me some credit. You didn't call because you're you."

"But then I ran into you on the street, and you were *so* mad, and I wanted to talk to you, but nothing coherent came out, and suddenly it all made sense: I didn't puke . . . because I like you." He looked proud, as if he'd presented a brilliant discovery: Earth is indeed flat!

"Imagine that—sleeping with someone you like. What a revolutionary idea. For a vapid, trust fund baby."

His face fell. "Ouch."

"It's the truth."

"I guess the truth hurts."

"Only if you have a soul."

Mac stopped walking, forcing Marjorie to stop too. "You're missing the point: I *like* you."

It was like being awarded a crummy watch for retirement, now that time no longer mattered. "Great. Thanks."

"That's it?"

"What else do you want? Over the years, I've heard you tell a million girls that they were 'the one,' the subtext being 'for the night.' It's your great gift to make people feel special, until you lose interest. You have the attention span of an ADD goldfish."

He shook his head firmly. "No. Not this time, Madge. I've been trying to talk myself out of wanting you for years. A decade, even. This is for real. Why won't you believe me?"

"Because I know you!"

"Fine." He kicked at a loose granite pebble with the toe of his oxford. Then, eyes sparkling anew, he looked up. "How about you?"

"What?"

"I know you know that there's something with us."

"I don't even know what you just said, let alone what it meant."

"You've been there with me all these years, sensing the same thing." Mac was so indulged that unrequited feelings were not on his radar. "Tell me you don't know what I mean. Admit it. You think about me sometimes."

"Not really. Nope."

"You never think about me?"

"The answer is no. Remember? I said it like two second ago."

"You're lying."

"You're right. I do think about hating you."

"That's a start."

"Seems more like an end to me."

"Madge, cut me some slack! Can we just have an honest conversation?" A pigeon strutted by and eyed Mac distrustfully.

"I don't know. Can we?"

"This is your life. It's not worth being stubborn." He tugged at his ear in frustration; the familiar gesture broke her resolve.

"Fine!" she choked. "Yes, I have thought about you once or twice *that* way. I have. But it's been at my worst times, when I'm in a terrible place. Don't you see? You're my quiet desperation guy!"

"You're going to have to translate that."

"You're the guy who pops into my head when life gets unbearably lame. When I walked to school on winter mornings at seven thirty, dreading the day, I'd think, 'Maybe Mac will be entertaining today.' When I flunked a college midterm and felt like a failure, I'd think, 'I bet Mac could distract me right now.' At bars in my early twenties, when I was bored with the same stupid people telling the same tired stories, I'd think, 'Maybe I should text Mac to liven things up.'"

Encouraged, Mac ran a hand through his coiffed hair. "See? Isn't that some version of love?"

"No, Mac. It's masochism. I only want you around when I feel low, to wallow with you, make bad decisions and feel worse."

"That's the most fucked-up, ridiculous thing I've ever heard."

"That's hard to believe."

"Take a moment, just one second, and imagine that maybe there's another reason why I pop into your mind at your most hopeless moments—which, by the way, sound pretty pathetic."

"Funny."

"I'm not being funny."

"Agreed. Look, Mac, it doesn't matter because it's all a fantasy. It's not *real*. In real life, we'd fight about what time to go to bed, what movie to see, who should buy the paper towels."

"My housekeeper, Wanda, buys the paper towels."

"Mac!"

"Madge, I want that. I mean, not *that*. But our life doesn't have to get tired like everyone else's. And, if it does, we'll handle it."

"You don't even know me!"

"I know you."

"Don't even bring up Aunt Gladys again."

"Aunt Gladys?"

"You always ask me how she's doing like that's supposed to demonstrate that you *know* me. I'm not an idiot. You do it with everyone. You asked Vera about her dog! He's been dead for years!"

"So? How was I supposed to know?"

"I've heard you ask her three times before!"

"Look." Mac sighed. "I won't pretend I know every detail of your life. But same here: You think you have me figured out, but you don't know who the real Mac O'Shea is."

"Someone who talks about himself in the third person."

"You're impossible!" Color rose to Mac's cheeks. "Look, I'm going to say one last thing, and then you're going to give me a chance—because you know you want to, because your life looks pretty sorry over here, and because I trekked to motherfucking Brooklyn and I don't cross bridges unnecessarily."

You're going to give me chance. Wasn't that what he'd said to her when they were fifteen, before he kissed her, then sauntered away? In that moment, Marjorie realized that she would. She sighed. Mac could see that he'd won her over.

"I may not know your aunt Gladys or your favorite board game or even your college major—which is probably meaningless because you went to General Studies at NYU—but I know *you*, Madgesty Plum. I've known you from the moment I met you. And that's the truth."

Marjorie said quietly, "I need to know why you did what you did in high school."

"Can you be more specific?"

"Why did you kiss me, then tell everyone that you didn't like me?"

"Oh, that." They resumed walking. After a silence, he said, "I knew you were into Bryce. I couldn't handle you picking him; I figured I'd save face. It was stupid."

Why had that never occurred to her? They arrived at the bodega, but instead of going in, they settled on a bench outside in unspoken agreement. Mac grunted, as he sat.

Marjorie smiled. "Was that a creak? Could Mac O'Shea be getting old?"

"Never! I'm just sad. I still can't believe old Grinch died."

Marjorie laughed and whacked him lightly in the arm.

"Hey! Don't hit me. I'm in mourning."

She sat back. "You're an incorrigible person, Mac O'Shea. But I guess I am too."

"So, you'll have dinner with me this week?"

"Yeah. I guess. But not at DIRT."

"Done." Mac smiled, placing a proprietary hand on Marjorie's thigh. Feigning nonchalance, he added, "So, who was that guy you were talking to, anyway?"

Marjorie's memory of earlier that evening before Mac's arrival was blurry thanks to the vodka she drank and also the marijuana that Roberta had in fact baked into the brownies. But also because it officially became the night not when Marjorie sobbed into a stranger's lap but when the wrong guy, who might just be right, fought to win her back, though she wasn't his in the first place. It was the night she elected to give Mac a chance.

17

On Monday, Gatherers was crowded with worker bees, who had re-buffed home offices and taken their laptops, like so many 1950s secretaries, out on the town.

Belinda walked in wearing a T-shirt that declared I LOVE MUSIC! above a cartoonish electric guitar, shorts, and brand-new Doc Martens. When her eyes rested on Marjorie, a shy smile spread across her face; she waved. How incredible, Marjorie thought, that anyone could be so happy to see her.

"I've decided I want a nickname!" Belinda slung her backpack across the chair's rungs and flopped into her seat. Apparently, there would be no performance of skepticism this time.

"You do, do you?"

"Yes. And not 'Four Eyes.'"

"Someone called you 'Four Eyes'? When? In 1962?"

"This boy Johnny Snarlson, who the kids at camp call 'Snarls.' We don't usually play coed sports, but they combined us for softball. Lord knows why!"

"Lord knows indeed."

"Anyway, I missed a pop-up fly because, really, I don't even know what that is! That's why they put me out in right field in the first place. So he called me names."

Marjorie cringed. "Did you cry?"

"What? No! Are you crazy? Johnny Snarlson is an idiot. I told him to shut up because he'd be working for me one day."

"Ha! That's my girl! Are all eleven-year-olds like you?"

"Not really. Anyway, our counselor Becky didn't find it funny. She made us both sit out for the rest of the game. As if skipping sports is a punishment." Belinda rolled her eyes.

"Is Johnny cute?"

"Snarls? Ugh. No."

"Like, ugh, no, boys are gross?"

"Like, ugh, no, Snarls looks like someone squished him."

"Got it," Marjorie laughed. "So, down to business! What are we having for snack?"

"The usual!"

Marjorie placed their order at the counter with Bandana Girl. When she returned, Belinda's spiral notebook was open before her, a pink pen idling beside it.

"I couldn't help but notice that you walked here by yourself today," said Marjorie. "How'd you swing that?"

"I told Mom H. that I'd text when I got here, which I did. She probably followed me anyway." Harriet was indeed now clomping toward her chiropractor's office and away from Gatherers, having confirmed that her daughter arrived without incident.

"Good. The best way to gain your parents' trust is to be reliable. I learned that the hard way."

"Why hard?"

"Because I forgot a lot and then my parents would ground me or make the phone off-limits. I messed up so many times that they finally made me wear a reminder bracelet that said CALL."

Belinda's mouth dropped open. "They did not!"

"They did."

She considered the idea. "Was it cute?"

"Sort of. Like a pink and blue friendship bracelet."

"Some girls in my grade wear those—Sabrina Wilkinson, who is, you know, the girl the boys all like."

"But you don't?"

"I think they're cute. I like the rubber ones with words even better, but I don't know where to get them. Also, there are other things I want more."

"Like what?"

"Like books. And these shoes." She stuck her leg out from under the table to show off her electric blue combat boots.

"Very cool. I definitely approve."

"Oh, good. I was hoping you'd like them." She blushed, too

obvious. "The kids at camp mostly wear Converse and Keds, but the urbs wear these."

"'Urbs'?"

"The older kids who wear band T-shirts and skinny jeans and tattoos and stuff."

"Ah. We called them 'indie.' I had a pair just like those in eighth grade, Belly."

"Belly? Is that my nickname?"

"Could be. Let's see if it sticks. Anyway, it's good that you do your own thing. Don't worry about kids who are popular in seventh grade. It's not an indicator of future success. I know, firsthand. Jimmy Snarlson probably *will* work for you one day! And so will Sabrina whatever."

"Sabrina is actually really really rich. Her dad like owns Staten Island. She probably won't work for anyone."

"Lucky Sabrina. But the point still stands. In fact, here's another assignment: Watch the movie *Romy and Michele's High School Reunion*." Belinda scribbled dutifully. "Now, let's *really* get down to business."

"Okay! I'll review last week's assignments." Belinda's expression grew serious, as if she was addressing a board meeting agenda. "The headband is gone, as you can see. Mom H. wouldn't budge on the allergy list, but she did agree to add an addendum, explaining that I don't have allergies. (She also taught me the word 'addendum.') And she agreed to strike diarrhea from the list of symptoms, so it's less humiliating."

"No fecal matter. Always a win."

"What else? Mom D. downloaded the Liz Phair song for me when she got home from her corporate retreat while Mom H. was at book club. I figured she was the safer bet to ask. She's kind of clueless about what's age appropriate, and some of the songs had curses."

"Why is Mom D. clueless?"

"Oh, you know. She works all the time, so she's home less. And when she is, I guess she's tired, so she mostly reads the newspaper on her iPad."

"Does Harriet, um Mom H., work?"

"She has hobbies . . . besides harassing me. I heard them fighting last night, though, about how they don't have 'shared interests.' Mom H. is big on quality time, but sometimes it's less stressful with Mom D. She even lets me call her 'Dinah.' *And* she doesn't make me eat bean curd. We order pizza and go out for ice cream. It's a secret." The household sounded pretty traditional, not unlike Marjorie's own. "Now that I'm older I can go to pizza myself with friends for lunch sometimes. But it's still a special thing."

The barista arrived with their iced tea and cookies. "For Belly, right?"

Belinda giggled.

"So, did you like the song 'Girls' Room'?"

"It reminded me of our school. We also have a couple girls who wear super tight clothes." Belinda took a big bite of her M&M cookie, dropping crumbs on the pad. "They didn't have *He's Just Not That Into You* at school and, I gotta say, the librarian looked at me like I was insane. I'll try the public library. Oh. And I tried to make my hair wavy like yours, but it didn't work."

"That definitely wasn't an assignment, Belly. Everyone wants shiny straight hair like yours! As we speak, women are shelling out thousands of dollars to poison themselves with keratin treatments for it."

"But I want it wavy. And Mom H. won't get me a curling iron."

"Just let your hair dry in a braid."

Belinda copied the instructions down. "So, that's it for last week."

"Um. You left one off."

"Did I?"

"Belinda! Tell me you made the list of experiences for the actual writing assignment!"

"I tried." She frowned, turning a page and handed the notebook over.

5 Things I've Done in My Life
By Belinda

1. Nothing interesting. Ever.
2. Went to Arizona to visit Nanny and Grandpa. Made a friend at their country club, who was cool and older and swore she'd smoked a cigarette before, but she left the next day.
3. Met a dog and a chicken who were friends in Mom H.'s friend's backyard in Greenpoint.
4. Saw an actress from some TV show in front of Franny's (favorite pizza place, where you have to wait two years for a table).
5. Saw a bicyclist get hit by a car.

"Okay, well, good job. But you need to replace #1 unless you want to write about a boring character."

"Too close to home."

"Did anything new happen this week?"

Belinda rested her cheek on her fist, pushing her lips cockeyed. "I did meet a kid at camp, who is going to be new at my school next year."

"Perfect! Now, of the five ideas, which would be best to describe?"

"None of them are going to be *War and Peace*."

"Belinda. Even *War and Peace* isn't *War and Peace*. The battle parts are so dense—everyone skims them! Now, which one?"

"You pick."

"I can't know what's most interesting to you." Belinda didn't budge, so Marjorie reread the list. "Fine: I say no chickens unless you want to write about farmers. The cigarette thing will probably land you in therapy, as will the bicycle crash. And seeing famous people is fun, but they can be disappointing."

"How do you know?"

"It used to be my job to throw fancy parties for celebrities."

"That sounds so awesome."

"Do not, under any circumstances, even think about wasting your life doing that."

Belinda looked surprised. "Why?"

"I mean, I'm not being fair. PR can be great," Marjorie admitted, "but you should be an op-ed journalist or a foreign correspondent or a neurosurgeon or something, not checking on the white hydrangeas for J-Lo's greenroom."

"So, if you did that, then why are you a tutor now? No offense, but like why are you free to teach me during the day on Mondays?"

The too astute question flummoxed Marjorie. The only answer she could muster was the truth. "I'm kind of a loser, Belly. I was one of those popular kids, then I got confused about how to be an adult. I'm here now because I like cookies and writing. You're okay too."

On Saturday, after their talk, Marjorie and Mac had eschewed the bodega's Rold Gold pretzels for meatballs, roasted vegetable salad, and pork braciola at Frankies 457. Mac had flirted throughout, making lewd remarks while she ate gelato and wondering aloud about the shade of tonight's neon underwear. It all felt surprisingly normal. And, when they said good night outside her building, Marjorie had to fight the urge to drag him upstairs and show him her new bedroom. She reminded herself to be wary: This was *Mac,* after all. She pecked him goodbye and sprinted inside before she could change her mind.

A few remaining guests lounged on the floor. Fred was passed out on the sofa like a rag doll. Marjorie headed upstairs to bed but had trouble falling asleep; the night was too sticky, her air conditioner too weak. Mac was a ticket back to her old life. For the first time, she wondered if that was a good thing.

The next morning, as she and Fred Swiffered the floor and Method-sprayed the counters, she didn't mention Mac's appearance, loath to explain what she did not yet understand. Luckily, Fred's headache made her less amenable to chitchat, until the afternoon, when Marjorie slipped out to meet Belinda.

"Where are you going?" asked the subdued pixie.

"Just running errands."

"I'll come with! I can show you that cool mural I found."

Thinking quickly, Marjorie blurted out, "I kind of need alone time."

"Oh." Fred looked injured. "I guess I understand that."

Now, Belinda gave her tutor a measured assessment, then announced, "I'm pretty positive that you're not a loser." Marjorie wasn't so sure.

"Thanks, Belly. But, hey, time is a-wasting and we need to choose your topic. For next week, make a list of what you learned about this new girl at camp."

"Boy."

"Even better. Brainstorm ten facts—about where you met him, what you know about his past, how you think he'll fit in at your school. And come prepared to work. We're going to do a writing exercise."

"We? Like you'll do it too?"

"Like I'm going to help you with yours." Marjorie watched Belinda crumple like someone had run over her puppy. "All right, all right, all right. Maybe I'll do one too."

"You always repeat things three times."

"I do? That's funny. I never noticed."

"Well you do, do, do."

Before packing it away, Belinda scanned her to-do list:

1. Borrow "He's Just Not That Into You" from public library.
2. Make "Belly" stick.
3. Watch "Romy & Michele's High School Reunion."
4. 10 Facts About Meeting Mitch.
5. Find out what really makes someone a loser.

18

"You're sure you don't want to come with me instead?"

"Thank you, Fred. But I'm good, good, good."

"Positive? The art opening is in Chinatown and it's going to be *pretty* cool."

Marjorie applied makeup at the full-length mirror that hung on the inside of her bedroom door; Fred lay on her floor in a racer-backed, blue-and-yellow leaf-patterned jumpsuit, and enormous round sunglasses. A wide-brimmed felt hat and high platform sandals sat to her left like loyal pups.

"It's called 'Pictures My Camera Took.' The artist printed photos she accidentally took with her camera phone—like of her feet, her bag's interior, the inside of her pocket. You know: ART!"

"It should be called 'Pictures My Butt Took.' Sounds cultured, but you know I have plans."

Fred propped herself up on her elbows. "So, we're really doing this? Going out with the stalker?"

"No. *I'm* really doing this. *I'm* going out with the stalker. And I'd love to stop talking about it. Wouldn't you rather hear about my latest rejection?"

"Stop changing the subject!"

Marjorie had begun job hunting online, and the descriptions that most matched her skill set were so ambiguous that she was never quite sure for what she was applying: Executive Associate, Associate Executive, Associate Assistant, Assistant Associate to the Executive, Manager of Associate & Assistant Relations, Assistant Associate Managerial Coordinator for Northeastern Territories . . .

Decoding the listings became a game. "Hands-on experience" meant long hours for paltry pay. "Competitive salary" meant comparable to teenage babysitting rates. And, for out-of-touch employers, required skills like "optimization experience" and "social media acumen" seemed satisfied by an active Twitter account and a postmillennial graduation date.

By and large, the jobs sounded soul-sucking, but Marjorie could not afford to be picky. A recommendation from Brianne was as likely as a lottery win, and as antithetically toxic. And her experience was rarely applicable: As it turned out, the Newark, New Jersey, bezel manufacturer was not in need of a "celebrity liaison."

While eating Union Market's gourmet samples for lunch to save cash, Marjorie had confessed to Fred about her panic attack at the party, Mac's arrival, the urge to draw a cat nose and whiskers on a passed-out Fred's face. Disapproval wasn't her roommate's style, but she seemed unimpressed with Mac's grand gesture. "He sounds like Bruce Wayne." Fred shrugged. "I've always been a Clark Kent girl myself."

"Speaking of which, what was with the Abercrombie model?"

"Who, James?"

"'Who, *Jaaaames*?'" Marjorie teased, grabbing a shameless handful of rice cracker samples and dipping them in hummus marked "vegan" (as if there is any other kind). "Of course, I mean James. He was the only guy at the party who owns a brush."

Fred and James had first met a couple years before in Prospect Park. She'd set off on a solo nature hike, only to get caught in a torrential downpour in an open meadow. (The experience later inspired her song "Buckets of Pain.") Foreshadowing their future dynamic, James appeared—a knight in shining chinos with an umbrella as shield—and escorted Fred home. He wasn't her type—being employed and groomed—but she deigned to give him a chance. And they were happy until Fred played a disastrous Hoboken show eight months later. Her punk female followers protested the too melodic, cheerful riffs of her new song, "Happy to Be Anywhere." She almost lost their faith. Fred promptly broke off the relationship, she claimed, without irony, to focus on her music.

"You couldn't do that with an adorable boyfriend?" Marjorie speared a chunk of soy cheese with a toothpick, tasted it, then spit it out into a napkin.

"He was too supportive!" complained Fred. "He paid for everything, bought me presents, forgave my mistakes. How is a girl supposed to channel angst with that? What was I supposed to write about? The 401(k) he set up for me? Really, he set up a 401(k)."

"He sounds awful. I don't know why you still speak to him." Marjorie watched her friend feign interest in a can of organic vegetable soup before taking a Dixie cup sample. "Fred! He's the goddamn Holy Grail! Why is he still hanging around?"

"We're friends."

"Friends? No."

Fred planted a hand on her hip. "Why can't we be friends?"

"The *When Harry Met Sally* theory aside, how about the fact that he's in love with you?"

"He's not!"

"Oh, please. I saw him looking at you. Be honest: Do you call him when you're lonely? Stay up nights on the phone together? Does he drive you to Fairway in Red Hook for groceries?"

"What's wrong with that?"

"You're dry dating him until someone better comes along. It's unkind. No one wants to be a backup plan."

"This from the girl dating *American Psycho*!"

Now they hung in Marjorie's room, each in defense of her questionable relationship. Marjorie finished drawing a black liquid line across her lids and turned around. The dress was a Pickles castoff: short, tight, black Lanvin. "How do I look?"

"Better than your date deserves," said Fred, without looking up. But then she actually glanced over. "Wow. Smokin'! Men must love you."

Marjorie snorted. "Boys, sometimes. Men, never. I gotta go." She grabbed her yellow leather Crossbody bag.

"Have fun with the stalker!" said Fred. "Just remember: Never go to the second location. That's the kiss of death."

Marjorie left Fred staring at the ceiling and considering the band name Cracked Paint.

En route to the subway, Marjorie had felt nervous. Mac, not so much, or so it seemed.

Toward the end of their dimly lit dinner at the Dutch on charming

Sullivan Street in the West Village, he sat across from her, self-assured as ever, musing about their future: "How many children should we have? I've always imagined one or two, but now I'm thinking eight."

"Oh. I think you have me confused with your second and third wives."

"Right, Greta and Paige."

"Paige. That's it. She's the one with the childbearing hips."

"Any flesh is good flesh as long as it's not wrinkled. That became my motto at eighty-two years old, when I married her."

"Hmm. But that raises the issue of how to dispose of me." Marjorie tossed back the dregs of her martini. "Divorce? Tragic death? *Suicide*?"

"Depends on the prenup. Did we have one? Or were we so in love that we believed it was forever? Because, without one, I might have to murder you."

"Alas, no prenup. You refused to listen to advice from your parents and lawyers! And, as a gold digger, of course I egged you on. Poor Paige may have had six of your eight children, but she gets none of the cash."

"Poor Paige!"

"Poor Paige? Poor Greta née Pippi West End!"

"Pippi West End?"

"Greta's stripper name."

"Of course." Mac nodded.

"Greta thought she'd found her ticket out of 'the life,' when this dashing middle-aged gentleman stumbled into her Vegas club and fell in lust. But she was a mere stepping-stone out of heartbreak hotel after the crushing end of his first marriage to the brilliant and magnificent Marjorie Plum!"

"Marjorie O'Shea."

"Well, that," said Marjorie, sliding her cocktail's olive off the toothpick and onto her tongue, "is up for debate."

"I like it. Good story." Mac considered her from across the table.

"You're insanely hot, you know that? I have no idea how you kept me at bay for all these years. Let's get out of here and start on kids one and two."

"Oh, May and Milo! So adorable, those sweeties, in their matching tennis whites . . ."

Marjorie thought maybe she should let the make-believe marriage game drop. This was *Mac*. She'd trained herself never to believe a word he said and now she was taking him seriously? Same repartee, different outcome. Normally, after a similar exchange, she'd have watched him slither into a cab with their waitress (a pretty aspiring actress, who kept asking—without subtlety—if he wanted "anything else?").

"I am not naming my child Milo, but I'll let May pass if we leave for my apartment now and make up for the other night's chaste peck. I'm still having nightmares."

"What's the rush?"

"Gotta seal the deal before you remember I'm despicable. You ready?"

Marjorie did want to go home with Mac. To her surprise, she would have attacked him right there, over sliced five-grain baguette and extra-virgin olive oil. But she was leery. The stakes were higher now. Last time seemed like an isolated mistake that she'd pay for in mild embarrassment. Now he was sucking her into his vortex, getting her good and addicted to feeling wanted and . . . *special*.

"You look unsure." He reached over and toyed with the slim rose gold bangles encircling her wrist. "Okay. You win. Milo it is."

She returned his gaze over the Syrah-stained white tablecloth. "I'm ready."

He didn't move. "This isn't like before, Madge. You think I'm kidding, but I'm not. We can do whatever we want together: have stupid adventures, fly to the Amalfi Coast or Tokyo for no good reason, Milo and May, and whatever the hell else. That can be our life."

Suddenly seized with fear, Marjorie fought the urge to run from this new intense and sincere Mac—the future sounded so permanent.

Was she ready for him every day? When she had the flu, when she was feeling down, when he was eighty-two years old? Did she want this life of cocktails hours and red eyes? And, jokes aside, would he be able to pass up Greta and Paige? The questions felt oppressive.

She forced herself to stand, flashing her best come-hither smile. "Let's blow this joint," she said, pushing past the "what if's." And they did.

She needn't have worried, at least for the night. Back at the loft, awkwardness dropped away. They lounged on the bed, as she made fun of how few of his books he'd read. Somewhere in the midst of it, he kissed her and, the rest, as they say, was not so ancient history.

This was the first of many nights they would spend together over the next weeks, as their coupledom and shared stories began to replace memories of each other as friends. A blur of events included a party reintroducing his sister Natalie into "civilized society" postrehab—or so his blotto mother put it at the sober function. The O'Sheas were a cold brood and, though they had known Marjorie for years, they sniffed around her like bloodhounds, suspicious of her new role in Mac's life.

Still, soon enough, for Marjorie, the smell of his Old Spice deodorant and musky sheets and the straying of his naked leg to her side of the bed ceased being strange. Shuffling to the bathroom in her underwear, the bearskin rug sprouting between her toes, became the norm. She grew accustomed to finding Mac and Fred debating music in the kitchen on mornings after his occasional stays in Brooklyn.

And yet she could never quite shake the sense—after he dropped off to sleep and she lay awake listening to buses wheeze outside—that he was unknown to her. It was as if she appeared next to a new character, having missed the story's middle.

19

There are few things as demoralizing as being rejected by those you only deigned to engage.

Thirty-five résumés later, Marjorie was still unemployed. Her desk was a monument to organized chaos, strewn with printed applications. She lay on her unmade bed, refreshing her e-mail over and over again, and had just begun to imagine that the entire Internet was broken, when she received a new message:

Hi, Girl,

I'm e-mailing from my personal account because the Witch has been on the prowl since you left, demanding that every employee profess loyalty like she's the Gestapo or something. Next she'll make us wear armbands designed by Galliano. You know mine better be purple!

She's always looking over my shoulder to see what I'm working on, and yesterday I caught her searching Herb's cubicle because she suspects you were friends, even though he screwed you over. She tried to fake like she lost an earring. In his file cabinet?! She's lost it. I'm telling you. I even heard her ask sweet old security guard Bill whether he's seen you. Like you're hanging around, waiting to strike, like you're actually crazy like she told people. I think without you to abuse, she's got rage constipation.

Here's the punch line: The Snow Lite liquor people appreciated your honest feedback. They're changing the "flavor profiles." So, there you go. You could probably get a job there, if you wanted. Tell them you pulled a Jerry Maguire; that's why she called you insane. They'll think it's inspiring!

But I'm really writing to see how you're doing. The girls and I have been good. I took them to see *Madagascar 3* last week; I'm a sucker for a singing lion. What else? The coffee machine broke, so Brianne bought one of those fancy Nespresso situations to curry favor. Of course, she can't work the damn thing, so I hear her cursing at Herb about Americanos from the kitchen. Luckily, I don't have to watch her—this was a Botox and Restylane month, and you know how creepy it is when she tries to form expressions right after the injections. It's like her forehead is fighting her skin. Nasty.

In the end, she did send that horrible e-mail to her entire address book like she threatened. First time that woman ever figured out how to work anything on her own. Figures.

Anyway, keep your head up! Hopefully, you're somewhere fabulous with your friend Pickles, licking your wounds and feeling free. Maybe you already have a new job! Either way, I know you're on to something bigger and better.

It's not the same here without you. I miss our midafternoon "street hot dog breaks" (Brianne trashing sessions!) at Bryant Park.

xoxo Tina

Marjorie sat back, one leg dangling off the bed. The Bacht-Chit office was all-consuming. Brianne tunneled into her employees' psyches, forcing them to think about her nonstop. Even grounded Tina couldn't help but obsess over that psychopath's bad behavior.

Tina was right: Marjorie had the chance to find something fulfilling. She didn't have to wind up working for some Tumblr-obsessed former frat boy for minimum wage (*plus, free Starbucks!*). She was—what had Tina said?—"on to something bigger and better." She opened a new e-mail that had materialized from some guy named Mark at Blinter Blotters. The prospective employer—who she suspected was actually a bored thirteen-year-old boy, messing around—asked her to list her three best and worst qualities. Emboldened by her newfound perspective, she replied:

WORST: Too hard a worker, too committed to perfection, too beloved by clients.

BEST: Not remotely interested in this job.

By that evening, when Marjorie arrived to see Fred perform at a pop-up music venue and art installation space in Greenpoint, she felt cheerful. She paused in the entryway: To one side sat six disemboweled toilets, either a sculpture or plumbing mishap, and tall cocktail tables were littered with flyers.

The crowd was Fred's usual, though some of the men were more put together with hair pomaded in a skate-rat-meets-Clark-Gable comb-over. James—a sore thumb in his Polo and loafers—saluted congenially but stayed near the stage for the best view of Fred.

Marjorie passed the time playing quarters with Elmo's new girlfriend, Lou. The now couple had connected over a shared love of stale Peeps at Fred's party. And, since, Marjorie had developed her own friend crush.

She successfully bounced a coin (she didn't want to think how dirty) into Lou's Dixie cup of watered-down beer. "Drink, Drink, Drink!" she chanted. Her companion's cheeks were already flushed from alcohol, the allergy her Korean birthright. Lou brought the cup to her lips, then, instead of chugging, took a dainty sip.

"That's how old people like us play quarters," Lou said.

Marjorie laughed. "That's right. It's after nine P.M.!"

"Please. I'm just glad this isn't one of their eleven o'clock shows that really start at one. I may be too old to date a musician."

Marjorie smiled. It was obvious to everyone how much Lou and Elmo liked each other. "Just wait out the honeymoon period, until he's hooked, then let him know you're elderly.'"

"Deception. Always a good call."

"That's what women be doing." Marjorie slouched over the table, giggling. "Bitches, man."

Fred's brother appeared at their side. "What's so funny?"

Michael could be mistaken for vanilla by the unwitting observer. He used his sunny demeanor and appearance to his advantage, with clients, employers, women. But behind that Mayberry exterior lurked a sardonic sense of humor and an impatience with the dumb or rude. He planted a kiss on each girl's cheek.

"No Celeste tonight?" asked Lou, after Michael's girlfriend.

Lou was a filmmaker who moonlit as a Forever 21 salesperson, and had met Michael years before at a small upstate festival. He'd been impressed with her work and they kept in touch. That's why he'd invited her to the party where—to the accidental matchmaker's surprise—she'd fallen for Elmo, or "the Bearded Man" as Michael called him.

"We're leaving day after tomorrow for Italy, so she's getting ready."

"You don't have to pack?" asked Marjorie.

"Celeste packs for me. Otherwise she doesn't like what I wear."

"Rough life," said Lou. "I wish she didn't like what I wore." She turned to Marjorie. "Have you met Celeste? It gets worse: She looks like a supermodel and cooks like Julia Child."

"Wow. Can I date her?" Marjorie took a swig of beer.

Michael shook his head. "Sorry. I'm hoping to take her off the market. On this trip, actually."

The girls cooed on cue so sweetly that they moved a passerby to decide to adopt a kitten, his roommate's life-threatening allergies be damned!

"I thought you were going with her parents?"

"We are. She's really close with them, and this is like a *Roots* tour. They're taking us to Taormina, Sicily, where her great-grandmother grew up."

"Ooh! There are amazing cliffs there overlooking the water, and cafés where famous writers hung out!" said Marjorie. "Isn't that where they shot *The Godfather*?"

"That's the place."

"You're so lucky! I almost went once from Tuscany with my friend Pickles, but we got roped into some annoying Milan fashion thing instead."

"Pickles? Milan? Who are you and why can't I be you?" Lou frowned.

"Oh, you don't want to be me." Marjorie chugged the rest of her warm craft brew, which she suspected was Bud Light. "Today I got rejected by Teddy's Trolley Barn, among other prospective employers. I'm thinking I need one of those green jobs that Obama and Romney keep talking about. By green, they mean *cash,* right?"

"That's right, sweetie." Lou raised her eyebrows in mock horror and patted Marjorie's shoulder. "You're going to be just fine." She shook her head at Michael. The threesome laughed, Marjorie with less conviction.

"You know what?" said Michael. "We need someone."

"We do?" said Marjorie. "For what?"

"You know how we have this film distribution company? The one employee who was our support staff, Cleo, just left to pursue a graduate degree in star fucking as assistant to some reality TV star, which would be fine if I had time to hire anyone before my trip. That's my responsibility, since Gus . . . well, Gus hates people." He paused to consider this, deemed it apt, then continued. "It's temporary, glorified assistant work, but we have festivals coming up that Gus will need help covering without me around. Interested?"

"Are you kidding? I'm more than interested. I'm fascinated, intrigued—"

"A thesaurus?" said Lou.

"I'll e-mail you the info. You can start Monday."

Marjorie's shoulders relaxed inches with relief. "Michael. I can't thank you enough."

"My pleasure! I'd been meaning to mention it. Any friend of Fred's . . . well, is usually strange. But you're welcome." He blushed, and Marjorie thought that, as amazing as this Celeste was, she was lucky to have such a good guy to love her.

Just then, the lights went down, then up, then down again. Some guy in a rumpled trench coat walked out onto the makeshift stage and introduced Fred and her band, the Cracked Walnuts.

"Here we go." Lou smiled.

Fred's voice, more beautiful and sincere in performance than Marjorie had imagined, teased a soft melody that trilled into a punk shout, then wound back down, pouring itself through Marjorie's ears like liquid hope.

Later, with the van packed up, the group left the venue, ears ringing, in search of lo mein. Elmo's arm was parked around Lou's shoulders.

"They're in love," said Fred, watching Marjorie watch the couple. "And you look happier?"

"Your pipes lifted the spirit of the wretched. I was so proud!"

"Mac couldn't come?"

"I didn't invite him."

"How come?"

"I don't know. Do you think that's bad?"

Fred bit her lip—and her tongue. "What do I know? I'm only the voice of an angel."

20

At their regular table, Marjorie scanned Belinda's information about the new boy at camp.

10 Facts About Mitch

1. His last name is Kaplan.
2. He's going to the Math & Science Exploratory School with me next year.
3. He lives 10 blocks from me, but doesn't know the neighborhood.
4. He is really good at basketball, swimming, and soccer.
5. He's funny.
6. He moved here from Seattle and says that's why he likes outdoor sports.
7. When we met on Taco Day at the mess hall, none of the other girls were eating hot sauce and he called me "bold."
8. His parents are also too overprotective to send him to sleepaway. We're like the oldest kids at day camp.
9. We have an overnight in a couple weeks and he asked me to sit with him at the evening activity movie. (Unfortunately, his best friend is that kid Snarls—who looks like a bulldog—and he seems less psyched about me tagging along.)
10. Mitch's favorite color is blue, I think. He wears it all the time.
11. (I know we said 10 facts, but this is more of a confession.) When school starts, I'm worried he'll meet the more girly girls and stop liking me.

Number eleven cracked Marjorie's heart in two. How was it possible to be so young and so grown up at the same time? Some of the hardest lessons are learned early.

The crown of Belinda's head bobbed, as she picked the remaining cookie crumbs from her napkin. A sugar-starved kid with sweets is like a lion devouring raw meat—graphic.

"Perfect," said Marjorie. "This gives us physical and emotional cues, and a sense of place, even some supporting characters."

Belinda looked doubtful. "Where's *your* list?"

"I brought a short story I wrote when I was a little younger than you instead. You can read it when we're done." Marjorie pulled a photocopy of her flip book story from her bag. "Yours will be much better."

Belinda took the page and began to read.

"Hey, put that away! We need to get cracking. It's mid-July and we don't have a first draft!"

Belinda tucked the paper away in her backpack. "Can I ask you a personal question?"

"No. Stop stalling! I'm on to you." Marjorie performed her best no-nonsense look. "Okay. We're going to take four of these facts and turn them into fiction."

"Which ones?"

"Let's figure that out." Marjorie scanned the page. "First, you might want to change his name . . . to protect the innocent."

"Definitely. Let's call him Henry!"

"Perfect. Henry goes to your school, lives in your hood, is athletic, from Seattle. Hmm. What if he moved from somewhere more exotic?"

"How about Bath?"

"Bath, like in England?"

"I like Jane Austen and she's from there. Mom H. read *Pride and Prejudice* with me."

"Exotic Bath, it is! Three more facts to go. He's funny. Well, we don't want him to be dull. Taco Day and overprotective parents are things you have in common." Marjorie tapped her pen against the table. "Do you want to write a happy or sad ending?"

"Maybe somewhere in between? The best books have both."

"What if you weren't going to school together next year? And he had to go back to Bath instead?"

"How tragic!" said Belinda.

"Exactly. One last detail to be fictionalized. Let's see, let's see, let's see."

Belinda eyes popped open like an anime character. "I know! What if Snarls is a dog instead of a person?"

"Belly! You're a genius. That's brilliant."

"Did I tell you he snatched my glasses during tennis yesterday? I almost got smacked in the head with a flying ball. It's all fun and games until someone gets hurt."

"He needs a new name."

"How about Trash Bag McGee?" Belinda giggled. Suddenly, she was a child again, back from the brink of teenage cynicism. Was this the age when Marjorie had gone wrong?

Marjorie shook her head clear. "Done. For next week, you'll write a plot outline."

"But I don't know what the story should be!"

"Just tell the truth about meeting Mitch, ahem, Henry. Then think about what it would be like if he left. Good?"

Belinda scowled; the adolescent had returned. "I guess."

Marjorie took a sip of her iced tea. "You may ask your personal question now."

Belinda perked up. She pulled her hair into a ponytail, then let it fall back down her back (a Marjorie mannerism). She had fought with Harriet for forty-five minutes that morning about wearing it loose. "So, do you, like, have a boyfriend?"

"Good question," grunted Marjorie.

"You don't know?" The kid looked disappointed.

Marjorie folded, unfolded, and refolded her straw's paper wrapping. "Well, it's complicated. He's an old friend and I'm giving him a shot."

Belinda scrutinized Marjorie's face. "How come you don't seem excited?"

"You sound like my roommate, Fred."

"The one who was supposed to be my tutor!"

Panic caught in Marjorie's throat before she realized she hadn't been caught in a lie. "Yes. *That* Fred. Anyway, I am excited. It's just that after years of dating different guys—"

"How many different guys?"

"Don't worry about it. Let's just say I'm cautiously optimistic."

Belinda turned that over in her mind. "Makes sense, I guess. But if Mitch was my boyfriend, I'd be psyched."

"If Mitch was your boyfriend, he'd be the lucky one." Marjorie glanced at her cell phone. "Time to go. We don't want Mom H. to worry."

Marjorie and Belinda gathered their belongings.

"Actually, Mom H. hasn't been home much lately. I didn't think it was possible, but I'm getting sick of pizza."

"Where's she been?"

"Pottery class, a lecture series on chia seeds, candlelight yoga class." They wove, like a caterpillar, around tables toward the exit. "She says Mom D. has work and I have school and camp and she needs something for herself. Really she just wants time away from Mom D., I think. Normally, they try to hide their fights with these loud whispers they think I can't hear, but lately they've been outright yelling." She paused. "Hey, what are 'intimacy issues'?"

As they stood outside the air-conditioned restaurant in the heat, Marjorie neither wanted to cause alarm nor lie. "I think Mom H. would probably like more attention from Mom D. Life can get busy and stressful; it's not always easy to find time to make the people we love feel important."

"Does your boyfriend make you feel important?"

"Mac? Sure. But he could make a rock garden feel special."

"Hey, BTW, I've decided you're not a loser."

"Oh. Well, thank you. I did get a new job, actually."

Belinda looked stricken. "Does that mean no more tutoring?"

"No, no, no. It's temporary and part-time. I need you around to tell me I'm a winner!"

The preteen didn't crack a smile. "I'm serious. I asked Mom D. what makes someone a 'loser.' First she said I shouldn't call people *losers.*" Belinda rolled her eyes. "Then she said that losers are selfish people, who are too busy blaming others for their problems to get their lives together. So you're not one because, for one thing, you're helping me."

"That's not exactly charity," said Marjorie. "I hear you, though: I'm not a loser. But maybe I used to be."

21

Monday's forecast was hot and disgusting with a humidity index of a billion percent and winds from the east carrying the stench of rotting half-eaten hot dogs, urine, and ten thousand yellowed armpits of five thousand commuting executives.

Against all odds, Marjorie awoke feeling hopeful, the first indicator that her mood could only plummet.

Unrest came in the form of an early phone call. Marjorie had made the rookie mistake of calling to share career news with her parents, forgetting her mother's propensity for the buzzkill. Barbara Plum was too embroiled in a client's Sunday night crisis to chat and hung up abruptly, as if the interruption had been audacious. Now she called and demanded an update.

"My new job starts today," said Marjorie, sorting through her closet.

"Today? Are you late? It's nine thirty!"

"I know what time it is, Mom. I start in the afternoon."

"Why?"

"I guess Michael's partner needs to get me up to speed but has morning meetings. This is when you say, 'A job? That's great!'"

"That *is* great. This is doing what?"

"It's an assistant job for a film distribution company."

"Oh! A big one?"

"A tiny boutique one, I think."

"Oh. Does it pay well?"

"I don't know. I needed a job; they offered one; I took it."

"You didn't ask about salary?"

"Mom, I'm desperate. Michael is a lovely guy. He wouldn't take advantage of me."

"Okay. I'm sure the stability is comforting."

"Yes, for now." The cordless phone almost slipped from between Marjorie's shoulder and chin, as she pulled a dress off a black velour hanger. "It's only for a few weeks. Temp, temp, temp."

"I see." Barbara paused, loudly. "Are you doing 'morning pages' as I suggested? Writing down your thoughts first thing can clear your head and help you find direction."

"Sometimes, Mom. Not every day." By that she meant *no*.

There was silence on the line, as each woman waited for the other to speak. Marjorie got distracted by a toothpaste smudge on her garment's collar, Barbara by Mina the Cat crying for fresh dry food—as if that wasn't an oxymoron.

"I should have seen this coming." The elder sighed.

"Seen *what* coming?"

"You. This. I tried to steer you in the right direction as a child, but you spoiled easily. You expect opportunities to come to you."

"I *spoiled easily*?" Marjorie threw her poor innocent frock onto the bed. "Like a tangerine?"

"I guess they do rot quickly."

Marjorie fell silent. She crossed to the mirror and examined her skin for imperfections.

Barbara Plum sensed the error in her approach, though she could not understand how she'd stepped in it once again. Had a life-coaching client relayed the same conversation verbatim—set in a different household, delivered by another mother—she would have seen that the child's unrealistic expectations resulted directly from the mother's being set too high. But so goes the blindness of parenting. She could so clearly see the future that Marjorie deserved but was letting slip away. Perhaps if she reminded her daughter of her flaws, she might avoid having them.

"Marjorie? Are you still there?"

Marjorie pulled a tweezer from her makeup bag and began plucking stray blond hairs from below her brow line. "Yes. How *convenient* that the problem was not with your parenting, but with my character."

"I've offended you."

Marjorie took a deep breath. "I don't care about being offended." Her mother often made these damning pronouncements, then appeared genuinely surprised by the negative response. Barbara Plum had thick skin; she assumed everyone else did too. "I just want to be in the right mind-set for my first day at a new job. This isn't helping."

"Right. Good thinking." Barbara grimaced. "Well, good luck!"

Marjorie gritted her teeth. "Thanks. Wait, Mom. Did Mac O'Shea ask you for my address?"

"Oh, yes, he did."

"You didn't think to give me a heads-up?"

"Why would I? I assumed he was inviting you to one of his mother's charity galas or whatever." Fair enough. "I better go. I'm teaching an Owning Your Passion seminar at the college. Your father would like to say a quick hello. Bye, honey."

Barbara Plum shrugged at her husband, a gesture that said, *I guess I said the wrong thing . . . again,* and handed him the phone.

"Hey, Bozo!" said Chipper, cheerleading. "I heard you got a job."

"Just for a week or so," Marjorie grunted. "But they may eventually hire someone full-time." *Shit!* Never pluck angry. In her suppressed rage, she'd created a tiny bald spot toward the tail of her left brow, a symbol of her absent sense.

"To prepare, may I suggest watching *Working Girl*?"

Marjorie had to smile. "Dad. It's not 1988. I'll try to fit in a rerun of *The Office* before I leave, though."

"Touché, dear daughter! I've taught you well." Chipper's attempt to repair the damage from Hurricane Barbara was valiant, but

Marjorie needed to get off the phone and refocus. "I'll let you go. But have a great day."

"Thanks, Dad. You too."

Doubt took root and became a stubborn splinter. And that cast a pall over the the rest of the morning. From the front desk at the wellness clinic, Fred texted, "Break a leg!" and, as Marjorie left their brownstone, she almost did. Roberta had accidentally—or perhaps as vengeance for the stolen tomato—trailed gardening topsoil on the front steps. Unstable in her platform heels, Marjorie slipped and caught herself inches before landing in a pile of manure. She carefully righted herself and went on her way.

The heat was the epic kind that erases all memories of showers. Instantly, the strands of Marjorie's hair experienced a collective schizophrenic break triggered by the humidity and turned so puffy that a passing old man was reminded of fond trips to the groomer with his deceased poodle, Muffin.

Marjorie's dress stuck to her back and her sandal strap rubbed her heel in an ominous way that spelled blister. She couldn't drown out her mother's voice no matter how loud she turned the volume on her iPod. The songs seemed cloying anyway.

The old Marjorie would have jumped in an air-conditioned cab, saved herself the literal sweat, blood, and tears of the subway trip, so she could arrive looking professional and long-term hirable. But she was dead broke and unsure that a taxi ride would give her the desired sense of personal satisfaction. (She had indeed watched *Working Girl* the night before despite her denial and was now determined to break the glass ceiling on foot!) After all, this felt like her first real job, one that she hadn't been offered only because she was cute and knew Justin Timberlake a little.

As she neared the subway, her phone rang. She pulled it from her bag, ready to ignore her mother's call back. Instead VERA flashed on the screen, an Amber Alert for lost friendship.

"Hello?"

"Hi." Her old pal's voice was clipped. "I'm calling because Victor contacted me about the security deposit check. I didn't know where you wanted it sent, so I gave him your parents' address."

Great. Marjorie would have to endure another family dinner. "That's fine. Thanks." Silence. "So, how are you?"

"I'm great. Not that *you* care, but Brian and I love our new place. I'm headed to ABC Carpet right now to look at end tables. My lunch meeting canceled, so . . ."

"That's nice, Vera."

"I think so. But I'm sure you don't."

"Jesus! I don't understand why you're so angry. You left *me* high and dry."

"Oh, please," huffed Vera. Hers was a rage born of late-night stewing, things left unsaid. "I know you told Brian to 'Get the fuck out!' of the apartment."

"Want to know what he said to provoke that?"

"Not really."

Perhaps the heat accelerated her temper, but Marjorie hit her boiling point fast. "Your loser frat boy appendage told me he'd hit on me a year too early because I'm an easier target now."

Seconds passed, during which, Marjorie assumed, Vera ingested this information, decided it didn't suit her taste, and spit it back out.

"Well, aren't you? Easy these days?" said her once best friend. "Everyone *knows* you're Mac O'Shea's latest piece of trash."

"Trash?" Marjorie felt actual pain in her chest.

"You're such an idiot. You think you're the exception? That he actually *likes* you?"

"You don't know what you're talking about. He's my *boyfriend,* Vera. It's not a fling."

She cackled. "You're even sadder than I thought."

"Yeah, well, you're horrible. I spent years defending and protecting you. Now I finally see why people called you 'bitter' and worse. Some advice: If you're jealous and feel overshadowed, don't wait twenty years to say something. It makes you ugly—ugli*er.*"

Marjorie hung up. Dizzy with adrenaline, she leaned against the subway's exterior. A grandmotherly woman stopped and approached. "Are you feeling faint, dear?"

"I'm fine. Thank you." She willed herself not to cry under the lady's kind gaze, even as her chin wobbled.

"It's hot today. Make sure you hydrate." She continued on her way.

Marjorie couldn't afford—practically or emotionally—to show up weepy to work. Anger was another story.

She stomped down the stairs, swiped her MetroCard, and almost kicked the turnstile when an error message—PLEASE SWIPE AGAIN— flashed. Cursing, she reswiped and entered. Rats frolicked in and around the third rail.

Marjorie was trying to start from scratch. How dare Vera invade and squash her newfound hope with pettiness! What did she know about Mac, or even Marjorie, except that she represented all things unequal? How could she just shake off Brian's betrayal? Did she have no self-respect?

Marjorie thought about that photograph of them as kids, their arms wrapped around each other, their only worry the next day's algebra quiz. How long had Vera hated her? One year? Six? Had she only pretended to be a sister from day one, commiserating about unfair parental rules and making inside jokes, while harboring secret scorn? Once, they had complemented each other: Marjorie a relaxed, outgoing foil to Vera's organized, controlled being.

Grief hit like a punch to the gut. Overcome, Marjorie slumped onto a nearby bench. How could she feel both betrayed and mournful? Her breath came short and labored. Panic. *This is a subway station. This is sweat down my back, a McDonald's bag in the tracks, a friendship ending.*

The F train pulled up and Marjorie climbed on board. The car was air-conditioned, but there were no free seats. She propped herself against a pole by a set of doors and stared out the window into blackness. Based on her reflection, looking back with tired eyes, her makeup had not worn well in the heat.

The jostling had a calming effect. Six stops later, at 2nd Avenue in Manhattan, Marjorie was starting to breathe evenly when a drunk man boarded and started mumbling, then ranting about the mayor. More alert passengers hopped off and onto the next car, sensing unpleasantness. Others watched the doors close with regret. Readers concentrated more closely on books, iPod listeners studied their fingers hoping to turn invisible. Some sturdy older women, longtime veterans of the New York City transit system, looked on with unflinching disinterest.

"First he took cigarettes, made 'em, how much—they cost, they're . . . stogies on the black market, Canal Street, with their Chinese," raved the man. "What is this? Russhhhia? Ain't no Communist—this is— New York motherfucking City—this is—and no giant drink. I want me a big-ass soda! This ain't a police state . . . Russia! This ain't ching chong China." A nearby Chinese passenger adjusted her pocketbook strap.

He made his way through the car, swinging between poles, stopping short before a seated thirty-something man in a tailored shirt and Ray-Bans. "They took—where's my—polluting the damn air, man. We're taking—cancer in our lungs, in *your* lungs!" He stuck a finger in the guy's face; the passenger scratched an imaginary itch behind his ear and pretended not to mind being accosted.

That's when the drunk spotted Marjorie, the lone person standing.

"You!" he yelped, pointing at her. "Women, man. Women, you're—like flowerrrrs. You gotta—" He readdressed the sunglass wearer, who had wrongly assumed he was off the hook. "Gotta take care of women. 'Cause they flowers. They need water and . . . care!"

At least he didn't think women were spawns of Satan, thought Marjorie. But then he stepped toward her. "I think—you look sad. You need a kiss."

Horrified, Marjorie backed into the corner. He was so close she could smell metallic liquor and nicotine on his breath.

"Excuse me, sir," came a nasal command from behind. The voice belonged to a pudgy middle-aged man, who—judging by his loafers and beat-up briefcase—commuted to the city for business from somewhere like New Rochelle, where his lovely family was looking forward to that night's viewing of *America's Got Talent*. "The lady would prefer to be left alone."

Marjorie shot him a grateful look. Never before had she loved a gentleman in a Men's Warehouse suit. She cursed her past prejudices. This guy was ten times the person she was, helping a total stranger.

"How'd you know what she want? You—her *boyfriend,* fatty? Mind your bid—business or I'll hit you." The drunk took a threatening lunge forward.

Of all things, Marjorie wondered, in that moment, what her actual boyfriend might do in this situation. Charm the guy out of kissing her? Offer him money? Let her get molested, then poke fun later? Right: He would never have set foot on a subway in the first place.

"No one wants a problem," said the businessman. "She just wants to go about her day."

The homeless man looked unsure. "Then why she's not saying that?"

Both men looked to her for confirmation. Barely above a whisper, she managed, "I'd prefer if you didn't kiss me. I'd like to be left alone."

As they pulled into the station at Broadway-Lafayette in lower Manhattan, the drunk considered this, shrugged, and exited the train.

She exhaled. "Thank you so much!" she gushed to her savior, whose name, as it happens, was Fred, suggesting something supreme about the moniker.

"No problem."

"What you did—I'm having a bad day. That's not the point, but, well, thank you for restoring my faith in humanity."

Only then did Marjorie realize that she was missing her stop. She leapt off the train, as the doors closed around her lucky Alexander Wang bag. She tugged at it, but nothing budged. From inside the car, businessman Fred came to her rescue again, prying the doors open. Just as she almost let go, watched her wallet, keys, and all fly away with the train, the doors opened, releasing her. She stumbled backward, falling to the platform floor.

"Thank you!" she shouted. Fred nodded at her with pity, vowing never to let his daughters move to the city.

22

There have been prettier sights than what showed up at Michael's office that day and introduced herself as "Marjorie."

At the front desk was one of two NYU film students who worked part-time as interns for Grover & Grouch Entertainment (named for the two *Sesame Street* characters who most resembled affable Michael and curmudgeonly Gus). She wore a porkpie hat atop thin blond hair and a too narrow face, a romper, and Keds that looked self-splatter-painted. (In fact, an art major from her dorm had created the master-pieces with tinted Wite-Out, after they'd inhaled a cumulous cloud of vaporized weed.)

"We've been expecting you!" she sang. "Wow. That sounded creepy, right? Mahahuhuh!" She giggled at her own Dracula impres-sion. "I'm Lydia. And that's Kate!"

The second intern appeared from inside a room labeled VIDEO VAULT/FILM LIBRARY and nodded. She was as short and round as her cohort was gangly. She wore a Flaming Lips T-shirt, faded jeans, and Janeane Garofalo circa *Reality Bites* bangs (extra short). Marjorie wondered if the girls were too young to have seen the movie. She felt ancient.

"Now you've met 'the staff'"—Lydia mimed air quotes—"welcome to G & G! Do you want some water or iced tea? Hey! That rhymes!"

"That it does," replied Kate, an alto to Lydia's chirping soprano. "I'm a poet."

"Yes, you should start a blog. Oh, wait. You already did and I had to hear about it for all of yesterday."

"I'm like obsessed with my blog," confided Lydia. "I know that's so 2009, but whatever! It's called Feathery Weather, and I talk about cool art and film projects by kids in my dorm. It's a platform for launching my clothing line, when I'm ready."

"That sounds cool." Marjorie smiled. Lydia's dreams had yet to be tempered.

"Want to have a seat? His grumpiness will be right out." So much for the drink offer. Lydia gestured toward three folding chairs pushed against a wall.

As the girls returned to work, Marjorie slid onto a cold metal chair and tried to collect herself. This looked nothing like Bacht-Chit PR. The space was bare bones: There were framed posters for indie movies she assumed they'd distributed, some of which she recognized. The reception furniture was unmistakably IKEA—well designed but not meant to stand the test of time. She could make out a small kitchen at the entrance of the hallway, which led to offices.

Gus emerged moments later. He turned to his intern. "Were you planning to tell me that someone arrived?"

"Oops!" Lydia grinned. "I knew I forgot something. Gus, *someone* has arrived."

"Well done. Come talk to me about that raise."

She smiled, wiggled, and resumed collating. Kate appeared in the vault's doorway. "I like this one. Let's keep her." Next to tall Gus, she looked like a friendly stump.

"I'll take that under advisement."

For all the talk about Gus's moods, they didn't seem afraid of him.

He wore a Fugazzi T-shirt, jeans, and old school Nikes; Marjorie chided herself for dressing formally. This was her cue. She rose and stepped toward him.

"Hi. I'm Marjorie."

His smile disappeared. "You *can't* be serious. You weren't *that* drunk."

She shifted in her heels. "I'm sorry?"

"We met at Fred's party."

"Right. Of course. I remember. I wasn't sure that you'd remember me."

Under normal circumstances, Marjorie would have done a better performance of recognition or might have even mustered the brain power to recall meeting Gus. But today she lacked the wherewithal to fake anything.

"Amazing." He shook his head. Kate and Lydia looked on with unabashed interest, as if the conversation was an episode of *Scandal*.

"No, really. I know. You're Gus. Gus, Gus, Gus." He was unmoved. Marjorie sighed, not at him but with impatience at herself—an act promptly misinterpreted. "Okay. I'm sorry. I do remember meeting you, vaguely. That night is a blur. I was a train wreck. Not my finest moment."

"Neither is this." Gus started toward his office, then snapped, "You coming or not?"

Taken aback, but accustomed to abuse in an office environment, Marjorie followed him down the hall. Behind her, Lydia grimaced, then resumed bopping to whatever song played perpetually in her head.

Gus's office was sparse and impersonal, especially—Marjorie would later note—by comparison to Michael's homey nook across the hall, appointed with framed photos of Celeste and a desktop rock garden. In Gus's lair, an unworn Yankees cap teetered on the arm of a rolling desk chair and fell several times a day. On the desk, beside a laptop, sat beat-up issues of *The New Yorker, Atlantic Monthly,* and *Vanity Fair.* Philip Roth's *I Married a Communist,* J. D. Salinger's *Franny and Zooey,* and Jonathan Franzen's *Freedom*—with a receipt as a bookmark—sat stacked.

A half-eaten pack of gum lay alongside a landline and two in- and out-boxes, empty save outdated junk mail. (No one in history has ever used them as intended.) A random green-and-blue-swirled rubber ball sat poised, ready to roll. Even Gus's coffee cup—from a neighborhood spot called Java the Hutt—was disposable.

Against the back wall, below a window, leaned an Ork map of Philadelphia and a small signed photograph of Bruce Springsteen. The only mounted object was a black wall clock with a white face. A large flat-screen TV sat to the left on a metal rack above disordered piles of plastic DVD cases.

"Close the door," Gus grunted.

Marjorie did as told, rolling her eyes as if she and the wall were in cahoots. As Gus futzed on his computer, letting her stew, she sat upright in the other chair, feeling that somehow her posture and pride were correlated.

He continued interfacing with his laptop, perhaps answering an e-mail. Apparently, the task trumped basic civility. Marjorie cleared her throat and smiled tightly. "Hot day. Hot, hot, hot day."

"Yup. Couldn't be grosser."

She had the uncanny sense that he wasn't talking about the weather. She pulled her hair up off her damp neck. The office was much cooler than outside, but she was still decompressing from her en route adventure. Her body felt like a furnace with a stuck valve.

Gus finally looked up at—almost *through*—her, his eyes grazing the exposed nape of her neck. "So, Mike didn't tell me much," he said. "What experience do you have in film?"

Marjorie was caught off guard. She hadn't expected an interview. "I've actually never worked in film before. I worked in PR and—"

"Oh, great. PR."

"But there are skills that may transfer, and my father—"

"Lemme guess: Daddy has buddies in the movie biz. He once invested his Wall Street capital in a failed indie film on a lark? Lost a bundle?"

"No, actually—"

"Look, it doesn't matter." Gus ran a hand along his stubbled cheek, then over his brown mop. "I was hoping Mike had found someone with chops, but you'll have to do."

Chops?

"You'll basically be an assistant. Hope that's not below you."

The statement had to be rhetorical, never mind insulting, but he sat silent as if he expected a response. "No. Being an assistant is not below me." Why did they need her, if they had Lydia and Kate?

He seemed to read her thoughts. "Lydia is the receptionist and a personal assistant for me and Mike. Kate keeps the vault intact and deals with deliveries, but they're both part-time. What's left is administrative. Hours might be long."

"That's fine."

Gus stood. "Great. Wonderful. Fucking fantastic. Let's get you started. Ready, Train Wreck?"

"Excuse me?"

"Isn't that what you called yourself?"

This man was to be her boss for the next week at least, and Marjorie knew she should be respectful, but his snideness was too much. He swung the door open and headed into the hallway. Presumably, she was to follow again.

"Perfect," Marjorie said aloud to herself, grabbing her bag.

She caught up to Gus in a small conference room with another large-flat screen and a plexiglass table surrounded by midcentury-modern-style chairs, surely Michael's choice. Three enormous cardboard boxes sat parked in a corner. Gus was plugging in a laptop.

"You'll work here. I'll get you a scissor."

"A scissor?"

"How else are you going to open the boxes?" He cracked the door and called, "Lydia! A scissor!"

The intern appeared with it in hand. "You rang?"

He didn't smile. She set down the scissor and, when he turned his back, opened her eyes wide at Marjorie and mimed tiptoeing away. Gus turned to leave too.

"Wait!" said Marjorie. "What am I doing here?" Gus sighed, as if he was wondering the same thing. She was getting annoyed: Should she have miraculously intuited the details? "You don't have to groan; just explain."

"It's simple. The boxes are filled with DVDs from three upcoming small film festivals." He spoke at a maddeningly slow pace, as if she might be too dumb to understand. "They're still old school. No streaming. The programmers send us screeners beforehand, so we can get a jump on reaching out to filmmakers and make our pitch for anything we like. You need to open those boxes, then create spreadsheets for each festival. For each movie, log the title, date, running time, filmmaker, and contact information. Leave a column open for notes. And list whatever log line they include." He turned to leave and then pivoted back. "A log line is the one-sentence description or synopsis of the film."

"I know what a log line is."

"Kudos."

"Is that it?"

"Yup. E-mail me the spreadsheets as they're finished. Gus at ggfilms dot com. Think you can handle that?"

Marjorie was incredulous at his arrogance. "Yes. Because I'm not a fucking moron."

Gus was momentarily taken aback, but then nodded sharply. "That remains to be seen." Leaving, he mumbled loudly enough for her to hear, "Michael sure knows how to pick 'em."

Alone in the conference room, Marjorie wondered what had possessed her to curse at an *employer* when she so badly needed work. In the nine years she'd worked for Brianne, she had never come close to speaking that way, and that woman had thrown mugs at her head.

She inflated her cheeks and let the air drain, with a whistle, from her lips. She tossed her bag on a chair, picked up the "scissor," and got to work.

Pulling packing tape from the boxes' seams turned out to be the stimulating part of the job. Logging was mind-numbing. Three hours later, Marjorie was sorting the second festival's haul. The air conditioner was set at "frigid" and she hadn't brought a sweater; she shivered violently. No way she would give Gus the pleasure of admitting discomfort. She was rubbing her hands together to boost her circulation and wondering about symptoms of hypothermia, when Lydia popped her head in.

"Holy Jaysus! It's faaareeezing in here! Aren't you cold?"

Marjorie nodded, teeth chattering. "They should put the polar ice caps in here. Might save the polar bears."

"I have an extra sweatshirt! Come with me." Grateful for the kindness, Marjorie followed Lydia into the hallway, a Bahamian resort by comparison. "We had you set up in the extra office, but Gus e-mailed us to move the computer after you arrived. I don't know why. He knows the building keeps the conference room arctic on hot days. It's like torture!"

That's exactly what it's like, thought Marjorie.

Lydia ducked under the reception desk and pulled out a baby blue sweatshirt with SEXY BEAST ironed on the front. It looked stupid over Marjorie's dress, but it was warm. If only she had footie pajamas, maybe she'd have a fighting chance of feeling her toes again one day.

"Poor thing! You're like blue!" Lydia rubbed her hands clumsily over one of Marjorie's, more slapping it around than anything; a sweet gesture nonetheless. "Kate! Come help me defrost Marjorie!"

Kate popped her round head out. "You want some tea?"

"Or hot chocolate?" suggested Lydia. "And OMG you must be starving! I have protein bars."

"I have an extra yogurt too."

Marjorie felt her stomach groan. "You wouldn't mind?"

"Not at all."

"Then, yes. Yes, yes, yes."

The three ladies huddled in the kitchen, as Lydia began rummaging through the cabinets. "Where did that chocolate powder go, from that LA place that Gus loves? What's it called?"

"Coffee Bean," said Kate.

"Right! Together we have one full brain!"

"And one full lunch. Ish."

"So, you guys met here?" asked Marjorie.

"We're both film majors," answered Kate, "so we already knew each other, but we've gotten closer here."

"Kate is my best friend!" Lydia smiled.

"For eva." Kate held up four fingers.

Lydia was like a sweet but manic jack-in-the-box, while Kate seemed of sturdier stock—and not just because she was built like a tank. They complemented each other.

At the sound of footsteps, the three girls looked toward the corridor, catching Gus on his way out.

"Going somewhere?" Lydia raised an eyebrow.

"That Fox Searchlight thing. Hold down the fort."

"We're busy saving this poor girl from hypothermia. The conference room is Abu Ghraib with icicles!"

"It's not that bad," he mumbled, then loped out of view.

The door banged closed. Lydia giggled. "Of course, Gus might spell the end of our friendship."

"Really? Why?" Marjorie tore the wrapper off a s'mores-flavored Luna bar.

"Because! We're in love with the same man! A classic Shakespearean tragedy."

Kate nodded. "Tragic."

"Yeah, right," grunted Marjorie. "Love, love, love."

When she looked up from her power bar, the girls were eyeing her curiously.

"You don't think he's dreamy?" asked Lydia.

"Honestly? I hadn't thought about it."

"You didn't notice his arms? His biceps alone are catfight-worthy."

"He's got the guns of a gladiator," seconded Kate. "And by that I mean Russell Crowe. But not as bulky."

"I guess that's true. But isn't he kind of . . . a jerk?"

"So he likes to pretend," said Lydia. "But he can't help but be sweet. He practically forced cab money on me last week when I suggested taking the train uptown by myself at nine o'clock!"

"When my grandfather had a stroke, he took me to the airport and sent my mother this enormous fruit and cheese basket," reported Kate. "He made her day. My mother really likes Gouda."

"Also, Michael says Gus can play the guitar like really well. And that's just hot."

"So, have you told him you like him?" asked Marjorie. "Either of you?"

"Oh, no. He is way too proper for that!" exclaimed Lydia. "He'd never. That's part of why we adore him."

Marjorie was having trouble reconciling this characterization with the man who had dismissed and berated her earlier. "He must not like me."

"Don't worry," said Lydia, "he'll warm up to you."

"I hope so. Otherwise I might freeze to death."

Marjorie returned to her igloo soon after and worked until Gus popped his head in, hours later. He looked surprised. "Oh. You're still here."

"No one told me to leave and I'm not done, so . . ."

"Sorry. I'm used to the girls coming and going on their own. I didn't think to let you off the hook."

"It's fine. I'm about finished with the second box. I'll send you the spreadsheet now." Biting her lip in concentration, Marjorie entered one last date, then saved and attached the file and e-mailed it.

When she looked up, Gus was watching her. He glanced away, as if caught.

"What?" Marjorie brushed at her mouth. Did she have leftover crumbs on her face from the three protein bars she'd eaten for lunch?

"Nothing," Gus said, his face redrawn in a scowl. He looked her up and down.

"What?" she repeated. "What is it?" Marjorie chided herself silently for her tone, but the man was infuriating.

"Nice sweatshirt. You look like a twelve-year-old mall rat, Train Wreck."

"It's not mine!" she yelped. "And that's not my name!" But he'd already stalked back to his dungeon.

23

Marjorie had no time the next morning for an argument with her mother or a face-off with her former friend.

She'd arrived home the previous evening around 9:00, planning to gorge herself on sesame chicken and dumplings with her roommate—compensation for the day's deprivation. But Fred had a last-minute gig, so she'd have to wait for the scoop on Gus's attitude problem. Mac was hosting a St. Germain cocktail–sponsored party at DIRT in honor of a new coffee table book and the socialite author's ease at calling in favors.

Left to her own devices, Marjorie channel surfed, lamented the suckiness of summer TV, then gave up. In her room, she applied a blue clay face masque, then lit her candle, more for entertainment than contemplation.

Bored, she turned to cyberstalking. Gus's Facebook profile revealed no clues as to why he hated tall redheads. His wall was blank except for perfunctory birthday greetings and posts from Michael, ribbing him about the Phillies. He was tagged in some pictures: on a beach at sundown, in a dark bar, manning a BBQ—all with hot women. He was good-looking, she conceded. He had options. Propriety was probably not the only thing keeping him from a "love affair" with Lydia or Kate.

Marjorie made a turkey sandwich for work the next day, soggy bread being preferable to protein bars. Then she climbed into bed and fell fast asleep.

By 9:30 the next morning she was back in the conference room in cutoffs and a tank, but with layers close at hand, sorting the third box of DVDs. Kate was at a class and Gus was at a meeting, but Lydia welcomed her back with a tooth-cluttered smile and the offer of a caffeine fix.

"There's a coffee machine here?"

"Of course! Did you think we were heathens?"

Marjorie got the sense that Lydia only feigned addiction to project sophistication. "I noticed Gus with a cup from somewhere else yesterday."

"Yeah, something about liking the place's owner? He's a mysterious man." Lydia floated back to reception.

At half past noon, Marjorie sent the final spreadsheet to Gus. She opened the door of her cave; the front desk was unmanned. In the kitchen, she pulled her now gloppy sandwich from the fridge and ate it standing up, tossing the crumb-filled ziplock into the garbage. Then, on second thought, she moved it to the recycling bin; on second thought *again,* she moved it back to the trash. Who could keep the rules straight?

With time to kill, she explored the cabinets and settled on a cup of Twinings English Breakfast tea. Playing a solo game of bartender, she added nondairy creamer, brown sugar, cinnamon, and honey, then sipped, winced, and tossed it.

Empty-handed, she wandered back to her "office." Gus hadn't responded in the fifteen minutes that had passed. She checked her personal e-mail—just a note from her mother, solidifying future dinner plans. At a loss, she turned to Instagram. Perusing the feed, her heart sank: Pickles had posted a picture with Vera and Brian from July 4th. So they *had* gotten together without her. She was officially odd woman out. And, sitting in a foreign office in July, wearing a fisherman's sweater and skullcap, she looked like the odd woman too. She stared at their sun-kissed faces, reminding herself that Pickles likely spent the weekend delivering fascistic lectures on the importance of breast-feeding and the dangers of vaccinations, while the others namedropped and exchanged dull stories about boats and traffic patterns. Marjorie didn't want to be there anyway. *Right?*

Suddenly, she was desperate for distraction. Pushing down nerves, she left the conference room and approached her boss's half-open door. Inside, Gus looked anxious. His hands were planted on either side of his head, fingertips pressing into his temples. He grumbled an expletive and pulled his palms down his face, kneading his eyes like a sleepy baby.

"Knock, knock," she said and immediately regretted it. Why not just *knock*?

Gus glared at Marjorie like she was the most annoying person on earth, a Hayden Panettiere–Rush Limbaugh–Carrot Top hybrid.

"I finished the spreadsheets and, since you're paying me, I thought you might want me to do something else." She crossed her arms over her chest.

"Whatever."

She exhaled. "Look. You're clearly stressed. *You* look like a train wreck. I don't really care, but maybe I could help. If the problem is work-related, that is. If it's to do with your personal life, from what I've witnessed of your social skills, I'm sure that would require years of professional intervention."

He shrugged. "I guess I have no alternative."

"I'm gonna choose to ignore that. So, shoot." She paused. "That's an expression, BTW. I'm not sure how much you hate me, so to be clear: I'm not inviting you to shoot me."

"The films you've been logging are from festivals we need covered." Gus leaned back, his chair sighing. "We're supposed to have four days to review them before other distribution companies get access. That's important because we can make early offers."

"Right, I get that. Remember when I said I wasn't a moron?"

"Remember when I said that remains to be seen?" He paused. "Anyway, now they're saying we only have two days."

"Are these important festivals?"

"They're not flashy, but they're big ones for short films, and our bread and butter is from licensing those to airlines and cable networks."

"So now you have to go through hundreds of movies in two days."

"Yup."

"And Michael isn't here."

"Yes."

"Why don't you ask Lydia and Kate for help?"

"They both have class this afternoon and all day tomorrow. And even if they were available, we've tried to farm stuff out to them before. They're both whip smart, especially Kate, but they're not that sophisticated yet." He covered his face with his hands again, as if their youth was the final insult.

Marjorie brought a hand to her hip. "Well, here's a crazy idea, boss. Why don't you let *me* watch some?"

"You?" He peeked through his fingers. "But you don't know anything."

"Why, thanks."

He dropped his hands to his lap. "No. I mean you've worked here for less than two days. You don't know what we need for our markets."

"I've seen movies before. It's not that rarefied a concept. Let me watch some. Since I don't know your buyers, I'll write up minidescriptions with recommendations about whether they're good and you can decide which to bother rewatching."

Gus frowned. "Like coverage. Not a terrible idea."

"Occasionally, I have a decent one."

"I'll start you off with something unimportant in case you suck at it."

Marjorie dropped her arms to her sides. "*Wow*. Don't mince words for my sake."

Gus motioned her over to his side of the desk. She wove around, then stood awkwardly beside him, careful to keep her distance. At this proximity, she couldn't help but notice that Lydia and Kate were right: His arms were kind of incredible. She cursed the girls for pointing that out and tried to focus on what he was saying.

"You can't see from there." Gus motioned Marjorie closer, so close, in fact, that she could smell peppermint gum on his breath. He pulled up the second of her spreadsheets and scrolled down. "See the titles marked 'Experimental Video' and 'Social Commentary'?"

"Yes. I made the spreadsheets, remember?" It was hard to snap effectively within a foot of him. What the hell was wrong with her? Why was she eyeing the tanned back of his neck, wondering if Lydia and Kate had noticed that too?

"I need reports on those. You can watch in the conference room."

Marjorie backed toward the door, tripping over a stack of DVDs and toppling them. "Shit." She bent to pick them up.

"Don't worry about it." He gestured her toward the door. "Just start."

"Sorry, sorry, sorry," she said, hurrying out.

"Hey, Train Wreck?"

She turned before she could stop herself from responding. "What?"

"Why are you wearing a wool hat? It's the middle of summer."

"Unbelievable." She glared at him, returning to her icy nook.

24

Marjorie spent the afternoon and evening watching what seemed like the most god-awful films ever made. (But then she had not attended the feelings-themed, Cymbalta-sponsored Seattle high school festival the previous week, where teen angst met two hundred days of nonstop rain and digital video cameras. Parents actually fled the auditorium.)

Nevertheless, Marjorie's afternoon was not without agony. Watching and synopsizing largely unedited experimental films was almost as torturous than having to create spreadsheets in the tundra. Though she applauded the filmmakers' initiative, even the better films were too offbeat for distribution.

Just after 10:00 P.M., she pulled off her hat, sweater, scarf, and leg warmers (yup, *leg warmers*) and left the conference room. How strange to bundle up indoors and strip down to go outside. She knocked; Gus looked up from his TV screen, pressing Pause.

"You look different." He eyed her, standing in his doorway in short shorts and a thin tank top.

"I took off my snowsuit."

He swallowed hard, then coughed. "No. I mean, you look bleary-eyed."

"I finished those films and sent you descriptions. Nothing good yet."

"Ah. That explains the exhaustion. Sorry. I meant to order us dinner."

"No problem. Do you need me to stay and watch more?"

"Nah." Gus looked around his office at nothing in particular. "I'll leave soon too. We should both get some rest. Especially you. You look awful."

"Gee, thanks. Can you repeat that at least one more time?"

"Tomorrow may be a late night, assuming these summaries are okay. I'll pay you overtime, don't worry." He raised a hand in good-bye, already absorbed in the document she had sent. "See you tomorrow."

Marjorie returned to the conference room, shut down the computer, and organized her pens. She was starting to feel ownership over this subarctic enclave. As she reached the exit, she heard a booming laugh from inside Gus's office. And she smiled, despite herself.

EXPERIMENTAL VIDEO Short Films
Descriptions by Marjorie Plum

1. ELECTRIC KOOL-AID & ALL THAT JAZZ
In b&w. The shadow of a fan plays on a white wall in a dim, cavernous room. The shadow of a fan plays on a white wall in a dim, cavernous room. The shadow of a fan plays on a white wall in a dim, cavernous room. A door opens. A door shuts. The shadow of a fan plays on a white wall in a dim, cavernous room for 22 more minutes. Why, God? Why???! [27 minutes]

2. A BAD NIGHT
A 24-year-old filmmaker playing a hard-living 64-year-old (read: stuffed midriff, sprayed gray hair) saddles up to a bar and orders a drink from an underage bartender with a very real Road Runner tattoo on his arm. The drinker has had a rough day, but don't get too excited because we never find out why. This is a silent film, after all. The only text: "This is the worst night of my

life, a very bad night." And then "May I please have a Budweiser. I don't like Coors." Superbowl ad? [19 minutes]

3. SURREALISM & THE MELTING CLOCK
A young film student wants to be Fellini. Sadly, he is not. [32 minutes (I will never get back)]

SOCIAL COMMENTARY Short Films

1. TWITTER BUG
To the tune of a jitterbug, sepia-filtered screen shots of Twitter feeds, Pinterest boards, Facebook pages, Instagram photos, Tumblr accounts, Linkedin connections, and even Friendster and MySpace profiles, proving that old people (aka the film festival judges) still fall for it when twenty-somethings drop the term "social media." [11 minutes]

2. MAN ON THE TOWN
Man sees girl in park. Man stalks girl. Man buys weird large fake flower for girl, perhaps like a clown? I start to think Man is special needs. Man follows girl home. Girl goes inside. Girl's boyfriend comes over. We realize that girl does not know Man exists. Man goes home and discontinues his Match.com profile. We pan to Man's wall. It is (gasp!) plastered with pictures of girl. He goes to sleep wearing a T-shirt with her picture on it and masturbating. Then I die of boredom. Why not disgust, you ask? Hard to say. [38 painful minutes]

3. PASS THE BUCK
We've all seen this in other incarnations. It's the pass-the-dollar movie, questioning currency's inherent value. At a gas station store in "Nebraska" (actually off I-95 in NJ), a man buys cigarettes with a crumpled dollar. Then a NYC "career woman" on a business trip gets it as change for Certs. She takes the bill to the Museum of Natural History. It goes on from there, making its

way to fake Africa (Brighton Beach, maybe?), where the dollar
buys a pen of chickens for a happy Kenyan family. No irony
included. [22 minutes]

25

That night, to Marjorie's chagrin, Fred was out again, but she'd left a
note on the kitchen counter:

> My Dearest Marjorie Morningblatt!
>
> I haven't seen you in eons! Don't we live together or
> something? Save Thursday. That's the real party night
> anyway. We're going to get crazy at the club (couch)
> with bottle service (box wine), farm-to-table haute
> cuisine (takeout & stolen tomatoes), and foreign films
> (something terrible with Katherine Heigl).
>
> I'm expecting some good stories about your stalker/
> lover. Prepare accordingly.
>
> Love, Moonlight, & Twinkletoes 'til then!
> xoFredericka

Marjorie smiled. Fred was out of her mind in the best way.
   She managed a half-civil phone conversation with her mother,
watched an episode of MTV's *Awkward,* remembered how awful

being fifteen could feel, then packed a bag—she'd stay at Mac's after tomorrow's film marathon. Then she went to sleep.

At the office the next day, the reception desk was unmanned. Apparently, Gus hadn't gotten desperate enough to rally the college troops. Marjorie poured herself a cup of coffee and threw her lunch in the fridge. She hadn't gone grocery shopping, and the sandwiches were getting progressively sadder. Today's special was almond butter and marmalade on stale olive bread, an innately bad combination. She walked down the hall and swung the conference room door open, ready to settle in.

Marjorie froze in the entrance. All her supplies were gone: her office laptop, her organized pens, the scissor—*her* scissor! Had she mistaken Gus's laughter at her summaries the night before for approval when it was mockery? Was she about to get fired?

As Marjorie stared at her disassembled workstation, PTSD from years of Brianne's abuse reared its head. Her surprise turned to anger; her hands balled into fists. She would lecture Gus on disrespect, citing his arrogance and the misery that no doubt awaited him when he died alone!

Startled by a tap on her shoulder, she whipped around and almost smashed into the scoundrel himself. He ducked, protecting the Java the Hutt cup in his hand.

"Whoa! I was about to give you this coffee, but maybe you've had enough caffeine this morning."

Flushed—from humiliation or fury?—Marjorie glared. She cursed how relaxed and golden tan he looked in his thin blue button-down, untucked, over jeans. In place of an articulate insult, she managed a petulant, "Where's my stuff?"

Gus didn't register her upset. He nodded toward the hall. "I moved you to Michael's office. Can't have you freezing your ass off all day. Plus, you looked ridiculous in that wool hat." She peered at him, uncomprehending. He held out the coffee; she took it. "I got you a soy latte. No idea what you like, but that's what they do best and I figured it was safe in case you can't do milk."

The thoughtful gesture only confused her more. Marjorie stood for a stupid beat, staring at the drink like she'd never seen one before. Gus pried the cup of crappy office coffee from her other hand and tossed it in the trash. He beckoned her to follow. "C'mon. I'll show you."

He'd transferred Michael's belongings to a cardboard box in the corner. In their place sat Marjorie's work computer and office supplies (the scissor!), plus a packet of highlighters gathered in a red Moroccan-style cup. A thermostat pronounced the room a very temperate seventy-two degrees. Recovering herself, Marjorie ran a finger along the penholder's etched glass. "This is really pretty."

"Yeah. It's just a festival giveaway, but it seemed girly and . . . well, you're a girl, so . . ."

"I am a girl. That is correct." Marjorie turned toward Gus, touched and humbled. "Thank you for moving me. It was . . . considerate." She gave his forearm a friendly squeeze, but he jumped like she was radioactive. Then, embarrassed, he shuffled his feet, peering down at his sneakers like an overgrown child. He looked up at her, parted his lips to speak, then shook his head and closed his mouth tightly.

"Okay. Time to work. I e-mailed you which films to cover. Don't summarize them all—just the ones you like or think are commercial."

Marjorie grinned. "Does that mean you trust me?"

"Let's not overstate it. I'm desperate, remember? But your work last night wasn't horrible."

"Wow." She pressed a hand to her chest in mock swoon. "An *almost* compliment from the great Gus Rinehart."

"You know my last name."

"Yes. Because I'm not a moron. Remember?"

"So you keep claiming, Train Wreck." With that, Gus crossed to his office and shut the door. Marjorie set down her coffee and settled into Michael's ergonomic chair, sighing happily.

She mucked through many films: long, short, Technicolor, black and white, pretentious, goofy—almost all were poor matches for G & G. She wrote only a couple summaries, but something about Gus's trust in her made the process feel more satisfying.

1. EAR WAX

A man walks into a doctor's office (no, this is not a borscht belt joke) to get his ears professionally cleaned. The wax gets sucked through mad-scientist's-lab-style glass tubing and into a beaker (gnarly). The man leaves, thrilled with his new supersonic hearing. But outside, the traffic and ambient noise is too loud. He can't focus. At his office, he overhears people's deep dark secrets and coworkers saying terrible things about him. Finally, he can't take it anymore. He runs back to the doctor and demands his wax back. Alas, says the nurse, it cannot be retrieved. The doctor is an amateur artist; the wax is now part of a sculpture of his dachshund. THE END. Good for Science Channel? Discovery? Comedy Central? [13 minutes]

2. CALL 9/11

I'm skeptical about 9/11 movies because they're automatically emotional, good filmmaking or not. (Plus, no one wants to hear other people's 9/11 stories—it's like sharing dreams.) BUT, this is from the perspective of a child. Overwrought, but also kind of good. The main character, a 2nd grader, finds out what happened at school. While the teacher explains, he draws a picture of the towers and then erases it. The image comes back; it disappears. He goes home and watches his mother watching TV from the doorway of his living room; the camera work reflects his confusion. [7 minutes]

After a film about U.S. reliance on foreign oil through the lens of cartoon hip-hop lab rats, Marjorie needed a break; she was hearing squeaky rodent voices in her head. Plus, it was lunchtime. She set the computer to sleep and rose, cringing at her atrophied muscles.

In the kitchen, she pulled her sandwich from its baggy and stared at it ominously before going to take a bite.

"What is that?" Gus's voice boomed from the doorway.

"My lunch."

"No. It's not." He took the thing from her hand and threw it in the garbage.

"Hey! You can't keep doing that to me!"

"That's disgusting. And you need fuel to keep working."

"Who are you? My middle school health teacher?"

"No, I'm an adult, who eats grown-up food. We'll order from Cafe Gitane around the corner. It's good and it's on me."

The restaurant was on Marjorie's former block in NoLIta—euro, hipster, lots of aviator sunglasses. And it *was* good. "Fine. But that doesn't mean it's okay to throw away someone else's food."

"If that came from Fred's fridge, I probably saved you from *E. coli* poisoning."

Marjorie sighed. She had wondered about the worn-off expiration date on that jar of almond butter. "I'll have the hearts of palm salad with chicken."

Gus was dialing. "So you're a regular, I guess?"

"I used to live around here."

He placed their order. Afterward, they walked down the hall to their offices, parting at the entries. Neither closed his or her door, though, and once they sat, they had only to look up to face each other. Marjorie tried to focus on work, but a mixture of hunger and curiosity kept her stealing glances across the way.

They made inadvertent eye contact for a third time, and Gus laughed quietly. "Mike and I set it up this way so we could talk easily."

"Ah."

"I can close the door, if you need. It just gets kinda stuffy."

"No, that's fine." She trained her eyes back on her computer screen. "I'm good. Good, good, good."

"You know, you do that all the time."

"What?"

"That repeating thing. Thing, thing, thing."

"Oh! You know, someone else pointed that out to me recently. It's unconscious. Sorry."

"It's not bad. Just . . . distinct."

Marjorie cringed. "'Distinct' is code for weird. I hope it's not a habit I picked up from my mother."

Gus considered that. "Why? Does she drive you nuts?"

"Often. Yours?"

"I don't see my mother that much, so less so. But she's her own special case. That's the thing with family: You miss them, then they make you insane."

Why didn't Gus see his mother? Marjorie wondered. Fred said they lived close by in Philly. "My parents are uptown in the apartment I grew up in. Some distance might not hurt."

"You didn't leave New York for college? How come?"

"It's a question I've been asking myself a lot lately: What would have happened if I'd left?"

Marjorie and Gus had stopped pretending to work. He sat back in his chair, rolling a pen between his fingers, listening. She rested her cheek against her palm in thought.

"Because of your work situation?"

She hesitated. Should she be honest? This was a strange conversation to have with a boss with whom she did not get along and by whom she hoped to be hired long term. But she felt compelled to "confess," just as Mac had in her presence.

"Yes. Because of my work, living, and everything else situation. I got offered a job while I was in college, so I never left after graduation either." She bit down on her thumbnail. "I think maybe I was afraid of something different."

"And now?" Gus tilted his head in question.

"Now I'm here. Living with Fred in Brooklyn—"

"Instead of NoLIta."

"Instead of NoLIta, which I loved. And working here. This week." She forced a grin. "So."

Instead of returning her smile, he furrowed his brow. "Is the change bad?"

She glanced around, as if trying to decide, her eyes resting on Michael's silly wall calendar: fruits with felt eyes, noses, and mouths to represent each month. "I don't think so. I love Fred. I'm so lucky to have met her. I guess I have my mother to thank for that."

He nodded. "They're a good bunch, those Reynolds kids."

"Yeah. Plus, I actually like Carroll Gardens. And this work is great: writing, watching movies. It's just weird to be peripheral to everything you've known. Suddenly, I have a different life. I moved a couple weeks ago, but it seems like it's been a millennium."

"So how come you know something about film?"

"Ah, so you admit it!" She pointed a finger, *J'accuse*.

"I admit nothing."

"Of course not." She shook her head. "My father is a media studies professor; he's obsessed with film and TV. I spent my child-hood watching seminal, and not so seminal, pieces of art and enter-tainment. It's sort of the religion of my household. That and secular Judaism. Okay. Now it's my turn. You've asked me twenty questions. I get one."

"Fair enough." Gus opened his arms, as if to present himself.

"What's with the books? There's nothing else in your office. What's the deal?"

"Seriously? You know nothing about me; you can ask *anything*. And that's what you choose? You must be lousy at Truth or Dare."

"I didn't know I could ask those kinds of questions!"

"You can't." He smirked. "Well, *Freedom* I'm reading—not too fas-cinating. The others are my favorites. I bring them everywhere I spend chunks of time, then reread them—or at least passages—regularly, to keep in touch with strong storytelling. I can get jaded. These help me remember what constitutes 'good.'"

"So Franny and Zooey, huh?"

An unfamiliar voice rang out from the front of the office: "Hello? Delivery!"

"Shit, I almost forgot." Gus jumped up and jogged toward the front. Marjorie could tell he was athletic. *Ugh*. If only Lydia and Kate hadn't mentioned his arms. Ever since, she couldn't help checking him out: his back, his hands, the imperfect speckle in his left eye. She pushed down the thoughts, chalking up the odd accompanying feeling to low blood sugar from hunger.

Gus dropped her salad off at her desk. And they went back to work, doors closed.

26

Seven cups of tea, three Coke Zeros, six bathroom breaks, countless snacks, one dinner, and one sunset later, an almost deaf and dumb Marjorie finished watching her allotted movies. When she stood, a crick in her back threatened to take her back down. Kneading her muscles, she turned her back to the door, stretched upward, her hands pressed together, and dove down to touch her toes, her hair spilling over her legs.

At that moment, Gus opened the door to find Marjorie ass foremost—a compromising position considering her miniskirt. "Hey, I—" He stopped short. "What are you doing? Is that Downward-Facing Dog?"

Marjorie shot to standing, yanking her skirt down over her thighs and her shirt over her stomach. "I was just—my back. It's—"

He smirked. "C'mon. I want to show you something."

Gus led a mortified Marjorie into his office, where the TV was paused on an image of butterflies. She'd half expected C-SPAN, as he'd grumbled nonstop since she met him about Congress and gerrymandering. His obsession with politics had motivated Marjorie to bone up in case he ever paused for a response. He rolled the second office chair around to his side of the desk and motioned for her to sit.

"It's a documentary about monarchs," he explained. "It takes three generations for them to complete their migration. Somehow the off-spring intuit the directions—like they're biologically programmed. Just look."

He sat beside her and aimed the remote at the screen. Unable to sit still, Marjorie sat up straight, slouched, crossed and uncrossed her legs, pressed her thighs together, stuck, unstuck. She could feel him next to her, could smell that damn gum.

On-screen, butterflies swarmed, as the narrator described the culmination of their southern migration; they settled over their Mexican nesting place like an orange-and-black blanket. And Gus was right, it was beautiful. Not just the images, but also the concept that personal and even ancestral memories could be embedded in the body's neurons, arteries, blood, muscles, and bones. In her exhausted state, Marjorie almost began to cry.

The film was over; credits rolled.

"How cool is that?" said Gus.

"Pretty cool."

The nature documentary's requisite instrumentals soared.

"So, you almost finished?"

"I'm actually done."

Gus exhaled. "Great work today."

"Maybe. I went brain-dead three hours ago and have no idea what I've watched since."

"Part of the process." His gaze lingered on her face: cheekbone, earlobe, mouth.

"What time is it?"

They both glanced at the clock. "After one."

"Hey." Marjorie hoped to sound offhand. "Before you do something atrocious to make me feel otherwise, I want to say I'm grateful."

"For?"

"The chance to do more interesting work."

"You earned it." Gus shrugged. "You can do yoga in my office anytime."

Marjorie shot him a feigned dirty look, suppressing a smile. "Seriously, it means a lot." She reached out to squeeze his shoulder, then pulled her hand back, unsure.

"So," he said.

"So, so, so," she said.

In the unadorned room at that advanced hour, beneath dimmed halogens and white-painted pipes, a charge sparked between these two individuals, surprising them both in its intensity. Outside, bulbs from a thousand apartments twinkled and fell, a fluid strobe. Goose bumps rose against Marjorie's shirt sleeves. She could chart the distance to Gus's hands, could feel the air between them emulsify. The clock's second hand hesitated.

Slowly, carefully, Gus raised a palm and rubbed at the back of his neck. He took a steadying breath, stealing himself. "Okay." He swiveled his chair to face Marjorie and leaned in close, elbows resting on his knees. "Here's the thing—"

That's when a voice broke in from down the hall, startling them. "Hello!"

Gus and Marjorie both blinked as if blinded by harsh bar lights, having lingered after last call. Suddenly, they remembered the world outside, where people were sleeping or talking, kissing or fighting, and the moment combusted, too easily shattered.

"Madge! You here?" called the voice again.

Marjorie shot to standing. "I forgot, I texted him; he said he'd come grab me."

Gus sat frozen, slouched over his legs. "Right. Him?"

"Coming!"

She flipped on the light and pulled the door open, rushing down the corridor to greet Mac. Reaching him, she planted a kiss on his lips that lingered too long. He tasted faintly of rum; she, of guilt.

"Now, that's a greeting." He winked. "You ready?"

"Just have to grab my stuff."

He followed her back to Michael's office, his hands in his pockets as he strolled. Mac took his time; it was not in his nature to rush. Once there, he peeked inside, assessed the fruit calendar, then turned and started when he spotted Gus behind his desk.

"Oh, it's *you*," said Mac. "You work here." Marjorie might have forgotten her chance meeting with Gus at Fred's party (she was no monarch butterfly), but Mac had not.

"It's Gus's company." Marjorie slipped her tote onto her shoulder. "With Fred's brother. I mentioned that."

"Got it." Mac's darkened expression said he most certainly did. "I didn't make the connection." He strode over to Gus, never breaking eye contact. "Good to remeet you." He offered his hand; they shook. "Mac O'Shea."

"The imaginary friend."

Mac shook his head, a decisive jerk. "The boyfriend."

Oblivious, Marjorie bustled in, smacking her many bags against the door. She examined them both—Gus in his now wrinkled shirt and sneakers; Mac in his immaculate short-sleeved button-down and shiny shoes—and thought, *A man dressed like a boy; a boy dressed like a man.*

"Okay, I'm ready! Thanks again for everything, Gus."

"Like I said, you did a good job."

Mac edged toward the exit. "Shall we, Madgesty?"

Gus seemed to process the nickname with alarm, looking to Marjorie for confirmation. She didn't meet his eyes as she left. "Well, bye."

Walking down the concrete hall, she thought ahead with detachment to Mac's air-conditioned loft, the stiff books, king-size platform bed with ironed sheets, all edges.

"Shoot! I forgot something!" she said. "I'll meet you by the elevator."

As Mac exited, she reappeared, breathless, in Gus's doorway. "You were about to say something."

"What?"

"You said, 'Here's the thing,' then Mac came in. You were about to say something."

Gus shrugged. "I don't remember. Must have been about the butterflies."

Marjorie bit her lip. "Well, if you think of it, you have my number."

"I do . . . *Madgesty*."

She took a step, rethought it, and returned once more. "Don't ever
call me that, okay? I don't like it."

"Fair enough." Gus forced a smile. Then, when he finally heard
Marjorie close the front door, he covered his eyes with his hand and
groaned.

27

Outside, the air was muddy, viscous. Since Monday morning, mois-
ture had been building. Humidity had collected in insidious pockets,
coating the region and its inhabitants like a parasitic blanket, causing
fingers to stick together, hair to crinkle, and tempers to hover somewhere between homicidal and burner lethargic.

Joan Didion famously wrote about LA's arid Santa Ana winds that
steal breath and make people's minds go funny. This was New York's
equivalent. And there was no lake, pool, weeping willow, Mexican
taco stand or Southern pie shop to render the mugginess worthwhile.
Marjorie felt mad and overcome by a desire to escape.

Mac was unperturbed by the heat. "It's fine," he assured Marjorie, as if his feelings made it universally so. Suddenly, his jaunty gait,
staccato voice, and old stories about John, Matt, and Carlos (all of
whom he'd seen that night) bugged her. His cavalier attitude seemed
like a dearth of personal insight.

Waiting to cross the street at a red light, he placed a palm on her
shoulder. She turned on him with murderous eyes. "Please don't
touch me."

"Whoa." He removed his hand, lest it get bit. "We need to get you
into a cab."

And because he was Mac and so impossibly charmed, a yellow taxi pulled up at the next corner. They slid inside. The air conditioner, though not frigid enough for Marjorie's taste, helped. After a couple minutes, during which Mac remained sagely quiet, she decompressed. Mac was fine. Mac was great. She was losing her mind.

Marjorie sighed, a signal that her mood was improving. Mac gazed out at the blur of passing streets. "So, that's your boss, huh? You didn't say he was the guy from the party."

"I didn't remember that you had met. I really do think those were pot brownies." They fell silent. She examined Mac's aristocratic profile, as he stared hard out the window. "Did you expect someone different?"

"Sure. You made him sound blustery, like a hard-ass. I pictured him older, balder, thicker through the middle."

Marjorie snorted. "Oh! Not at all. You should see the two interns falling all over him."

Mac faced her, his tone casual. "What about you?"

"They like me fine, I think."

"No. I mean, you don't think he's *dreamy*? It's fine if you do."

His white lie tumbled out easily, as similar ones have from thousands of other mouths on tense nights. The pat response returned automatically like a boomerang from Marjorie's own lips: "Me? No. He's not my type. Too tall."

Mac chose to believe her fib. He sidled up closer, pressed his clothed right leg against her bare left one, and settled a possessive hand on her knee, as her head dropped against his shoulder. They screeched to a stop at a red light, Marjorie's body traveling ahead of her insides, her soul playing catch-up, a millisecond late. It felt like free-falling.

"You still too hot?"

"Much better, thank you. But I need a cold shower."

"That's doable. Just like you."

Upstairs, Marjorie did shower, but not alone. Mac's company worked just fine for her. Pressed however awkwardly against the cool ceramic tiles, she felt nice and distracted.

Nervous energy thus expended, she threw on Mac's old oversize Radiohead T-shirt and stood before his bookshelves, brushing tangles from her wet hair. She thought she remembered seeing a leather-bound first edition of *Franny and Zooey* among the untouched tomes. *Yes!* On tiptoe, she nudged at its rough bottom corner until it dropped and caught it midfall. She rubbed a hand over the cover, enjoying the embossed lettering against her fingertips. Had she finished the book when it was assigned in school? Or was she too busy sneaking vodka and Cokes in Mac's den with the other stoned fifteen-year-olds?

He emerged from the bathroom, smelling of pine soap, his cheeks pink from steam, a towel wrapped around his waist. Considering the late hour, he looked refreshed, ready for a morning jog. Eyeing Marjorie bent over a book, the girl he'd had lodged at the back of his mind for longer than he cared to acknowledge, he felt good too.

He flipped off the light and collapsed into the memory foam mattress like a fingerprint. Her bedside lamp cast a soft glow.

"It's weird. I know we showered, but I feel dirtier. In a good way. Should we go again?"

She glanced at him, unseeing. "You're funny." She wasn't listening.

It was late. He was, despite appearances, tired. He threw his towel toward the laundry hamper in a rare instance of sloppiness and climbed under the covers.

"Let's go to bed." He was already drifting. Before Marjorie, he had stayed up nights, plagued by hypochondria and heartburn. Now, he slept like the dead.

"One sec." Marjorie slipped between the sheets too and reread a sentence, having failed to absorb it the first time: "Lane spotted her immediately, and despite whatever it was he was trying to do with his face, his arm that shot up into the air was the whole truth."

Mac opened one eye. "Is that for work?"

"No. It's for life." She giggled at echoing Belinda's words.

"Why is that funny?" Mac felt suddenly glum. "You're a nerd. G'night. I'm already sleeping. Don't try to cuddle with me. Okay, you can."

Marjorie hardly heard him. Soon after, though, she did begin to nod off, forgetting each sentence as she read it, words tumbling in and out of comprehension. She closed the book and drooped toward her pillow for the night's slumber.

That is until 4:23 A.M., when a crack of thunder erupted, signaling the city's release from Big Mama Nature's smothering, chesty embrace. The humidity broke. Dreamers relaxed into REM cycles, cooled down, and breathed easier. But Marjorie was wide awake. A dam had broken in her too.

She stared at the ceiling, her thoughts nonlinear. She wasn't sure from what dream she'd awoken, but suddenly she could more than recall, she could *feel* the sensation of cavorting toward Central Park with a pack of other at once insecure and cocky teenage girls—the wind at their backs, the boys at their destination, the ghostly trails of chatter and teasing shoves, the sense of her own grace as she navigated sidewalks' cracks. She could taste her faintly perfumed mocha-colored lipstick, could sense the gazes of passing strangers, who recalled, with nostalgic pangs, their own disappeared youths. A cigarette lit, mostly for effect. Ferocity, strength, freedom. She'd been a nuclear conductor, unchecked, alive, awake. Awake, like she was now.

That time in her life was hard to release because it felt so electric— all gusto, no consequences, like peeling off a sweater on the first day of spring. Now Marjorie recognized its ephemerality. Sooner or later the sun dipped behind a cloud and a confident strut was deflated by an imperfect reflection in a mirror, another girl's nasty barb, a crush missing from among the crew of roughhousing boys or, worse, a crush focused elsewhere. To move on, she would have to let go and accept reality.

Marjorie almost woke Mac to commiserate but stopped herself. She had naïvely assumed that her friends lived in homes as safe as her own, until he told her otherwise. Adolescence had been fraught for Mac. At school, it took effort to be the charming, funny guy, the one you couldn't trust but did; his home was no better. His family members made bad choices, perpetuating "a cycle of semifunctional codependence," so described the countless experts in their lop-sided glasses, dishes of hard coffee candies on their tables. Cast as martyr—and, finally, brute—he had thanklessly tried to corral his drunk mother, reckless sister, and gruff father (who resorted to withholding silence). Mac wouldn't recognize the romance Marjorie chased.

She gave up on sleep. A pair of Uniqlo socks, made from some unearthly synthetic material, waited like a fuzzy friend at her bedside. She pulled them on, then slid along the floor toward the living room like a child.

On the couch, Marjorie tucked a leg underneath her and wrapped herself in a chenille throw that she suspected was for show. On the authentic Noguchi coffee table was one large clicker in place of the requisite three remotes. Of course, Mac had hired someone to stream-line the system. He would not tolerate anarchy.

She clicked Power, muting before the picture manifested for volume's sake, then began flipping through channels. In the dark, the TV's light pulsed, the kind of relentless stimuli that cause seizures, Marjorie imagined. She considered watching *Sweet Home Alabama* on TBS and then *Fargo* on HBO.

But, as she clicked past, CNN's "Breaking News" ticker caught her eye. Somewhere far outside Mac's apartment, something sinister had happened: a shooting in a place called Aurora. The tension had broken in New York City but descended 1,621 miles away. There, brows furrowed midsleep, as locals osmosed terrible news.

The Colorado shooting would make most Americans think of 1999's Columbine massacre, when two boys, gangly and acne-dotted, hid semiautomatic weapons in trench coats and terrorized their school's teachers and student body, killing twelve students and one teacher before killing themselves.

Marjorie was no exception. She shuddered, turning up the volume a notch. An unfamiliar anchor was getting her big break, while the tragedy brigade—Anderson Cooper, Wolf Blitzer, Soledad O'Brien—was no doubt summoned. Experts were surely being woken for interviews on shooter psychology, the impact of violent film on today's youth, and gun control.

"A gunman opened fire at a midnight showing of the new Batman film, *The Dark Knight Rises,*" the anchor was saying.

Marjorie's unease mounted; movie theaters were like temples to her. Growing up, she had gone with her father every Saturday, first for kids' fare like *Mary Poppins* at the revival house or, when she begged, *The Last Unicorn*. Then, later, he took her to grown-up films before she wholly understood them: *Radio Days, My Own Private Idaho, Misery, Goodfellas*. Even horror movies seemed safe as she sat beside him.

What were the loved ones of these victims doing in the late hours before the shooting occurred? Watching syndicated sitcoms? Double-checking their alarms? They couldn't have known how much they were about to lose.

Suddenly, Marjorie had the urge to call her parents—to be picked up halfway through a sleepover party. As her eyes welled, she realized that the numbness that had characterized her last few years—*was it that long?*—was lifting. She was inside the world again, vulnerable to its joys and misgivings.

"What's up?" asked Mac from the doorway, making her jump.

She recovered and tucked his blanket out of view, feeling that she'd somehow overstepped bounds by using it. "Sorry. I didn't mean to wake you. Go back to sleep."

He squinted, eyes glassy. He'd taken the time to throw on gray boxer briefs. "No, *you* come back to sleep."

She nodded toward the TV. "There's been a shooting."

"Oh, no. Where?"

"In Colorado."

"Of course. Colorado. Their biggest import."

"At a midnight showing of *Batman*. They don't know how many people were killed. But there were babies there."

"People brought their babies to a midnight movie?" Mac sighed. "Well, I'm sorry to hear that." He nodded toward the darkened bedroom. "C'mon. Let's go back to sleep."

"But it's so terrible."

"It is. But sitting here watching the news isn't helping anyone. You're gonna be exhausted."

She looked from him to the gigantic television screen. In her fantasy, would he sit down? Comfort and watch with her? "Don't you want to know what happened?"

Mac frowned. "Honestly? Do I want to hear how some lunatic ruined people's lives? Not really."

"But what about empathy?"

"I have empathy. I do. But you can't feel everything for everyone, Marjorie. And I don't choose to marinate in other people's misery."

She stared into his sleep-imprinted face. Mac had learned survival in the O'Shea household, where concern only won him disdain. He reached out a hand to her.

"Let's go to bed. You can save the world by watching CNN tomorrow."

Marjorie relented, though unsure. She did need sleep. She felt pressure behind her eyes. She switched off the TV and began folding the throw. Mac liberated it from her grasp and threw it over the couch. "We can do that in the morning." He placed his hands on Marjorie's shoulders and steered her toward the bedroom, a two-person conga line.

As she lay cocooned next to him, his arm and leg thrown over her like a rag doll, she reasoned that emotional boundaries could be a good thing. Mac balanced out her neuroses.

Later, along with the rest of the country, Marjorie would scrutinize unsettling photographs of a young man with an expression of constant alarm, hair dyed a comic orange to mimic the Joker. She'd learn that he entered the theater with a ticket, left through an emergency exit, and reentered with tear gas and guns, injuring over seventy people, killing twelve.

Now, as she drifted off to sleep, she tried not to think about the people who would awake from dreams into nightmares.

28

The next morning, Marjorie was like a zombie—jerky and slow.

After his morning meetings, Gus stopped by her office and proclaimed that she looked terrible again.

"Gee, thanks." She sat back, too tired to argue. "I couldn't sleep. Then I turned on the TV and the shooting . . ."

"Yeah, me too." The only sign that Gus had lost rest was tousled hair. Why did sleep deprivation render him fashionably disheveled, but her *undead*? He sighed. "At five A.M., I wrote a letter about gun control to the *New York Times*."

"Oh! You're *that* guy."

"Guilty. It's probably good that I was alone, so no one had to listen to me rant, you know?"

"Totally. Not that I was alone, but I get it." Why did she feel the need to say that?

Gus's jaw tensed. "Right. Anyway, leave early. Leave now, if you want." He turned to go, then reconsidered and pivoted back to face her. "So, that guy is your boyfriend now, the imaginary friend?"

"Yup."

"Huh."

"'Huh?' What does that mean?"

"It means nothing. It means, *huh*."

"It obviously means *something*."

"Not to me."

"What's *that* supposed to mean?"

"Nothing! Jesus. So paranoid. Go get some sleep; relocate your sanity." Miffed, Marjorie narrowed her puffy eyes at him. He grunted. "Fine. You just seemed pissed at him at Fred's party, and . . . I wouldn't have pegged him as your type."

"What type is that?"

"The type who would date you, I guess." Marjorie's jaw dropped, as he added, "Can I go now?"

"Please do!"

"Okay, bye." Gus didn't move; he rested a forearm against the doorjamb. "But if you feel judged, you may want to examine why. Just saying. The truth will set you free."

Before Marjorie could protest, he flashed her a rare million-dollar grin and left, for real this time.

Eyes drooping, Marjorie headed home and passed out cold for several hours. When she emerged, Fred was downstairs, sorting through take-out menus and humming Roberta Flack, periodically spinning away from the counter *Saturday Night Fever*–style. It was so good to see her. Soon after, a delivery man arrived with enough aluminum containers of spaghetti and meatballs in marinara sauce, plump mozzarella sticks, and iceberg salad drenched in unnaturally yellow Italian dressing for a small army. God bless Brooklyn.

Fred wasted no time. From the mountain on her plate, she slurped a strand of spaghetti, splattering her vintage AC/DC muscle T-shirt. "Oops!" She grabbed a napkin, dabbed ineptly, and returned to stuffing her delicate face.

Watching from the kitchen, Marjorie couldn't help but compare her to Vera, who expressed caloric guilt after fat-free Tasti D-Lite and would have treated the stain like an international incident. Fred didn't stress such things; she was happier. A pang of sympathy snuck through Marjorie's anger; she poured a little Dr. Brown's Cream Soda out in the sink for her tightly-wound former homey.

Rounding the island with her own plate, she settled next to her roommate on the battered couch. "So, I've waited a hundred years: Give me the dirt on Gus!"

"Mmllhhm!" Fred was attempting, against all odds, to chew through a baseball-size meatball. "Righffft. Sorry. I'm not sure how much I have. He's lovely!"

"Yeah, yeah. So I've heard. Now tell me the truth." Marjorie took a bite of her pasta—tangy. "Why is he such a grouch? How did he and sweet Michael become friends? Does he have a girlfriend?"

Fred, having just swigged from her beer, clapped a hand over her mouth to stop a spit-take. "Mmphph, moppph!" She choked back the liquid. "Phew, that was close." She turned to Marjorie, her upper lip ringed with a faint tomato sauce mustache. "Did you just ask if he has a *girlfriend*?"

"Yes. I mean, *no*. Not the way you think. I was asking for details, you know? That wasn't—I didn't mean—that's a normal question to ask about someone."

The pixie raised an eyebrow. "If you say so, Morningblatt."

Fred returned to eating, forgetting the issue at hand. Marjorie nudged, "So?"

"Oh, right! So, Gus. Well, he's sweet, brilliant, loyal. He and Michael were freshman roommates. In some ways they're unlikely friends, but I think they were meant to meet. They needed each other, you know? Like us!" Fred beamed at Marjorie.

"Right, right, right. Like us. And . . . ?"

"And Gus has been a lifesaver for our whole family, really. We love him. I practically have to stop my aunt from humping him whenever he's around."

"That sounds disturbing," said Marjorie, through a mouthful of cheese. "I guess he's okay looking."

Fred shot her an incredulous look. "You *guess* so?"

Marjorie avoided her eyes. "Continue, please."

"To answer your not at all suspect question, no, he does not have a girlfriend."

"What kinds of girls does he date?"

"I guess this is another totally normal inquiry? His girlfriends tend to be beautiful but too serious. His hookups are usually hot and dumb. But then it's LA and he's a dude."

"What's LA?"

"Where he meets girls."

"He only meets women in LA?"

"For the most part."

"That's weird and location specific. Okay, tell me about his family."

"I don't know his parents well. They have one of those divorced but amicable relationships. They live in Philly. They're both high school teachers. His mother has some mental illness stuff that he never talks about. I know he's close with them and gets bummed that he can't see them more often."

"Why can't he? Isn't Philly only two hours away?"

Fred wiped her mouth with a paper napkin; it came away fluorescent orange. "Not from LA."

"Wait, *what*?" Marjorie was being willfully slow on the uptake.

"Morningshade, he lives in LA!"

"O-ooh. I see." The pieces puzzled together, revealing an image that was not to Marjorie's taste.

"He's here covering while Michael's in Italy. When my brother comes home this weekend, Gus goes back."

"Okay. Got it."

Marjorie returned to eating, though her heaping plate seemed less enthralling.

Fred considered her suspiciously. "So, how's Big Mac?"

"He's fine."

"Just fine?"

"He's *good*. I slept at his place last night. Well, not slept exactly . . ."

Fred wiggled her eyebrows, "No sleep, huh?" She affected the nasal voice of an old school gangster. "Sounds like a wild night, buddy boy. A wild ride, see!"

"No, not like that. I mean, yes like that. But I stayed at the office late, working with Gus and then . . . I just couldn't stop thinking."

"About Gus?"

Marjorie shook her head. "Maybe he triggered it because he's an adult, something I haven't figured out how to be." She fell quiet. "Do you ever feel stuck in the past?"

Fred thought for second, plunking her plate down on the coffee table and pulling her knees to her chest. "I'm more of a forget-the-past-at-all-costs kinda gal, but that has its problems too. You're just sentimental."

Marjorie let her head fall onto the couch's tufted back. "I just can't believe I wasted so much time. I spent ten years chasing this phantom feeling that's left over from being a teenager, a *child*. It's pathetic. I look at Belinda . . ."

"Who's Belinda?"

"Oh. No one. A preteen girl I know. A family friend. Anyway, I see how young she is and I think, how can I be stuck on something from so long ago? I still *ache* to feel that excited again. I guess you don't get to peak twice."

Fred rested her chin on her knees. "I don't think it works that way. Life isn't fair, for better or worse. You can peak a thousand times or never. So you liked being a kid 'cause you got great feedback for just being you. That doesn't mean the rest of your life will be disappointing. You just have to figure out what you're missing and replace it!"

"Maybe it was the thrill of all the firsts: first kiss, first beer, first love. Maybe it was feeling successful?" Marjorie thought hard, struggling to identify the sensation as it whizzed past. "I got validation from kids at school, my mom; I never figured out how to *earn* it. And now I lie next to this amazing guy at night, who has always had the power to make me feel compelling and compelled, and I still feel empty. Obviously, I'm the problem."

"Hey, easy does it. A month ago, you were still tunneling backward. This is progress!" A bleat rang out from Fred's bag, which sat slumped on the counter. "Oh, shoot. One sec!" She jumped up, pulled her phone out, grimaced, and pressed Ignore.

"Who was that?"

"No one. James. You were saying?"

"He's still calling all the time?"

"Not *all* the time.

"Fred! You have to date him or let him go! I'm about to make 'Free James' T-shirts."

"He *is* free!" She collapsed back onto the couch. "Let's finish talking about you."

"I'm sick of myself. Let's talk about you."

"No."

"Fred."

"Morningfield."

They sat in standoff. Finally, Fred picked up the remote and offered a truce: "Bad TV?" Marjorie nodded.

29

Marjorie had agreed to stop by the office on Saturday to tie up loose ends. She arrived with an adjusted attitude: Gus lived in LA; he was a nonissue. Even if G & G hired her full-time, she'd report to Michael. Who cared if she and Gus got along?

Before she even got to her desk, the man himself stuck his head out his office door and called, "Oh, good. You're here! I need to talk to you."

"The doctor will see you now." Lydia giggled.

"Seems you got over your discord," Kate said with a wink. "You guys all alone in the office for two days and now, voilà! He needs to *talk* to you."

"You guys are ridiculous."

"If you say so, friend. If you say so."

Marjorie dropped her tote in Michael's office, then entered Gus's. It made sense now: the unadorned space, unmounted pictures. He only used his office sporadically. "So, here's a funny thing," she said, dropping into the seat across from him. "I thought you lived in New York."

Gus looked up from the papers on his desk. "No. LA."

Feeling awkward under his gaze, she crossed her legs, adjusting her high-waisted sailor shorts, smoothing her sleeveless buttercup-

colored button-down. "Across the country!" she offered enthusiasti-
cally. "Three thousand miles away!"

"Yup. That's where California is." He shook his head. "You know
we have an LA office. Who did you think ran it?"

"I don't know."

Gus focused back on his paperwork. "That's kind of stupid."

"Hey! A good manager would have explained the company's in-
frastructure!"

He grunted. *Maybe*. "That's sort of what I need to talk to you
about."

"All ears. Well, not *all* ears." She shimmied her shoulders, trying
to crack his steely, businesslike tone, then felt like an idiot.

Gus looked at her blankly. He seemed to have misplaced his sense
of humor.

"There's been a hiccup."

"Hiccup?"

Apparently, after too many bottles of Prosecco in celebration of
their engagement, Michael and Celeste were walking back to their
villa, when the bride-to-be turned her ankle on a loose cobblestone.
(That did not detract from the evening's romance, since she literally
swooned and was caught by the man she loved.) But Celeste's ankle,
possibly in protest over leaving Italy, promptly swelled to the size of
a grapefruit. The couple could make it home, explained Michael, but
not without considerable discomfort. And, since Celeste's parents—
Michael's future in-laws—were there to pressure the duo into staying an extra week, he felt it best to avoid engendering their displeasure.
(As if they could be displeased by the introduction of an affable
son-in-law, the kind of boy, to the irritation of certain ex-girlfriends
who knew better, who parents loved.)

The extended vacation would have been fine but for the following
week's Silver Screen Film Festival in LA. Michael was scheduled to fly
in and help Gus cover the event, as the organizers allowed select distributors to screen the movies in advance, but—for fear of pirating—
only in the safety of screening rooms at the American Film Institute.

"I need you to come to LA," said Gus.

"You need me to—"

"Stand in for Michael, help me screen the films, be my wingman—"

"Wingwoman. I'm a girl."

"Whatever—at some mixers. Michael usually does most of the . . . mingling."

"That's so surprising considering your warm and fuzzy nature."

"Do you want to come or not?" Gus scowled.

"With you?"

"Yes, with *me*. You might think that's a hardship, but believe it or not, some people like to spend time with me." He leaned back in his chair. "We'll put you up in a hotel and compensate you, obviously."

"Sure, sure, sure. I guess I'm in. When do we leave?"

"Tuesday."

Marjorie was over the moon. This meant that Gus and Michael believed in her. Plus, she might make contacts at the festival. She would have to tolerate Gus's surliness, but that was a small price to pay for a much-needed escape from home.

"You're grinning." Gus wore a look of distaste.

"Yeah? So?"

"It's kind of creepy."

Back behind the closed door of Michael's office, Marjorie plopped down in the desk chair, which swiveled with contagious exuberance, and dialed her mother's number. At that moment, Barbara Plum was clomping down the street like a drunk dockworker spoiling for a fight. She was en route to Fairway for Chipper's favorite fresh apricots and cranberry muffins, but six decades as a New Yorker had trained her to bob, weave, and juke like a thuggish linebacker bent on a touchdown.

"Hello?" she half shouted.

"Hi, Mom. It's me."

"What?" Whoosh. Whoosh.

"It's me!" There was a pause and another *whoosh* of air. "Mom. It's Marjorie."

"Oh, hi, sweetie. I can't hear you so well. Must be the wind."
Whoosh.

In fact, there was no breeze on that blinding, midsummer day, though the weather was unseasonably lovely sans humidity. *Whoosh* was the sound of Barbara's rushing.

"Where are you, Mom?"

"Broadway. It's gorgeous out. Just beautiful. Where are you?"

"In the office, actually."

"Sinful! I hope you can get out for lunch. Speaking of which, are we on for Tuesday night dinner? Your father was just saying we haven't seen you in ages."

"Sorry. Brooklyn is so far from uptown. But Tuesday is what I wanted to talk about."

"Oh, good, because I have something to talk to you about too."

Marjorie felt her stomach drop. "What is it?"

"No, you go first." *Whoosh.*

"No, now I'm nervous. *You* go first."

"Well, *excuse* me! It's called a walk sign!" Barbara scolded the driver of a passing car, who answered with a long "screw you" honk and a burst of bass-heavy Eminem.

"Mom! Mom, mom, mom."

"What?"

"What's your news?"

"I don't know, sweetie. I can't hear a word you're saying. I think you have a bad connection."

Marjorie mouthed, *Oh, my God!* to a googly-eyed strawberry picnicking with a banana on Michael's fruit calendar. The strawberry did not respond.

"I'm on a landline. It's—"

"This never happens to me." Whoosh, whoosh, whoosh.

Marjorie considered hanging up and blaming the connection. She took a deep breath. "Mom. Can you veer onto a side street and stop walking for a second?"

"All right, done. Veering now." Marjorie waited as the sounds of pedestrian chatter faded. Barbara was out of the throng and jam. "Phew."

"Okay, what did you have to tell me?"

"Right. I ran into Ramona Schulman."

Uh-oh. Here it came. Her mother had learned about her rift with her two best childhood pals, that she'd been cast out of their precious world. Barbara had been thrilled when Marjorie befriended Pickles. Other mothers might have worried about the influence of this reckless girl, but Barbara Plum saw Pickles as "adventurous." It didn't hurt, Marjorie had suspected, that her new friend hailed from an "important" family.

"She mentioned something. I hope you won't feel I'm prying."

Marjorie braced herself. "I won't, Mom. What did she say?"

"She said you were *dating*—is that the word you use these days?—that you were dating Mac O'Shea."

"Ah."

"I wouldn't ask," Barbara rushed on, "but I hate learning about my *child* from another mother. She was surprised I didn't know. She said it was *serious*. Is that true? He called the house for your address, so that seems odd if it's serious."

Of course. Far from disappointed, Barbara was poised for bliss. The Schulman fortune was chump change compared with the O'Sheas'. Her mother was not shallow enough to be concerned with the cash itself, but she coveted their access and boundless opportunities on her daughter's behalf. Suddenly, Marjorie was overcome by both guilt and rage, frequent partners.

"I'm sorry. I'm being nosy."

Marjorie swallowed her irritation. "No, I just wasn't expecting the question. I haven't mentioned anything because it wasn't official until recently."

"So it's true?" Barbara's voice rose with excitement.

"Yes, Mom. Mac O'Shea is my boyfriend." Only now, as the sentence rolled off Marjorie's tongue, did she realize how odd it sounded. *Mac O'Shea is my boyfriend.* Pickles had described the relationship as "serious." That conflicted with Vera's take.

"You know, we've always liked him." Marjorie doubted if her father could pick Mac out of a lineup. "Oh! Have him join us for dinner on Tuesday!"

"Oh, shoot. Mom, no, the thing is, I'm calling because I can't make dinner."

"Oh. That's too bad. How is Thursday, then? I have an afternoon seminar, but I'll be out by six thirty. I just have to check with your father."

"Actually, I'm going out of town. On a business trip." It sounded fantastic out loud.

"Really?"

"Yeah. They asked me to cover a film festival in LA. I think this could turn into a full-time job. He thinks I have potential."

"That's great news! Who is he?"

"Who is who?"

"*He.* You said 'he.'"

"Oh, Gus. My boss. At first, I didn't like him. He was a jerk—*is* a jerk. The girls here, the interns, think he's a god. I didn't see it, but, now, even though he's sort of impossible"—she giggled—"I also think that he's . . . well, I respect him. He's smart and Dad would love him because he's a total film nerd."

"He sounds great," said a suspicious Barbara.

"Sort of. He's a pain. But he's also—like, interested in things my friends aren't: books, politics, and—not that he's my friend. We don't even like each other. So, yeah," she paused midbabble. "That's Gus. And that's why I'm going to LA."

"But you're dating Mac?"

"Yes. What does that have to do with anything?"

"Nothing. Just don't forget to behave professionally."

"Seriously, Mom?"

"We can all use a reminder now and then, you know, not to wear shorts to the office, etc."

Marjorie looked down at her bare thighs. "Right."

"Anywa—" The phone burped a pause, interrupting Barbara. "I think I have call waiting. The stupid thing never works."

"Go ahead, Mom. I'll try to call before I leave. Sorry I've been neglectful."

"Please do. Your father misses you. And let's make plans to have Mac over when you get back. Bye, sweetie!" *Whoosh.* And off marched Barbara to rejoin the throngs.

30

At Gatherers on Sunday, Belinda eyed Marjorie with alarm. "What do you *mean* you're leaving?"

"It's less than a week. We can e-mail and then I'll be back for our next meeting."

"But I was going to ask you for a makeup lesson," Belinda complained. Her lids were bordered by broken strokes of eyeliner, a first attempt.

"Be excited for me, Belly! I get to see palm trees."

"My grandmother lives in Boca Raton. They have palm trees there. They're nice, I guess."

"Well, then you know. When I come back, we'll do a makeup lesson—or you could just ask your mothers?"

"No way!" Belinda sank her chin between her hands. "Mom D.'s idea of makeup is ChapStick. And Mom H. is still MIA. She joined an a cappella group."

"Wow, really? What do they sing?"

"Mostly Indigo Girls and Lady Gaga. I watched them practice. She's really excited about it." Belinda examined her hands.

"Something wrong, Belly?"

She hesitated. "Mom D. is kind of a mess, I think. She keeps asking me strange questions about Mom H. I didn't tell her, but I'm worried that Mom H. might like this lady, Charity, who runs the singing group. Like as more than a friend."

Marjorie censored her grimace. Didn't they see their perceptive child watching? "There's probably a good explanation, Bells. It's really difficult to accept, but you can't control your parents. They're just people who make mistakes too. Sometimes they have to be stupid before they can be smart. We can't all pop out as brilliant as you."

Belinda blushed, then smiled. "You don't even know what happened to me at camp!" Kids are so resilient.

"Do tell. Quick, 'cause we need to work. It's almost the end of July!"

"Remember Snarls?"

"How could I forget? Last I heard he was trying to get between you and Mitch at movie night."

"Oh, he was trying to get between us all right. If you know what I mean."

"Um. I do not know. Please explain."

"He came up to me a few hours before, you know? And he asked me to sit with *him,* as if he and I weren't already sitting on the same blanket because Mitch asked me."

"You're kidding! The nerve." Marjorie suppressed a grin.

"Can you believe it? He said he likes me and he is never going to be happy until Mitch and I break up!"

"Break up? Were you together?"

"I knoooooow." Belinda flipped her hair. "He's crazy, crazy, crazy."

"So what did you do?"

"Well, I couldn't be mean. So I said we could all sit together, not *with* anyone, and sort it out later. But that meanwhile he should stop destroying my macaroni sculptures to get my attention!"

"You told him!"

"I did!"

"Well, I'm proud of you, Bell. You did the right thing."

"It's just the beginning of the saga, I fear."

So dramatic, and not even twelve years old. Marjorie wished

she could freeze Belinda as she was, before she was exposed to the corrupting influences of high school—the superficiality and cynicism.

"That *He's Just Not That Into You* book may not have been totally right," Belinda said. "Sometimes boys do act like jerks when they like you."

"True!" Marjorie laughed. "Okay, back to work. It sounds like you have good fodder."

"What's fodder?"

"Material for the story."

Belinda shrugged, handing over her outline; Marjorie scanned it.

I. Henry meets Chloe on taco day in the mess hall. (Chloe is the main character's name because only cool, beautiful girls have that name.)

II. Henry is from England (Bath to be exact!). He's at day camp outside of NYC because his overprotective parents have dragged him with them on a summer-long business trip. His dad works in advertising. (No idea what that means, but it sounds good?)

III. Henry and Chloe bond over guacamole, despite confusion over his British accent. He has this dog Snarls. (What's his fake name again?)

IV. The dog HATES Chloe. Won't let them near each other.

V. Finally, Henry and Chloe find themselves alone, away from the other campers and the dog (who Chloe has now won over with treats for his FAT BUTT). But, sadly, it's the last day of camp and they must part.

VI. They have a tearful good-bye, but, at the last minute, he decides to leave Chloe a memento: the dog! She loses Henry, but she gains a new slobbering, drooling pet.

"Belly! I love this ending!"

"You do? I thought it could be funny. Like your flip book story—what seems bad ends up good, you know?"

"It *will* be funny! The image of Chloe and the dog left alone together, grumpy and resigned? I love it! It's an unexpected twist." Marjorie leaned over, her long hair pooling on the page. She drew a star at the top.

Belinda beamed. "I didn't know I was being graded, but I'll take it!"

"That's big of you. To settle for being left with Snarls."

"Yeah." Belinda brushed cookie crumbs from her palms. "Maybe the dog isn't *that* bad."

31

What the hell am I doing here?

Marjorie watched a uniformed doorman press the elevator's call button. (She—like every other able-bodied person—was up to the task herself, but Fifth Avenue residents paid exorbitant maintenance fees to avoid lifting a finger, literally.)

The circular button lit up bright, like a good idea, which this was not. Marjorie tapped her foot on the lobby's gaudy marble floor.

She had been surprised when Pickles chose an Upper East Side apartment, blocks from her childhood home, over a more fashionable West Village brownstone. One of many expectations proved wrong.

Tonight was another surprise: Marjorie had received the "Code Orange" alert from Pickles while packing for the next day's trip to LA. She couldn't bring herself to ignore the call.

Pickles was her usual unmodulated self. "Oh, thank God! Madgesty, dearie. It's me!"

"I know, P. I have caller ID. Everyone in the world has caller ID."

"Riiiight. So true, so true. Anyway, it's been ages. *Ages.*"

Marjorie rolled her eyes. "It has, Pickles. Because you haven't called."

"Oh. Did I miss *your* calls?"

"Excuse me?"

"I didn't get any messages from you either."

"I didn't leave any. I also didn't spend July Fourth with all of our friends and exclude you. Did you toast to ditching me with Vera's Skinny Bitch margaritas?"

"For goodness' sake, Madge. They're called Skinny*girl*. And, yes, we drank them, but for the love of all things holier than thou, it was Vera's birthday. I couldn't very well invite you!"

Right. Vera's birthday is July 3rd. Marjorie had completely forgotten. She was shamed into dumb silence.

Pickles was not one to hold a grudge. "I'm sorry, Doodlebug. You know I love you forever."

"But you never called to see how I was doing either . . . after everything."

"Sweets, I don't even *know* what happened! You disappeared off the face of the earth, moved and didn't tell me where! Even your mother was cryptic with mine. Ramona called raving about how you might be in Rikers, Barbara was being so tight-lipped."

Marjorie was touched at the image of her mother, handbag poised at the ready, protecting the details of her whereabouts.

"Fair enough," Marjorie grunted. *Fair enough?* She never used that expression. Where had she picked it up? *Mac? Ugh, no. Gus.*

"Anyway, we have bigger fish to fry. And I mean *fry.* A crisis demands your attention."

"'*We*' as in you and me?"

Pickles cleared her throat. That spelled trouble. "Me and Vera actually. Well, just Vera."

Seriously? "What could she possibly want from me?"

"There's a bit of . . . an issue. With Brian." Pickles dropped her voice to a whisper. "Madge, she's sitting on my bed, sobbing. You know I'm no good in these situations. I can barely comfort my kids when they fall on the playground. She needs *you*."

"Pickles. She called me 'trash' last week. Never mind what her boyfriend said."

"Oh, dear." Pickles sighed. What was with these people? "Well, under the circumstances, I'd say Brian is now a nonissue."

"They broke up?"

"Something like that. Involving another girl."

Marjorie sat cross-legged on the floor, surveying the leaning towers of clothing that surrounded her. Her half-packed suitcase gaped. She still had a lot to do but felt a pang of—responsibility, sympathy, being right? "She must be sad."

"She is. She's doing that thing where she cries silently, then suddenly heaves like a rhino. I mean, it's terrifying. Like watching Animal Planet!"

So up Marjorie trekked to 81st Street to confront the rhinoceros in the room.

Vera had been wailing for hours. Pickles's husband, Steve, was hiding in the panic room (or den), clutching his iPad like an emergency flashlight as he waited out the storm. He received Marjorie with a wicked smile, whispering "Good luck!" in disbelief.

Vera was slumped against the guest room bed's headboard in a hooded Dartmouth sweatshirt and yoga pants, a tear-stained pillow tucked under her arm like a teddy bear. Her eyes were puffy from ugly crying; her bob was pulled severely back in a headband; her lips were chapped and pale. In this state, her features looked almost cubist.

In contrast to the apartment, the room's decor evoked a beach house with bleached-out wooden furniture and turquoise prints. Marjorie clocked a half-empty *Felicity* box set and realized this must be where Pickles escaped for alone time, her sanctum from Diaper Genies. No doubt Pickles not only wanted her friend to feel better;

she wanted her space back. She stood behind Marjorie in the door-way, whispering, "It's all you!" as if coaxing a trapped bird out the window.

Vera sobbed into cupped hands.

"It's okay, Vee." Marjorie slipped off her ballet flats, scooted onto the bed, and put an arm around her old friend's quaking shoulders. "I know you feel awful right now, but I promise it's not forever."

Vera responded with a loud sniff and a vibrato exhale. She turned into Marjorie's shoulder, crying harder. Marjorie could smell Vera's fruity shampoo and the familiar scent of her Coco Mademoiselle per-fume.

She'd comforted Vera like this before: When girls at school said she looked like a witch, when her crush kissed Katie Brandwin, when the School of American Ballet's rejection letter arrived. Marjorie had witnessed her lows.

Vera took deep breaths, looking up through watery eyes. "I can't believe this is happening. How could I be so stupid?"

"You're not stupid, Vee." Marjorie brushed stray hair from Vera's face and tucked it behind her ear. "You love him."

"But you knew and tried to tell me. Why didn't I listen?"

"I didn't *know*. I suspected and wanted you to make the best decision . . . for you."

"Then I called you and was so awful, I said—I didn't mean—"

"Don't worry about that now. We'll hash it out another time." Friendship issues would have to wait.

Vera wiped ineffectually at her cheeks and came away with a moist hand. Marjorie grabbed a Puffs Plus from a porcelain tissue case on the nightstand, a box inside a box, and handed it over. "Did Pickles tell you what happened?"

"No."

"I found a text from someone named Stacy on his cell. It's his birthday next month. I wanted to buy him golf clubs, but I don't know anything about the lame-ass sport. I was looking for his brother's number to ask for help. I'm such a fucking idiot."

"You're not an idiot for expecting him to act like he's in a relationship."

She nodded. "I called him on it. He admitted that they met up once. He kissed her and claims he's been tortured about it ever since."

"Well, he didn't deny it. That's good, right?"

"He *had* to tell me. Even if I hadn't seen the text. Jen Bradley saw him with the girl, and he knew it. Jen *fucking* Bradley. I'm sure the entire city knows by now." The whimpering recommenced. "I'm so embarrassed."

Jen Bradley had been their high school's information trader, a tan, spoiled, rotund girl with a "pretty face" (never a more backhanded compliment did exist), who collected details about her peers in exchange for simulated friendship. Everyone lived in fear of awakening the beast, as her vendettas ended in humiliation and tears. Not that Marjorie had ever seen Jen behave anything but kindly to the faces of her enemies. She'd smile, then "accidentally" tell the entire class about your parents' divorce, your mother's affair, and your unfortunate case of crabs (*"Poor thing!"*)—then she'd remind everyone about how you wet your bed at a sleepover in third grade. (Jen had the world's longest memory too.) She delivered all this with a mournful head shake and tongue cluck, as if spreading your personal information was a show of concern rather than a cynical mind game, designed to protect herself. (She, in fact, had parents who divorced because her father was getting nasty with his young male assistant.)

If Jen Bradley knew, *everyone* knew. "You shouldn't be embarrassed. He should be."

"At least it was just a kiss," said Vera.

Marjorie doubted that. A skilled liar offered enough information to mimic a confession, as the lesser offense might allow for redemption. When does a guy call "Stacy" with the intention of only swapping saliva? Surely other fluids were involved. Marjorie shook the image of Brian's no doubt pimpled and dimpled ass from her head.

Pickles flopped onto her stomach on the bed, propping her chin on both hands. "How goes it, girls? Anyone feeling a teensy bit better? I know I am."

Vera gave a weak nod, *yes*.

"Good. Let's not do this whole 'ignoring each other' thing again. It cramps my style."

Vera laughed faintly. Marjorie pretended to readjust the coral-colored pillow behind her. This makeup session was a bit quick.

"Okay! Now, let's get the 411 on Mr. O'Shea, from our Madge," continued Pickles. "I've heard some salacious rumors about commitment and, dare I say, coupledom?"

Marjorie looked at Vera in question. *Do you really want to hear this?* At the same time, she wondered, *Do I really want to share?* This girl had said such hateful things only days before. Marjorie suddenly felt protective of what she had with Mac.

Vera nodded. "I'd appreciate the distraction."

Pickles patted Vera's knee, then turned to Marjorie. "Ready, set, dish!"

Marjorie shrugged. "What is there to say? I made what I thought was a stupid slip-up with him that night—after you left DIRT, Vee. He didn't call. Not surprising. But then he stalked me until I agreed to give him a chance, and has been trying to convince me he's 'boyfriend material' ever since."

"Look who harpooned the White Whale." Pickles giggled. "How's he demonstrating this so-called dedication?"

"Dinners, nights in alone. He picks me up from work, keeps my almond milk in the fridge. You know."

"How very plebeian! How positively run-of-the-mill and domestic!"

Vera nodded. "Word is he means what he says to you." Marjorie flinched; she didn't need confirmation from some outside source. "He's professing his affection all over town. It's disgusting," she joked, though Marjorie caught an edge of bitterness. "It would be our Madge who snagged Mac O'Shea *by accident*."

When Marjorie left hours later, after take-out sushi and two escapist reruns of *Friends* to calm Vera, she realized that neither girl had asked about her life beyond Mac, about where she lived or how she was surviving. Instead, she had struggled to show interest in their chatter about longtime acquaintances and elaborate upcoming weddings.

Still, as she nodded good night to the doorman and stepped out into the warm night, she told herself that she was glad to have her real friends back. And she fought to ignore those lingering question marks.

32

A chorus of chimes erupted as the plane coursed onto the runway at LAX and passengers groped for and then resuscitated their smartphones.

Marjorie and her fellow passengers had boarded toting caloric snacks, trashy novels, and tabloid magazines in blue plastic shopping bags from airport newsstands. There is a silent understanding that, thirty thousand miles above the earth, normal rules of respectability don't apply. In this limbic state, reading about some starlet's DUI is acceptable, even culturally responsible.

The New Yorkers wore blazers, determined expressions, and the occasional colorful accent to nod to LA. They battled for overhead compartment space and, when deplaning hours later, aisle position. Once in California, they would merge into threatening freeway traffic in their Chevy Malibu and Honda Civic rentals, grow panic filled, then arrive at outdoor macrobiotic cafés to wax—with revisionist abandon—about how *relaxing* the experience was compared to the East Coast bustle, how soothing the sun, how wrong their tailored black clothing.

The Angelenos, on the other hand, were on their way home and, boy, were they ready. They loved New York; they *did*. They were *so*

New York at heart. But during the visit, they'd pushed too hard, drunk too much, stayed up too late, eaten too much cheese, and collected grime and blisters navigating the urban sprawl. They'd expended so much energy feigning nonchalance. Now, in soft James Perse uniforms, they anticipated their cars' leather interiors and spacious Spanish-style homes, radio songs to which they could sing along sans judgment—"Free Falling," "Bohemian Rhapsody," "Firecracker"— and *This American Life*–filled Saturday morning drives. They craved hemp milk, algae and cacao smoothies, fish tacos, fresh sushi, and juice cleanses. They ached for the yogic stench of stagnant sweat and essential oils, the daily, almost competitive game of star sighting, hikes past well-preserved women in bedazzled sports bras.

Meanwhile, Marjorie had spent the flight inwardly raging against the pushy middle-aged Long Island woman to her left who insisted on leaning against Marjorie, spilling pretzel crumbs onto her thigh. And though her acrylic warm-up jacket kept slipping onto Marjorie's seat, she remained unapologetic, even snide, shooting angry looks as if the world should cater to her.

Marjorie was ready to escape. As she shoved her book back into her bag, Gus popped up from in front of her, leaning an impressive forearm against the top of the seat. "Welcome to LA . . . dude. That's what we call people here."

Marjorie shook her head at the lame joke but smiled. "Thanks, bro."

Gus had insisted on picking her up in a town car—the seedy kind with cracked leather seats and copious legroom—en route to their flight. She'd been nervous about spending a travel day alone with him, but conversation was smooth from the get-go. By the time they'd checked her bag with mild teasing ("*Is there a dead body in that enormous thing?*") and cleared security, Marjorie was learning about Gus's childhood, about the guitar lessons that stuck and the piano lessons that did not, about his dog Radicchio and his cat Matilda. (Marjorie did note that he barely mentioned his mother.) In fact, they were so engrossed that they realized only while boarding that they weren't seated together. The sharp-featured stewardess in pancake makeup at the desk would not help, even when Gus flashed her that rare, winning smile.

He shrugged at Marjorie. "Not my demographic. Too young."

"Older women like you?"

"Older women *love* me."

Other passengers refused to trade, too relieved to finally be sitting to switch designated rows. Marjorie offered her aisle seat to the dark-haired woman in the middle next to Gus, but she declined. She was afraid of flying and preferred to sit beside a strong man (especially one who looked like him). Apparently, he had more than one demographic.

Now Marjorie jostled for exit position and escaped the plane's claustrophobic innards, as Gus allowed every man, woman, and child off before him, pulling their monogrammed suitcases and FAO Schwarz shopping bags from the overhead compartments for them. He finally emerged into the gate area, shaking his head. "Where's the fire?"

They made their way toward Baggage Claim C. "So you're one of those," he continued.

"Those?"

"The rude ones."

"No! I just hate being trapped on the plane."

"Like I said. Rude."

Marjorie sighed. "Whatever, *dude*." With Gus, it was one step forward, one judgmental step back. For the rest of the walk—on a maze of escalators, past kiosks selling groat-filled neck pillows and La Brea Bakery bread—Gus pointed out elderly people whom Marjorie might like to push over for better position. "You're so annoying!" she snapped. He made it impossible for her to behave like a professional.

Once at their destination, Gus moved toward the automatic doors. "I'll go get my car from long-term parking, then come get you."

Marjorie was incredulous. "So you help strangers off the plane, but I'm on my own pulling my suitcase from the conveyer belt?"

He paused, looking her up and down until she felt stripped bare. "Yeah."

Gus left Marjorie there, crowded by vaguely familiar fellow passengers. The morning marine layer had lifted, and Southern California sun shot through the windows—the sky blue, without a cloud. Marjorie felt bolstered by the vitamin D, catching the eau de LA scent of In-N-Out Burger's Animal Style drive-thrus, taco stands serving al pastor pork with pineapple, avocado, and cilantro, and top notes of ocean breeze, exhaust, billboard paint and celebrity perfumes.

The giant conveyer belt belched, indelicately announcing its impending rotation. Bags began to thud from the metal ramp. Marjorie sent a quick text to her parents and Mac to announce her safe arrival.

Her mother responded right away. "Enjoy! Don't forget sunblock!" (It was an unnecessary reminder; Barbara Plum had beaten daily SPF use into her daughter's head years before. *Skin cancer, wrinkles, sunburns, oh my!*)

Mac was slower to respond. Marjorie had scooped him up in a cab heading downtown from Pickles's the night before, so he could sleep at her place, and he'd been almost too reassuring. "The trip will be great. You'll have a great time. That's great!"

Finally, she called him on it. "All right, O'Shea. Nothing is that 'great.' What's up?"

"Nothing." He fell onto her bed and rested on his side to demonstrate his fineness. "I'm *great.*" He returned to studying his iPhone.

"You have your head buried in that device." She walked to the foot of the bed and peered down at him.

"I'm a very important man." He looked up, catching her eye. "What?"

"So you're refusing to tell me what's bothering you? It's only a matter of time before we become an after-school special: you, bottling up resentment and finding solace in your secretary, Lorraine; me, looking for love at the bottom of a bottle."

He smirked. "A bottle of what, lightweight? Seltzer?"

Marjorie climbed onto the bed and crawled over to him. "If you don't tell me what's wrong, I'm gonna sit on you."

"With that fat ass?" He looked unconcerned.

"That's it!" Marjorie sat squarely on Mac's stomach, letting her weight fall as heavily as possible. Then she bounced up and down.

"Holy shit. You've lost your mind. You think you're going to get away with this?" His voice bobbled with her movement. He grabbed her wrists and flipped her easily off him. She managed to climb back on, this time straddling his hips. He grinned. "That's better."

"Let go of my wrists or suffer the consequences," she warned.

"Not afraid of you."

"You should be."

Marjorie leaned down and licked Mac's left hand. He released her, laughing hard. "You've, ha, you've lost your mind. Seriously. You just *licked* me. Are you four?"

"My wrists are free! I win!"

Perched on top of him, Marjorie raised triumphant fists toward the ceiling.

"I think I win." He smiled up at her.

"Aw, thanks. Now, you wanna tell me what's wrong?"

"I'd rather just stay like this." He placed his hands on her thighs just below where her shorts ended, his fingers cool against her skin.

"You want me to lick you again?"

"Kind of."

"Mac!"

He sighed and propped himself up on his elbows. "Fine. I'm a little . . . I don't want to say 'concerned,' because he's no threat—The thing is, I finally have you and it's as good as, *better than* I imagined. I never thought I was relationship material, but it seems like maybe I can be."

"Maybe?"

"Definitely. I just don't like that guy."

"What guy?"

"Your boss. Russ."

"Gus."

"Whatever. I don't trust him. You need to be careful."

"Okay." Marjorie shrugged. "But do you know something I don't? Because he's a pain in the ass, but basically decent."

"That's what he wants you to think. I know men. He's that do-gooder type, acting all moral. I don't like it."

"Mac. Don't take this the wrong way, but could you maybe be . . . *jealous*?"

He frowned. "No. Why the fuck would I be jealous of that douche bag?"

"Well, he's not bad-looking and he's successful and—"

Mac shot her an impatient look. *Seriously?*

Marjorie contained a laugh. "Sorry. No jealousy, then. I promise to be careful. But don't worry. He's a nice guy. Unlike you."

Mac smiled wickedly. "Yeah, I'm not nice at all. I'm a bad, bad boy. You should punish me."

Marjorie dissolved into giggles, collapsing onto him, her head against his chest. He wrapped his arms around her.

"I love you," he mumbled into her neck, his lips a tickle against her skin. "I think you should move in with me."

Unsure of how to respond, Marjorie closed her eyes, hung on tight, and hoped that it was enough for now.

33

In LA, an ever sparser elder generation reminisces about a long lost era, when no barbed wire and security cameras protected the HOLLY-WOOD sign. In those days, the view of Santa Monica's shore was unobstructed from as far away as 12th Street, and gridlock wasn't a given.

Now, traffic is a point of pride. Spread across a bazillion miles, the city has a shared language unhampered by any Tower of Babel. Navigating freeways may be torture, but residents enjoy no greater pleasure than debating the merits of routes.

Marjorie was unaware of such things. When Gus picked her up in

his Prius—a Hollywood staple that revealed little about economic status but much about political affiliations—she assumed traffic was
terrible, but they were flying by the city's standards. They turned from
La Tijera onto La Cienega Boulevard, a long, wide thoroughfare that
squiggles toward the hills past strip malls, industrial warehouses–
cum–hipster galleries, and parkland. As the Clash clipped from the
stereo, Marjorie gazed out the window, a dry breeze whipping her face,
a pleasant lashing.

The drive was so nice that she was disappointed when they pulled
up to her boutique hotel, the Orlando. Gus pulled her suitcase from
the trunk, feigning injury under its weight.

A uniformed valet guy stepped forward and handed Gus a ticket.
"Checking in?"

Gus nodded and led Marjorie through automatic doors inside.
"The hotel isn't fancy, but it's nice and central," he explained. Of
course, all Angelenos believe that they live in convenient neighborhoods because they've oriented their experience that way. West siders and east siders alike brag about rarely crossing the divide. Gus
was no exception. "I live around the corner here on Blackburn, so
you won't need a car. I'm assuming that's best."

At the check-in desk, two attendants were busy helping other
guests. "Why would that be *best*?"

"I know you New York City kids can't drive."

"I will have you know that I am an excellent driver," protested
Marjorie. "Mostly."

"Oh, Lord."

"Well, I haven't driven that much! I only got my license two
years ago."

"See? NYC kids."

"Is that some kind of Philly snobbery? You're not proud enough
of your cheesesteaks? You have to disparage us?"

A clerk gestured them over. Soon, Marjorie was upstairs, unpack-
ing her suitcase, while Gus headed home. The room was modest but
sweet, with plush white pillows and a small sofa. How luxurious to

have space to herself, where unpaid bills, unread books, and unrealized dreams didn't stain the landscape, with gratis gardenia-scented bath products, and where someone else made the bed and washed the towels.

She pushed back hazy white curtains and looked out the window. The purple mountains, fuzzy from smog, lazed in the background like a homebody on a well-worn couch, the slighted valley at its back. Quaint buildings on West 3rd Street looked more suited to a small city than this sprawling metropolis, only a few stories tall and housing independent shops: a Magnolia Bakery, a nail salon, pizza joint, travel bookstore, bodega (called "convenience store" here).

This understated neighborhood bore no relationship to tourist destinations like Rodeo Drive, Universal Studios, or Hollywood Boulevard with its costumed character photo ops and stench of deterioration. En route to the airport in New York, Gus had promised that LA would surprise Marjorie. Suddenly, she felt inclined to believe him. Gazing out toward an uncertain future didn't make her feel lost. She was like a Jane Austen heroine, awaiting a visitor to render a boring drawing room exciting again. (Maybe Belinda was right about Bath.) She felt the buzz of possibility.

Marjorie let the curtain fall back. She and Gus would start watching films the next day. How should she occupy herself tonight? She hadn't contacted her acquaintances here, remembering—with a pang—that Brianne's e-mail had described her as deranged. She wouldn't let that ruin her time. She threw her hair into a bun, applied lip gloss, changed into sandals, and went out.

The air was amazing; July in Los Angeles was quite comfortable. The more torturous heat would come in September, somehow surprising residents year after year. Marjorie wandered past the hotel's busy restaurant and storefronts before arriving at gourmet market and eatery, Joan's on Third, LA's answer to Dean & DeLuca.

Diners—golden and glowing to Marjorie's eye—sat outside in aviator sunglasses with small pups tied to their metal chairs. They snacked on Chinese chicken salads, pretending not to assess each arrival's celebrity status. Women clutched oversized purses and "boyfriend" cardigans, as the weather could shift on a dime. Men wore fitted V-neck T-shirts and gelled faux hawks. Exaggerated hand gestures outed many as actors.

Marjorie was about to step inside, when a *bing!* alerted her to a text from Gus. Several bystanders checked their own phones, then visibly deflated.

> Have dinner mtg with fest organizer. Want
> to join?

> Sure! When?

> Meet at 6? Have to drag you to a pool party
> first. You'll get a dose of "LA."

> Bring it.

> My address: 8431 Blackburn. Need
> directions?

> No. I can walk around the corner all by
> myself.

> I knew I hired you for a reason.

> You didn't hire me. Michael did.

Later, primped and ready, Marjorie waited outside Gus's building, a Spanish-style house subdivided into an upper and a lower unit—what Angelenos refer to as a "duplex." A lone palm tree sprouted from a well-manicured lawn. The walk was lined with white night jasmine, which wafted a smell so sweet at sundown in summer that it reminded passersby of stolen kisses behind barns, cold lake swims, and first loves. A hummingbird zoomed from one bird-of-paradise flower to another, never idle.

The door swung open and out sauntered Gus, relaxed in his own element. His dark T-shirt, better manicured jeans, and high-tops apparently equaled evening attire.

"Hey. You found it."

"Confirming once again that I'm not mentally challenged."

"'Confirming' seems like a strong word, but this strengthens your case."

Marjorie thought she looked pretty good, bordering on risqué in the cleavage department, but Gus didn't glance in her direction. Not that she required his affirmation, but he was a straight man, right?

She sighed. "Nice place."

He looked back at his building, as if jogging his memory. "Thanks. The landlord says Charlie Chaplin once lived there."

"That's cool!"

"Honestly, if Charlie Chaplin lived in all the homes people claim, he would have had to move daily, but yeah."

As they walked to Gus's car past other charming façades, with dogs and cats strategically perched at windows, Marjorie envied the stress-free lives she imagined unfolding inside. (In fact, as they passed, an out-of-work actor received a rejection call from his commercial agent, who was one failed audition from dumping him; a couple argued about the price of their cable package; a hungover personal trainer—late for her next session—wondered why the hell she'd slept with *that guy,* again.)

"I think I like LA."

Gus smirked. "After all of two hours."

"When you know, you know." Marjorie ducked into the Prius and strapped on her seat belt. "So where are we going?"

"The Mondrian."

"Wait, Skybar?"

"That's right."

"No way! That's so classic!"

"My friend DJs an afternoon party there. I never go, but it's his birthday, and I swore I'd stop by."

Marjorie raised an eyebrow. "You have friends who are DJs?"

"I'm not a fucking geriatric." Gus tore his eyes from the road to shoot her a dirty look. "Don't make me regret bringing you."

That shut up Miss Plum.

Gus pulled into the tall white hotel's precarious driveway and collected a valet ticket, suggesting the attendant keep the car close as their visit would be short. The sparse lobby was all light woods, sharp angles, and mirrors. Women in heavy makeup wandered through, tight dresses dotted with grommets, Swarovski crystals, and sequins. This was the stuff of Los Angeles's breast-implanted rep.

Gus came up behind Marjorie, startling her. He whispered in her ear, "We're literally staying for ten minutes—one drink. Whichever comes first." The breath from his lips sent a shiver down her body. *Must be chilly in here.*

A door guy checked Gus's name off a list and let them pass. The party was in full swing. Revelers lounged in cabanas and on chaises around the rectangular pool. Some had stripped down to bikinis and trunks—showing off sculpted arms and abs—and dipped their toes, while sipping cocktails. Most were too busy bopping to trance and '80s pop remixes to notice, but the view was stunning: West Hollywood seemed to extend forever, the bar on the edge of the world. The sun faded, experiencing its own early evening ennui.

"I'm going to say hi to my friend, so he knows I showed. You want to come meet him?"

Marjorie envisioned standing dumbly to the side, while Gus tried to talk to his friend midrecord scratch. "I think I'll grab a drink."

"All right. You're okay?"

"I'm okay."

"Okay. See you in a sec."

Marjorie watched Gus beeline for the DJ booth. She wasn't the only one: A duo of bleached blondes followed shamelessly with their eyes. Marjorie shook her head and headed for the bar.

"Can you make a pisco sour?"

The beefcake bartender grinned. "I can, but I won't."

"Is that—are you're kidding?"

"No joke, Mama. We've just got the two signature cocktails with this new low-fat liquor."

Only then did Marjorie notice the bottles of Snow Lite vodka on display. She would have burst out laughing if she wasn't about to have to drink the stuff. "What flavors do you have?" *Please don't say "peanut butter."*

"Wheatgrass or kimchee."

Well, that was a stumper. "Whichever's better."

He mixed, then handed her the drink, pumping his head to the music. "Enjoy, Mama!"

Marjorie wandered to a corner to take a sip, in case she had to spit it out, when a disembodied voice demanded, "Who are *you*?"

She turned to discover an early twenty-something, bearing an uncanny resemblance to young Michael Jackson despite short shorts and neon Ray-Ban sunglasses.

"I'm sorry. Were you talking to me?"

"Yes. Who did you come with?"

"Gus." She pointed to the DJ booth, where her boss laughed with his friend.

"I don't know him. Is he a producer?"

She shook her head. "A distributor."

"Oh." The kid looked disappointed. Marjorie fought an irrational urge to apologize.

"What do *you* do?" she asked.

"I'm an actor, singer, writer/director/producer, hair stylist, makeup artist, T-shirt designer, and faith healer. But right now I'm a canine mobility companion."

"Like . . . a dog walker?"

He pursed his lips. "I work for a very upscale company called Raise the Woof, so. I took Henrietta Sweet's bichon frise up Runyon today. No big deal."

"I actually don't know who that is."

"OMG. Where have you *been*? She's the bad girl on season two of *The Waxers of Woodland Hills*. The one who freaked in the middle of a Brazilian and made her client leave with only half her pubes removed!"

Marjorie was not familiar. "For celebrity clients, do you have to go to puppy psychiatrists or animal psychics or whatever?"

"Only the first dog walker gets to do that. I'm the second assistant, but I'm hoping for a promotion. If my TV pilot doesn't sell before then."

"You wrote a TV pilot?"

"Not yet, but it's up here." He pointed to his egg-shaped cranium. "Melody—that girl by the daybed, the one with the good chin job—practically knows Chris Harrison, the host of *The Bachelor*. Her cousin serves him every morning at Coffee Bean. Melody thinks she can get herself on the show. That's instant access."

"I'll say I knew you—actually, I didn't get your name?"

"Stardom."

"Sorry?"

"I changed my name to manifest success. What's yours?"

"Marjorie."

"Oh. You should rethink that." Stardom examined her face. "You're very pale. Don't you spray tan?"

"No, I live in New York, land of pasty people."

"No way! I'm here for my career, but I'm totally a New Yorker at heart. "

"You visit a lot?"

"I've never been. But I watch tons of *Sex and the City* reruns with my girlfriend. Actually, I better go find her."

"You have a . . . girlfriend?"

"Melody. The one with the great chin, remember? We're in a polyamorous relationship, but Blake is at a v-o audition. Wait! Is that Jeremy Piven? I gotta say hi! I walk his aunt's poodle. We haven't met, but we're practically family. Instagram me! @Stardom4EVA."

Marjorie stood slack-jawed, as Gus approached. For once, he

seemed like a friendly face. "You ready?" he asked. "Looks like you didn't even start your drink yet."

"I think it's probably safer if I don't."

Marjorie was grateful to return to what Gus described as "the real LA." They arrived at an unassuming sushi restaurant, Hama, in Little Tokyo and, despite a substantial number of people waiting, were seated right away. Their "date" had put his name on the waiting list long before.

"Of course," murmured an amused Marjorie, as she followed Gus over to a middle-aged man who might have been the Unabomber with his salt-and-pepper beard, misshapen pharmacy sunglasses, and baseball cap.

"Marjorie, this is Benny Hamish."

"Nice to meet you." He nodded, taking her hand in his warm own. As they settled across the table, he tucked a *New York Times* underneath his chair and frowned at Gus. "This guy doesn't know squat about economic recovery. He's a goddamn used-car salesman, a haircut, telling people what they want to hear, swindling them out of their last dollars."

Marjorie peered around. What guy? Benny seemed more like an eccentric uncle than a film festival organizer.

"Mitt? We'll see if he releases those back taxes, I guess."

"Yeah, right!" exclaimed Benny, slamming his fist on the wooden table, causing the soy sauce canister to toggle. "This guy? This guy! He's never gonna do that. And our guy—he needs to step it up in the debates. Show this overprivileged, ass bag bully what's what."

"Ass bag," said Marjorie before realizing she'd spoken out loud. Benny peered at her, as she tried to recover: "That's new for me. I like it. Adding it to my repertoire."

He laughed, more a shout than anything joyful. "I like this one. She's got moxie. Where'd you find her?" Like Marjorie was a great umbrella or a new iPhone app.

"Two for one at Walmart. I picked her up and also this shirt." Gus pulled at his forest green T-shirt.

"Well, good choice. How long you been dating?"

"No!" Marjorie and Gus both protested, practically leaping across the table to correct him.

"We're not dating."

"She's my employee."

Benny shrugged. "She looks like your type." To Marjorie, he said, "But you're in film. Much more interesting." He took a sip of water. "That's funny, fucking Walmart. Don't get me started on goddamn them."

Against the odds, Marjorie found herself liking Benny—though not quite as much as the albacore sashimi. (This was the best sushi she'd ever had.) He was gruff and unpolished, but also substantial in a way she was coming to appreciate. When they parted ways later, he gave her a bear hug.

"You sure you're not dating?" he repeated, retreating down the block.

"Yes!" they chorused.

"Then you're idiots." Benny shook his head and continued toward his tiny Fiat.

Marjorie turned back to Gus, whose brow furrowed as he examined an e-mail on his BlackBerry.

"You know BlackBerry is going out of business, right? You're a dinosaur."

"They're easier to type on," he grunted, not bothering to look up.

"It gets—"

"Yeah, I know." He rolled his eyes. "Everyone says it gets easier, but I don't think typing on my phone is a skill I should have to cultivate."

"Fair enough."

"Anyway, I saw your hardcover book on the plane. How come you don't have a Kindle or iPad or whatever the kids are using these days?"

She smiled. "'Cause I'm a dinosaur too."

They strolled back toward the car. The air had turned chillier and Marjorie hugged herself for warmth. She looked at Gus—his gait loping and slouched, his T-shirt a little wrinkled as always. Was that sloppiness a tiny rebellion?

"So," she nudged, "I'm your type, huh?"

He looked up from his BlackBerry and groaned, "I *knew* you were going to say that. Benny doesn't know what he's talking about. He barely knows me."

"If you say so."

"It's superficial, anyway. I happen to have dated a few taller girls with that kind of hair or whatever before."

"I'm sorry, that kind of hair?"

"You know"—he gestured toward her head—"that color."

"Auburn."

"Whatever you call it. I'm not a wordsmith."

"'Wordsmith?' Hey, Gus, 1890 called. They want their lingo back."

"I'm not even going to dignify that with a response." He patted her shoulder, his hand heavy with condescension. "It's not your fault that you're young and dumb."

She gaped in mock shock at his insolence. "Older doesn't mean smarter. You may be demonstrating early signs of senility. Plus, that's not what Fred said about your type."

He looked stricken. "What did Fredericka say?"

"Wouldn't you like to know."

"I'm serious. Tell me."

"That you fluctuated between pretentious girls and dumb bimbos."

He was clearly relieved. "No. I only like smart bimbos. Why were you talking about my type, anyway?" Marjorie ignored the question.

Back on 3rd Street, Gus parked his car and insisted on walking Marjorie the half block to her hotel. They lingered outside.

"So is Benny a typical festival organizer? Not that I've met many, but he's not super solicitous."

Gus nodded. "He's involved, but he actually established a non-profit foundation that gives grants to the winning filmmakers mostly. It's his creative outlet, a side project. He made a bundle in supermarket chains, then he opened one of the first medical marijuana dispensaries in Venice. He offers reward cards for return customers. 'Buy one-eighth, get a joint free!'"

"What? That can't be real."

"Oh, that's real."

Marjorie snorted. "Ha! Well, now I don't like LA; I *love* it."

"Please. You couldn't handle *normal* brownies at Fred's party."

Suddenly, Marjorie was struck with a memory she'd lost from the night she met Gus, before Mac professed his undying . . . like.

Gus's hand was on her back for comfort.

"I must look like a mess," she'd said.

You look fine. Good, even. I'm thinking you've never looked bad. Let's be honest." She'd wiped her tears away with a crumpled brownie napkin, as he continued, *"At some point, we all go through this—growing pains are a rite of passage. This is what it feels like to be in transition. It's horrible, but it's en route to something better."*

She'd watched him talk, this handsome, sardonic, kind stranger. She'd known nothing about him and yet she'd felt comfortable. But now she felt nervous.

"Anyway," he said. "We should probably both get some rest. Long day tomorrow."

"See you in the morning." Marjorie was wide awake and hesitant to retreat alone to her room, but didn't dare express it. "Thanks for tonight!"

Before she realized her mistake, she threw her arms around Gus's neck and planted a kiss on his scruffy cheek. It took her a moment to realize he wasn't hugging her back. His arms remained at his sides, his hands held up, like a crossing guard stopping cars.

Suddenly, she couldn't distinguish between his warm skin and a panicked heat spreading up her own neck. She willed herself to step back—at least move her face away from his tanned jaw, where she was close enough to see the beginnings of laugh lines—but she couldn't bear to confront the awkwardness.

Finally, after seconds that felt like years, she let go, sliding down his front. Once on solid ground, she patted his upper arm, as if that final gesture somehow mitigated the rest.

Gus's phone began to ring. "Um." Barely meeting her eyes, he picked up the call, listened, then waved good-bye to Marjorie, retreating down the street, head bent in conversation.

Standing alone, Marjorie shifted in her shoes. Why did Gus have to be so stiff and make her feel like some heathen? She imagined a female coworker thrusting a similar embrace upon Mac in an innocent—barely inappropriate—show of enthusiasm. What would he do? Laugh it off, maybe make an off-color joke about his irresistibility. In the old days, before Marjorie, he would have bought her a drink, told her she was *by far* his prettiest employee, then taken her home. She frowned. Either way, he wouldn't have compounded the awkwardness by ducking away.

One hug and she'd likely undone all progress toward loosening Gus up and making her job easier, more pleasant. One hug and he was a stranger again.

She watched him disappear, then—still blushing—went inside to drown her humiliation in room service dessert.

34

The morning came too soon. When the hotel phone rang rudely, Marjorie awoke with a sugar hangover. (She'd ordered apple donuts and chocolate ice cream, then—while watching a poorly edited version of *Willy Wonka*—dug into gummy candy from the Joan's on Third-curated minibar.) She reached for the receiver. After a shrill beep, a recorded female voice chirped: *Good morning. This is your 7:30 A.M. wake-up call. Today is Friday, July 27th. The weather is sunny, with a high of 84 degrees Fahrenheit. Have a great day!*

"No, *you* have a great day," Marjorie grumbled. She slammed the phone back onto its cradle, wishing she too could return to her rightful place, sandwiched between the comforter and pillow-topped mattress.

Outside, the sky was a translucent periwinkle, having pushed the darkness out. All over LA, hungry producers and young actors pulled on Pilates, SoulCycle, and CrossFit gear, dreaming of soy lattes and hemp milk smoothies, taking advantage of extra energy from biweekly B_{12} shots. This was for them an average day.

Marjorie's body felt like lead. Staring down at her rounder than usual belly, she realized it was not possible to eat away embarrassment— only thinness.

She prepared for an uncomfortable interaction with Gus. Why did it feel like she'd pulled up her shirt and flashed him when she'd only pecked his cheek? He was *so damn uptight*. No matter. She resolved to be the model of stoicism from now on.

Awhile later, in the shade of the valet's overhang, there was a chill. She pulled her sweater over her head, realized it was backward, then got twisted up trying to fix it. When Gus arrived, she had the thing on upside down with one arm through one hole. He smirked. This was not the respectable first image she'd planned to present.

Yanking the sweater off, she slid onto the perforated passenger's seat and stared forward, her bag perched on her thighs like one of Stardom's lapdogs. "Good morning."

"Hey." The silent car whirred into action. Gus pulled out into the street, nodding toward the cup holder. "I got you coffee from Kings Road Café. It's the best."

"Thank you. That's considerate."

He narrowed his eyes at her formality. "You're welcome. How'd you sleep? Is the hotel okay?"

She thought back to the night before: candy strewn around her on the all-white bed, chocolate smeared across her face.

"It was quite nice. You?"

"Fine. I watched *Willy Wonka*."

"Me too. How amusing."

"Why are you talking like that?"

"I'm being *professional*."

"By 'professional,' do you mean *weird*?"

"Oh, I'm not the weird one." She sounded petulant again.

"What does *that* mean?" The car in front of them was driving about three miles an hour. "For the love of God! Is this person going to move?"

"It means that you're the weird one."

"Holy shit. Is this person crazy? It's rush hour in LA! Drive!"

"That's why you have a horn. Honk it."

"No. I don't like horns."

"Why?"

"Because they're loud and obnoxious and I don't like to add to the noise pollution."

Marjorie was incredulous. "You're worried about people on the street, but I have to listen to you curse inside the car?" She lowered the window, watching it glide halfway down.

Gus finally wove around the car and stopped at a red light. He looked over at Marjorie, bewildered. "What's with you this morning? You seem . . . are you angry or something?"

Marjorie took a deep breath. She needed to let this go. Why was she so pissed, anyway? "Nothing. I must have had bad dreams."

"That sucks," he said. "Were they about car horns?"

She glared at him. Then, mercilessly, Gus turned on the radio and they drove in silence the rest of the way to Hollywood.

The American Film Institute sits high above Western Avenue, as the thoroughfare curves dramatically and morphs into Los Feliz Boulevard; it's as if the cars, racing around the bend at warp speed, have transported themselves onto a different road. The scenery changes too: Gone are Hollywood's asphalt, graffiti, hopeless cases, and dilapidated storefronts with perpetual security gates. Just north, Griffith Park appears like a revelation, a nourishing explosion of green. The neighborhood is filled with pretty old apartment buildings and homes against a panorama of leaves. AFI seemed to bridge the gap, reigning over both parts of the kingdom, Sodom and Gomorrah and Eden.

As Gus wound up the drive, Marjorie had a fantasy of being in some amazing old movie, crackly, off-speed, and black and white. Instead of climbing out of the hybrid, she would step—with the help of a white-gloved valet—onto the running board of a classic Hispano-Suiza.

No such luck. They parked. Gus introduced himself to the front desk clerk in a main building and, shortly thereafter, a man named Tom appeared and led them to a modern and unromantic edit bay. Three rolling chairs were splayed about, as if punch-drunk. A gnarly old love seat was pushed against a back wall; several screens sat atop a long table with tangled cords hanging down. A box of DVDs waited in a corner. Tom pointed out the bathrooms, kitchen (with water, tea, and coffee), and a vending machine stocked with unsavory snacks, then left Gus and Marjorie alone.

"Ready?" Gus peeled off his navy blue hoodie and threw it on the sofa's arm, revealing another worn T-shirt, straining against his arms.

"Oh, are we doing this . . . together?" Marjorie regretted the phrasing immediately. "I mean, we aren't splitting the movies up?"

"Nope. They only gave us the one suite." He sat down in one of the rolling chairs, as a wheel spun out, and grabbed a remote control.

"I just thought that's why I'm here."

"No, Train Wreck, you're here to play yin to my yang, for your brilliant insight and taste and your uncanny knack for not boring me. Although, the longer you stand there staring at me, the more I wonder if this was an ill-advised idea. You gonna sit?"

Gus pushed some buttons. When nothing happened, he began checking for loose plugs. Marjorie's gaze lingered on the space between his T-shirt and the top of his boxer briefs; the sliver of skin drew her eye like a shiny penny. Why was that always attractive to her? Was it some throwback to when skateboarders and homeboys wore jeans that sagged?

Marjorie forced her eyes elsewhere, as the largest screen came to life, with a bright haze like dawn. She put her sweater aside and sat in a rolling chair, as Gus slid across the floor to the light switch and flipped them into darkness. As the first movie began, he sat close up, adjusting the settings; his face was bathed in light, as if he was the screen and the film projected onto him. Marjorie moved her chair another foot away for reasons she could not (*would* not) entertain, and tried to focus on the task at hand.

Over the next several hours, Marjorie wound herself into pretzels from rods to twists. She hugged both legs to her chest, let one dangle, rested her hands behind her head, her head on her hand, her elbow on the arm of the chair. She was slumped low with one leg hanging over the seat's arm, when it started to tip. She almost faceplanted onto the dusty floor. That's when she moved to the couch.

There were bathroom, water, and sad food breaks (Snickers, Wheat Thins, peanut M&Ms)—and one extended pause when a dark-haired woman named Susan, whom Gus knew from his Paramount assistant days, showed up and insisted that they "must grab a drink—no excuses!" She chided him for not calling, while pawing at his forearms. Marjorie watched, first with amusement, then irritation. Gus didn't recoil when Susan pressed a palm to his chest or nudged his calf with her open-toe gold sandals. When she winked, he winked back. *What was his problem?*

Susan slithered away. They watched movies, movies, and more movies. Eventually, Marjorie awoke—she hadn't realized she'd been sleeping—with vague impressions of an aimless man driving the country in a rusted Buick. She looked down and realized she was snuggling against Gus's hoodie, laid over her as a makeshift blanket. It smelled like his soap, grassy and clean; she inhaled. She rubbed her fists against her eyes like a child postnap and stretched, muscles tight, head thick, body chilled. White credits rolled down the black screen. Gus rubbed his neck and sighed, existentially.

"How long was I out?" she asked, startling him. He almost toppled backward, but the chair leveled out in time.

"Jesus! When did you wake up? You're like a fucking ninja."

"Did I miss the whole movie?"

"The last one and a half, actually."

"Oh, my God. I'm so sorry. That's so unprofessional."

"It's fine. You didn't miss much. Though there was an Old West standoff in a diner parking lot. Lots of dust and french fries. An actual tumbleweed blew by, thanks to some diligent production assistant." Gus stood. "Wow. I'm ancient. My knees actually creaked." But he didn't seem to mind. When Marjorie said the same thing to Mac, he'd been resolute about his youthfulness.

Could Mac O'Shea be getting old?

Never!

"What's the next movie?" she asked.

"Nothing tonight. It's been a crazy long day."

Marjorie swung her feet onto the floor. "Who knew watching movies could be so exhausting?"

He yawned. "I did."

"So, what are we—or do you have festival stuff tonight?"

"Nope. No big plans. You hungry?"

"I could go for something besides vending machine junk."

"How 'bout I take you to Dan Tana's?"

Marjorie was too dazed to recall her earlier irritation. "I'd love it! What's a Dan Tana?"

"You're ridiculous." Gus laughed. "It's a red-checkered-tablecloth Italian place, but famous. An old Rat Pack hangout."

"Perfect. Is anyone else coming?"

"Oh. No. I didn't make plans. It would just be . . . us."

There was a prolonged silence, as their eyes locked.

"Okay, great! Pick me up . . . now," said Marjorie, trying to break the tension.

He nodded. "It's a date. I mean, not a *date*. We don't even have to go—we could just go to bed."

"You want to go to bed?"

"I meant *separately*. Obviously. I didn't mean we could sleep *together*." Flustered, Gus grabbed his backpack and headed for the door. "Why would I mean that? I wouldn't. I don't even know why I'm still talking. I must be really tired. Are you tired? Of course you are. You fell asleep. We should take it easy tonight. I'll see you tomorrow."

Marjorie stared at him. "Um, Gus."

He turned reluctantly in the doorway. "Yeah?"

"You're my ride, remember?"

"Right. Of course. I'll meet you out front. By the door. You know what I mean." He left.

Marjorie shook her head. Had any man ever been so concerned with propriety? Here she was, passed out during work, and *he's* embarrassed because he said something barely suggestive? She stumbled out of the screening room, still disoriented, and found Gus at the front, pacing. They were on different speeds.

"You ready? Good." He climbed in the car and started the engine without waiting for a reply. "Look, sorry, Marjorie, but something came up. I have to rain-check dinner."

"Oh. Okay."

"But you don't care, right? You'll have more fun without your boss."

Marjorie forced a smile. On the way home, they barely spoke. Her mind was still half in REM cycle, half on Gus's retracted invitation. His was somewhere far off, perhaps down his ex-coworker Susan's low-cut shirt. Back at the hotel, Marjorie climbed out of the Prius and dropped Gus's hoodie onto his lap. He looked at the sweatshirt without recognition, picked it up between his thumb and index finger like something corroded, and tossed it into the backseat.

In a last effort to resuscitate what Marjorie had thought was an improved rapport, she said, "Thanks, by the way, for covering me while I slept. That was nice of you."

"No big deal. I would have done it for anyone. Anyone at all."

"Well, good, then. I'll make sure to not feel special."

"Wait!" he called, as she slammed the door.

Reluctantly, Marjorie popped her head back inside the window frame. "Yeah?"

"I didn't mean anything before."

"About what?"

"About going to bed."

"I'm not going to sue you for sexual harassment—okay, Clarence Thomas? You can stop being so uptight."

Gus opened his mouth to respond. Instead, he frowned. "Fine. Good. Pick you up tomorrow morning."

"Great. Fan-fucking-tastic."

"Just don't be late," he barked.

"I'm never late!" Marjorie protested. But he'd already peeled away—a feat in a Prius.

Up in her room, Marjorie pulled on her pink sweatpants and shirt and collapsed into bed. But she was too antsy to enjoy the hotel room.

She opened her laptop, resting it on her crossed legs, and checked her e-mail, then left a message for Mac. They'd had trouble connecting with the time difference. His nightly calls—carrying unsubtle suggestions of phone sex—came too early.

She scanned the *New York Times* online for Gail Collins's latest column mentioning Mitt Romney's dog. Marjorie was raised to be politically aware. Her mother was a card-carrying member of the ACLU, NAACP, NPR, NOW, MADD, and several other acronymic organizations. The son of a local politician, her father had government in his blood. But lately she'd tried to stay extra informed. The upcoming election was growing tenser daily, but also—though she hated to admit it—she was impacted by a sobering new influence in her life.

Unable to control herself, Marjorie navigated to Gus's Facebook page again, searching his list of "Friends" for that woman, Susan. She clapped a hand over her eyes, feeling embarrassed in front of herself. *What am I doing?*

She was about to slam the computer shut, when an instant message window popped open:

Madge?

The user's name, Dinah Levinson, was unfamiliar.

Yes?

Marjorie typed.

It's Belly!

Of course! Marjorie grinned. She missed the kid. A chat with Belinda was just what she needed.

Hi Bell! You're allowed on Facebook?

I'm only on for a second. This is Mom D.'s account.

Does she know you're using it?

Truth? No.

A few seconds passed.

Are you gonna tell on me or talk?

I'm not going to TELL, Belly. But why don't I just call you?

No. They'll hear and this is private! They think I'm in here working on my story.

You should be!

I will, but right now I need your help! It's Mitch and Snarls.

Uh-oh. Are they fighting over you?

Not exactly. It's just . . . You're going to think I'm crazy.

I doubt it, Bell.

Okay, Mitch totally likes me. He sits with me on the bus every morning and Snarls sits behind us and like pokes me the whole time.

How annoying!

Sort of. Anyway, Mitch asked me to sneak out during free period after lunch and go up to the goat farm.

Look at you, wild child.

It's no big deal. Our counselor never pays attention anyway 'cause she's too busy hitting on the swim instructor, Jose, who's all buff and stuff. It's just that I know what it means.

What what means?

The goat farm.

It means something other than a smelly place where goats live?

It's where older kids go to make out and like smoke pot and drink and stuff.

> Ah. I see. And you're nervous? About
> kissing him?

> Yes and no.

Marjorie furrowed her brow:

> ???

She wasn't going to let Belinda get pressured by some boy.

> If I confess something, do you promise
> not to laugh?

> Belly, if I laughed, you wouldn't know. I'm
> 3,000 miles away. But yes. I promise. No
> LOL.

> Okay. The thing is . . . I don't like
> Mitch.

> Belly, then forget it. You shouldn't kiss a
> boy you don't like!

> No, I know. Aargh. You're going to laugh
> at me.

> I'm not. Scout's honor.

Almost a minute passed while Marjorie waited.

> I like Snarls.

Marjorie didn't laugh. Far from it. For some reason, she felt slightly
betrayed.

But you said he looks like a bulldog.

I know.

He calls you "Four Eyes." He broke your
macaroni sculpture.

The heart wants what it wants.

Are you sure, Belly? Mitch is going to be
the new cute guy next year and you can
have him! Starting off 7th grade on the
right foot can be important for survival.
This isn't what we planned for you!

I know. I don't know what's wrong with
me. I'm sorry.

Marjorie took a deep breath and got a handle on herself. Why was
she exalting the same values that undid her and making this amazing
girl feel bad? Belinda didn't need some boy to give her confidence;
she was unique and independent.

No, Belly. I'm sorry! I am just surprised.

He's not as cool or good-looking, but he's
smart, you know? And he's funny. Mitch
is nice, but he's kind of boring. We don't
have much in common. He likes Lady
Gaga and I'm over her.

So, have you told Snarls?

Kind of. He wants to take me on a date.

Marjorie could feel Belinda's happy gamma waves through the computer.

> A date! Belly, that's so cute!
>
> But what do I wear? And what do I tell my moms?
>
> You're allowed to hang out with friends, right? Tell them that you're going to the movies, or whatever you're doing, with a friend. It's the truth.
>
> Ok. And, since Mom H. has been busier, Mom D. has been letting me go more places by myself. I'm no longer trapped in my personal organic prison.

Marjorie laughed.

> How are things between them?
>
> Not good. They've lapsed into silence. Three women silent at a dinner table every night is just wrong.
>
> I'm sorry, Bell.
>
> What can you do?

She sounded twice her age.

> You can work on your story, for one thing! How's it coming?

Good! I'm excited to show you when you
get home. But what about you?? Are you
having fun in LA? Have you seen famous
people? Is that jerky boss guy being okay?

Yeah, he's ok. I think he's just—

Not that into you? HA!

Marjorie's heart sank.

Yeah, I guess that's probably right.

Tell him to call me! I'll give him a piece of
my mind!

As long as your moms aren't around.

Right. And not after 9:30 'cause I go to
bed.

They said good-bye and Marjorie shut down her computer. How strange that she'd been a sworn kid hater weeks before. Homesick, she dialed Fred.

"Well, if it isn't Miss Morningstar, calling from the coast! Hi, Roomie. How's LA?"

Marjorie glanced around, as if an answer lay in the room's neutral carpet. "Good, good, good. What's up with you?" Examining her nails, she noticed a chip and went in search of a vanity kit in the bathroom.

"Nada. The Mad Hatters and I—"

"Nope. Bad name."

"Damn! That's what Elmo said too. Anyway, we're playing a show tonight. Same old. But I do have news. Ready?"

"Born ready."

"I'm going for drinks with James."

Marjorie exchanged an incredulous look with herself in the mirror. "Fred, how is that news? You see him all the time. Poor guy probably has pictures of you plastered to his ceiling."

"No! I'm letting him take me on a date. I'm giving him a real shot."

"Oooh. That's great! He's such a sweet guy."

"I figure, why not let myself be happy?"

"Totally. Plus, you can never have enough pairs of khakis."

"You're bad, friend. Bad to the bone!" Fred laughed, her incongruous boom. "So, how's our guy treating you out there?"

"Okay."

"Okay?" Fred groaned. "Out with it: What did the grouch do?"

"Nothing. Literally he's done nothing. He's at his place or maybe out to dinner with some trashy studio chick and I'm here at the hotel. It's fine."

The phone line crackled like damp Pop Rocks. When Fred finally spoke, her tone was carefully neutral. "Are you saying you *want* him to *do* something?"

"Are we speaking in code?"

"I don't know. Do you want me to say it out loud?"

"No, don't!" Marjorie looked away from her own reflection. "I just got lonely for a sec. He's been a gentleman."

"A gentleman, huh? That sounds lame."

"No. It's exactly as it should be. In fact, I should probably call Mac."

"Have you figured out what to do about that?"

"About . . . ?"

"Moving in with your boyfriend."

"Oh. That."

"Yes, *that*."

"I dunno. I don't want to leave you high and dry with no roommate."

"I was roommate free before. I'll be fine."

"Oh. Okay. Then I just need to wrap my mind around moving again so soon."

"If that's what you want."

"I think so."

"Up to you, girl. It's your life." Fred gasped. "OMG! I buried the lead: Elmo and Lou got engaged!"

"What?!"

"They decided, 'When you know, you know!' And apparently they know. Of course, Elmo wants to seal the deal before Lou realizes she's totally out of his league."

Love was in the air: Lou and Elmo, Belly and Snarls, Fred and James, her and Mac. So why did Marjorie feel like she swallowed an inflated balloon? People talk about love at first sight, about *knowing*. Marjorie didn't even *know* where her left sneaker had gone.

She was suddenly exhausted. There's nothing so tiring as a case of the shoulds.

35

Just before 10:00 the next morning, Marjorie and Gus found a winner. They were in what had become their respective screening room spots; he, with his arms and legs outstretched, as if the rolling desk chair was a beach lounge; she, curled into a ball against the corner of the couch.

Throughout the last few days, they had discovered some decent filmmakers to keep on their radar, but no truly memorable films. At least not in a good way.

The morning drive had been quiet; Marjorie stole glances at Gus as he drove. The edges of his mouth were downturned, dark circles had emerged under his eyes, and his stubble had graduated from five o'clock shadow to near beard. She wondered if he was hungover. Where had he gone last night after they parted ways?

"How was your evening?"

"Good. It was good."

"You look exhausted."

He flashed her a wry smile. Tired or not, he still looked good. "My dinner ran late and turned into drinks."

"With Susan?"

Gus looked confused. Then, as recognition set in, he tried to cover a laugh with a cough. "That's sort of none of your business, right?"

Marjorie stared ahead, missing the humor in Gus's eyes. "Just making conversation. Like a normal person. Do they not make emotional IQ flashcards for that?"

The rest of the drive was silent.

Their first film of the morning was *Writing on the Wall,* a documentary about a Hasidic graffiti artist in Williamsburg called Talmud (his tag). Gus and Marjorie were hooked by the notion of an Orthodox hipster—his Ray-Ban Wayfarers obscured on the sides by curling payos, his beard in keeping with his secularist peers but with meaning beyond style. He was a symbol of the neighborhood's spirit: Williamsburg might be the epicenter of cool, but the Hasidim were there first in long black coats and hats.

This ultra-Orthodox Jewish community had no relationship to Marjorie's Reformed one. But, during her childhood on the Upper West Side, the cultures coexisted and collided—all part of the "melting pot." Often she'd wondered what the Hasidic kids thought of passing bus ads for TV shows like *The Real World* and *Sex and the City,* nonkosher pizza joints hocking pepperoni slices, boutiques displaying short, tight, exposing clothing. Sometimes she saw the older men engaged in behavior that seemed antithetical to religious life: in strip clubs, for instance. (Marjorie had gone to "gentlemen's clubs" with male friends in her early twenties and pretended to feel blasé when confronted with the gyrating girls' open legs.)

Talmud's family did not understand his passion for graffiti. He was an artist, he explained. He had to create *artwork*. He followed their religious rules, never tagging on the Sabbath. Wary of depicting graven images, his pieces contained only words. But under the cover of night, he slipped outside and "threw up" masterpieces on city walls, an increasingly difficult act in recent, more policed years. Decades before, subway cars were like communal artworks, telling stories of dueling gangs and lost loves in bubbly text. But the trains had been rebuilt in graffiti-proof materials with conveniences like air-conditioning and digital signs.

Talmud's father, who was offended most profoundly by his son's tag name, reminded his son regularly of the book of Daniel, chapter 5, in which King Belshazzar disrespected sacred vessels from the Jerusalem Temple at his feast and, thus, writing appeared on the wall, spelling out the leader's death and the fall of Babylonian rule. Writing on walls was sacrilegious, he insisted. And the viewer empathized with both the artist's need for acceptance and a creative outlet and his father's panic amid a changing world. *Writing on the Wall* was about generation gaps, about art, identity, family, and the existence of God. As the credits rolled, so did Marjorie's tears; she missed her parents horribly. She resolved to make more time for them when she got home.

As always, Gus watched the credits until the end, a meditative ritual. He pressed Stop and looked at Marjorie.

"Are you crying?"

"It was so good!" she wept.

"What's wrong with you?"

"What's wrong with *you*, Tin Man?" She leaned across the couch's arm and flipped on the lights, catching Gus as he wiped his own eye.

"Allergies." He shrugged.

"Right." Marjorie fell back onto the love seat, its loose springs reverberating. "We *have* to get this movie."

"We'll try. A lot of people are going to want it."

"Yes, but you *need* it. You guys will do right by it."

"Yeah. We could really use this. Between you and me, it's been awhile since we got a great film. I've been stressed about it. We just have to convince the filmmaker." He studied the clear plastic DVD case. "Danny Hellerman."

"Let's call him right now! Before other people see it!"

"I'll see if he can meet tonight."

"That's too late!"

"Okay, Train Wreck. I think you're being a little dramatic. The official festival screenings start tomorrow. No one is going to see it before then."

"You don't understand!" Marjorie reached over and picked up Gus's iPad from a wooden side table, her shirt riding up. She yanked it back down, but not before catching Gus watching her. She pulled up the festival's site and clicked through to the film's profile page. "Yeah, that's what I thought. Gus, the filmmaker isn't Hasidic, but he's Orthodox. Look, he's wearing a yarmulke in the photo."

"So?"

"So it's Friday, and if we don't speak to him before sundown, we're not going to be able to get to him until tomorrow night, and by then everyone will have seen it."

Gus considered that. "You're right."

"Would you mind repeating that?"

"There's a luncheon today for the out-of-towners. I'll call Benny and tell him we're coming." Gus stood and opened the door to the suite. "Ladies first."

Marjorie grabbed her bag and slid past, within an inch of him; his chest rose and fell. In the doorway, she paused and looked up, as he looked down at her, their eyes meeting. A weightless sensation worked its way from the tips of her fingers to her toes, stealing her breath. A long second passed, as they stood, frozen.

He cleared his throat, his voice thick, "I guess we should go."

She nodded and walked out. She felt strange, unbalanced. In the car, sitting beside Gus, she texted Mac:

Hey. Just thinking about you.

He responded right away:

> Wish you were here, wearing a pair of my
> socks and nothing else.

> You're a strange one, O'Shea.

> When are you gonna move in with me
> already, Madgesty?

Just like that, a tidal wave of anxiety crashed over Marjorie. Her mind tumbled over her choices—which felt epic though they should have been simple—and the brackish tsunami grew fiercer, flooding her bloodstream with debris and threatening her feeble rationality. What was wrong with her? She was getting what she wanted! Her throat constricted, her knee thumped against the glove compartment door. She pulled at her fringed scarf. She was trapped in this car, in this strange city, in her body.

At a red light, she felt Gus glance over, as if he could sense her unease. He noted her pallor, the way she white-knuckled her phone but typed nothing.

"Are you okay?"

"I'm—fine."

"You sure?" She managed a nod. "Because you look like you're freaking out."

"I'm probably—it's just low blood sugar." Her voice sounded hoarse.

Gus considered her for a beat, not buying it. "Okay. I'll pull over at that gas station and get you peanuts or something. That helps, right?"

Not being hypoglycemic, Marjorie had no clue whether peanuts "helped." She was confident they wouldn't solve her current problem. "That's okay. We're going to lunch. I can make it."

The light turned green and the beat-up metallic blue Mitsubishi Galant in front of them glided forward, setting a snail's pace for traffic.

"Look, Marjorie, I saw you panic like this at the party, remember? On the off chance that this is anxiety, maybe take some deep breaths? Inhale for a count of five and then exhale for the same, a few times."

Marjorie didn't bother protesting. She took a first uneven breath in and exhaled, then repeated that over again. She wasn't cured, but she felt calmer, maybe just by virtue of his understanding.

"It's biofeedback," Gus explained. "It slows down your heart rate, stops the adrenaline from intensifying."

She took a few more breaths. "Why do you know about this?"

He shrugged. "My mom. She has these attacks, way worse than yours. She has fears that get in the way of her living her life."

"Oh. That's terrible. I don't want that to happen to me."

Gus looked at Marjorie with earnest concern. "Oh no, no. That won't happen to you. She's a wonderful person, but with real problems. She can't see the world clearly. You're fine. Just in flux. Happens to the best of us. I once went to the hospital in college for chest pains: I-don't-want-to-be-a-lawyer syndrome."

Gus was a private person. Marjorie understood how unnatural it must be for him to confide in her. *This is a car, this is Gus, someone who I trust to take care of me, this is a safe place.* She felt the floodwaters draw back, crisis averted. For now.

"Do you know what triggered this?"

"No," she lied.

"Maybe it's this lunch? Your first big filmmaker meeting? Don't worry. You'll be great."

She nodded, amused by the idea that she would panic in anticipation of meeting a fledgling filmmaker. As a PR person, she'd defused diva designers and actors, bipolar event planners, and anal Fortune 500 CEOs and their heavily drugged spouses.

Mac texted again:

Hello? Bueller? Were you kidnapped by
Russ?

She bit her lip and typed:

> Gotta run, ok? Off to film fest. Call you
> tonight.

> Look at you, Jet Set. Ok. Later

Within ten minutes (an LA miracle!), Marjorie and Gus arrived at the tiered garage at the Sunset Boulevard festival location, at the intersection of Denial and Subtext.

They pulled into a narrow spot, delineated by fat yellow lines. Stepping out of the car, Marjorie was sturdier on her feet than she expected. It was a clear day, blue skies, little smog. Through the gap in the cement guardrails, she could see the city laid out before her. Embedded in hills was the Hollywood sign, spotted with tufts of brush. They started down the steps to the building's entrance.

The lobby was abuzz. Organizers and staff wore laminated badges that dangled around their necks from red lanyards. Many were baby-faced college kids with telltale slept-on hair and USC and Cal Arts sweatshirts. Their focused expressions—as they unpacked and stacked schedules, brochures, and promotional postcards on folding tables—demonstrated a commitment that far outweighed the task. Perhaps creating an attractive display of complimentary pens would ensure their futures as studio executives or filmmakers! Their overseers looked unimpressed and worried, as they were every year, that the event would not resolve itself in time.

"That's it. I'm going to be fired," said a gangly male organizer in tortoiseshell glasses, raising a backhand to his forehead in despair. "It's the Omaha Horror Festival for me."

"I'd—*They'd* be lost without you," promised his squat female co-worker.

Marjorie and Gus were directed to a carpeted banquet hall, where a lunch buffet included everything from gluten-free, veggie wraps to kosher hot dogs and fruit salad, a step above the East Coast honeydew, grapes, and cantaloupe norm. Metal buckets held tropical neuro drinks, advertised to improve brain function—an event sponsor. Rushing attendees would imbibe these in place of water over the next days, so much that the flavors would become sense memory, tasting of the festival itself.

Benny introduced a pretty woman of ambiguous ethnicity, whom he described as his "counterpart, Kayla." They shook hands.

"I understand you're interested in meeting Danny Hellerman?"

"We are," said Gus. "His movie is fantastic."

"It's brilliant," Kayla effused. She sounded perpetually wistful, a habit formed from years of exaggerating her empathy for human suffering and love of art. "He's over there, in the striped shirt." She could have said the "yarmulke," but apparently that might be considered insensitive. "Shall I introduce you?"

Gus and Marjorie followed her to a round table, where Danny sat trapped by some long-winded fellow filmmaker (spiky hair, sunglasses inside, embellished jeans). "Excuse me, guys," Kayla interrupted. "I want you to meet some very important people: This is Gus Rinehart and Marjorie Plum from Grover & Grouch, a great art house distributor, especially for you, Danny." She waved a hand in the filmmakers' general direction. "This is Danny Hellerman of *Writing on the Wall* and Grant Vollbracht, who made *The Deep Emotions That I Feel*."

Gus and Marjorie made the proper addresses, as Kayla returned to work.

"Mind if we grab food and eat with you?" asked Gus.

Danny shook his head. "Not at all."

"Sit! The more the merrier!" Grant shouted, his sunglasses slipping down his nose, as his gelled hair remained frozen in time and space. "I'd love to hear your pitch. As you know, Danny and I represent the future of filmmaking."

Marjorie half expected Gus to lunge across the table and strangle Grant right then—they would *not* be kindred souls. Instead, he mumbled something incoherent before heading for the lunch spread. Marjorie slung her bag across a chair and, after confirming that Grant and Danny needed for nothing, sidled up next to Gus. He was eyeing the vegan egg salad distrustfully, as if it might jump onto his plate.

"That Grant guy is up your alley," Marjorie whispered.

"It took everything I had not to punch him on the spot."

"I don't remember his movie? Have we seen it yet?"

"You were lucky enough to sleep through it. It's this overwrought crap: The main character is too handsome and brilliant; his 'light shines too bright.' He has to wear a mask and hang out alone, contemplating the universe, heroin, suicide. It's 'autobiographical,' I'm sure. One day, a child pulls him out into daylight and tells people not to be intimidated. And the world is a better place. It's even worse than it sounds."

"Okay, well, stay calm."

"Yeah, I will. Of course."

"We can't make him feel ignored."

Gus turned to her, his face close. "Believe it or not, I've done this before, bossy."

"I'm just trying to help."

They settled into folding chairs back at the table, with filled plates.

"So, Danny," said Gus, "tell us about your movie. How did you first meet Talmud?"

Danny's face lit up, but before he could answer, Grant interrupted. "How does any artist find his subject? You hear a voice from the heavens, passion takes over, and the story arrives through . . . osmosis." He paused, as if the word had just come to him, though this was clearly a prepared speech. "For my short, when Tom Cruise *asked* to executive-produce and Beck said he'd score, I knew I'd created something special. We all did."

Gus wore an undisguised look of disgust.

"What a coup to get those people involved," rushed Marjorie. "Are you from LA?"

"I'm a citizen of the world, really. Been around, traveled the globe."

Danny looked perplexed. "I thought you were from Minnesota?"

"Among other places," said Grant with a flourish. "Did you see my film?"

"Unfortunately, no," said Marjorie, looking to Gus for confirmation.

"But I did." He gritted his teeth. "Good job."

"Thanks, thanks. Yeah, I heard some people buzzing about Danny's movie, and I thought we should team up, since we're the guys everyone is going to want to meet. Of course, I'm already down the road with a studio, can't say which, but I'm more than happy to talk to little guys like you too because what I create is *art*, you know? My film is a deeply personal character study. I'm not sure the big guys understand that vision."

Gus looked strained, like the Incredible Hulk about to burst forth, green and muscle-bound, from his clothes. "I see someone I know," he managed. "I'll be back." He left. It was better, Marjorie figured, than losing his temper.

Grant rambled on about his "process," petting a phantom goatee, as Marjorie and Danny sat captive. She caught the soft-spoken filmmaker's eye and shared a commiserating smile during a particularly absurd snippet of monologue. "People always remark on the depth of the character's struggle," Grant explained. "I guess that's why John Travolta says I'll change the face of film."

Mercifully, Grant's phone rang. "Sorry. I have to take this. It's my agent. At CAA."

Gus was nowhere to be seen, having wandered off in search of oxygen he didn't have to share with Grant. Danny, Marjorie noted, exhaled when the other filmmaker left. He looked younger than she'd expected, overwhelmed.

She smiled. "Big personality."

"Huge." He raised his eyebrows.

"I guess he's kind of glommed on to you?"

"Yeah. But I don't know anybody here, so . . ."

"Good to have someone to hang with."

"Right. And he does sound connected."

"He *sounds* that way, yeah. Operative word."

Danny nodded. "Are you from LA?"

"No way." She shook her head. "I live in Brooklyn."

"Oh!" The filmmaker brightened. "That's where I'm from."

"I know, I read. Crown Heights, right? This is a long way from there." She smiled. "I want to apologize for Gus leaving. He can't stand guys like Grant. But he is so incredibly excited about your film. We were both bowled over by the way you handled the subject. We only came to this lunch to meet you."

Danny blushed and looked down at his stained paper plate. "Thanks. That's really good to hear."

"During the course of this festival, you'll be approached by a lot of distributors and acquisitions executives."

"It's already started a little."

"And that's an incredible thing. Congratulations! I hope you'll take a second to appreciate what an accomplishment that is before you worry about making decisions."

"That seems like good advice."

Marjorie laughed. "My mother is a life coach. Like her, I'm good at giving advice and terrible at taking it."

"I'm like my father. Too quiet."

"No! You're taking it all in. I need to shut up more. Anyway, I don't want to monopolize you. We wanted to meet you because we've watched a bazillion movies over the last week and yours is our favorite. I'm new to the company, so you'd really be working with Gus and his partner, Michael, in New York, but I know they'd take good care of you and your movie, if you chose to go with us. This type of film is their forte. But you're going to have success no matter what you do. Just don't let the Grants of the world steal your thunder."

Danny grinned. "How do you think he got those famous people involved in his movie?"

"I wonder if he really did. LA is so weird."

"Yeah. But I kinda like it."

"Me too." Marjorie gathered her belongings. Danny trashed his plate and Grant's too.

"Will you guys be here all week?" Standing, Danny was stockier than he first appeared—more dockworker than documentarian.

"I'm headed back, sadly. But Gus will be floating around. I don't have cards yet, but I'll give you my e-mail and his cell." She scribbled on a napkin. "Maybe we can hang out in Brooklyn sometime!"

"That'd be cool. Nice meeting you, Marjorie!"

Grant appeared and threw an arm around Danny's shoulders. Marjorie escaped before getting sucked back into the walking name drop's vortex.

36

"I cannot *believe* you left me alone in there."

It was the third time Marjorie had repeated herself. She was enjoying getting under Gus's skin. She'd spent weeks feeling like an idiot, enduring his taunts. It was her moment.

"Okay. I get it. I shouldn't have left. But it was for everyone's good. I actually thought I was going to hit that jerk."

Marjorie looked at Gus. He was a big guy, maybe capable of doing some damage, but it was hard to imagine him getting rough. If he got caught in a brawl, he'd probably shake his head at the situation and stroll out unscathed. "Please. You don't fight."

Gus smirked at her. "You think you know me?"

"I can peg your type, yeah."

"Yeah? What's my type?"

"You know, judgmental, uptight, superior, smart-ass."

He smile faded. "Seriously? That's how you see me?"

"Well, those aren't the good traits."

"I have good traits?"

"So Fred and Michael claim."

"Like what?"

"Oh, they say you're loyal and have integrity. You're trustworthy and hardworking."

"Wow. I sound like a great time. What do you think?"

"What do I think of *you*?"

"C'mon. Tell me."

Marjorie was flustered. "I mean, I guess you're sort of funny. Maybe by accident."

"That's it?"

"And smart-ish."

He raised his eyebrows.

"Fine. Very smart. And a champion of the underdog. I've seen you be sweet, though not to me." She coughed. "This is an awkward conversation."

"Well, now it is."

"Fine. Then what do you think of me?"

Gus paused to consider the question, then said, "I think you have okay taste in clothes."

Marjorie's mouth dropped open so wide that her back molars had their first real view of the world and were enamored of it. "Are you kidding me? That's all you have to say?" Marjorie crossed her arms over her chest and huffed like a child midtantrum.

"What? Are you mad? You're mad."

"I'm not mad. Because I don't care what you think."

"Really? But I'm so smart and funny and a champion of the underdog."

"Oh, my God! I hate you!"

Gus unleashed a throaty, rumbling laugh that she'd not heard before. Marjorie wasn't thrilled about the inspiration.

"I have an idea," he said. "Let's blow off the afternoon and do something fun."

"Together?"

"Yes. Together."

"Is this you proving that you're not uptight?"

"This is me deciding that we need to blow off steam."

"What about the other movies? I leave tomorrow morning. And you already screwed up one deal today. Shouldn't we see the rest before they screen?"

"There's only a few more. I can watch them first thing tomorrow."

"Whatever you say, boss."

"Don't call me that."

"Why?"

"Because." Gus navigated the car south down Highland toward the hotel. "Did you bring sneakers and workout clothes?"

"Of course!"

He looked skeptical. "I didn't peg you as a big exerciser."

"Oh, I bring cute workout gear on trips in case I wake up in time for a resort yoga class."

Gus rolled his eyes. "Of course you do. Anyway, wear them."

"Why? Where are we going?"

"On a hike up Runyon Canyon."

"Wait, what? I thought we were doing something fun!" Marjorie shook her head. "You have me confused with one of those hearty girls who like camping and . . . sticks. My idea of a trek is up subway steps— at Bryant Park, for a drink."

"We'll do something like that too, afterward. Trust me." Gus pulled up to the Orlando's valet. "Go change. I'll pick you up in fifteen."

"If I must," said Marjorie, her lazy muscles already protesting.

Because fifteen minutes was hardly ample, a half hour later Marjorie emerged back outside in '70s-style mini gym shorts, a tank top, Nike sneakers, and ankle socks, her hair pulled into a ponytail. Gus, who'd been leaning against the car's hood, looked her up and down, his eyes lingering on her exposed thighs. Suddenly self-conscious, she checked herself out in the glass door's reflection and, finding little fault, said, "What? Why are you looking at me like that?"

"No reason." He ducked inside the car. "Except you look like a Harlem Globetrotter in all that gear. Where are your sweat-bands?"

She climbed in too. "Funny. At least I don't look homeless." She poked a finger through a hole in the shoulder of Gus's worn Brown T-shirt, touching his bare skin. Once again, he recoiled like she was radioactive. And, she did have to admit, she felt a strange charge at her fingertip. Wasn't static electricity more of a winter thing?

The air between the duo held a heightened vibration; it filled the air-conditioning vents and black plastic cup holders. From the radio, NPR mumbled, barely audible. Gus and Marjorie held their collective breath, their minds racing without clear direction toward some unknown finish line.

Suddenly, a piercing noise rang out, startling them both. Marjorie gasped like some Victorian fainter.

"It's my phone, on the car's Bluetooth," Gus explained. "I don't why it's so loud. Do you mind if I . . . ?"

"Go ahead."

Gus pressed a button on the steering wheel. "Hello?"

"G-man!" Michael's voice, amplified but not otherwise worse for wear, blared from the car's speakers. "What's up?"

"Not much, Mike. I'm actually—"

"So what happened with the Hasidic director?"

"It's not the filmmaker who's Hasidic. It's the graffiti artist, but—"

"Whatever. How'd it go? Did you work that ole Rinehart magic?"

"Not . . . exactly."

"What?! What happened?"

"I'll explain, but what I'm trying—"

"What? I missed that. You cut out for a second."

"He's trying to tell you that I'm in the car," piped Marjorie. "So you don't say anything risqué."

Gus shook his head. "That's not why I wanted him to know you're here. I thought—"

"Morningblatt! Do you mind if I call you that? I know it's Fred's name for you, but it has a nice ring."

"Mind? I love it! How was Italy?"

"Bellissimo."

"Buono! I want to hear all about the food!"

"Oh, Madge. We went to this little place on a vineyard near the—"

Gus interrupted, irritated, "Can you girls play catch-up later? When I'm not on the phone? Or in the state?"

A whistle shot from the car's speakers. "Someone woke up on the wrong side of the bed."

"*Someone* always does," said Marjorie.

"Fuck, you guys are annoying! Can we talk later, Mike? We're obviously not getting anywhere now."

"Aren't you gonna tell him what happened with Danny?" Marjorie feigned innocence.

"We'll talk tonight."

"Wait!" said Michael. "Madge, did I hear that you're moving in with your stalker?"

"We gotta go," barked the grouch.

"But—"

"Bye."

Gus pressed the steering wheel's End button with force, like he was releasing a bomb.

"Well, that wasn't very polite." Marjorie smiled.

They arrived at Runyon shortly thereafter and spent twenty-five minutes looking for parking—pre-exercise road rage is what burns the most calories for Angelenos. Jockeying for spots did not boost Gus's mood. Up the mountain's initial incline, he stomped silently, as Marjorie struggled to keep up. *Moody much?*

He offered to buy her a water from an honor kiosk at the entrance, but she declined in protest of his attitude. She regretted the decision. It might have been temperate for July, but this was the desert. Dogs from Chihuahuas to Great Danes raced past in pursuit of owners, panting less than Marjorie. She almost tumbled more than once to her death as her untread sneakers slipped on rocks and dirt.

She stopped at a plateau to catch her breath. They had cleared the steepest part of the climb, but ahead was another hill. Her chest stung. She propped a hand on each hip.

"You okay?" Gus asked.

"Fine, fine, fine. Just. One. Minute."

Gus nodded, amused. Nothing like some Marjorie-style humiliation to cheer him up. As she mentally drafted her own obituary, a bleached blonde—with breasts that stood separately at attention without the help of a bra—sauntered by in high heels. The shirtless, steroid-addled former *Real World* contestant at her side was also unfazed. He flashed a forearm tattoo of a Chinese symbol that he thought meant "success" but actually translated to "vacuum cleaner."

"How are they doing that?" Marjorie croaked.

"They're probably out-of-work actors. It's their job to stay in shape."

"But why would anyone hike in stilettos?"

He shrugged. "They're on a date."

Marjorie's mouth, hanging open in hopes of catching extra oxygen, dropped wider. "Wait, seriously? People do this on *dates*?"

"Of course."

"But you get all sweaty."

"Not everyone thinks that's bad." Nodding toward the trail, he said, "Let's go. It gets easier. Promise."

As they crested the last hill to the lookout, Marjorie was calling him a liar. "Nothing about this. Is. Easy."

"I didn't say, easy. I said *easier.*"

With no stamina left for fighting, Marjorie held up a hand in protest. She walked to the edge of the ridge and bent at the waist, taking deep, labored breaths.

"Over here!" called Gus, climbing onto a bench, tilted back and raised for the best view of the city. Marjorie collapsed beside him, relieved.

He pulled his water from his pocket. "You want?"

Marjorie nodded, humbled. Cooling down, she looked out at the skyline. LA was laid in front of them: Downtown to the left, Santa Monica to the right, buildings topped with turquoise pools ahead. The day was clear; a thin line of navy blue ocean sat in the distance. She couldn't help but think of the mountain metaphor Gus had used months ago on Fred's stoop—about climbing to lookouts instead of one peak.

"Pretty, huh?" Gus smiled, then returned his gaze to the landscape.

Marjorie nodded. But she wasn't looking at the view. Gus hadn't struggled like she had, but the uphill hike had been a workout. His T-shirt clung to his chest and back. Always a bigger fan of a toned, slim build than huge muscles, she thought the cheesy *Real World* guy had nothing on him.

"How come you don't have a girlfriend?" she asked before she could censor herself.

He looked surprised. "Um, I don't know. I guess I haven't met the right person recently."

"But you go on dates?"

"Sure."

"How often?"

"Enough."

"How much is enough?"

"What are you, my mother?"

"No. I'm pretty sure I'm not your mother."

"So nosy," he chided. "Ready to get going?"

Marjorie leaned back onto the bench. "You're going to have to carry me."

"Don't worry; it's all downhill from here."

Marjorie unstuck her thighs from the bench. "Why do people use that expression like it's a bad thing?"

37

Marjorie's hotel room door was propped open; the maid had just begun cleaning. She pulled out her cell and dialed Gus's number.

"Hey, I have to come to your house to change."

"What? I just dropped you off. Why?"

"Because my room is being cleaned and I need to shower before dinner."

"Can't you wait?"

"Where, Gus? In the lobby?"

He sighed. "Okay, fine. It's the upper doorbell."

Marjorie walked the block to Gus's place with a bulging tote bag. She rang the bell and he opened the wooden door, barefoot in a T-shirt and jeans, hair damp from the shower. How in the world did men get dressed so quickly?

"I'm letting you in," he said, blocking her entrance to the apartment, "but my housekeeper has been on vacation in Poland for the last couple weeks, so don't judge."

"Fine." She waited; he didn't move. "Are you going to let me in or not?"

Reluctantly, Gus stepped back to reveal a cozy living room—not spare like his New York office. A comfortable couch sat atop an oriental rug, probably inherited from a relative; magazines and books were scattered about in stacks.

"Stop looking at everything like you're trying to figure me out."

"I'm not!" Marjorie examined a black-and-white photo of toddler Gus with his mother on a carousel. "So cute!"

He put his hands on her shoulders—apparently willing to touch her, if it meant moving her along—and marched her toward the hallway. "The bathroom is through here."

As Gus disappeared back into the living room, Marjorie opened the door to her left, which turned out to be the bedroom: wrong door. But that's where she discovered the real surprise. It was bedlam—a total mess. Laundry tumbled from an overstuffed basket. The bed was unmade. A desk in the corner was piled so high with scripts and DVDs that no one could possibly have worked at it in years, let alone days.

"Oh, my God!" she exclaimed with delight. "You're human!"

"That's not the bathroom!" He rushed over and slammed the door.

"Too late, Gus. The secret's out: You're a horrible slob! And I feel it's my duty to torture you about it."

"I don't know if the word 'horrible' is appropriate."

"But 'slob' is, for sure."

Gus looked up at the ceiling's scalloped moldings, as if asking a higher power for mercy. "All right, fine. The secret is out. And the bathroom is in there." He crossed to a built-in cupboard and rotated a latch—stiff with white paint—to reveal linens. Some were folded, presumably by his housekeeper or an ex-girlfriend; the rest formed misshapen piles. He tossed a towel to Marjorie, who caught it, just. "Now, for the love of God, get in the shower and stop giving me shit."

"Fine, but water won't wash away this knowledge."

The French blue–tiled bathroom was clean, save two empty shampoo bottles that lined the tub's porcelain ridges. Marjorie resisted the urge to snoop in the medicine cabinet for possible Magnum XL condoms or telltale medications (herpes cream, antipsychotics, Rogaine). She wound her hair into a bun, so it wouldn't get wet, and turned on the shower. Stepping under the stream, she closed her eyes and relaxed her posture. The water ran down her shoulders. She sighed, content.

Then, suddenly, alarm bells went off in her head.

Marjorie's eyes popped open. She looked at her feet, submerged in pooled water at the tub's bottom. She was in LA, in a strange bathroom, far from everything she knew and loved. Once she climbed on a plane the next morning and flew back to real life, she would once again be unemployed. She had no financial security, no plans. She should have been panicked, but instead she felt better than she had in ages. *Why?*

In her defense, life was falling back into place. If she moved in with Mac, she wouldn't have to worry about paying rent. So there was no great rush to find full-time work. Plus, she'd proved herself employable. She was back on speaking terms with her best friends, whom she'd live close to again in Manhattan.

But it was those "reassuring" facts that made her uneasy.

Barbara Plum often suggested envisioning one's "happy place" to find peace and direction. To Marjorie's surprise, when she closed her eyes, her little room on the second floor of Fred's apartment came to mind. She saw the streets of Carroll Gardens, the old Italian men sitting in straining folding chairs, biscotti, meatballs, Roberta's garden, and her roommate's funny hats and beat-up guitars. In the midst of the chaos, Brooklyn had become her home.

She had to speed things up. How long had she been contemplating her existence, while Gus stood outside, wondering why she was lagging? She picked up his soap, something generic and milky green from the drugstore, maybe Irish Spring, something boys use.

She needed to finish up, calm down and get out. *This is a shower curtain with a world map on it: Peru, Texas, Canada. That is the scar on my knee from when I fell off a swing. That's Gus's phone ringing, the murmur of his conversation, too distant to decipher. That's the sound of his voice, upbeat. That is Gus. I like Gus. Oh, God. Oh, no. I like Gus!*

It was time to face the truth: Against all odds, this new life had grown on Marjorie. Change had busted its way in and, when her back was turned and eyes were shut, it had made itself at home. Why did that feel like a betrayal? And of whom or what?

There was Mac, of course, whom she'd "tamed." What about their life together, so like the one she'd unconsciously envisioned since her teenage years? What about Pickles, Vera, and her mother and the Marjorie they expected her to be?

And what about Gus? Her *boss,* who lived in California, who might not like her *like that,* who recoiled at her touch, who watched C-SPAN, who might have antipsychotics in his medicine cabinet, and who definitely had a surly disposition. What about Gus, in whose shower she now stood, *naked,* in every sense of the word? Too many unknowns.

"Marjorie!" he called above the din of water, at that moment, like he knew. "You almost out? I want to tell you something."

Just a wooden slab with hinges separated them. She could picture his hand on the knob; one twist and he'd open the door and see her through the transparent plastic. She sensed his closeness like a buzzing. She had to get it together. Gus couldn't read her thoughts, she reminded herself. There was still time to salvage her old life, escape, do the right thing.

"Yeah, one sec!"

"No problem." His footsteps faded away.

Marjorie finished, facing into the stream so water pinged her cheeks and forehead. She stepped out and dried off, then searched for her bag of clothing. *Shoot!* She'd left it in the living room. Minutes before, retrieving it might have been mildly awkward, deflected with a joke. But now Marjorie had tasted that Garden of Eden apple.

She had two options: She could ask Gus to pass the tote through the cracked door, which seemed strangely intimate, or she could act nonchalant and march into the living room in her towel. *Just grab the bag.*

Letting her hair drop to her shoulders, she looked at her reflection in the mirror for solidarity, then tucked the towel securely around her chest. At the door, she took a deep breath and reminded herself to act normal. *What was* normal *again?*

Marjorie stepped through the hallway into the living room. "Hey!" she said too loudly. "Just grabbing my bag, no big deal." (Nothing like saying "no big deal" to make something a big deal.)

Her bag sat two feet from where Gus leaned against the doorframe at the kitchen's entrance. *Of course.* He looked up from his iPhone, flushed, and looked back down. He seemed not to know where to rest his eyes. "Oh, I—you're in a towel. Which is fine because I gave you that towel . . . to use. Not to keep."

"You think I'm going to steal your towel?" Marjorie hadn't accounted for Gus's discomfort when she opted to feign poise; it had clearly been the wrong choice. Under much less inappropriate circumstances, Gus maintained strict professional boundaries.

"No. Just—you were in there for a while. I thought you might be dressed."

"Nope. Not dressed."

He held her gaze for a beat. "Not dressed."

Never had Marjorie been more aware of her nakedness under a swath of terry cloth. "Um. My bag is right there." She pointed.

"Oh." He looked down at it but didn't move. "Did you want me to—?"

"No, no, no. I'll grab it." She tiptoed to within a foot of him, feeling his eyes on her as she kneeled. The bag's handles had, of course, gotten tangled inside the bundle of clothing and toiletries—lavender shea butter lotion, calendula toner, pink underwear.

"You said you had something to tell me?" Marjorie peered up at Gus, desperate for normalcy. The sun shone through the window onto his face, emphasizing its angles.

He swallowed, hard. "Yeah, good news. Danny called. He wants us to distribute the film, at least internationally. He looked us up online and said we seem like the best fit."

"Oh, my God!" Marjorie forgot her discomfort and stood, beaming. "You're kidding? That's amazing!" Without thinking, she clasped his hands. "Gus! We did it!"

For once, he didn't flinch. Instead, he stood still, eyelids half lowered, gaze steady. "Actually, *you* did it. You were the deciding factor. Danny said he could tell that you were not only smart and, of course, from Brooklyn, but that you genuinely cared."

"Well, that's sweet, but I'm sure it wasn't me." She dropped her hands to her sides.

"It was you," Gus said. "Seems he's got a little crush."

"Imagine that."

"I can't."

"Hey!" Marjorie shoved his shoulder.

He gave her a lazy, cool half grin that would trail her for years to follow and pop into her head at unexpected moments like a surprise. "A *big* crush, on the other hand. Now that I get."

It happened so fast. The tension between them, Marjorie reasoned, had to be defused. Otherwise, the apartment's gas appliances, the pressure cooker, the BBQ's propane tank would surely have combusted in mass stainless steel wreckage. This was a public service for the safety of Gus's neighbors.

Time and space suspended their regular rules. The air thickened, charged and inevitable. As Gus drew close, Marjorie saw fragments of herself in his eyes, and sunlight, white splotches that persisted behind her lids once she closed them. He kissed her hesitantly, his lips a question mark against her own. But soon that propriety transformed to urgency, an exclamation. As she pressed against him, the balls of her feet pushed away the uneven wooden floor, osmosing its history in the Braille-like ridges against her skin. She slipped her hands under his shirt, following the crease up the path of his spine. He slid his palms behind her head, then down her still damp back and sides, tracing a nonsensical route, the long way home. He lifted her closer. And the thread of the story was lost in a jumbled tangent of terry cloth and skin.

It wasn't until the towel threatened to completely fall away that Marjorie's higher consciousness returned. Slowly, reluctantly, she remembered the existence of phones and planes and clocks, daylight streaming through the window, offering no cover. *This is not okay.* Her bare limbs felt so right against Gus's skin and rough jeans, this version of him a happy surprise. But she had to stop.

Pulling away was like stepping from a warm bath onto a cold tile floor. It took Gus a moment to realize what was happening, his expression dazed. But then he stepped back, raising his hands in surrender like she was holding a gun on him, like this was a *stickup*. And she felt depressed as his face clouded with concern. "I'm sorry. I'm—I thought you—"

"No, I do. It's just . . . Mac."

"Right. Mac." Gus's arms fell to his sides. "Your not so imaginary friend, who you're moving in with."

"That's the guy." She tightened the towel across her chest.

Gus's hair was ruffled; his T-shirt sat askew across his shoulders, riding up on one side. Marjorie's own hands had traversed that territory moments before, had displaced that shirt. She wanted to reach out again, prove that she'd been there. He rubbed the back of his neck, his head dropping toward the floor, a habit, she now realized, she found adorable. He looked up at her, hangdog, "I'm not that creepy boss, right? 'Cause that's my worst nightmare. To make you feel uncomfortable—"

"Oh, God, no. Please don't think that. Really, really, really. You could never be that guy, even if you tried."

"Good." He shot her a hint of a smile. "So, what now?"

"Um, I think maybe we should talk. Is that the worst idea ever? Am I *that* girl now?"

"That girl only exists in opposition to *that* guy, who doesn't give a shit but wants to keep sleeping with her."

"Don't say perfect things like that or I'll have to walk back over and let the towel drop this time."

"Don't say things like *that* unless you mean them."

They stared at each other.

Gus cleared his throat. "I sort of can't believe I'm saying this, but why don't you go get dressed? Then we can hash this out."

Marjorie nodded and bent to grab her bag, now dumped out at her feet. Standing, she caught her towel just before it fell, once again. Gus groaned, throwing a hand over his eyes. "Can you just put on some clothes?"

She couldn't help smiling.

Back in the bathroom, Marjorie threw on her outfit in record time. So much so that a drill sergeant at West Point felt a jolt of inexplicable joy.

She emerged in jean shorts and a sheer T-shirt. Gus was waiting on the couch. He looked up, a pained expression on his face. "Don't you have a snowsuit or something you could put on?"

"Sorry. It's summer."

"So it is."

Marjorie settled next to him. "So, so, so."

"That's a well-articulated point. Everything's much clearer now."

"I don't want you to feel responsible for what happened. This is all my doing."

He raised an eyebrow. "It is?"

"I mean, you haven't even wanted to hang out with me."

"What? Why do you think that?"

"Two nights ago, you ran away when I kissed your cheek." She was embarrassed just thinking about it. "And last night, you disinvited me from dinner."

"Marjorie. That's crazy. That isn't what happened."

"Then what did?"

"You surprised me with the kiss, sure. But that was encouraging. And last night I really did have another obligation."

"But you got so weird when you left the screening room."

Gus sighed. "The morning after dinner with Benny, you seemed angry. I thought you were behaving 'professionally' because I'd been somehow inappropriate. And last night, one of my best friends, who I never see, called to say he was in town. I would have included you, but he's having marital problems and needed to vent. And I wanted to get advice from him . . . about you."

Marjorie's eyes widened. "About *me*?" She tucked her legs underneath her and leaned an elbow on the back of the couch. "What about me?"

Gus pinched the bridge of his nose, willing himself to think clearly. He exhaled and looked at her. "I've had some . . . weird feelings for you since the night we met at Fred's."

"Weird feelings?" She smiled.

"Just shut up and listen, okay? I met you, I liked you. I haven't liked anyone in a long time. And you seemed single, if not slightly unhinged.

Mac showing up was a wrinkle, but I didn't think you were together. I knew you needed a job, so *I* suggested hiring you—not Mike, by the way."

"But you treated me like an idiot, like you resented my being at the office!"

"You acted like one, walking in with attitude."

"I did not!"

"Well, it seemed that way to me. And then"—he looked at his lap—"you barely remembered our conversation. I guess I was a little offended." He raised his eyes to meet hers. "Because it meant something to me."

Marjorie started to protest, but he raised hand to silence her, as he continued. "Anyway, I thought we were getting along better. When you left the job at the end of the week, I planned to ask you out. But then Mac picked you up at two A.M. and called you 'Madgesty . . .'" Gus grimaced. "I got the picture. So I kept my distance. I was trying to behave." He gestured to the spot where they'd kissed minutes before. "Now I guess I broke some kind of guy code."

"So then why invite me on this trip?"

"You turned out to be good at the job, really good. Since anything romantic was off the table, I figured I might as well get you some experience and me some help. It didn't go quite how I expected."

"That's for sure." Marjorie was distracted by Gus's hand inches from her knee. He smelled like something good: suntan lotion? coconuts? that soap?

"The more time we spent together, the more I liked you, despite your being a royal pain the ass and a pathetic hiker. I didn't think you felt the same way. I'm still not sure?"

She sighed. "I think I was in denial. Until I was in your shower."

"And I'm only human. You walked out in that little towel, which incidentally I'll never see the same way—"

"You gave me that towel!"

"I didn't know you were going to parade around in it! Then you got all excited about the movie thing. What's a guy to do?"

Marjorie felt a pang of guilt, though she wasn't sure toward which man. "I'm sorry."

"Please. Don't be. I'm not sorry. I hate the idea of you feeling that way . . . about this."

"You know, you have a funny way of showing that you like me. I said all those nice things about you in the car this morning and you keep calling me 'special'—and making fun of me."

Gus lifted a ringlet up off Marjorie's shoulder and yanked it softly. "I happen to think you're brilliant, sweet, beautiful, funny, and totally infuriating. In that order."

Before either realized, they were leaning in again, their lips millimeters apart. This time, Gus pulled back. "Okay. I can't fucking take this. We need to talk about that stupid boyfriend of yours or I need to leave."

"This is your house."

"I know." Gus rested his elbows on his lap and buried his head in his hands. "What if I take you to Dan Tana's?" he said, voice muffled. "No pressure. We'll talk, safely. In a public place. It's early. We should get a table without a wait."

She nodded. "I'm kind of hungry. And by that I mean I need a drink."

"Good. Let's go. Before I lose my mind."

Marjorie threw on lip gloss and collected her belongings, feeling intermittently sublime and wretched, and she and Gus left and walked to the car. They were about to pull out of the driveway, when he realized he'd forgotten his phone.

"Slob," she teased.

He ran upstairs, leaving the car running, as Marjorie waited in the passenger seat. Outside, the blue sky was infinite. The temperature would soon drop. Could she get used to cool summer evenings, when the heat disappeared with the sun?

Marjorie's thoughts turned to Mac, three thousand miles away and three hours later, maybe at the bar trading jabs with his friends, expecting her home the next day. Was this a childish dalliance on her part, a relationship panic, or was she really looking for something different?

For distraction, she e-mailed Belinda:

Coming home tomorrow, Belly! Can't wait to see the first real draft on Sunday. xo Madge.

Just then, Gus's cell phone rang from the car's speakers like an alarm, startling her. He'd left the Bluetooth on, and it was still connecting from inside the apartment. She searched for an Off button, but nothing on the dashboard looked right.

"Hello?" Gus's voice projected, clear as day.

"Hey G-Man."

"Mike. What's up, dude?"

"Got your message. Why do you sound so chipper?"

"Oh. 'Cause we got that movie, looks like. The filmmaker wants to sign with us."

"That's awesome! Good fucking job."

What choice did Marjorie have but to eavesdrop? She couldn't vacate a running car.

"It was our girl, actually. He loved Marjorie. Thought she was great and trusted her."

"You were right from the beginning. She's smart. We should keep her." There was silence on Gus's end of the line. "G-Man? You still there?"

"Yeah, I'm here."

"What do you think? Should we offer her the full-time gig?"

Marjorie was thrilled. They thought she was good! She was going to have a job!

"Uh. I don't think so."

Her heart sank. Was Gus kidding? She waited for a punch line.

"I don't get it. Why not?" asked Michael.

"It's not the best fit. She probably wouldn't stay for the long haul."

"But she made this deal."

"Yeah, because he had a crush on her. I just don't see this as her future."

It was like being slapped. Marjorie listened as Michael reluctantly agreed not to hire her. Then she zoned out, numb. They said their good-byes and clicked off.

Robotically, she pushed the car door open, climbed out, and started walking, as Gus jogged outside. He looked from the humming car to his former passenger. "Hey Marjorie! Where are you going?"

She stopped but didn't turn to face him. "To bed."

"It's six thirty. What about Dan Tana's?"

"I'm not in the mood anymore."

"I don't understand. What happened?" His voice broke, tugging at her heart, and she hated him even more for that. She turned to face him. "What happened is that the Bluetooth is on in your car."

"Yeah?" She watched him, waiting for recognition to set in. He winced. "Ah. You heard me talking to Mike."

"Yeah, Gus. I did."

He stepped toward her. "Marjorie, you don't understand."

"Actually, I do. You think I only got that deal because of how I look." She felt sick.

"No. Not at all."

"Really? 'Cause it sure sounded that way when you told Michael not to hire me."

"I just don't think we should work together. There are better things you could—"

"Gus, even if that's true, even if what you want is for us to be together, your solution is to sacrifice my credibility? God forbid you risk tarnishing your own image!"

He rubbed at the back of his neck. "I'm sorry. I panicked. We haven't talked about anything yet. You have a boyfriend. I don't know how much you want people to know. And it isn't just about us working together. I think you have other talents that—"

Marjorie was enraged. "What about asking what *I* want? I need to support myself! If this had happened months from now, it would have been bad, but at least we'd have had a foundation. This was already an impossible situation. Now . . ." She turned to leave.

"Marjorie, wait! Let's talk about this. I'll call Mike back right now and explain. You can have the job. It's not even close to too late."

"Actually, Gus, it's entirely too late." Marjorie trudged back to the hotel, leaving Gus standing on the street alone.

38

The woman behind Virgin America's check-in counter studied Marjorie's ticket. "This is for tomorrow morning."

"I know. I'd like to fly standby tonight instead."

"Let me see what I can do." She pressed some buttons on her keyboard. "In a rush to get home?"

"In a rush to get out of here."

Marjorie had tried to relax at the hotel. She'd stared unseeing at the Olympic opening ceremonies in London on TV, then wept as torch-wielding athletes ran into the stadium past its brick and mortar builders, who wore hard hats and suits.

She was devastated—about losing Gus, betraying Mac, compromising her self-respect. She wanted to go home. She could not have understood, because Gus barely did himself, that years of helping his mother through bouts of "the black dog" (her pet name for depression) had taught him to take the reins and make decisions for others. Even as Marjorie packed her bags and headed for the airport, he sat slumped on his couch, deflated and bewildered. In neglecting to consult Marjorie about her own future, he had exorcised himself from it.

Once through security, Marjorie stopped to grab pretzels and water for the flight. By the souvenir shop's register sat an impulse buy basket of rubber bracelets imprinted with words, the kind Belinda had mentioned liking. Marjorie chose a French blue one for her that read DREAM. Just imagining the kid's glee at receiving it bolstered her.

She had time to kill at the gate. She examined an unfamiliar mole on her arm and wondered if she had cancer. She scanned e-mails on her phone. Barack Obama's campaign was asking for a donation, pleading: *Marjorie, time is running out!*

You can say that again. But for what?

Nothing from Gus. He hadn't tried to explain himself. It was probably for the best.

Belinda had responded. Marjorie felt lifted at the prospect of hearing the latest in her prepubescent saga: Had she chosen the bulldog, after all?

Marjorie clicked on the e-mail. It opened. She read the message, then read it again and again and again before her brain would absorb its meaning:

Ms. Plum (If that is truly your name),

Please do <u>NOT</u> e-mail, call, or otherwise attempt to contact our daughter, Belinda, ever again. We recently discovered that you are not who you claim to be and are not associated with Write Her Tutoring or any other scholastic enterprise.

We're not sure what kind of <u>twisted</u> person pretends to be a <u>tutor/mentor</u> and dupes a <u>defenseless</u> child (who had come to admire you for mostly <u>superficial</u> and reprehensible traits that a <u>responsible</u> parent could hardly view as positive). Are you pleased with yourself?

We've come to understand from cursory Internet research that you're a former PR executive with nil integrity and a history of mental illness. As for the money, keep it to finance your next <u>rehab</u> stint.

Do not under <u>ANY</u> circumstances contact us again or risk police/legal action.

Harriet & Dinah Porter-Levinson

Marjorie stopped breathing, for real this time. *This is a metal chair connected to a row. This is me, a fraud, caught in a lie, in an airport, but going nowhere.* No amount of orientation was going to help. She gasped.

She was drowning in shame. How bizarre and frightening she must seem to these two mothers, trying to do right by their kid in a world full of threats from diseases to pedophiles, from tsunamis to car crashes—where disturbed young men shoot up movie theaters and politicians spout about the "sanctity of marriage," then sext pictures of their genitals and swap fluids with underage boys in public restrooms. How destructive of Marjorie to come into their lives and misrepresent herself, making them even less trustful. Poor Belinda was probably on lockdown.

What kind of person had Marjorie become? She'd done something she'd be too ashamed to tell even her parents, her best friends. Why had she misrepresented herself that first day instead of finding a sensible solution? Why had she continued to omit the truth?

She was upset at being exposed; nobody enjoys a threat of "police action." But more than that, the letter—an articulation of what she'd done—put the act into perspective and made it concrete. Through her own carelessness, her unwillingness to take responsibility for her choices, she'd lost Belinda, with whom she'd developed a true bond, who understood more about life at eleven years old than Marjorie did at twenty-eight.

The devastation set in, hot and heavy. Marjorie curled over her lap, almost sinking to the floor. She'd had promise, hadn't she, once upon a time? That's what everyone said. But then so did the suburban prom queen, passenger in a car that smells like stagnation, her taffeta mall dress ripping at the seams, where she is already starting to spread.

How could anyone still believe in her? That's when Marjorie remembered Fred. *Fred, Fred, Fred.* Shit! She had to call and explain what she'd done, so her friend could get ahead of the narrative with her tutoring employer. What would Fred think? Would she tell Michael? Would he tell Celeste? Would they tell *Gus*?

Marjorie took as deep a breath as possible, more of an accordion's wheeze, and dialed. It was late in New York. Fred might not answer.

The phone rang once. Then again. Then one more time.

"Hello."

"Fred! Oh, thank God I caught you. Do you have a second?"

"I guess."

"I don't know how to say this. I—I did something . . . bad. And it affects you."

"It would have been nice if you'd thought of that before." The pixie's voice was tinny: no chirps or twitters, flat affect. Marjorie was too late. She swiped at a wisp of hair that had fallen into her eyes, blurring her sight. "Write Her called me yesterday," Fred continued. "I know you pretended to work for them."

"Oh, Jesus, Fred. I'm so sorry. I went there that first day planning to tell the truth, but then, I don't know what happened. I never explained. I know it sounds pathetic."

"It does. And *insane.* I can't lie, Marjorie. I'm not a master manipulator like you."

"Fred, I—"

"No. Let me say something. Because I'm so incredibly mad at you. That job was my primary source of income." Marjorie cringed, as Fred's voice rose. "So I have every right to feel this way."

"I know. Of course you do."

"But more than anything, I'm *worried,* Marjorie. Because this was a really weird thing to do. You always say I'm open-minded: If you had told me that you never explained the situation that first day, I would have understood. Hell, I probably would have lent you cash, if you needed it. I saw you cracking under the weight of your crumbling world. That's why I welcomed you into my house, my life, and tried to help."

"You were amazing and generous from the start. I don't know what's wrong with me."

"Me neither." There was a pause. "We spent all this time together and you never mentioned a thing. I think maybe you need help."

"Fred. I hear you. I probably do need a psychiatrist or like a whole panel of therapists. But this was an anomaly. This isn't who I *am*."

"I don't think you know who you are. And as long as you straddle two identities and act passive about your life, you'll never figure it out." Fred sighed. "Honestly, I almost called your mother."

"My mother?"

"To keep this hidden, to be deceptive in that way? It's destructive. I just—I can't have that around me right now."

Marjorie's stomach dropped. "You want me to move out."

A silence. "I guess so, yeah. I don't know what else to do. I don't have the answer."

Marjorie willed her voice to stay steady. "Okay." What else was there to say? She couldn't blame Fred. She'd acted unstable, horrible.

"I gotta go."

"Okay." They each hesitated, as an announcement came over the airport loudspeaker: *Flight 852 to Cairo is now boarding.* Marjorie wished she could hop on board and disappear. "Fred, I am really sorry."

"Yeah. I'm sure you are."

Marjorie's eyes brimmed with—she knew *unearned*—tears, about to crest the ridge and flood her cheeks. She'd lost Belinda, Fred, even Gus, and, worst, the new life she'd come to love. And it was her fault; she'd taken it all for granted.

The boarding process began. On the redeye, she couldn't sleep; she was too uncomfortable. She didn't touch her pretzels, read her book, or watch TV. And when the flight landed early the next morning, she shuffled like a zombie toward baggage claim. The recycled air had sucked her dry: skin, throat, eyes.

At the taxi stand, the dispatcher asked where she was headed. She hesitated for so long that he prompted: "Manhattan? Brooklyn? The Bronx?" as if she needed a menu.

There was only one place left to go.

39

Marjorie rang the doorbell and waited, her suitcase beside her like a pewter bodyguard. She heard footsteps, and then the door swung open to reveal Mac in a T-shirt and boxer briefs, sleep written across his face.

He welcomed her with a sardonic smile. "Look who's here."

They had been together for over a month now, and yet she still felt like she was arriving for an illicit one-night stand.

"Look who."

"You're a sight for sore eyes. Or . . . is it an eyesore? I can never remember which is a good thing."

"I think I'm supposed to be a respite for your sore eyes."

He grinned. "I missed you, smarty." He leaned across the threshold and planted a kiss on her lips. "Actually, I *really* missed you."

"You were lying the first time?"

"I didn't realize how much." He opened the door wide. "Come on in. I didn't expect you until tonight."

"I was ready to come home." She grabbed her bag (since he didn't) and dragged it inside. She watched him pull a bottle of Advil from a kitchen cabinet. "Rough night?"

"John wants me to invest in this spiced rum company. It's pretty good with pineapple juice. Too good."

"Of course you like it. It's sweet."

"I like you and you're not sweet."

"No, I'm not. I'm disgusting. Plane, heat, ugh." Marjorie slipped off her shoes and collapsed on the couch with a thud. It was impossible to relax in this room with its sharp angles.

"What?" he called.

"Nothing."

Mac returned and sat down beside her, leaning back against the couch. "So, you've been a little . . . I wanna say *freaked-out* lately, not to put words in your articulate mouth."

Marjorie was taken aback. So he had noticed. "Oh, you know me." She waved him off.

"Yeah. I do." Mac had no intention of dismissing the topic. He let the silence compel her to answer. Was this a skill born of countless interventions for his sister?

Despite the context, it felt good to be known. Marjorie picked at the frayed wrist of her sweatshirt. "This has seen better days. Days, days, days."

"Ah. The nervous repetitive tic. Now I know you're stalling."

She exhaled. "Fine. You win. I guess maybe I've been a little . . . unsure."

"Ha! I knew it!"

She looked at him, surprised.

"*What?* I did."

"You seem oddly cheerful about it."

"I'm new to this relationship thing and, I'm just saying, I was right." He shrugged. "Plus, someone is freaking out and it's not me."

Marjorie laughed, despite herself. Only Mac O'Shea could turn a glitch into a personal success, spin straw into gold. She shoved him lightly and he caught her hand.

"Look, don't worry. I'm not bringing up the moving in thing again. I learned my lesson."

Marjorie felt drowsy. She tipped her head onto his shoulder and closed her eyes, as she had a hundred times since they were children. It was so comfortable.

"Hey Mac," she murmured. He smelled faintly of some expensive, sporty men's cologne. His arm slid around her; his hand rubbed her shoulder. "About our cohabitation, the invitation still stands?"

"Sure." The word vibrated through him, lulling her further.

"Then I accept."

"Oh, yeah?" She could feel Mac smile, his muscles contracting. "Okay, then."

She opened her eyes and peered up at him. "I missed you, stupid."

"Good to know, Madgesty."

As she settled her head onto his lap, he murmured, "Hey, while you're down there . . ." She smacked him and he snickered, as she fell into a dreamless sleep.

A decision made in haste and out of desperation is not well-endured.

Marjorie woke up a couple hours later on the couch to a shrill call from her mother that she ignored. As she rubbed her eyes, she remembered her conversation with Mac and her first impulse was to flee.

The shower was running. She cracked the door. "Mac! Just running out!"

Steam escaped. "Where to?" he called back.

Good question. "Um, coffee."

"You can use my espresso machine."

"Too lazy."

"I can do it for you when I'm out?"

"No, I want an iced half-caff cappuccino . . . with vanilla. Too complicated." She'd never had anything of the kind.

"Mmm. Sounds good. Get me one too!"

Outside, a bus belched exhaust; she breathed it in like sweet country air. She wasn't sure whom she felt more upset about betraying: Mac or herself? She just felt off.

Fumbling for her phone, Marjorie called the one person to whom she could confess without judgment. "Pickles? It's me."

"Oh, honey bunch," she cooed after Marjorie imparted the story, along with fresh tears. "That is tricky to say the least."

"Obviously, I need to tell Mac about Gus."

"No you don't."

"I don't? Are you sure?"

"If there's one thing I'm positive about, it's that. Telling him would only make him insecure. And an insecure Mac O'Shea sounds ugly. And like it might involve strippers."

"True."

"This was a one-time thing. Was it not?"

"No. I mean, yes. Gus and I are not an option."

Pickles paused. "Are you choosing Mac because Gus is not an option or because you want Mac?"

Marjorie shook her head. "I don't know. I'm not sure if I'm panicked about moving in with Mac or if . . . there's a lot going on. What do you think?"

"Oh, Madge, you know I can't answer that. Maybe it's not coincidental that this happened after Mac asked you to shack up. You could be afraid of a good thing?"

"So you think I just panicked?" Marjorie felt relieved. She was off the hook. She could write this off as a blip, return to her old life with Mac, be happy.

"I don't know. I've been watching you and Mac circle each other for years. When you finally took the plunge, I never thought you'd be the one to panic. But if this Gus guy—"

"Let's not talk about Gus." Marjorie spotted a coffee shop and headed across the street. She needed to get Mac that vanilla drink she'd invented—what was it again? "Let's talk about you: Actually, can you tell me how you knew that you wanted to marry Steve?"

"Me? Well, obviously, we fell in love. But also I guess I knew he could give me the life that *I* wanted, not my mother or anyone else. Everyone said I was too young and crazy, but I knew." Marjorie heard the squeak of a rocking chair; maybe Pickles was nursing. "Make sure your choices are your own, love, or you'll never be happy."

It occurred to Marjorie for the first time that Pickles's early

marriage and neurotic obsession with her children was in opposition
to her own upbringing. She'd come of age recklessly because her
parents had not bothered to *parent*. In a show of bravery and self-
knowledge, she chose something different; she opted for structure
and kale. Suddenly, Marjorie not only forgave Pickles for her ser-
mons on raw food and cloth diapers, but she respected them. (She'd
still avoid that mommy group, though. Those women terrified her.)

"Thanks, P." Marjorie pulled the door to the coffee shop open; air-
conditioning gusted out.

"Look, Madge, you may not want to hear it, but I think you and
this Gus guy—"

"Oh! There's Vera by the scones!" Marjorie would have done anything to stop Pickles from finishing that sentence, but she really did
spot her former roommate by the bakery display right then. "Gotta
go! Call you later."

"Wait! Vera is—" cried Pickles. But Marjorie had already hung
up and was waving to her old friend.

Vera didn't seem to see her. "Vera! Vee!" It wasn't until Marjorie
was within a couple feet that she realized Vera was not alone. Brian
drooped at her side like a slug. "Oh. Hi."

Vera shot her an icy look. "Oh. It's you."

"Yeah. I'm—what are you doing here?"

"We live around the corner. What are *you* doing here?"

"I'm just coming from Mac's. This is where you moved? I thought
you hated Meatpacking and thought it was cheesy?"

"I hate a lot of things. This neighborhood isn't one."

"Okay . . ."

"So, Mac sent you out for his coffee?" Vera smirked at Brian, who
grunted back.

Marjorie lowered her voice to a whisper, out of Brian's range.
"Vee, I don't understand. Why are you acting like we're not friends? I
thought we were okay."

"I'm not *acting*, Marjorie."

The words stung. So that was all it took: Vera was back on Brian's short, fat arm. Maybe she was embarrassed at having confessed the details of his philandering, then taken him back. Who knew? Either way, the bonding session at Pickles's house had been a temporary fix. For Marjorie, it had only underlined their disparate values, anyway.

"I better go," Marjorie said.

"Hear your master calling?" Vera laughed, a single sharp chord, then she and Brain left without a backward glance.

Marjorie left soon after too, stunned, without coffee. She was upset; she'd wasted valuable time chasing a relationship with someone unworthy while she took people like Fred for granted.

Her friendship with Vera was dead; the old Vera mourned months, even years, before. The buddy Marjorie missed—with whom she'd shared secrets and hugs like sisters—no longer existed. Sometimes what once seemed lifelong proves changeable and, finally, disposable.

40

This was the never-ending day. Back at the apartment, Marjorie found Mac lying in bed, messing around on his iPad. He looked up for a moment, then back at the screen.

"No coffee?"

"Sorry. They didn't have what we wanted."

"Ah. Too bad. Maybe I can figure out how to make it here."

"Mac, I have to tell you something," she began.

"Shoot."

"Can you put that down for a second and listen to me?"

Mac raised an eyebrow and put the device down. "Done, Miss Plum."

"I have to confess . . ." She steeled herself. "I got Fred fired." The words were hard to fathom even as they emerged from her lips. "The truth is, I can't go back to Fred's. I pretended to be her and took over a tutoring job of hers. The company and the parents found out. She's not speaking to me and they threatened legal action."

"Why?"

"Why did I do it?"

"No. Why would they sue you for tutoring their kid?"

"I guess because . . . I don't know."

"Did you do the work?"

"Of course."

"Well, then they're overreacting." He patted a spot next to him on the bed; she sat. "Everyone makes mistakes. It's just blown out of proportion. Fred will get over it."

"You think?" As Mac rubbed her back, Marjorie tried to appreciate his support, but she couldn't help judging him for not judging her more harshly. She'd done something pathological and strange—betrayed people she cared about, people who took care of her, whom she would now perhaps never see again. Yet he was prepared to forgive and forget without question. What did that say about her? What did that say about *him*?

"So, that's it," she said. "You can go back to reading . . . whatever that is."

"Reading?"

"On your iPad. Was it *The New York Times*? Is there election news?"

"Oh!" he gestured to the device. "No. I only read the sports page, if anything. I was playing Words With Friends."

Everything hung in the balance. The world spun wildly with potential change, threatening to propel itself from its axis, its inhabitants at once threatened and emboldened by climate change, global economic collapse, unemployment, terrorists, civil liberties, education, Medicare, Social Security, scientific innovation, women's reproductive rights, gay marriage, gerrymandering, military defense, war, taxes for services, taxes that no one wanted to pay. Greece—an entire country—was rendered a cautionary tale. US citizens were buying guns, selling stocks, blaming George W. Bush, blaming President

Obama, blaming Wall Street, blaming a CIA conspiracy and little green men. People from trailer parks to mansions bit their nails in fear of too little income, of winding up on the street (or a less pretty street, as the case may be). America as a superpower seemed to hang in the balance. But Mac O'Shea didn't bother to follow the news.

He picked his iPad back up and resumed playing.

Who the hell was this guy, whom Marjorie might eventually marry? She knew his dignified profile, his unintentionally austere posture. She'd spent years watching him clown during Human Sexuality seminars and breeze through Precalculus pop quizzes with the answers in his back pocket like the entitled boys before him. She'd seen him try not to cough from a first Marlboro Medium cigarette and get too drunk at a first teenage house party. But who was he *really*?

He tugged on his ear. Suddenly, she found the habit so irksome that she wanted to rip the lobe off and throw it across the room.

That was when she noticed. Maybe the timing was coincidental. Or maybe an atomic shift caught her attention. Whatever it was, Marjorie glanced at Mac's screen and noticed a pop-up ad, which he clicked closed to reveal a Web site: Unscramble.com. He reviewed his tiles, typed in the letters, pressed Enter, and waited while they rearranged themselves into viable words.

Marjorie hadn't caught Mac with another woman, stealing cash, or shooting intravenous drugs. He hadn't done much of anything. And yet she was outraged.

"You're cheating," she said, her tone acid.

"What? At the game? No I'm not."

"Yeah, Mac. *You are.* You're using that Web site to find words. If that's not cheating, then what the hell is?"

"Whoa. First of all, *calm down.*"

"Don't tell me to calm down! It's condescending."

"*I'm* condescending?" He smirked and returned to his game.

"Hey! Wipe that self-satisfied look off your face."

He looked up, surprised. "What the fuck is your problem? Why are you starting with me?"

"My problem is that you're a cheater—to your core. Cheater, cheater, cheater. Sorry if I don't respect that."

"Because of Words With Friends?"

"You can look at me like I'm crazy, but *yes*. What's the value in winning if you cheat?"

"When you play online, all bets are off, the rules change. Dude, what's up with you?"

"Stop changing the subject!"

"What *is* the subject, Marjorie?" Her full name fell off his tongue with a clunk, crashing on impact. "My online Scrabble game against John?"

"You need to cheat to beat John? That's even more pathetic."

He narrowed his eyes. "So now you're insulting my best friend. What the hell is *that* supposed to mean?"

She shrugged, picked *Franny and Zooey* up off her bedside table— its edges satisfyingly rough against her thumbs—and pretended to read. "Take it however you want."

Mac slammed his iPad into the mattress, then pressed Marjorie's book down toward her chest, so he could look into her eyes. His face was blotchy and pink. He looked angrier than she had ever seen him, except maybe freshman year when a senior threw a strawberry at him in the lunchroom and hit him in the eye. "Fine, Marjorie. I look up words. Here's a news flash, everybody does it."

"Not everyone, Mac. Just the people you spend time with."

"Oh, I'm sorry. I didn't realize how scrupulous you were. Tell me again about pretending to be a tutor and getting Fred *fired*?"

She had supplied the fodder, and he had a point. But it was dirty play. "Seriously?" she whispered, her eyes brimming. "Can't you see that I'm . . . that I can't—"

As the tears came on, she caught the overflow in her hands, ineffectual dams.

Mac exhaled. "Marjorie, you know who I am, who I've always been. I'm sorry I brought that up, but I don't know what to say. I'm trying. Just tell me what the *hell* is wrong. How can I make you fun again? *Please.*"

Marjorie sniffled. He was right. He didn't deserve her scorn. "I'm sorry. I don't know what my deal is lately."

He placed a hand atop her head, tentatively, as if she might snap like a tortoise and draw blood. Then he ruffled her hair, sliding his hand down to the juncture where her neck met her shoulders. "It's been a hard time. The whole thing with your job kinda crushed you."

Marjorie nodded. It was true. During her brief stint at G & G, she had tasted what it was like to feel valued, to contribute. She'd liked the work. The detox from that satisfaction would prove painful.

"That's why," Mac continued, "I talked to Brianne."

The words were so unexpected, so out of left field, that it took Marjorie a few beats to comprehend. The muscles in her body seized up, as she sputtered, "Sorry. You—*what*?"

Mac smiled like he'd done a good deed for which he deserved gold stars, pats on the back, and letterpress thank-you notes, written in cursive with fountain pens and real ink. "She met me for a drink at DIRT. And I convinced her to take you back!"

"You *convinced* her?"

"She wants me as a client and, you know, you weren't *that* bad at the job. It didn't take much cajoling."

"Ca—*cajoling*?"

"Yeah." He grinned. "Your big words are rubbing off on me."

"Mac."

"Yes?"

Marjorie struggled to remain calm, to breathe. "Are you kidding me?"

He was too busy basking in his own glow to notice Marjorie's hands curled into fists. "It's no joke, Madgesty. You'll have to start at a junior level and climb back up, but don't worry! You have your job back." He brought his hand to Marjorie's cheek. That's when he noticed the dangerous look in her eyes. "Are you okay?"

"Mac. I don't want that job back. *Ever.*"

"What?" His jaw went slack.

"Brianne told people I was in an *insane asylum.*"

Mac gaped at Marjorie as if she belonged in one. "I know Brianne is psycho, but isn't everyone in that industry?"

"No, Mac. Everyone does not get their jollies by humiliating employees!"

"But you said you miss your job."

"Yes. My job with Michael and Gus."

He grimaced. "Gus? Really?" Mac almost never tried. In a rare act of selflessness, he had taken initiative with Brianne and he expected appreciation. "Well, guess what? That ship sailed. Maybe swallow your pride. It's not like you have other offers."

"It's not about pride. I hated myself in that job, every excruciating second I spent babysitting washed-up celebrities and socialite brides cost me self-respect."

Mac stood and began pacing across the bearskin rug. Sweat had collected on his clean-shaven upper lip; a vein in his forehead bulged. "What do you want from me, Marjorie? Because I'm trying." He threw his hands up, literally. "But this is *me.*"

He had meant well, that much was obvious. Suddenly, Marjorie saw the problem: She *did* know who he was, and it wasn't enough. As much as she adored him, spent years (she now realized) wondering about him. He was self-involved and cavalier; he cut corners and took the easy, if not debauched, route. Instead of helping her solve their problems, he wanting to press Reset to make her fun again like a glitching video game console. He charmed and bought his way in and out of situations. That was his *gift,* one that Marjorie had once admired. But now she realized that effort made life feel rewarding. Once upon a time, she and Mac might have made the perfect couple, their lives neatly tied in Tiffany blue bows. But they no longer made sense.

This is me about to blow up the last of my old life. No job, no place to live, no plan, no money, no clear path, no friends. She felt surprisingly calm; her tears had dried.

"Do you not want to be with me anymore?" Mac was asking, a look of realization, then hurt, crossing his face. "After all these years, is this just it? Why did you even agree to live with me?"

She opened her mouth to offer an explanation, but all that came out was, "I'm sorry."

They stood looking at each other for a while. Finally, he sighed and slumped down onto the bed to sit. "I guess I should have seen this coming."

"It's not your fault. I think I changed."

"Maybe." He shot her a resigned smile. "But you'll always be Madgesty to me."

"I think that's part of the problem."

In the living room, Marjorie gathered her belongings and dragged her rolling suitcase to the door. Mac handed her the edition of *Franny and Zooey.* "I'd like you to have it."

"Are you sure?"

"Yeah. It's not like I'll read it." He walked out with her. "I'll take you down."

Outside, the doorman hailed Marjorie a cab. She and Mac stood reading each other, a silent discussion, layered and messy. He looked sad.

She started, "About before—"

"Hey, Madgesty. Let's not, okay? I'm trying to keep it classy."

"I know, and I appreciate it."

"We gave it a good try, right?"

"I think so. You were great."

"Thanks," he nodded. "Okay. I'm gonna go now, if that's okay . . . if you're okay."

Marjorie nodded, *okay.* He kissed her on the cheek, a whisper against her skin.

As Mac walked away, growing smaller as he strolled back into the lobby, his hands in his pockets, relaxed even now, he turned at the last moment and tipped an imaginary hat to Marjorie. In his wake, she could see a teenage Mac, loping down the street after a stolen kiss, just the same.

41

Marjorie let herself into her parents' apartment.

"Hello? Anyone home?"

Not even Mina the Cat came to the door, though she meowed in greeting from the kitchen. Marjorie followed her cry and found the feline on top of the table, drinking milk from a half-eaten bowl of cereal.

That was odd. It was unlike either of her parents to leave food out. She picked up the dirty dish and brought it to the sink, accidentally kicking an object in her path. She bent down to pick it up: the cordless phone.

Why was it on the floor? What the hell was going on?

A key turned audibly in the front door. She called out, "Hello? Mom? Dad?"

"Marjorie? Is that you?"

"Yes!" Marjorie walked to meet her mother in the entryway. "Unless somebody else calls you M—"

She stopped in her tracks. Her mother looked like a wreck. Barbara Plum never left the house without makeup, yet here she was bare faced, wearing a stained T-shirt, yoga pants, and a strained expression.

"Mom? What's wrong?"

Barbara sighed. "I guess you didn't get my messages."

"No. I'm so sorry. I know I've been hard to reach. I've had kind of a crazy—actually, it doesn't matter. Are you okay?"

"There's been an incident." Barbara Plum's voice was a creepy, measured sort of calm, a surefire sign that something was wrong. Marjorie recognized the tone from when her aunt lost her savings in a Ponzi scheme, when her cousin got into a car accident, when her grandfather died.

"Is everything okay?" Marjorie knew the answer was no.

Chipper had been teaching a class on the advent of reality TV (an understandably upsetting topic), when his heart launched a protest against the lobster mac 'n' cheese he'd eaten the night before and the unfilled Lipitor prescription buried under papers on his desk.

No sooner had the word "Snooki" escaped his lips, when a clot surrounding a plaque deposit grew one-hundredth of a millimeter, damming the flow of oxygen-rich blood to the heart, starving the organ and refusing to budge like some warty gatekeeper from one of Chipper's beloved *Lord of the Rings* movies.

Many of the students—finishing notes on *Newlyweds: Nick & Jessica*—mistook Chipper's heart attack for a dramatic reenactment before realizing that he was clutching his chest in pain. Luckily, the university's Language & Letters building was situated next to the medical school. Before medics arrived, Chipper's coworker, Dr. Rupert Rubenstein (who had often found himself on the opposite side of the aisle when it came to interdepartmental politics), had already begun treating him, administering IV aspirin to thin the blood and limit damage to the heart. Some faculty members speculated that perhaps now Chipper would be more generous when voting to allocate funds to the medical school. *Just saying.*

Within three minutes and thirty-eight seconds, an ambulance full of EMTs showed up, only the first of many acronyms from EKGs to ICUs that would define the experience. Ultimately, Chipper suffered a very mild coronary and would be fine, though he would certainly endure more nagging about his diet from his wife.

"I'm just here to pack a bag for him," Barbara explained.

Marjorie sat down, her knees weak. "Mom, that must have been terrifying. Thank God he's okay."

Barbara sat down too. "It wasn't a fun call to get, that's for sure. But we were lucky."

"I'm sorry I didn't pick up my phone. And that I haven't been answering your e-mails."

"Oh, sweetie. You're busy. It's fine."

"It's actually not fine at all. I owe you more than that."

"But why are you back from LA early? And why are you here? Was the trip okay? Are you okay?"

Marjorie forced a smile. "Mom, LA was great. I'm great. Don't worry about me. Let me support you guys for a change. I can handle it. I'm ready to take responsibility—for myself, for you guys. It's about time."

"I guess I could use the help. I need to call the insurance company. He has his university health care. Thank God he didn't leave to write that book full-time like he threatened. And I'm trying to stay on top of the nurses without irritating them. On NPR, they say you have to be your own advocate to get decent treatment."

"Whatever you need."

Barbara tucked a strand of hair behind her daughter's ear. "You're a good girl, you know that? We're so fortunate."

Marjorie smiled back weakly. Guilt sat on her chest like a brick. She had avoided her parents for weeks for fear of facing the truth about her own poor choices. She hadn't wanted to answer the tough questions. And, now, she couldn't recall her last movie excursion or marathon TV session with her father. She'd been so arrogant to imagine she'd been in bad shape when people were mourning post-Aurora, women were dying in Darfur, and her father was in the hospital. She hadn't known what bottom was.

Marjorie made her mother a cup of tea and forced her to lie down for a few minutes, while she packed a bag for her father. Once alone, she allowed herself some deep breaths and then counted her lucky stars that her selfishness hadn't done permanent damage. She could still make things up to her parents, to herself. She had arrived at their house with plans to grow up and start anew, for real this time. No more limp gestures that did nothing to propel change.

When she reemerged, Barbara was waiting, wearing a smear of purplish lipstick—Marjorie felt an affectionate pang for her mother, ever presentable.

"Ready?" asked Marjorie, anxious to see her father.

"Yes." They headed for the door. "Do you need to call Mac?" asked Barbara. "Tell him what happened?"

"Um. No. Mac and I are—questionable."

"I see." Barbara locked the door behind them, and they waited in the hallway for the elevator. "What about Fred?"

"Questionable too. Which is entirely my fault."

"And the job didn't become full-time?" Barbara feigned indifference. *Just asking.*

"I was good at it, but it wasn't . . . a fit. Gus and I, well, we're—"

"Questionable?"

"Right. I should call Pickles at some point, though, before she hears from someone else."

"But not Vera? Is that friendship questionable too?"

"No. That's just over."

"Huh. I guess she couldn't be Care Bear Club VP forever." Barbara smashed her lips together, anxiously. "I *thought* maybe you liked Gus, the way you talked about him."

"Mom, please." Marjorie placed a hand on her mother's shoulder. "Don't worry about me. I'm fine. I know you're disappointed that Mac and I didn't work out, but—"

"Why would I be disappointed?"

"Wasn't becoming Mrs. Mac O'Shea the dream for me?"

Barbara looked genuinely surprised. "Marjorie, 'the dream' isn't *marrying* anyone! It's about building a life for yourself. It's about being fulfilled."

"Sure, but it wouldn't hurt if that 'life' came equipped with a palatial Fifth Avenue apartment."

Marjorie's mother winced. "I never meant to give you that impression."

"That status matters?"

"That you should move to the Upper East Side. So stodgy." Barbara smiled at Marjorie; they both giggled despite themselves.

"There's this random quote that keeps popping into my head," Marjorie said. "It's 'The only person you are destined to become is the person you decide to be.'"

Barbara Plum crossed her arms over her chest. "You learned that from me, young lady. I use it in every one of my life-coaching seminars. I can't believe you don't know that!"

"Oh, do you use that quote?" Marjorie teased, and slid her arm around her mother's shoulders and squeezed.

42

Chipper required an angiogram, but no bypass surgery, *thank goodness.*

"You missed my big moment!" he announced hoarsely, as Marjorie entered his room in the cardiac wing. "It was dramatic! And with a live studio audience."

She bent to kiss his cheek. "Let's not do a rerun of it."

"At least this whole near death thing gets me out of scooping the cat box for a few weeks."

"Impossible!" Barbara sat down in a metal chair against the wall, her smile equal parts relief and strain.

Marjorie stood at her father's side, the window and cityscape to her back, and tried not to imagine him on a stretcher, as if in some schlocky medical drama he'd criticize but still watch. "So how are you feeling, Dad?"

"I've been better . . . and worse." He sighed. "Just makes you feel old."

"Don't be ridiculous. Martin Sheen had a heart attack at thirty-six years old. And he went on to be president."

"Fictional president." Chipper laughed, a hand flying nervously to his chest. "That's the rub with this mortality shit, honey. It's real."

"Maybe it can be a reminder to enjoy your life."

"Yeah," he rolled his eyes. "But with less cheese."

"*No* cheese! Not *less* cheese," piped Barbara. "So, Chipper, I've asked Marjorie to move in with us for a while." She'd asked no such thing; she was throwing Marjorie a bone.

"What? No! Marjorie, don't sacrifice your fabulous lifestyle on our account."

"No, Dad. Mom is being generous. I want to stay with you guys for a while." Her parents exchanged a look, happiness tinged with worry. "I need to start fresh. Besides, I haven't had much time with you lately and apparently you're not long for this world."

"Marjorie!" her mother exclaimed.

Chipper grinned. "We'd be delighted to have you. Give us some movie catch-up time."

A nurse with a kind face and a name tag that read ANDREA interrupted gently to suggest they give "Mr. Chipper" time to rest after she took his vitals.

"Naptime like kindergarten," he grunted. "But without the snacks."

Over the next week, Marjorie spent hours at the hospital, drinking lukewarm English breakfast tea and making friends with the nurses, who nicknamed her "Bonita Ciruela" or "Pretty Plum."

By the time Chipper moved home, she was settled into her renovated bedroom, admittedly now more age-appropriate without the gummy remnants of old unicorn stickers on the walls. The only remaining clue to its past incarnation were the old flip books her mother had organized on a shelf.

Marjorie and Mac never discussed their relationship's demise, though he did send a text saying he hoped Chipper was thriving. It was over; a postmortem seemed gratuitous.

Marjorie helped her parents. She intervened when they argued about how to use the cable remote (they were both wrong) and enticed Chipper into eating healthier foods. She brought him nonedible treats from the outside world too, like magazines, books, and reports of the horrible humidity, so he'd know he wasn't missing anything by being stuck indoors. When the Republican convention began at the end of August, she forbade him from watching, except via the lens of *The Daily Show*. Too stressful!

Together, they wondered whether vice presidential nominee Wisconsin congressman Paul Ryan—with his workout regimen, Ayn Rand obsession, and widow's peak hairline—would lend Mitt Romney enough "policy muscle" to take the election. They dropped Nate Silver's statistics and took their own inaccurate straw polls. (Mina the Cat had concerns about Obama's environmental record and remained a swing vote.)

Pickles and her mother, Ramona, visited twice a week, bearing quinoa and kale salads, and hemp milk and cacao smoothies with chia seeds. "Superfoods packed with antioxidants!" exclaimed a delighted Pickles, as she presented the dishes.

"Super tasteless," Chipper grumbled, once she was out of earshot. "But sweet."

Meanwhile, Pickles was miffed. So many weeks ago, she'd been prompted to call Marjorie for help, only to have Vera behave spinelessly, *ungratefully*. Of her own volition, the young mother pledged allegiance to Madge, creating a separation with Vera too. The lines were drawn in the Montauk sand.

Marjorie did enjoy seeing Pickles, Steve, and the kids on a couple social occasions (when they weren't ranting about preschool applications), but she felt the old boredom with the other familiar faces, as they debated fast cars, investment strategies, and tentpole movies, bragging about friendships with cheesy celebrities.

Mostly, she and Chipper binge-watched TV series and films together, a nod to late summers of her childhood. (Before the Plums left for their annual weeklong seafood-packed stay with Nana Judy every August, and while Marjorie's friends were off on fancy family vacations, she and her father survived the heat by screening movies.) Now they watched back episodes of *Homeland* and *Breaking Bad;* movies like *Casablanca, Blade Runner,* and *Wedding Crashers.* They got absorbed by stories of tragedy, perseverance, and stupidity, of hope and defeat, stories of stories of stories.

Meanwhile, Marjorie regaled her parents with descriptions of the worst and best of the films she'd watched at G & G, moving them to tears of laughter with her impression of pretentious Grant Vollbracht, performed during dinner one evening.

"And he kept his sunglasses on the whole time?" giggled her mother.

"I can't blame Gus for walking out." Chipper shook his head. "Sounds like a man after my own heart. It's one of the reasons I went into academia instead of to Hollywood."

"Yeah. He couldn't take it." Marjorie's smile faded.

Barbara read her daughter's look. "Have you thought about getting in touch, either socially or for work opportunities?"

"It wouldn't make sense right now." In truth, she had thought a million times about calling Gus and hearing him out. But he hadn't contacted her since the incident. He'd probably heard about the tutoring debacle and thought she was nuts.

"I have a thought," said her father.

"Yeah? Just one?"

"Grow up." He grinned. "I know you're applying for writing jobs right now, and I think that's great. But I have some friends who produce TV shows. Now, I'm not saying they'd hire you right away. But if you were willing to start at the bottom, maybe you could work as a writing assistant, then story editor, and become a full-fledged writer, assuming you liked it. Of course, that might eventually mean moving to LA."

"Chipper!" Barbara admonished.

He shrugged. "Or not. But you'd have to write some spec scripts first, as samples for me to show them."

"Dad! Are you kidding me?" That did the trick. Marjorie pushed her seat back, stood and walked around the table, throwing her arms around her father. "Thank you! Thank you! Thank you!"

"Don't squeeze me too tight, honey. I might drop dead."

She planted a kiss on his cheek. "That would be very inconvenient."

Chipper said, "You know there are no guarantees, right, honey?"

"Oh, trust me, Dad. If there's one thing I've learned, it's that."

Marjorie worked harder than ever before over the next weeks. Each morning, she brushed her teeth, threw her hair in a bun, checked on her father, and sat down at her computer to write.

Immediately, she could tell she was cut out for a writer's life—something she'd begun to suspect while working with Belinda. She felt at ease editing and reediting wrongly worded sentences and tweaking lines of dialogue that rang insincere. She had an outlet for those invented backstories about strangers on trains. And she felt directed in a way she hadn't since before she became "Madgesty."

Once she finished a draft, Marjorie brought the script to her father, ignoring her jitters. She pretended not assess his every head scratch as he read. After turning the last page, he peered up at her as she stopped pacing: "Have you done this before?"

"What? No! You know that. Is it that bad?"

"No, Marjorie." He looked down at the coffee-stained, paper-clipped document on his lap, then back up at his daughter. "It's *that* good."

"Good? Good, good, good!"

Chipper had notes, of course: The stakes should be higher, the climax more pronounced, one quirky supporting character less of a caricature. But he marveled at her ability. She wasn't sure whether to be proud or insulted by his surprise.

Barbara Plum announced, after Chipper's glowing report, that

she'd always known Marjorie would harness her talents for success—
never mind that just months before she had also "known" that Marjorie would wind up an impoverished old maid in an even more remote
outer borough than Brooklyn. All was forgotten, history revised. As
far as Barbara was concerned, Marjorie had never wavered on the path
to greatness.

Even Mina the Cat seemed pleased by Marjorie's tenaciousness,
perching on her lap as she wrote.

One evening, Marjorie received an e-mail from Tina, thankfully
not about scheduling her reentry meeting with Brianne thanks to Mac.
When hell freezes over.

> Girl, it's been too long. I miss seeing your tall ass around
> this place. (That said, I heard rumors about you coming
> back. Don't do it! Have you lost your mind? I'd be gone in a
> flash if she didn't pay me so well.)
>
> Meanwhile, I do have some amazing gossip to share. Get
> ready to pick your jaw up off the FLOOR.
>
> Seems our favorite acne-covered, kiss-ass intern Herb
> was not who he seemed. That puny dude is actually a
> writer for the *New York Post*. He was a Page 6 intern, who
> pitched the idea of infiltrating a bigwig PR company (that
> they'd already heard insane rumors about). He's been
> collecting the goods on Brianne for months!
>
> Even more nuts, I've heard rumblings that she was having
> SEX with that hot mess. That kid is barely legal and uglier
> than a bag of hair! You know I'm right. Hopefully that part
> isn't true.
>
> Anyway, I wanted to let you know because karma's
> one awesome bitch, right? The story is running next week.

Also, if you called the *Post* and talked to Herb, maybe he
would include your sabotage in the story? Maybe clear
your name, make it plain to those folks Brianne e-mailed
that you aren't crazy?

That's all for now. Would love to see you and hear what
you've been doing. You around?

xoxo Tina

Marjorie grinned as she read the e-mail, but she also felt a pang.
That was a lot of public humiliation, even for a terrible person like
Brianne.

Either way, Marjorie wouldn't call Herb. At this point, she
didn't care much what those contacts thought of her mental health,
since not one had called to verify the tale. Plus, bringing up the
story would only keep the narrative in circulation. And, whether
Herb had been playing a role or not, it would be a cold day in
Death Valley before she asked that whiny Benedict Arnold for a
favor.

Skimming Facebook updates about last gasps of summer, she happened upon an announcement from her high school boyfriend,
Bryce. Beneath a lo-fi-filtered image of him and his wife cradling a
stuffed toy armadillo, the caption read: "We're pregnant!" The post
already had eighty-six Likes.

Marjorie got to cyberstalking. As far as she could tell, he and his
adorable wife were both graphic artists—a fact that she vaguely
recalled—who loved taking international bike trips. Pictures showed
them in myriad settings, smiling and flushed, in athletic gear. Marjorie was glad for him. If only she liked riding bikes; maybe she'd be as
happy as these two, one day.

She sent Bryce a private instant message:

Congratulations! So are you nervous about
being a dad?

He responded right away:

> A little. But Carrie is so good with kids.
> It'll be fine.

> It will be more than fine! You'll be great.
> No question.

> BTW I heard about your dad's heart
> attack. I'm so glad he's ok.

> Oh! Thank you. I didn't realize you
> knew.

> I talk to Mac pretty often.

> Ah. I should have realized.

She hesitated, then typed:

> So then I guess Mac told you we were
> dating? But not anymore.

> He did.

> Can I ask you a weird question?

> Anytime.

> Did you ever worry about me and Mac,
> back when you and I were together?

> Not really. But it makes sense. You guys
> always sort of had a connection. Don't get

me wrong. Even now, it stings a little. Old
habits . . .

I hear you.

But I pictured something different for
you than Mac's life. You're weirder than
that.

Gee, thanks!

In a good way. Ha! Remember that story
you showed me that you wrote when you
were a kid? The one about being stuck
inside a book? That was crazy creative.

I can't believe you remember that.

It stayed with me for some reason. You've
always been different from that group,
you know? That's part of why I liked you.

I don't think I knew that.

Look, I found it hard to be a regular
person in NYC after college. It's
hard. That's why I moved to Austin.
It never seemed like enough just to
be functioning—like if I wasn't doing
something flashy, I didn't count. And I
didn't want to be that guy who peaked in
high school, you know?

Yeah. I know something about that.

The next day was Chipper's first postheart-attack (PHA or "FA!" as the family had come to call it) stress test, and Marjorie was tagging along, despite her father's objections to being "babysat."

But when they stepped into her parents' lobby from the elevator, she stopped dead in her tracks. The pixie, in one of her signature get-ups (tassels, high-waisted striped pants, heeled boots), was waiting to ride up.

"Fred! What are you doing here?"

"Coming to see you, of course. What else? No one answered the buzzer, but the nice doorman thought you were home. I convinced him to let me go up and ring the doorbell."

"Of course you did."

Fred glanced at Marjorie's parents, standing by the exit. Barbara had hustled a clueless Chipper away to give the girls space when she realized that this was *the* Fred. "Looks like you're on your way out."

"We are, but wait, wait, wait. These are my parents." Marjorie made the proper introductions. Everyone smiled and nodded, though Chipper—feeling he'd earned the right at his advanced age—shook Fred's hand, accepted well wishes, then promptly forgot her. She joined the blurred ranks of Marjorie's other nameless, faceless friends.

"You girls go talk," Marjorie's mother said, opening the door to the outside world.

"But what about the doctor?"

Barbara brought a hand to her hip. "Marjorie, we survived before you and we can survive without you now! Go!"

The duos parted ways outside.

The former roommates headed down the sloped sidewalk toward Riverside Park, stopping on the outskirts to appreciate the old fountain beside which Marjorie and Mac had kissed so many years before. Marjorie had recently read a *New York Times* article about the Tennessee pink marble relic she had taken for granted: It was a horse trough designed by Warren & Wetmore (architects integral to Grand Central Terminal), funded posthumously in 1906 by a descendant of

Alexander Hamilton's, whose "adventuress" wife ruined his political career through scandal. The same man was believed to have
been murdered by his best friend on a hunting trip in Yellowstone
National Park. And Marjorie thought *she* was a bad judge of character.

They started down stone steps toward the basketball courts,
chatting about summer's abrupt end, a phenomenon that continues
to flabbergast year after year.

"I can't take it anymore!" Fred finally exclaimed. "I didn't just
come here to get my Upper West Side on! Let's talk."

Marjorie smiled. "You want to start, or should I?"

"Me! Because, Morningblatt, I feel *terrible*. I had no idea about your
father's heart attack. And when I heard . . . I'm so sorry I wasn't there
for you."

"Fred, no! You had every right to be mad."

"Maybe." The pixie scratched her head like a cartoon character.
"But I should have been more understanding. We all have our pockets of crazy. Like I once stalked an ex-boyfriend."

"Wait, what?"

"He dumped me. I was brokenhearted, so I started walking past
his building every day, hoping to run into him—normal breakup stuff
like that. Before long, I was at his coffee shop most mornings, 'running into him' near his gym on weekends. It got out of hand."

"It happens?"

"No. It doesn't. Finally, we ran into each outside his building, by
my design, and he asked me to stop. His doorman heard the whole
thing. It was the most humiliating moment of my life. The point is,
do you know why I stalked him?"

Marjorie shook her head. "You were in love?"

"No." Fred shook her head firmly. "He was a music exec with terrible taste, an affinity for bad funk. He didn't get my songs; I didn't
even respect him. But he was the kind of guy who never likes me and
he thought I was adorable—until he didn't. I was in a terrible place: I
wasn't writing music, I was still trying to keep a nine-to-five office

job. For the three seconds we were together, he made me feel accepted, bourgeois."

"Makes sense."

"Anyhow, we all act loony sometimes because we aren't in our right minds or because we have some image of who we're trying to be. As your friend, I should have given you some insanity leeway, considering everything that was going on."

"Fred, that's super generous. But I got you *fired*."

"Yeah, there's that." She kicked at one of the first fallen leaves standing out against the pavement. "But whatever. I got more shifts and a raise at the acupuncture place."

"Thank God."

"Speaking of tutoring, someone came by the house looking for you."

"Who?" Marjorie was disgusted with herself for hoping it was Gus.

"Belinda."

"Belinda! What? How? By *herself*?"

"No, she was with some chubby kid—Growl or something?"

"Snarls!"

"That sounds right."

"Was she mad? Did she look happy?"

"She didn't seem angry. She wanted me to give you this." Fred rifled through her bag and pulled out a thin stack of paper, stapled together. The top sheet read: "A short story by Belinda Porter-Levinson."

Marjorie clutched the papers to her chest, welling up. "Oh! Thank you!"

"She seemed pretty impressed by you, despite her mothers' threat of a restraining order." Fred did a little dance, for no reason except she was Fred. "So, what's up with Mac?" Marjorie mimed an axe across her neck. "Over? For good? Are you sad?"

"A little." There was a chill in the air, a whisper of autumn that seemed unimaginable days before. "But we weren't right."

Fred furrowed her brow. "Remember how you once said you and

Mac seemed 'meant to be' because the universe kept bringing you together in random places?"

Marjorie nodded.

"Well, I thought of it differently. Maybe you ran into him because
he represented everything you needed to let go? Style over substance
and unearned rewards. Looking for reassurance in all the wrong
places."

"I do think in retrospect that maybe he always hated Vera because
he recognized her need for approval as an unattractive quality in himself, though better hidden. I can understand why I got the reactions
I did from each of them."

"Why?"

"Because I *coasted*. I did nothing to deserve the attention. But the
joke was on me because it was fleeting, worthless. I kept waiting for
something to make me feel special again, but I never did anything but
mope. I thought maybe I had become less fabulous, but really people
moved on because that's what they do. I stayed in that horrible job,
with a boss who *literally* threw things at me, because it never occurred
to me that satisfaction isn't about validation. You could wait a lifetime
for that. I know. I waited a decade."

Fred examined her hands. "I ended things with James too." And
a million single female New Yorkers felt suddenly lighter, like something had righted itself.

"Again?"

"For real this time. He showed up for our date all cute and preppy,
ready to pick up where we left off. But I wasn't feeling it. I told him
he had to move on. No showing up at my shows or parties. Maybe
my 'focusing on work' line was an excuse all along."

"Or maybe you changed."

"It happens."

"That's what I hear." Marjorie linked her arm through Fred's.

Later, as the girls readied to part ways, Fred said, "Your bedroom
is waiting for you, if and when you want to come home. You need your
stuff!"

Home. "Thanks, Fred. I'll get it . . . at some point. I guess I can't live out of a suitcase forever."

The pixie sighed. "Look, I don't know what happened in LA, Morningblatt. Gus won't talk and apparently neither will you. But I refuse to have you annexed from my world because you're avoiding him. I can't have you both moping around!"

"He's moping?"

"Mope City, here we come. Maybe I can at least coerce you into coming to a Stolen Ivory show?" She paused. "Aren't you going to tell me the name sucks?"

"It's actually not that bad."

"Really? Maybe your taste is slipping."

Upstairs, once Fred left, Marjorie pulled out Belinda's story and began to read. It was different from what they'd worked on:

Once upon a time, in a land of Vespas and taxicabs instead of those horse-drawn carriages, there lived a royal princess named Chloe. Her parents, the King and Queen, meant well, but were overprotective pains in the butt by nature, too obsessed with their own arguments and seasonal dinners of mutton chop, kale, and quinoa to notice that their daughter was desperately lonely.

Eventually, the princess became so despondent that she refused to even dress herself, so they hired a Lady-in-Waiting to help her prep for festivals and events. What they didn't realize is that this particular maid, named Star because of how brightly she shined, had magical powers. Every time she entered the room, the princess got a little happier and more animated again.

Princess Chloe began reading books and watching TV shows that weren't for children, when the King and Queen weren't looking. She particularly liked *Homeland, New Girl,* and *The Good Wife.*

Meanwhile, the Queen had a suitor in mind for young Chloe, who she assumed would be her future husband (or at least boyfriend): the Duke of Prospect Park. He was nice enough, but Chloe was "just not that into him."

One day, Star took Chloe to Bodega Stables to see horses and buy Doritos. There, the princess met a boy named Ruff. At first, Chloe scoffed at his crass comments and stupid jokes, although the attention was nice. He was not polished like the Duke of PP, but he was funny and smart. Star had never intended to pair Chloe with anyone, but she had taught the princess to think for herself and grow into an independent teenager, who didn't follow a pack or blindly adopt her mother's values.

For a while, the King and Queen were too busy arguing about bedspread colors to notice. But eventually Princess Chloe decided that she favored Ruff and would prefer him as a date to the big Barclays Center ball, where Jay-Z would perform before a gladiator battle (after which they would go eat organic hot dogs at Bark). Busy night!

The Queen flipped out, to say the least. The woman lost her mind. Even the King was totally unreasonable. They could see it was too late to convince Princess Chloe to change her mind. She'd already been given her own voice by the magical Lady-in-Waiting. But they blamed Star and, so, to punish everyone involved, they (wrongly, if that's not clear) acted like losers and banished her from the kingdom—especially from the corner vegetarian bakery.

Star was not seen in the kingdom for some time. She went to live in Bath and had the amazing life she dreamed about with tons of beautiful, cool boyfriends, who were lead singers of super famous bands.

Princess Chloe and Ruff had a ball at the ball. Even the King and Queen were happier, because they bonded over hating Star and stopped fighting so much, though they weren't smart enough to know it. And they all lived happily ever after.

THE END

On the back, Belinda had scrawled:

To The Coolest Tutor Ever,
    I'll never forget you! I'm keeping your flip book story safe.
Hopefully, you rubbed off on me a lot.
    LOVE, BELLY

P.S. Do you like that I got "despondent" in there? Total vocab word!

EPILOGUE

Marjorie closed down her computer for the day, then rinsed her Zabar's coffee mug in the communal kitchen sink. She dropped it back on her desk and slung her bag over her shoulder.

She looked out over the open-floor-plan office, where the team's graphic artists were still squinting at their screens, enacting last-minute changes to ads. A new tune by the National—Brooklyn's favorite indie band—played from someone's Spotify; somebody else hummed along. Far away at reception, the landline rang. Out the window was a view of the East River and, from the right spot, the Statue of Liberty.

"You taking off?" asked Darren, Marjorie's new boss, startling her. She hadn't seen him standing nearby, his expression unreadable.

"I was going to. I promised my best friend I'd meet her for an early drink before I see her band play." She paused, bracing herself. "Is that okay? 'Cause I can stay."

"Totally okay." He smiled. "Unless I have to go. I hate live music. Better you than me."

Marjorie laughed. "Then you're off the hook." She was going to have to get used to this whole sane boss thing. He was a tech type, stilted but sweet.

"Hey, good work on the Gosling movie Twitter text," he said while heading back to his office. "It looks great."

"Thanks, Darren. I'm so glad you liked it."

Outside, in Dumbo, as Marjorie walked past art galleries and converted lofts toward the subway, her phone rang.

"Fredericka?"

"Morningblatt!"

Marjorie smiled. "I was just heading back to my place to drop off my work stuff, then come to you."

"Yeah, about that: change of plans."

"What's up?"

"Up? Nothing's up. Can't a girl change plans without something being up?"

"Um. Fred?"

"Okay, sorry. Just messing around. So, I have to meet now instead. There's no time for you to drop your stuff off. And I'm not home. Do you mind meeting somewhere else?"

"Sure. Is everything okay with the show?"

"Yes! I just need you to meet me now. I'm nervous. I need you to distract me."

"Okay. Done. Where?"

"The Maryland Monument in Prospect Park."

"Seriously? I don't even know where that is."

"C'mon! It's beautiful out and I need somewhere serene to relax. Hurry!"

"Fine, fine, fine."

The train would take too long. Marjorie signaled and, at the corner, a cab slowed to a stop. She climbed in: "Fifteenth Street and Prospect Park West, please. And make it snappy." She snorted. "Just kidding about that last part."

"You got it," said the driver, Mo, who was in a much better mood now that his infant son was sleeping through the night. Plus, the Yankees looked likely to make it to the playoffs, Jorge Posada or not.

Marjorie opened the window and inhaled the crisp air, which smelled of fireplace, sautéed garlic, and damp leaves. The day was winding down but some sun still lingered. Unconsciously, she brought a hand to her neck, where her Tiffany graduation necklace used to lie. She'd decided to take it off for a while. It felt like time. Instead, she was wearing a beloved new bird toile cashmere scarf that Fred bought her at a vintage store.

The taxi wove past Cobble Hill's shops, over the ripe Gowanus

Canal and into Park Slope, by Gatherers, then uphill toward the park. Marjorie sighed. She sometimes hoped to catch a glimpse of Belinda. In an envelope with no return address, Marjorie had sent her former tutee the DREAM bracelet she'd bought at the airport. She couldn't risk including a note. Would Belinda know it was from her? Maybe; maybe not. It didn't really matter. Marjorie just liked to picture her, sitting down to her homework at the kitchen table, over a dish of hummus and carrots, the bracelet dangling from her tiny wrist.

Though so far September had been fraught, today felt hopeful. The election was heating up, tempers were testy, the promise of autumn rode in on the tips of shorter, dimmer days.

Across the world, J. Christopher Stevens, the US ambassador to Libya, had been killed during terrorist attacks in Benghazi, the botched reaction to which sparked criticism of President Obama's administration. The unemployed were angry. Mitt Romney kept putting his foot in his mouth. No one would let Paul Ryan forget his lie about his marathon running time. Both sides were sure that the wrong duo in power would spell the end of America.

The Summer Olympics were over, but the women's gymnastics team's "Fierce Five" gold medalists continued to tour, looking toward a final exhibition at Brooklyn's Barclays Center stadium. *The Dark Knight*'s box office numbers were disappointing thanks to the Aurora shooting, but they bounced back worldwide. Fall TV shows started up again; that put some people at ease. But this was to be the last season for favorites like *The Office* and *30 Rock*. It was impossible not to feel, even as a new school year began, that something larger was drawing to a close. Change was near: an end, but also a beginning.

No exception, Marjorie had walked around like a live wire, nerves exposed, knees bumping against the underside of restaurant tabletops. In her case, it was a good kind of adrenaline, as she stood on the precipice of something hard-earned. She was still working on her spec scripts, but—after getting the chance to write some humor recaps for a popular TV Web site—the editor had suggested Darren hire her as an ad copy and social media writer for his movie-marketing company.

Her PR experience met her love of media and writing—for now, it was a perfect fit.

Chipper's health had fast improved. He returned to teaching, and Marjorie's mother resumed work, along with reminding her daughter to wear blush. That was one of many factors that pushed Marjorie to move back to Brooklyn. She loved Carroll Gardens, but Vera had been right about one thing: A twenty-eight-year-old should have her own place. She found a sweet studio a few blocks from Fred. It was tiny, but it had its own garden. The pixie had already made some not very subtle suggestions about growing tomatoes; she could not be trusted.

The exposé on Brianne hit stands and, although a bazillion people e-mailed Marjorie to commiserate, she avoided reading the story. She was as disgusted by Herb's self-serving deception as she was at herself for wasting years at that job. And though she couldn't help herself from flipping her old office building the bird each time she passed in a cab, she didn't like to feel glee at Brianne's misfortune. Admittedly, the one excerpt Pickles e-mailed her to read, about how Brianne threatened to beat Herb with her yoga mat, was pretty genius, though. Apparently doing tree pose now and then does not make you a good person. *Namaste.*

Now, the cab sped up tree- and brownstone-lined 6th, 7th, and 8th Avenues and finally crossed grandiose Prospect Park West to meet leafy green. Marjorie paid, got out, and checked a posted map for directions.

As she strolled past plush lawns, the breeze prickled her cheeks and she felt energized. Rounding the bend of a dirt path, she came upon the marble, granite, and copper monument, on a rise that served as the base of a steep hill. She looked around for Fred, then checked the time. Where was that girl? She was the one in a rush!

A short fence surrounded the statue. In the meantime, Marjorie leaned over it to read the George Washington–attributed inscription: GOOD GOD! WHAT BRAVE FELLOWS I MUST THIS DAY LOSE. Then she lost her footing and almost fell over.

"You have terrible balance," said a voice from behind her. Marjorie turned, her heart thumping. There stood Gus—tall, tan, straight-faced, looking back at her steadily.

"It's you." An uncomfortable silence bloomed between them. "I'm supposed to meet Fred."

"Yeah. She's not coming."

Marjorie scanned the area. "You didn't kidnap her, did you? Because she gets really cranky without her daily Flintstone vitamins."

"I did not." He examined his shoes like a bashful kid. "I may have coerced her into helping me get you here."

Marjorie was taken aback. "I'm so dumb. She's the worst liar."

"Ah, well. It was my best bet. You know Fred. She wanted to help. She loves anything covert. And she loves both of us."

"That damn pixie!"

"Don't blame her. I called, fishing. She said you've been working on some scripts?"

Marjorie was still having trouble believing that Gus stood in front of her, in the flesh. She thought about him all the time. "Yeah. I've been writing TV specs."

Gus smiled. "That's really good. I bet they're fantastic."

"But, Gus, why call Fred? Why not . . . call me?" She still felt hurt.

He rubbed the back of his neck; she realized how much she had missed seeing him do that. "I didn't think you'd talk to me after I waited this long. I wanted to see you in person to explain."

"Should we sit?" she asked. "You seem squirrelly."

"Yeah, well, you make me nervous."

"I make *you* nervous?"

"I was hoping we could climb the hill. I've heard there's a great view. Maybe we could walk and talk? If you can swing it without your workout gear."

She laughed. "I think I can handle it." They started up the path.

"First, I want to say I'm sorry," he began. "I shouldn't have made any decision about the job without asking you, but I honestly believed it was what you wanted."

"Why would I have wanted that?"

"We couldn't be together if you worked for me. I thought if you liked me as much as I liked you . . ." He trailed off. To their left, an enthusiastic sheepdog knocked over its owner, then ran laps around him. Gus shook his head, laughed. She loved that sound.

"But why didn't you call and explain?"

"Marjorie, you ran like a spooked herd of wildebeest."

"An entire herd?"

He looked her up and down. "Maybe a few more wildebeest than the last time I saw you."

"Gus!" She hit him on the arm.

"No, you look perfect. The most beautiful wildebeest of all the wildebeests."

"Gus."

"What? Right. When you got so damn spooked, I realized I was out of my mind. You have a *boyfriend*."

"I—!" Marjorie tripped on a tree root.

Gus caught her elbow to steady her, then shook his head. "Such a spaz."

"That's 'Train Wreck' to you."

He held on to her arm. Neither moved.

"What was I saying?"

She grinned. "I think you were talking about how much you like me."

Gus cleared his throat. "Um, no. I was saying that you have a boyfriend, and not only did that seem wrong, I figured you were also panicking about moving in with him. I was just a test."

Marjorie could smell Gus's mint gum, that same flavor, and the soap on his skin, could see behind his stubble, where that laugh line was emerging, making his smile more pronounced. *Stay focused.*

He continued: "And I was pissed at you for leaving so quickly. I was hurt." He looked at the ground, then back up to her face, meeting her eyes. "Plus, I can't be around you without wanting to kiss you, especially after the towel episode. I wasn't sure how to be friends."

They stood quietly for a moment, as that information settled. Marjorie felt a rising glee that threatened to burst out, embarrassing and obvious, if she didn't speak up soon. "I guess Fred told you that Mac and I broke up."

Gus's gaze was steady. "Oh. I'm so—oh, fuck it. I was going to say 'I'm sorry,' but we're past that, I think."

"It was my decision. It wasn't right. Plus," she said, nudging his knee with her own, edging closer to him, "I was distracted by someone else."

"Oh, really? Who?"

"Someone grumpier and much more difficult. He's kind of a huge pain in the ass."

"Hmm. That guy sounds awesome." Gus leaned in close to her ear, so she could almost feel his lips on her skin. "So you're available?"

"I am."

"Interesting. Maybe I could take you on a date sometime."

"Sure. You wanna take me to a wedding?"

"That seems kind of fast, but okay. You're cute, for a wildebeest. I guess I'll marry you."

"Not *our* wedding, dummy. Michael and Celeste's, next month."

"Hmm. You don't have anything sooner?"

"Nope. No professions of love on my calendar until then."

"Maybe we can muster one up."

Gus moved to kiss Marjorie, but she stopped him just before their lips met.

"But what about the distance? You live in LA, I'm in New York."

"I'm sure we can rectify that."

"Really? You would move to New York?"

"Nope." He grinned. She opened her mouth to protest. "Oh, shut up, Marjorie Plum." He winked. "We'll work it out later."

Gus pressed his lips against Marjorie's own, and they lost all sense of propriety.

At the sound of a polite clearing of the throat, they looked up to see an older couple strolling past them down the hill. The man grumbled something about "getting a room," while, behind his back, the woman gave them a thumbs-up. Marjorie and Gus laughed.

They walked the rest of the way to the top, where they were rewarded with views of changing leaves all the way to Coney Island. People were like ants, biking, pushing strollers, jogging, rushing. Gus put an arm around Marjorie's shoulders and gave her a squeeze.

"What is this place?" she asked, breathless from the quick walk.

"Lookout Hill. Seemed appropriate."

Oddly, in this blissful moment, Marjorie was reminded of a Maharishi Mahesh quotation that Brianne kept framed on her desk, left over from one of her failed self-improvement phases: "The important thing is this: to be able, at any moment, to sacrifice what we are for what we could become."

In a few months' time, President Barack Obama, the country's first African American leader, would win his second term in office, a landslide relative to expectations. Congress remained Republican controlled in what spelled another four years of warring between the extremist factions of both parties, particularly the Tea Party fringe. All was not necessarily right with the world. But, in this instant, Marjorie was just fine.

To preserve the moment in her memory, she oriented herself: *This is the view from a lookout; not a peak. This is the smell of trees and wind; this is a guy, with flaws, but maybe the right guy, standing beside me. This is my life: my nose cold, a blister on my heel, nerves about my new job and what's to come. This is awake. This is now.*

Marjorie Plum was the most popular girl in school, but it had been over a decade since anyone cared, least of all her.

Flip, flip, flip and then she was whole.

THE END

ACKNOWLEDGMENTS

Shortly after relocating from LA, I wrote *Will You Won't You Want Me?* while seated at a tiny kitchen table in an equally tiny, but very sweet, apartment in Park Slope. So, first and foremost, I am thankful to Brooklyn for that same charm at which I sometimes poke fun.

I am forever indebted to my agent, Anne Bohner, of Pen & Ink Literary, for her attentiveness, rigorous standards, and taste; and to my editor, Vicki Lame, at St. Martin's Press, for her apparently boundless patience, faith, and enthusiasm.

I have not been a preteen for quite some time, so I sought insight—and slang—from a few brilliant young women. Thank you to Sandy Radin, Lily Weisberg, and my beautiful cousins, Noa Elliott, Eden Elliott, and Georgia Eggers.

Reading an entire rough manuscript can be onerous. So I must thank my sister, Claudia, for wading through the first draft and for being the only person who truly understands my obsession with bodega beverages. Also, to my fellow writers Pete Soldinger and Laura Tremaine: I am beyond appreciative of the time you took out of your busy lives to offer invaluable notes.

To my mother, Lynn Zelevansky, on whom I can always count for honest feedback (she knows no other way): Thank you for teaching me to write during marathon essay-editing sessions throughout my formative years.

Thank you to my father, Paul Zelevansky, for his thought-provoking questions, dislike of adverbs, and his unusual perspective. (That is not code.)

Thank you to the Weiners and the Tabers, for all their love and support. And to my very best friends, for helping me be my "best Nora."

Last, thank you to my husband, Andrew, for helping me find my ending and, most important, for giving me our beautiful, trouble-making monkey, Estella Rose.

1. When we first meet Marjorie, she is barely present in her own life. Why do you think she makes self-destructive decisions and is so passive? Is she conscious of this abdication of control? What does it offer her?

2. Marjorie is stuck and can't seem to grow up. But she is also very hard on herself, as if she should already have life figured out. In what ways is she childish? In what ways is she just engaging in an earnest search? Does anyone really know who he or she will ultimately be at twenty-eight years old?

3. Marjorie's job is terrible. Why does she stay for so long? Can you think of times when you remained in a friendship or relationship or work situation because you were afraid of change? Why is change so frightening?

4. Usually, when people picture former quarterbacks and prom queens, they're not in the middle of a cosmopolitan city. Is it necessary to get out of your comfort zone in order to evolve, or does it depend on the person and circumstances?

5. Mac is a complicated character who adores Marjorie and wants what he thinks is best for her. Ultimately, is he a villain or a hero? Or is he neither? Why?

6. Marjorie's mother drives her crazy. Why do you think it can be so hard for daughters to take advice from their mothers and for mothers to offer suggestions in a helpful way?

7. On the surface, Fred doesn't have her life any more together than Marjorie does. What makes her so much more evolved than Marjorie? How is Fred advanced in terms of her worldview?

8. Belinda becomes deeply important to Marjorie very quickly. Why do you think Marjorie becomes so invested in Belinda's choices? Is she concerned for Belinda, or is she living vicariously through the eleven-year-old on some level? Ultimately, was her choice to stay on as Belinda's tutor immoral?

9. We learn a bit about Gus's relationship with his mother, who struggles with depression and can't make decisions for herself. How does Gus's relationship with her affect his actions toward Marjorie? Is what he does patently wrong?

10. On her personal journey, Marjorie has to let go of everything from old friendships to outdated perspectives. In general, how can we tell when something has run its course and should be discarded? Or whether we should keep trying? Is Marjorie's ultimate attitude toward Vera the right one, or should they both have fought harder because of their history? And why do you think Vera behaves the way she does at their last meeting?

11. What is the symbolism of both Marjorie's interest in flip books and her own story about being stuck inside a book?

12. By the end, what has Marjorie learned about herself and the world and how to approach life? What does the final climb to the lookout represent?